Unexpected

OTHER BOOKS AND AUDIO BOOKS
BY KAREN TUFT

Reality Check

Unexpected

A NOVEL

KAREN TUFT

Covenant Communications, Inc.

Cover image *Hot Chocolate and Macarons* © Verdina Anna, Courtesy of Getty Images.

Cover design copyright © 2013 by Covenant Communications, Inc.

Published by Covenant Communications, Inc.
American Fork, Utah

Printed in the United States of America
First Printing: September 2013

19 18 17 16 15 14 13   10 9 8 7 6 5 4 3 2 1

ISBN 13: 978-1-60861-229-1

For Stephen, always.

Acknowledgments

A SPECIAL THANKS TO CAROLYN, the original Bob, for allowing me to channel her essence into a heroine with a happily-ever-after ending.

And many thanks to my editor and friend, Samantha Millburn, who generously shares her talents and insights in order to make my words the best they can be.

Prologue

THE SKY, WHEN HE COULD see the sky through the towering buildings, was a gray shroud, and the air was thick with bone-cutting moisture, the temperature nearly subzero. Gusts of wind tore at his coat and whipped his cheeks into fiery redness. Newspapers pitched and dove wildly, slapping his legs like angry, flapping birds. Steam billowed out of the shop grates in the sidewalks, ripe with the smell of garlic and garbage.

But Ross McConnell could not stop grinning. It was a glorious day in New York.

His thumb, nearly numb from the cold, ran smoothly over the soft velvet of the small blue box in his pocket just as a large man in a heavy woolen overcoat, his hat pulled low against the weather, bumped into him, cursed, and hurried on. Startled briefly from his reverie, Ross did a mental check of the bundle he held carefully against his chest inside his coat—a dozen pink roses. Pink was Liz's favorite color.

He was nearly there.

A taxi shrieked past, spraying slush at him in its wake. Ross sidestepped, nearly managing to escape, but the brown sludge splattered his jeans below his knee and seeped rapidly through the denim. He could feel it ooze slowly down his shin, soaking his sock. And he grinned. It was a magnificent day in New York.

Ross was in love.

Liz had missed class again today; she had mentioned to Ross when he'd called to check on her yesterday that she thought she was coming down with something. She'd asked if she could get his class notes later, and he'd assured her she could. He loved her. He loved everything about her and had since they'd begun dating at the beginning of the semester. Besides, they were in the same study group, so sharing notes was no big deal.

This sudden illness of hers, he thought, still grinning like a fool, played so neatly into his plans. He was able to leave the law library early this morning and get to the jeweler, and with Liz conveniently not around, she wouldn't suspect anything. The ring had set him back quite a bit; he'd be paying for it, along with his law school loans, for a few years, but Liz was worth it. He wasn't about to scrimp on a diamond simply because he was a poor student. Not for Liz. He wanted that ring to clearly show her how special she was, how perfect.

And she was perfect. He wanted to yell it to the sky.

He took the steps of her apartment building two at a time. He imagined her in her oversized Boston College hoodie and matching sweatpants cut off and frayed. He would tuck her into a blanket on the sofa, all propped up with pillows, and brew a nice hot cup of herbal tea for her. Not cocoa, her usual favorite, not if she was under the weather. Once he had her all toasty warm and under his spell, he would cuddle up with her, take her hand, and—Whew! How was it possible that his hands could sweat when they were nearly blue from the cold?

He would tell her how wonderful the past few months had been with her. He would tell her he wanted her to stay by his side and be his bride, his queen, forever. He could envision her beautiful brown eyes brimming with tears of joy, her sweet mouth trembling with emotion. He would pull that ever-present elastic from her golden ponytail, run his fingers through her silky hair, and kiss that soft, sweet, trembling mouth. He would tell her how proud he was of her and her decision to be baptized. It was scheduled to occur a week from Saturday, and he hoped this little germ she had wouldn't create any delay there. He was confident that her decision to meet with the missionaries had been based on her own interest generated by his example. He was certain enough of her character that she would not agree to be baptized merely because she knew it would make him happy. She was not the type of woman to be swayed from her personal beliefs by a man's opinion. Elizabeth Turner, hopefully soon to be Elizabeth McConnell, was the most honest person he'd ever met.

Just as Ross was wiping his waterlogged shoes on the mat, Liz's neighbor opened the lobby door, allowing him to slip inside without buzzing Liz for entry. Even better. He could surprise her right at her door. Taking a deep breath, still grinning with excitement and nerves, he made his way to her door and knocked. His hand trembled. He chuckled and shook his head. He, Ross McConnell, at the top of his law class, editor of the *Columbia Law Review*, a man who had secured *the* plum internship with a prestigious law firm and had the amazing good fortune of a job offer with them upon graduation, was shaking like a callow boy simply because he would be asking a slender reed of a girl from Boston to be his wife.

And he couldn't be happier.

The door opened a crack, the chain still in place. He could see Liz, her eyes widening in surprise. "Ross! What are you doing here?"

He chuckled. "Let me in, and I'll show you, sweetheart."

She glanced over her shoulder and edged the door nearly closed. "Now really isn't a good time, Ross," she whispered. "You should have called first."

"I wanted to surprise you. How are you feeling, Liz? Take the chain off and let me in, honey. I want to make sure you're all right." He nudged gently on the door, trying to open it wider. Her face had paled, and he was growing concerned.

She shook her head. "Oh, Ross, please go. I can't see you right now. I'm not well. It's not a good time. I'll call you. Tomorrow, okay?" She pushed back against the gentle force he was maintaining on the door. "Tomorrow, I promise."

"Lizzie, someone at the door?" a deep male voice called from behind her. Her eyes lowered. Ross felt every cell of his body go on high alert. "Is it the pizza delivery? About time. I'm starving."

Ross pushed less gently on the door now. "Take off the chain, Liz. What is going on? Who's here?"

He looked over her shoulder. A tall, well-built guy was coming toward the door, pulling a shirt on as he came. He saw Ross, scowled, then threw a possessive arm over Liz's shoulders. "Friend of yours, baby?"

Liz dropped her head and removed the chain. "Ross, this is my—this is Clay. Clay, this is my friend Ross. We're in the same study group."

What? My friend? *Same study group? We're more than that,* Ross wanted to yell. He wanted to grab her and shake her, but his hands wouldn't move. *We're so much more than that! We've spent nearly every day, every evening together for months. We've talked about our goals and our families. We've pulled each other through tough study sessions and raced each other through the falling leaves at Riverside Park. We've fed french fries to the ducks, shared ice cream.* He knew every contour of her face and the sweetness of her mouth. And now she was leaning back against some guy named Clay, and her eyes had gone distant, the light snuffed out.

Clay wrapped his arms around Liz's waist and stared hard at Ross like he was drawing battle lines. "This must be that 'friend' of yours I've heard rumors about." He smirked, and Ross wanted to plant his fist in the guy's arrogant face. Clay laughed mockingly. "It appears I know more about him than he does about me. He's shocked speechless. You really know how to play it, baby. I didn't give you enough credit. But obviously, this guy doesn't know you well enough, or he'd know you belong to me. Game's over, buddy. You lose."

Ross's raging pulse quickened and rammed at the wall of his throat. He could feel an intense cold taking over, a cold that had nothing to do with the freezing temperatures. He couldn't feel his hands. He wondered abstractedly if the numbness in his extremities would stop his heart beating altogether if it were to reach that far.

"Five minutes, Liz. I deserve five minutes." Ross looked from Liz's dull eyes to Clay's glinting ones. "Then I'm gone."

Liz glanced at Clay. He shrugged, whacked her gently on the bottom, and walked out of the room. Liz quietly slid through the door and eased it nearly shut. She was hugging herself. Ross wanted to grab her, hold her, shake her senseless, yell at her. Cry. Instead, he stood rigidly, waiting. Waiting for the words that would shatter him.

Liz heaved a huge sigh and then spoke quietly. "Clay and I are a couple. We've been together for a long time, really. Until this year, actually. We just hit a rough patch for a while. But he came to town the other day, and we decided to give it another try."

Ross could hear the words and knew what she was saying. He also knew she wasn't telling him everything. His hand clenched in his coat pocket, and he was only slightly aware of the velvet box that rubbed against his knuckles. His other hand clutched the bunch of roses still hidden inside his coat, a thorn stabbing him. How appropriate. "Explain this rough patch." She wouldn't look at him. "Explain it!"

Now she glared at him, her back stiff. "Fine! Clay and I are together. You don't know how hard I worked to get him away from the other girls. Everyone wanted him, and I got him. I got him," she said almost to herself. "He's everything. He has everything. A prominent family, money, looks, connections. He can trace his family all the way back to the *Mayflower* on one side and the Boston Tea Party on the other. He's perfect. Things were great for a while; then I came to New York for law school, and he decided to be a jerk. The first year, it wasn't so bad. Then I guess he figured if I wasn't around to see what he was doing, I would never find out. Oh, but my friends saw him with other women, and they told me all about it. Over and over again. Until I'd had enough and decided it was payback time."

"I was payback," he said.

She rubbed at her arms unconsciously. "I'll admit it started out that way. I had to find the type of guy he would really see as a threat. That's why I asked to join the study group."

"I see. I should be flattered, I suppose," he said.

"I said it started out that way, but it didn't stay like that. Not exactly." Liz crossed and uncrossed her arms. She reached toward him then backed her hand away. "I do care about you, Ross. We had great times together."

Great times together building ammunition to make her ex-boyfriend Clay jealous. Ross just stood there. He had no words at the moment. Liz's face was a stranger's face. He was sure the thorn was making him bleed, so he unbuttoned his coat and removed the pink roses. He held the bunch loosely in his hand.

Liz looked up miserably. "Oh, Ross. Pink roses."

"Yeah. Your favorite."

"You were always so thoughtful, made me feel special. There were so many times I thought maybe . . . it was real between us, Ross. Times I'd forget about Clay, times I'd think of him and wonder if he was really who I wanted to be with."

Don't go there, Ross thought. *Don't say it.* It was one thing for him to play the dupe and be fooled by a consummate manipulator. Only his pride would suffer with that. But if she told him he'd been considered and rejected in favor of the clod he'd just met, it would kill him. On a very deep level, he wasn't sure he would survive it.

"Clay and I have a history. He loves me; really, he does. I made him see it. We'll be married this summer at his parents' home. It's what I've dreamed of for so long."

"You've dreamed of a vain, philandering husband, all for the sake of money and appearances?"

"It won't be like that. He won't be like that."

"You're an intelligent woman. You say you have a history with him. Can you not see the pattern? History repeats itself, Liz."

"Sometimes people recognize their mistakes and grow stronger. They change."

He could tell she really wanted to believe that. He knew he had lost her. But Ross loved her enough to take one final risk. He was not begging. He was arguing his case. "I love you, Liz. Marry me, not him. He may have money now, but I'll have money—all you could ever need or want. Connections? Those are formed easily enough, and you know I have the beginnings of those already established. You want a pedigree. Easy. I can trace mine back to Robert the Bruce. There. Scottish royalty. And I'll be faithful to you, Liz." His voice softened. "You won't ever have to wonder where I am or with whom. Marry *me*." He pulled the blue box out of his pocket, flipping it open for her to see its contents. This was not the way he had planned to propose to her, standing in a freezing hallway, desperate, dying inside.

Liz touched the brilliant two-carat diamond gently with the tip of her forefinger, then pulled her hand slowly away. "You must have robbed a bank or held the jeweler at gunpoint." She gave him a watery smile.

"Only for you, Liz."

Her face crumpled then, and Ross's heart sank. "I can't do it. I can't do it, Ross. It's too much. I worked too hard for too long to get Clay. I can't start all over again with only promises and no guarantees. I can't. And I can't be baptized next Saturday."

"Liz, that is an entirely different matter. It has nothing to do with us, or at least it shouldn't. Don't—"

"I can't say the things I learned weren't valuable. I really think I believed a lot of it, on some intrinsic level. But now I—Clay just laughed and said I couldn't be serious about pursuing such a quaint little idea. And my family won't understand. I'm sorry. You'll let the elders know?"

Ross nodded slightly. Looking down, he realized he still held the roses. He shrugged and started to hand them to her. She shook her head, and he dropped his hand.

"Well, there's nothing more to say except congratulations, I guess. Be happy in your choice."

He started to leave, ring in one hand, roses in the other. Liz stopped him with a touch. He turned and looked at her, her large brown eyes overflowing with tears. Her lips trembled. She brushed them softly over his cheek. He could feel the dampness of her tears on his skin. "Remember all of the good times, okay?" she whispered. "I do love you, Ross, and I'm sorry."

He looked at her then, this woman he'd known so well and didn't know at all. The numbness consumed him at last. "Yeah. I'm sorry I love you too," he said flatly.

Ross turned and walked out of the building. He didn't look back, but he heard the door shut behind him. He had been afraid his heart would break. Instead, it turned to stone.

Outside, the clouds had begun to part. Blue sky was breaking through, and there were tiny purple crocuses peeking out of the crusty snow in a small garden patch as Ross walked by. He chucked the roses on top of them.

New York was a lousy place to be.

Chapter 1

Eleven years later

NATALIE FORRESTER STEPPED INTO THE Lisles' house, loaded with her cleaning tools, only to stumble upon an eruption of empty pizza and Chinese-food boxes, potato chip bags, and cookie crumbs. Various beverage bottles and cans were strewn from room to room with the wild abandon of indulgent, wealthy youth, the cans' contents forming sticky sprays on walls and puddles on tables and floors. Valerie Lisle, Mrs. Lisle to Natalie, even though Natalie had cleaned the Lisles' spacious eastside Salt Lake City home for nearly two years, had left a note for Natalie the previous Friday saying she and Mr. Lisle were leaving for a cruise to the Panama Canal but that the boys would be expecting Natalie to clean up. That was obvious, Natalie thought as she looked around. The note had included a fifty-dollar bonus and a penned apology from Mrs. Lisle, stating she suspected the eighteen-year-old twins, Justin and Jeremy, would be "less than tidy" with their mother gone. Natalie's eyebrows rose in ironic agreement as she viewed the disaster before her, sent up a silent prayer of gratitude for three basically well-mannered children, and grabbed a bucket and rag. Her usual Friday-morning cleaning job of three hours had climbed to at least six. The extra fifty from Mrs. Lisle wouldn't even come close to covering the extra time and work.

She plunged her rag into a bucket of hot, soapy water, wrung it out, and attacked the living room walls. Golden droplets of beer and caramel cola fanned out like fireworks on the living room walls. A shake and spray stunt, no doubt. Next to the fireplace, someone had spelled an offensive word out of Oreos on the wall. Natalie had been tempted to rearrange them into a smiley face and leave them for the Lisle twins to find, but she wasn't sure when the mister and missus would be home and didn't think they'd appreciate the humor. She snagged one of the remaining cookies from the package on the counter and nibbled it as she threw the others away and pushed the soapy rag through Oreo goo.

Natalie moved to the master bedroom next; it appeared a little too disorderly to simply presume Mrs. Lisle had gone into a frenzy packing. More likely amorous party guests. She grimaced and pulled the luxury 520-thread-count sheets off the king-size bed and packed them downstairs to the laundry room, where she immediately put them in the washing machine.

She murmured words of relief that she only had to quickly make the beds in the boys' rooms and collect their dirty laundry from the floor. Slayer and Megadeth glared down at her from Justin's walls. Maxim girls smiled invitations from Jeremy's. Natalie knew as much about Jeremy and Justin as she cared to know. She was more than willing to let them live with their dust bunnies and whatever else lurked in the dark corners.

Several long hours later, Natalie loaded her cleaning tools into the trunk of her Ford Focus and collapsed behind the steering wheel. She pushed a few sweaty strands of hair off her face as she went through her mental checklist: The floors were mopped—hand scrubbed, actually, to remove all the crud. The hand scrubbing had also included the living room and kitchen walls. Oreo graffiti was now a thing of the past. The carpets were thoroughly vacuumed, everything dusted. Linens washed and folded, beds made. Her lower back throbbed, and her arms and shoulders were stiff and sore.

She was tired—tired of cleaning houses for a living. Other people's— rich people's—houses. Tired of her bank balance running in the red. Tired of feeling dependent on her ex-husband, a man she no longer trusted, for her children's well-being. Tired of feeling controlled by him.

Next to her on the passenger seat was a printout of the classes offered through the community college. It would be tough with a son on a mission and two teenage girls, but Natalie was on a mission too, a mission of independence, both financial and emotional. She wasn't trained to do anything besides clean houses, so she'd hoarded her hard-earned money and enrolled in a couple of college courses, just to get her feet wet. She would start with the basics, work toward earning her associate degree, and go from there. *My time has more than arrived*, she thought as she jammed her key into the ignition. She wanted a respectable job that could give her a respectable income. If education and experience were what good-paying employers wanted, she would get them. Somehow. By herself.

Her cell phone rang. She was tempted to ignore it, since it wasn't the programmed ring of either of her girls, but she checked the ID and, succumbing to the inevitable, answered.

"Natalie! It's Tori. I spoke to Ron. Are you still planning on tonight?"

Tori was Natalie's best friend, and Ron was Tori's boss, whom Natalie had met when she and Tori went out to lunch a few weeks back. Ron had mentioned at the time that his old college roommate would be in town this weekend and expressed interest in setting Natalie up with him. Ron seemed like a nice enough guy, and Tori liked working for him, so Natalie, having been caught off guard once again, agreed to the blind date. She figured she was one of the few single women either Tori or Ron knew, which was why she had been chosen.

She buckled her seat belt and started the car. "I guess so, but you're going to owe me."

Ugh. She really hated the pressure she felt on dates, especially blind dates, but "Sure, okay" had come out of her mouth anyway. Going out on the date did fall loosely into her current social philosophy, she rationalized, that of affording her occasional contact with supposedly real people—adult people—other than her kids, something mothering and cleaning empty houses rarely allowed her to do. Church services on Sunday were the exception. Natalie's social philosophy was two pronged: one, an occasional date kept her verbal skills semipolished in the event of a potential job interview, and two, it took pressure off her kids to feel they had to keep her company all of the time. She herself was through with men on a permanent basis.

"I think Ron's the one who owes you, but I get it." Tori laughed. "By the way, he heard from this Doug guy about an hour ago. He got into town last night for the conference and will be tied up at the convention center until this evening. He has your address. Ron told me to tell you to expect Doug at six. Will that work? He said to dress casual. And Nat? Call me as soon as you get home. I'm dying to hear how it goes."

"Count on it," Natalie said, "unless, of course, we decide to run off to Vegas and elope."

Tori laughed again and said good-bye.

Natalie really wished Tori and her husband, James, were doubling with them, or even Ron and his wife, even though she didn't know them. She wasn't opposed to blind dates, in theory—it was only when she was actually on the blind date, dressing for the blind date, or being lined up on the blind date that she tended to object. She really wasn't opposed to men as people—

except when they were strange men she had to deal with one-on-one. Or not even strange men, actually. Any man.

And this particular blind date felt pretty blind. She wished her black pants weren't still at the cleaners so she could wear them tonight.

But mostly she wished she'd just told Tori and Ron no to the whole thing.

* * *

"Dad called."

"Did he?" Natalie smiled thinly and tossed her keys on the kitchen table. "Did he say what he wanted?"

"He said he was going to pick Callie and me up at five thirty instead of five o'clock and that he wanted to talk to you when he came by." Emma looked up from her fashion magazine. "I told him I thought that was okay. Is it okay?"

Natalie now had one hour instead of four, thanks to the adorable Lisle twins, to run to the bank, grab Callie from her dance lesson, collect the dry cleaning, straighten up the living room, shower, and be ready for her blind date before her ex walked through the front door, hopefully not late, all smiles, to take her girls for the weekend.

"Sure, it's okay, honey. I need to run to the bank before I go get Callie. Will you straighten up the living room before your dad gets here?" She smiled and winked. "Make him think we remain remotely civilized around here after all this time—even without his constant good influence."

Emma rolled her eyes but grabbed her sweatshirt and backpack from the sofa. She hip bumped her mother as she walked by and waved her sweatshirt with the flourish of a seasoned matador. "I suppose," she retorted, trying to sound as put upon as possible.

Natalie chuckled at Emma's antics and then watched in utter amazement as her daughter responded to her request the first time. Of course, her Em was a sweet, agreeable girl, but to automatically grab the vacuum and drag it into the living room was not an everyday occurrence. Natalie started to make a joking retort, but she realized that even though they were sparring comfortably with each other, Emma's eyes had looked strained when she'd told Natalie her dad had called. Darn that Wade. What lasting damage had he done to all of them?

Natalie scooped up her keys and bag again, squeezed Emma's shoulders, and yelled "Thanks!" over the din of the vacuum before heading back out the door. She didn't much like Wade Forrester, not anymore, but he had given her two wonderful gifts in the form of Emmaline and Callisandra Forrester, and he'd been decent enough to Ryan, her son from marriage number one. For that, at least, she supposed she would always be grateful in a way. Whatever.

She mentally prepared for her encounter with Wade as she quickly drove to the bank on her first errand. She knew the drill. He'd tell her he'd have Callie and Emma back early Sunday evening (although he'd undoubtedly call late on Sunday to tell her he'd gotten hung up and could she pick them up, which, of course, she would do). When he got to the house, she'd ask him nicely when the child support checks would resume, and he'd condescendingly remind her he was not made of money, implying that if she weren't incompetent, it wouldn't be an issue—in fact, if she weren't incompetent, they would still be married—and when he closed on the two big real-estate deals in the works, the ones he always seemed to have in the works, he'd get her a check, so she shouldn't get all worked up. If she was really lucky, he would be gone before Blind Date Doug showed up on the doorstep; otherwise, she could look forward to a "let me give you the lowdown on Natalie" monologue directed at her date.

Because it was Friday afternoon, the bank was swamped. Natalie could see that all the drive-through lines were three to four cars deep. Sighing, she cruised into a parking spot and ran inside. Entering the bank meant using her best cloak-and-dagger skills. Keeping her face averted from the offices on the north side of the lobby, she quickly moved into the teller line. *Just keep moving, just keep moving, just keep moving,* she mentally prodded the tellers and customers. She tapped her toes on the marble floor and checked her watch. Four forty. Callie would be expecting her at four forty-five, and there definitely wouldn't be time afterward to get the dry cleaning, which meant no black slacks for tonight.

With the dire need for black slacks greatly reduced after tonight's big date, there was no rush to get to the cleaners this afternoon or even Saturday morning, since Saturday morning would be her only time all week to relax and catch up on her own house and laundry. She was booked Saturday afternoon cleaning the Masons' house. Adele Mason was having a big dinner party that evening and had scheduled Natalie weeks ago. Natalie had hated tying up part of her only free day, but since the girls would be with Wade and she needed the cash, she'd agreed. The couple of college classes she'd signed up for started on Monday, and afterward, she would have to squeeze in the quick straighten-up she'd promised Terri Larrabee.

She'd head to the cleaners on Tuesday—sometime Tuesday—and Emma would just have to live without her little pink sweater for a few extra days. And Natalie would have to live without the black slacks. She had really wanted them for tonight. They made her feel more slim and confident, something she really needed to feel going on this blind date into which she'd been maneuvered. Oh well. She would just have to see if she had any other kind of confidence-builder hanging in her meager closet.

Four forty-five and still there were three people in line ahead of her. Callie wouldn't start fretting yet. Natalie cautiously glanced over at the north office doors again. No sign of life there, which was a good thing, and Natalie felt herself relax.

Only one person stood in front of her in line now.

"Mrs. Forrester—Natalie—is that you? What a pleasant surprise!" a deep voice resounded.

Curses! Caught unawares from behind.

Heaving a huge sigh, Natalie turned and pasted on her friendliest smile. "Mr. Childs, how are you?"

Mr. Childs, the branch manager, was a large, robust man in his midfifties, with a sagging paunch that was disproportionate to his tall frame and dark hair slicked back like a mob boss. He was also one of the reasons Natalie dreaded being back on single status. At five foot four inches, she had to look up to maintain eye contact, which was difficult at best. She always found herself particularly distracted by his black caterpillar eyebrows.

"Good. Great! Never better." His partial was showing. Three teeth? No, four. She'd always wondered about that. He really needed to find a new dentist—one who wouldn't make him look like Austin Powers. "I've been trying to reach you, you know. Thought maybe that was why you were here. Left several messages on your machine at home. You got them, I hope."

"Yes, well, I apologize for not getting back to you sooner. Sorry about that." The last time she'd returned his telephone calls, she had assumed his call was because she was a few days late making a payment on her overdraft. Okay, the few days had been closer to ten. Instead, he had used the bank's commercial phone line to invite her to dinner. As she had been caught totally off guard, she hadn't had a ready excuse, and that evening she'd found herself watching him plow through three plates of food at the local all-you-can-eat buffet. They had discussed his grandchildren (Harvard bound, no doubt), his ex-wife (trying to bleed him dry even after all these years), his plans to remarry (a man has needs even at his age). Nauseated, Natalie had vowed there would be no repeat. Fool me once, shame on you, she thought; fool me twice, just take aim at me and fire. She would not ever be returning any of his voice mail messages. Unless, of course, some unforeseen financial disaster loomed and her overdraft became subject to collections. She mentally crossed her fingers. Even at that point, she'd probably rather sell a kidney.

"Not a problem," he said. "Noticed your loan is overdue. Thought maybe we should discuss payment options for you."

And perhaps maneuver a little social encounter out if it, she speculated to herself, grimacing inwardly.

Natalie's smile was getting tighter with each passing minute. "As we speak, I'm making a payment on it, Mr. Childs. Hopefully that will resolve any outstanding issue we may have."

"Earl, please. Well, good, good, fine." He moved in for the kill and lowered his voice. "I enjoyed myself the other evening; maybe we can do it again sometime."

Hallelujah, a teller is open. Stay cool. "Earl. That's so nice. I'll have to get back to you. Things are a little dicey right now schedule-wise. New school year and all. The kids, you understand. But thanks so much!"

She turned to hand her checks to the teller, flushing with embarrassment at the smirk on the young man's face. "Put these into checking, and make the minimum payment on the overdraft, please," she murmured.

The teller nodded, and Natalie thought she heard him snort.

She couldn't get out of the bank fast enough.

"What took you so long?" Callie plopped into the passenger seat of Natalie's little Focus and snapped the seat belt around her skinny hips.

The car had been her son Ryan's until he'd left on his mission; then she had taken over the payments and sold the ten-year-old Corolla Wade had so graciously allowed her to keep after the divorce. That sale had paid for Callie's orthodontics. What she had received after the divorce from the sale of the house she and Wade had shared wasn't much and was tucked away in a long-term CD. She couldn't touch that—it was her children's security, so she had scraped long and hard for enough money to take care of their needs and for tuition so she could start school again.

She glanced over at Callie and pulled out into traffic. Callie's elfin features were contorted from stress, with worry creases between her large eyes and a lemon pucker on her lips.

"I got hung up at the bank. I tried to call you, but you didn't answer." Natalie knew darn well Callie had left her phone at home because she'd seen it on the counter earlier. What good was paying for her kid to have a cell phone so she could keep tabs on her if the kid didn't have it with her? "Listen,

Cal-pal, your dad is picking you up at five thirty, but I'll need your help when we get home, so you'll need to hurry and pack quickly. You need to be all ready to go the moment he shows up." She glanced at her watch. It was already after five.

"What do you need me to do?" She tossed her purple dance bag on the floor by her feet.

"You had dish duty last night, remember? Except you had too much homework and promised you'd get right on it when you got home from school?"

She knew Callie remembered. She also knew that if Callie could manage her packing and a bathroom break just right, she might be able to avoid dish duty entirely.

Natalie swerved to miss an aggressive Acura trying to merge into her lane. Her hands tightened on the steering wheel. "I really want the house straightened before you and Em disappear for the weekend. And your dad always prefers things tidy."

Wade could spot a smudge blindfolded. His critical eye had honed Natalie's housekeeping skills to the point that she felt confident walking into strangers' homes to clean and walking out with them spotless and the owners pleased. It was the only thing she felt confident about these days. Not that she had the time or energy to do exactly the same in her own house.

Callie slumped farther into the seat. "I know. Last time he told us we might get away with slovenly living at our mother's house, but he had higher expectations for us and his home."

Slovenly. Natalie clenched her teeth. She tried so hard to put a positive spin on Wade for the girls. It was getting more difficult to do from her perspective, but she felt that staying positive, or at least neutral, about their father was important for the girls. The divorce had been difficult enough on them; Emma had adored her dad and felt betrayed now, and Callie, the little worrier, had been overwhelmed by loss and guilt. His sharp comments speared the girls like shards of glass. Natalie was used to it, expected it, but she hated the effect it had on her daughters.

The elf sitting next to her was fast becoming a troll. "Is Sandy going to be there? I don't want to go if Sandy's going to be there."

Wade's new bride wasn't Natalie's favorite person either, but frankly, new brides usually lived in the same houses as their husbands, regardless of what their stepchildren hoped. At least Wade had married this one. "I'm sure she will be. Just make the best of it."

"She hates me."

"I doubt she hates you. Not my little love pumpkin."

"She does."

"She's just getting to know you." How could Natalie reason with a thirteen-year-old female worrier who was all what-ifs and hormones? Sometimes she wasn't sure what to do or say, even though she herself had once been thirteen years old. "Smile, be helpful, don't touch her things, and stay out of her way. It'll be fine."

"Gwen's having a sleepover. Can I stay home this weekend and go to Gwen's instead?"

A knot started twisting in the pit of Natalie's stomach. Rearranging custody privileges with Wade was next to impossible. It was tough enough doing the pep talk to get the girls out the door every other weekend. Running interference between the girls and Wade was teaching her the skills of a hostage negotiator. And tonight, she just didn't have the time. "You know how much your dad looks forward to spending time with you."

"No, he doesn't. He just wants to make sure you don't get to have us more than you're supposed to. Once we get to his place, he expects Em and me to watch Sandy's two little brats while he and Sandy just go off and . . . you know. They're always hanging all over each other and kissing. It's sick. All they want is free babysitters. And we can't even get a snack without Sandy having a fit. Gwen's having everyone over, and I have to miss another party with my friends, and it's not fair."

Well, life certainly wasn't fair, Natalie conceded. "I'll talk to him, Cal. I can probably get him to be a little more discreet with Sandy, but I suspect your campaign to stay home this weekend will fall on deaf ears."

Callie sighed. Natalie pushed her sunglasses up her nose and tried not to sigh as well. After nearly four years, all of this should be easier. Somewhere in the *Cosmic Book of Life* there had to be a rule that fathers were to act like heroes and little girls were allowed to idolize them until they were replaced by loving husbands. Unfortunately, she thought ironically, Natalie's own circumstances seemed to subscribe to the *Comic Book of Life* instead, where she continually encountered men who were more like cartoon bullies, gorillas, or clowns. She wished she had chosen better for her girls.

The only man Natalie had ever really been able to count on at all was her own dad, and even he had faltered for a while when she was a teen and had needed him most.

A black SUV with temporary plates sat in front of Natalie's small rental house as she pulled into the drive. She exhaled loudly and threw the car into park. Callie slipped out of the car and slid into the house through the kitchen door. Natalie knew Cal was escaping the storm that was about to blow.

After intentionally telling them he would be there at five thirty, Wade had shown up early. It was one of his little tactics, Natalie had learned, to catch her off balance. *And* he was behind on child support—way behind—yet there sat a new luxury vehicle.

She found him seated comfortably on the floral chintz sofa he and Natalie had bought their first year of marriage, his legs stretched out in front of him and crossed at the ankles. Now the old couch wore a striped slipcover. He nudged a few colorful pillows out of his way and shifted to cross a leg over his knee. He had told her several times that he had graciously allowed her to keep most of the furniture after their divorce: the living room furniture and certainly the bedroom set. The dining room set had been a gift from his parents, so naturally that was his, as were all of the office furnishings. Natalie had no use for that kind of stuff anyway, he'd said. Her head was full of the impractical: art, photography, craftsy things. No reason not to claim all of the tech stuff too. He'd handpicked the TV and audio components, so they were his by right. And she barely knew how to turn on a computer, let alone use it in any practical manner.

She had challenged him over his claim to the computer system, saying she knew more about them than he gave her credit, but he'd asked her accusingly if she expected him to set up all of his programs and files in a new system when this one was virtually brand-new. He had assured her she would do better with something small, like a tablet, one she could master more easily once she could afford it. She thought about all of the time, the odd hours she had spent at the library, looking up college information. It would have been so much more convenient to do it at home.

Wade started rubbing a spot on the slipcover that was looking a little threadbare and gave her a reproachful look.

"Wade." Her tone had an edge, despite her best intentions.

"The girls ready, Nat?" His tone matched hers.

Natalie took a cleansing breath and opted for calmer tactics. "Wade, that's a new SUV out front. You owe me four months of back child support, and there's a brand-new SUV sitting in front of my house."

His face hardened into a look Natalie knew well. "Yes, there is. And my finances are really none of your business ever since you signed your name on that little dotted line."

"I suppose on one level that's true, Wade, but we depend on the child sup—"

"We've talked this subject to death over the years, Natalie. Emma, Callie! Are you girls ready yet? Get out here now. We're going."

"Hold on just a minute, Wade." Natalie could feel the muscles in her shoulders bunch into knots. She raised her hand to her neck and rubbed. She was getting too worked up over this, she knew; those Lisle twins and their house wrecking had really wasted her time and frayed her patience. She should stop right now and continue this conversation when she felt more in control and could discuss things with Wade rationally. That was the best approach. But there was a brand-new SUV sitting in front of her house, for heaven's sake! "The girls have school fees, and Emmaline needs a graphing calculator. You promised me last month that this month you'd come through. Callie has outgrown her winter coat, and I owe her dance teacher for lessons. I wouldn't have signed her up for this year's class if you hadn't promised them to her and if I'd known you were going to renege—" She snapped her mouth shut. The minute she had said it, she wished she could take it back. It was too far to go with Wade.

"Enough." Wade stood, his face as cold and rigid as a stone. "Now, girls," he called in a loud voice. "Out." He turned the coldness directly on Natalie.

She involuntarily flinched.

His words were sharp daggers. "I love my girls. And I take care of them. Generously. Don't you dare imply that I don't. And giving their inept, uneducated *mother*"—the word was said with disdainful emphasis—"the right to determine how that money is spent is beyond contemptible to me. I refuse to do it any longer. If you have a problem with that, contact your lawyer."

She knew he had her there. Her lawyer had gently informed her that waging constant legal battles with Wade, as he so often threatened, would only be a huge waste of her lawyer's time and her money and would ultimately resolve nothing.

Wade jerked the front door open and herded two quiet girls through it. The door slammed, and Natalie stood, her eyes squeezed shut, hands clenched, until she heard the SUV speed away.

Chapter 2

NATALIE GOT READY FOR HER date with all of the enthusiasm of a condemned prisoner facing execution. She applied her eye shadow and mascara, fluffed her hair, freshened her lip gloss, and looked down at her slim denim skirt and black tee. She wore a necklace with a hammered silver pendant shaped like a crescent moon—her own creation—and wide silver hoops shimmered through the blonde strands of her hair. It was six o'clock, the hour of reckoning. The doorbell rang, and she practiced smiling at herself once in the mirror, decided she had failed miserably, and went to answer the door.

Quietly slipping into the living room, Natalie wedged two of her fingers between the closed slats of her living room blinds and peeked out. *Comic Book of Life* gorilla man stood on her porch. "You will owe me until Judgment Day, Tori," she muttered to herself. "And Ron will die."

Gorilla Man hailed from Southern California and looked like he could have personally created the San Andreas Fault by stamping his foot. He was of slightly above-average height, but that was the only thing average about him. His shoulders and chest were the size of a Humvee and were bunched with muscles Natalie was sure were only obtainable with exposure to cosmic rays (make that comic rays) or primordial goo. His muscles rippled under his plum-colored golf shirt, and around his hulking biceps, a pair of Maori tattoos arched and writhed like snakes as he reached out to shake her hand. Doug had his California sun-bleached blond hair pulled back from his receding hairline into a ponytail longer than hers would have been had she chosen to wear her hair that way tonight. Not that she was philosophically opposed to tattoos, Maori art, or muscles if a person chose to have them— or even ponytails; she often wore ponytails—she was just philosophically opposed, as a general rule, to tattoos, Maori art, muscles, and ponytails when they appeared in profusion on her date. She smiled politely as he greeted her, and shook his hand. In some oblique attempt at fairness to mankind, she decided the night and her opinions were still young. She would maintain a cautious but open mind—for now.

* * *

Ross McConnell dug into his entrée and tried to listen to the conversation going on around him at the table, a group that included three of Ross's colleagues. Ross's good friend Barclay, aka Bud, Atwood and his law partner, Dave Somebody—his last name had slipped Ross's mind—had spent the last week in Belize and had stopped in Salt Lake on their way back to Seattle. Right at the moment, Bud was entertaining Allen, a divorced, middle-aged coworker, and Trevor and Sean, two of the younger members of the firm, with amusing anecdotes from the trip.

Bud and Ross had been on law review at Columbia together and had become close friends. Bud had chosen to return to his native Seattle to practice international law rather than work in the Big Apple with Ross, but the two had remained close despite the geographic distance between them. The guy was tall and blond and gave the impression of being easygoing and gregarious, like a big golden retriever, although Ross thought Bud's personality was more like a pit bull's: smart, friendly with people, ruthlessly aggressive when necessary.

As Bud regaled the men with an exaggerated tale about snorkeling with stingrays, Ross gazed idly around the restaurant, glanced surreptitiously at his watch, and calculated the minutes until he could excuse himself diplomatically and go home. He still wanted to go to the gym and needed to pack for his business trip, and frankly, he was bored. He noticed an older couple in the booth across from them, the man tall and lank, wearing a pearl-gray Western-style suit, the woman short and plump with dimpled elbows and cheeks, sporting a bright pink floral dress. Jack Spratt and his wife. The woman reminded Ross of a cupcake with strawberry icing, all sweet and sugary, the kind of woman a little child could securely pillow into for a bedtime story. The corners of Ross's mouth twitched slightly; he decided to make a quick call to his mother on the way home—not that his mother was a cupcake, exactly.

Ross watched as a man who could wrestle in the WWF led his date to the booth behind Jack Sprat and the strawberry cupcake. He was built like a behemoth, with massive arms and no visible neck. His dinner partner was a slender blonde, but that was all Ross could see from this angle. Bruiser and his bimbo out for a bite to eat. The table by the window hosted a family of five: two harried parents, two irritable adolescents, and a boy about five who was proving he was as bored as Ross. At least Ross, he mentally congratulated himself, had managed to learn not to act out in public. The five-year-old slipped under the table for the umpteenth time, receiving hissed recriminations from his mother and eliciting squeals from his older siblings as he attempted to grab their shoelaces.

It suddenly struck Ross that the parents were younger, quite a bit younger than he. The thought twisted his gut. He shifted his attention back to the blonde.

* * *

Gorilla Man—Doug—took Natalie's hand possessively and seated her at the booth in the steakhouse at the Little America Hotel, where he was staying. The lighting was dim and subtle, and their booth was in a corner that afforded a modicum of privacy. She ordered the grilled salmon, and Doug decided, not surprisingly, on the twenty-four-ounce porterhouse. As they waited for their salads, Natalie sipped her diet Pepsi and hoped the slight boost of caffeine would help her keep up her end of the small talk. Doug ordered a Bud. She wasn't philosophically opposed to other people choosing to drink alcohol, but she kept a close eye on him when he started a second round after their entrées arrived. She began to mentally plan an emergency escape if he got too far into a third. Surprisingly, conversation wasn't as awkward as she had thought it would be, and she tried to relax. As the meal progressed, however, Doug's glances became half-lidded, and he found ways to brush her leg with his and touch her hand. She casually tried to withdraw her hand from his, and his grip tightened just enough to keep it there. As he slid his thumb slowly across her palm and softly murmured suggestive comments, she realized he had not intended to watch his alcohol consumption because he'd had no intention of driving her home—at least not that evening. And *that* she *was* philosophically opposed to.

She needed a plan, and she needed one quickly. She glanced over her shoulder to assess her surroundings, like she'd done, however unsuccessfully, in the bank to avoid Earl Childs. Directly across from her was a table with a large, noisy family. In the booth behind her was an older couple, and across from them was a table of professional businessmen. Just beyond, Natalie observed, was a route that would allow her to surreptitiously detour to the hotel lobby. Natalie politely excused herself, saying she was going to the ladies' room. She didn't exactly think of Doug as Gorilla Man anymore, but he wasn't going to be making a love connection with her this evening.

* * *

The blonde rose from the booth and turned. Ross glanced at her briefly, then did a double take to study her. His eyebrows lifted in surprise. Bruiser's bimbo was no such thing. She was a little older than he'd expected, for one, but still appealing in a fresh way, not the heavily made-up style of the good-time girl he'd thought she was. Still, she was probably not too bright, considering the company.

Maybe with a tree-trunk neck and a couple of tattoos I too can find the woman of my dreams, he thought humorlessly. Nothing else had seemed to work. Not that he'd been trying too hard lately. He could count on one hand the number of women he'd met since moving back to Utah, the semidecent ones on his pinky.

"And what's your opinion?" Bud said, and Ross resurfaced from his thoughts, grateful to find the question had been directed at Sean and that he had not made himself the focus of attention at the table.

"UCLA over Oregon by seven," Sean responded coolly.

Football. The conversation had progressed from SCUBA and hot Latin bodies in bikinis to safer conversational territory.

"Come on, Sean. UCLA isn't even ranked this season, and Oregon is ranked at number four." That from Trevor, the leading fantasy football player in the firm and a walking stat savant.

"Injuries, man. Their top wideout is still sidelined for the next two weeks, and Taylor wrenched his throwing arm last game. They may say he's fit to play, but he's going to be below par."

The blonde strode past their table, apparently on her way to the ladies' restroom. There were no women like her in Ross's home ward, that was for sure—maybe because they were hanging out in bars, angling for guys built like the Incredible Hulk.

There was something singular about her. He found himself anticipating the blonde's return, and he turned his head in time to see her slip out of the restaurant. What was that about? He glanced at the Hulk, who was downing his beer straight from the bottle and drumming his fingers impatiently. As an attorney, Ross had developed a skill for assessing situations and people quickly. He'd learned to be analytical and intuitive. He thought of the woman again. What was it about her that piqued his curiosity? If he'd been paying closer attention, he would have a better read on her. What had been in her look as she'd walked by?

Then it dawned on him; she had seemed agitated.

He interrupted Allen, excused himself briefly from the table, and made for the door. "I'm checking on something," he whispered to the hostess, handing her a fifty as collateral. "I'll be right back."

* * *

Natalie snatched her cell phone out of her purse and called Tori. "Tor, answer the phone." It rang multiple times. "Dang it, Tor, pick up."

"Hi,"—Natalie started to breathe a sigh of relief—"it's Tori. Leave a message." Natalie clamped her teeth together and made a low growling sound in her throat. "I'll get back to you as soon as I can. Byeee."

"Victoria, it's Natalie. You and Ron are *both* going to die, slowly and painfully," Natalie hissed into the phone, then hit the end button and scrolled through her cell phone directory. Who to call now? How could she find a ride home? It was Friday night. Only people like her were home on a Friday night. That's where she wanted to be right now. Owning a smartphone would have been handy right at the moment—not that she'd ever be able to afford that type of luxury—but it would have made finding a decent cab company a whole lot easier. She would either ask the concierge or just catch the light-rail and walk the rest of the way home if she had to.

She'd known something like this was going to happen tonight. The only men she knew who were worth spending time with were fictional. *Give me Mr. Darcy and Rhett Butler any old day*, she thought. *You can take Doug and*—her thoughts slipped away as she sensed someone standing near her, too close. She shut her eyes briefly, took a cleansing breath, and casually dropped her cell phone into her purse. If it was Doug and he'd come out to the lobby looking for her, she would die.

She turned her head toward the person and raised her eyes. A man, a stranger, stood there. Not Doug.

This man was not a *Doug* either, not a comic-book gorilla but perhaps just as dangerous. He was very tall and had dark hair and dark, intense eyes. His charcoal-gray suit added to his formal, formidable presence, and though he carried himself with a poised, relaxed stance, Natalie had the impression she was up against something impenetrable, like a castle wall, his Italian suit akin to chain mail. A dark knight. A modern knight but just as fierce a warrior as his medieval counterpart. She glanced at his eyes and then fumbled with her purse, looking for nothing but searching for something to keep her hands occupied.

"Excuse me. Everything okay here?" the dark knight asked in a deep, low voice.

Natalie pulled her hand from her purse and swallowed. She wasn't even sure if she was still breathing.

"Are you okay?" he asked again, one eyebrow lifting slightly as if to suggest that, perhaps, she couldn't understand simple English.

Get a grip, Natalie thought. *Get a grip on yourself.*

She had learned in her marriage to Wade that independence was preferable to living with someone bent on controlling and dominating her. While she might be getting more comfortable with her independence, it didn't make her an expert at confronting strong, powerful men by any stretch of the imagination. Exhibit A was how she had dealt with Wade that very afternoon. And now she had two strangers, two terrifyingly powerful men, to contend with in the space of one evening. She had the urge to flee.

Resisting that urge as best she could, she raised her chin slightly and attempted to look him squarely in the eye.

She couldn't do it.

Her eyes dropped to his tie, an elegant silver stripe that matched the suit perfectly. "I'm fine. Thank you," she mumbled, then turned and walked quickly to the concierge's counter.

The concierge was very helpful, offering to call her a cab if needed. That put Natalie a little more at ease. It had crossed her mind, after she had run away—yes, she conceded, she had run away—from the dark knight, that Doug knew where she lived, and if he was truly the unsavory sort, he could follow her without any trouble at all. And while his advances were of no interest to Natalie, she really didn't get the feeling he was actually a serial killer.

She sighed and ran a hand through her hair. She was going to have to face Doug again. Her batting average stank when it came to holding her own with men. She'd come out on the short end of the confrontation with Wade earlier and cowered in the face of a concerned stranger, and she just wanted to slip away and avoid things this time, but she knew she couldn't do it. Dating was such a nuisance.

Then she remembered Earl Childs at the bank that afternoon and how she'd maneuvered around him okay. He wasn't intimidating, just disgusting. Still, maybe she could deal with Doug after all.

She straightened her spine, took a deep breath, and walked back into the steakhouse. Out of her peripheral vision, she could see the dark knight sitting with the group of businessmen. Feeling a flush spread to her cheeks, she turned her head away and slipped back into the booth, where Doug sat nursing his beer.

He smiled his most charming smile at her, but she could tell he had gotten edgy waiting for her to return from her lengthy "restroom break."

"Everything okay here?" he asked.

She looked at him, startled. That was exactly what the dark knight had asked her. She glanced over her shoulder at the group of businessmen. The dark knight caught her gaze and held it briefly. She turned back to Doug and mustered a smile. "What makes you think something might not be okay?"

Doug shrugged. "You were gone a long time." He reached for her hand before she could react. His eyelids and smile were relaxed, but the glint Natalie saw in his eyes made her swallow hard. "I thought maybe we could have dessert in my suite."

She knew what kind of dessert Doug was suggesting. This was precisely the reason nice, quiet evenings with a good book or an art project appealed to her more often than not. Right now she needed to find any speck of courage she could that might be buried within her and make sure it didn't abandon her. She steeled herself and took a deep breath. "Doug. I'm flattered, truly. And I am having a nice time. But you need to know that I am actually a very nice Mormon girl, and nice Mormon girls do not have dessert—of any kind—in men's hotel rooms." His face went blank, and he tensed, so Natalie lowered her voice to gentle his mood. "I am, however, in favor of dessert in restaurants with nice men—especially when the company and the conversation are pleasant."

His eyes narrowed, and he looked intently at her, studying her. She held his gaze like a poker player holding a pair of deuces and held her breath as well. She'd lost the stare-down with the dark knight. She really needed to win *this* stare-down contest. The tension in the air pulsed around her. Finally, a corner of Doug's mouth turned up slightly, he made a sound that was almost a chuckle, and he said, "No dessert, huh?"

She picked up the dessert menu. "I didn't say no to dessert. I said no to your suite."

He drummed his fingers on the table and stared at her again.

Natalie kept her eyes on the menu and held her breath. She wasn't home free yet. He still hadn't reconciled himself to having a dessert with calories and no action. Finally, she gave up pretending to read the menu and set it down. She watched the range of emotions flash across Doug's face as he came to terms with what she'd said. Insult, aggravation, resignation. Acceptance.

Finally, he shrugged. "Well, then, Natalie, what do nice Mormon girls consider *pleasant* conversation?"

Natalie exhaled slowly. "I can't answer for everyone, but I'd be interested in learning more about the person sitting across the table from me. Tell me about your family, Doug, and I'll tell you about my boy and my two girls."

His face shifted from vague disinterest to astonishment. "You've got three kids? Wow, I never would've guessed. A boy and two girls. What's it like having two girls? I've got a little girl myself." His eyes sparkled, and then for a moment, he looked past Natalie's shoulder at some far-off scene. "She's my angel."

Natalie smiled and inwardly breathed a sigh of relief. She'd held her own and prevailed. "Lucky you, Doug."

* * *

Allen was bemoaning the faithlessness of women, Bud and Dave were giving each other pained looks, and Sean and Trevor were huddled over napkin scribblings, comparing their fantasy football picks. Much to Ross's surprise, the blonde had slipped past their table a few minutes earlier and had slid back into her booth across from the Hulk. Out in the lobby, Ross had watched her retreat from him and head to the safety of the concierge. She had tried to put on a brave face, but Ross had scared her. He'd seen a trapped, vulnerable look in her eyes—startlingly green eyes—and since she'd returned, he'd found himself glancing over at the couple frequently. Ross had sensed several minutes of tension there and then had watched the behemoth relax visibly.

Ross was certain he'd read the situation outside the restaurant correctly. He was sure she didn't want to be here with that guy. Or maybe it was wishful thinking on Ross's part.

The Hulk laughed then, and Ross actually felt a slash of unease cut through his chest. If he didn't know better, he might have thought he was jealous. He almost chuckled. Jealous. That was ridiculous.

"And what's your story, Mac?" Allen asked Ross, referring to him as Mac like they did in the office because of his last name, McConnell.

Ross dragged his eyes away from the booth just after the blonde crossed her very attractive legs. "Sorry? What story? I lost the thread there for a minute."

Dave smiled sardonically at him. "Allen here got the guys away from talking football long enough to try to make us weep over his heartbreaking story. Trevor says he'll write a country-western song based on the saddest one. You're up."

Trevor looked up from his napkin scribblings and rolled his eyes.

Ross smiled diplomatically. Allen was pathetic and really needed to get over his bitterness and move on. In his best western twang, Ross said, "I guess I've broken my poor ol' ma's heart because I haven't found the perfect little woman yet."

"Too easy," Allen grunted. "There's no such creature."

And didn't Ross know it. But his pathetic attempt at humor had not diverted the hounds from their scent. They were lawyers, after all.

Bud gave him a searching look, his brows narrowing. Ross looked back at him, his face expressionless, so Bud stared grimly at his plate and carved off a large bite of steak. Ross knew Bud well enough, trusted him as a friend enough to know he would not dredge up their law school past, more specifically, Ross's past with Liz—not for the casual entertainment of mere acquaintances. Besides, that was exactly what it was: the past. Long past. Liz was long forgotten. Suddenly tasting something bitter, Ross picked up his water glass and drank deeply. He wanted to get out of the restaurant, get to the gym. He wanted to run. He smiled casually and said, "Well, there was Misty Harwood."

Bud visibly relaxed. He was a good friend, a concerned friend who obviously remembered how things had gone south with Liz back then. But there was nothing for Bud to be concerned about now, not after all this time.

"Misty Harwood. Sounds intriguing," Dave said.

"Yes," Bud added, following Dave's lead. "I thought I knew all about you, pal, but you've never mentioned a Misty Harwood."

Ross sighed for dramatic effect. "She had long blonde hair and big blue eyes. All the guys were in love with her, but she chose me. We were blissfully happy. We started making wedding plans."

He paused. A good attorney knew how to keep the courtroom with him, play his audience just right. He picked up his napkin, dabbed his mouth with it, and tossed it on his plate. He saw Bud's eyes narrow speculatively. Bud knew more about Ross than Ross's family did. Probably more than was safe.

He noticed he even had Trevor's interest now. "Okay, you were blissfully happy. And then what happened?"

"Total devastation. She pulled out the rug, took me out at the knees. Told me she couldn't see me anymore, that things weren't going to work out between us." Ross glanced at Bud, who was still eyeing him with suspicion.

"There was someone else, right?" Allen smirked. "Just when you think you can trust them—bam! They tell you they're sorry, but they can't help the way they feel. It's nothing to do with you; it's just the way it is. They still care about you, *but*. Then they look at you, all sad and earnest, and say, 'We can still be friends, right?' like they really mean it. Women!"

Ross found he was grinding his teeth. He felt sorry for Allen. It would be hard to be that angry, that hurt. Ross was glad he didn't feel that way. He unclenched his jaw. Time to lighten the mood. "Sorry to disappoint you, Allen, but it wasn't quite like that." He paused and looked wistful. "I'm not sure which hurt worse, the fact that her family was moving to Michigan or that Misty told me her mom wouldn't let her get married at seven years old."

They all groaned in unison. Trevor hooted. Allen's face went purple, his mouth drawn in a thin line. Ross belatedly realized that Allen didn't have the benefit of time that Ross had when it came to rejection and therefore couldn't see the irony. He watched in frank admiration as Allen, obviously embarrassed, got himself under control. He probably shouldn't have used Allen as the straight man of a joke he didn't know was coming.

"That was a cute little story, Ross. Really had us going for a minute." Allen smiled tightly. "But it seems to me that a man of your age ought to have more in the way of experience than seven-year-old Misty Harwood. One only has to watch the secretaries at the office to conclude that."

"Maybe Misty Harwood is the only story worth repeating."

"Well, that might be the case. But it isn't your only story." Allen took a sip of water and reached in his back pocket for his wallet. "I'm older and wiser than I was just a year ago. Maybe more bitter too, I won't deny it." He stood and pulled out some bills for a tip. "That wall you've got around you is so well constructed you don't even see it anymore. But you don't fool me. I'm becoming an expert on walls myself. I've laid a few stones in my own wall this past year. Some little skirt must have messed with you big time. You're licking your male wounds just like all the rest of us, only I suspect you've been doing it a lot longer and you're a lot better at it." He clasped Ross on the shoulder. Ross felt himself go rigid. "Good night, gentlemen; it's been a pleasure."

Trevor and Sean looked uncomfortably at Ross, and Trevor laughed awkwardly. "Where did that come from?" he asked vaguely to no one in particular. They paid their tabs, said their farewells to Bud and Ross, and Dave excused himself from the table as well.

Bud looked carefully at Ross. "I don't know Allen well, but he seems like a decent enough guy."

"Yeah, probably." Ross shrugged. "Shall we go?"

"How close was he to hitting the mark?"

Ross tossed a generous tip on the table, but not before he heard the Hulk laugh at something the blonde said. He abstractedly glanced in their direction and then returned his attention to Bud. "Barclay, old man," he said, swinging his arm casually around his friend's shoulders as they left the restaurant, "you worry way too much." He smiled at his friend convincingly, he thought, but his temples were starting to pound.

Bud shook his head. "Don't play me, man. I was there. I watched your guts get ripped out. I pulled you through that last semester, remember? Liz did a number on you; we both know it. And we both know you haven't had a relationship that went much beyond a second dinner date since."

"You should talk. How many women have gone through the revolving door of your love life since law school? Seven? Eight—hundred?"

"This isn't about me, and you know it. Besides, Rachel and I have been together for almost two years now, and we've even been discussing the *m* word, sort of." He lowered his voice and glanced at some hotel guests as they passed. "But you're the one with the whole religion thing going, that whole 'family forever' business hanging over your head. You thought you had that with Liz, and I just want to make sure you've really gotten over her and moved on. I don't see it, and it's been more than ten stinking years."

They were at the elevator that led to the underground parking lot. There was a hammer banging on Ross's head now. "Bud, you're a great friend. That was a rough time; I admit it. I made mistakes. Things I overlooked, was willing to overlook." It was a lie, and he knew it. Liz had been perfect, everything he was looking for. So perfect, in fact, that he had carefully searched his feelings for her just to be sure. He hadn't wanted to tell his family he was in love, contemplating marriage even, until he was certain. And he'd been certain in the end. That had been the devastation. Now he knew what he was looking for, really looking for, in a woman. And he'd be dead certain she *was* perfect before he allowed anything like that to happen again. "So I haven't found anyone yet. It will happen when it happens."

"I want to believe you, Ross, but I'm not sure I do," Bud said.

"Duly noted. I appreciate your concern, Bud, but I'm fine. Really. Give my regards to Rachel when you get back to Seattle, and stay in touch."

Bud shook hands with Ross and clapped him on the back with his free hand, bringing him in close. "Take care of yourself, old friend. Don't let a semester with Liz affect the rest of your life."

"I'm not," Ross assured him. "I promise."

If only that were true.

Chapter 3

As the evening progressed, Gorilla Man Doug evolved into Doug Merrill from Carlsbad. He was a thirty-two-year-old, self-made, successful entrepreneur who was in town for the Outdoor Recreational Expo. He had a six-year-old daughter, Bethany, from a past long-term relationship. Her mother lived in Las Vegas, and he didn't get to see Bethany very often. He'd had to push straight through from California to get to the expo, but he hoped Bethany's mother would let him see her on his way home. He was definitely into bodybuilding; he also liked deep-sea fishing, rock climbing, and four-wheeling. He planned to be in town until Sunday, and Natalie, ever the pushover, sacrificed her Saturday morning and agreed to go four-wheeling with him. They arranged to meet early because she still had her commitment to clean for Adele Mason in the afternoon, and Adele would be a wreck if the promised cleaning edged too close to party time. Natalie said she'd provide a picnic brunch, and Doug put himself in charge of pulling a few strings to have the four-wheelers ready. He also paid for her cab ride home that evening.

He showed up punctually the next morning in long, baggy shorts and a Grateful Dead T-shirt. He had a small trailer hitched to his Jeep Cherokee, with a couple of hot little four-wheelers on it, and they spent the morning barreling up Mineral Fork, drinking in the mountain scenery, and eating cold fried chicken, fudge brownies dripping with frosting, and a few fresh peaches, all thanks to the deli section of the twenty-four-hour grocery store near Natalie's home. Natalie brought along her old digital camera and snapped up the vibrant autumn colors: the auburns and scarlets of the oaks, the aspens fluttering their gold coin leaves like gypsies, the deep Navajo turquoise of the September sky.

When their adventure ended, Natalie asked Doug for his e-mail address. "I got a few great shots of you," she said as he walked her to her front door. "I'd like to send a couple of them to you. Maybe you can give one to Bethany."

"I'd like that," he said. "Very much." Then he held up his forefinger, gesturing for her to wait a moment, pulled his cell phone from his pocket, and punched in a number. "Ron," he said. "It's Doug. I'm good; thanks for asking. Hey, I heard through the grapevine than you may have been receiving death threats lately." He glanced at Natalie with a twinkle in his eye.

Natalie choked back a laugh.

"Uh-huh," Doug continued. "That's what I heard. Anyway, I thought you'd be happy to know that the coast is clear. The lady in question has given you a stay of execution." He paused. "Let's just say my blind date didn't turn out to be what I was expecting. I'll see you in a few hours, buddy."

He ended the call. "I meant what I told Ron, Natalie. This blind date wasn't at all what I expected it to be. It was much better." He leaned in and kissed Natalie on the cheek. "You take care, honey."

* * *

Hiking and four-wheeling with Doug had turned out to be a plus. Grinding the gears on her four-wheeler, spitting out dirt, and chewing up the terrain had worked out kinks she'd avoided acknowledging. The wind had blown her worries from her mind as easily as it had whipped her hair around her cheeks. She'd found some great old boards from a long-forgotten fence, gray and weathered, that would make great frames for some of the pictures she'd shot in the canyon.

After Natalie had said good-bye to Doug, she'd hurried over to Adele's house, where she then spent the afternoon helping her clean for her big dinner.

Now, Natalie thought as she tossed her keys on the kitchen counter, she was ready to relax and immerse herself in her latest crazy art project.

The weekends the girls were with their father were hard on Natalie, so she usually spent them doing what she called her "crazy art"—therapy in the form of creativity, recharging herself and preparing for the damage control that lay ahead. Natalie knew Emma and Callie needed to spend time with their dad, but she worried. They seemed to grow more distant from their father the more time they spent with him. Emma often returned home on Sundays in a brittle mood, and Callie was usually withdrawn. Natalie always spent the next couple of days talking brightly and making the girls' favorite meals. By midweek, she was emotionally exhausted, but the girls seemed more like their old selves.

The particular crazy art Natalie had planned for this evening involved an old lamp she'd rescued from an estate sale the week before that had grabbed her visually and hadn't let her go. It was a Tiffany knockoff, not great as it was, but Natalie had seen dual potential in it. The base was a dark bronze, a rough, knuckled sculpture that reminded Natalie of roots or fists. She could envision it perfectly next to her bed on the nightstand. The bedroom furniture, a large arts-and-crafts-style, woody, and welcoming set that Wade had actually allowed her to keep after their divorce had been her favorite furniture, so she'd been content. The lamp would blend in well with it after she found a different lamp shade for it. She would either get one cheap somewhere—something simple that wouldn't detract from the strong lines of the base—or she'd find an old one at a thrift shop and refit it with a new covering. Maybe she'd do something funky with it. She'd follow her muse.

It was the original stained-glass lamp shade that now sat on the worktable in her garage that held her full attention. It was a huge garish thing that had even overpowered the amazingly strong and sturdy base. But Natalie had seen beyond the lamp shade itself to the potential it offered for her to create something entirely new. She had seen colors: greens from the many Tiffany-styled leaves, blues and purples from the pansies that flourished around the rim, butterflies and dragonflies that could be taken apart for their pinks and deep golden yellows. The ugly lamp shade on the table was already transformed in her mind into a wonderful, abstract flash of brilliance that would adorn the arched transom window above her front door. She had briefly dabbled with stained glass years earlier in high school, and she had kept the tools and the few supplies she had purchased at the time. She had also harvested interesting glass from previous thrift shop finds.

She picked up the lamp shade and ran her fingers back and forth over the images, then slid it carefully over the narrow strip of plywood she had clamped to her work board. The first step was to cut the individual pieces of glass carefully from the solder holding the lamp shade together, salvaging as much of each piece as possible. Natalie had studied the shade carefully, determining which pieces to remove first. She put on her safety glasses and picked up her glass cutter. The thought crossed her mind that maybe what she was doing was a waste of time. Wade would have thought so, would have told her so in no uncertain terms. But she always found she felt better and was more focused when she'd had a chance to create something from nothing. Or recreate something from something else. A silk purse from a sow's ear, her mother would say when Natalie would present her with her crude little bits of handiwork as a child.

She remembered a particularly awful T-shirt she had decorated for Mother's Day when she was nine. Natalie had seen a book on modern art at the library and had been fascinated by the boldness she'd seen reproduced there. Works by Jackson Pollock and Wassily Kandinsky had leaped off the pages. She hadn't understood what she was looking at, but the images had gripped her. She had done her own Pollock interpretation on the front of a big old yellow T-shirt she'd found in her bottom drawer, using acrylic paints she'd purchased with allowance money. The result was less than spectacular, but her mother had exclaimed it was the best gift ever and had worn it all day long. Of course, after that, Natalie thought with a wry grin, her mother had worn it to weed the vegetable garden. Still, her mother's enthusiasm and encouragement had outweighed her diplomatic handling of the worst of the pieces. Natalie's creative efforts had improved since then, she believed. She'd even sold them occasionally, usually to friends. They knew she needed money, she figured. Well, it was true. She did. And there was always another mad creation, another art piece waiting to spring to life in her hands, so she parted with most of them easily enough.

Natalie worked carefully, cutting each glass shape from its soldered bond. When she eventually pulled off her safety glasses and wiped the sweat from her forehead, she realized her stomach was growling. She pushed up the sleeve of her sweatshirt to look at her watch. Nine thirty. No wonder she was hungry. The time had flown by. She quickly sorted the glass pieces into small boxes and cleaned up her glass-cutting tools.

Natalie fixed an easy dinner of leftover picnic chicken and tossed salad and then washed her dishes. A quiet soak in the bathtub would be relaxing and help her sleep, she decided, so she grabbed her old chenille bathrobe from the bedroom closet and headed for the bathroom. She poured a generous amount of her favorite bubble bath into the rushing tap water, its steamy fragrance immediately filling the small room. She breathed in deeply, then rounded up a few extra candles and added them to the few she kept on hand in the bathroom already. Money was admittedly scarce, but a candlelit bubble bath was a treat she'd decided she could afford—and deserved—occasionally. So in celebration of surviving the Lisle-twin disaster and the most unusual blind date she'd ever had, not to mention her run-in with Wade, she allowed herself to indulge. Candles now lit, she turned off the light and stepped into the hot bubbles that frothed to the rim of her old tub. She slid in up to her chin and let the soothing heat seep deeply into her aching muscles. She was used to sore muscles; she didn't take on the physical challenge of heavy housework day after day and not expect to have them, but today she also noticed a pull in her lower back and thighs and a tightness in her arms that came from matching wills with a four-wheeler. She closed her eyes and sighed heavily, breathing in the lavender fragrance from the bubbles as they blended with the vanilla scent of the candles.

She lifted a leg above the bubbles and soaped it from thigh to toe. It always surprised her to see some definition in her calves and quads. It was ironic, really. She'd never been athletic. In fact, after marrying Wade and having the girls, she had put on a little weight. While she had referred to it jokingly as baby fat, Wade had bluntly told her it was unattractive. Dieting and exercising were hard enough under normal circumstances, but after Emma's birth, nursing had made her ravenous, and exercising had been next to impossible in her sleep-deprived state, between the baby's regular nightly feedings and keeping a then-four-year-old Ryan out of mischief during the daytime.

Still, she'd tried hard to diet and exercise as soon as her doctor gave her the okay. But Wade had already begun to lace their conversations with subtle digs about her appearance, and though she hadn't consciously realized it at the time, she'd allowed the weight to remain as a deterrent to Wade. She'd discovered the hard way that a handsome man could actually be rendered unattractive by virtue of his behavior and comments.

By the time Callie had been born, the comments had expanded to include all of her general inadequacies, of which Natalie apparently had an overabundance. She had responded by gaining more weight, neglecting to do her hair and make-up, deferring to Wade on all decisions involving the household, and immersing herself in her art projects and her children's lives.

Natalie dragged a big soapy loofah down her arms. They too had muscle definition that surprised her. She should make an online exercise video and call it "Body by Bissell" or "Mop and Tone."

She remembered the anniversary she and Wade had celebrated when Callie was about five months old. Natalie had decided to work hard, despite nursing, to try to fit back into her regular clothes, realizing that even those were two sizes larger than she'd worn when she'd married Wade. Her relationship with Wade had been in a serious downslide, and she'd felt it was her fault. If only she had eaten less, hadn't let herself go as badly as she had. If only she had kept the house cleaner, ironed his shirts just right, made his favorite meals more often. If only she'd gone to college. All of their extra money had gone to getting him through school, and by the time he'd finished, she'd had two kids at home. Then Callie had arrived on the scene, and there had been three. Wade had worked long hours, and she'd been so tired after a long day with three little kids that she hadn't given him the attention he'd needed. He'd become distant all of the time, and they'd stopped talking to each other. He would come home late and eat his dinner alone (it was hard to make the kids wait until after eight to have dinner with him); she tried to convince him to come home earlier and spend a little time with them, but he always insisted his work was too demanding.

So she resolved to make this anniversary special, show him she loved him and was committed to making their marriage a happy one—although, at this point, she really suspected she was just attempting to keep it alive. She reserved a table at Cedars of Lebanon, where Wade had taken her on their first date. She fit herself into a borrowed dress she hoped made her look sultry as opposed to simply fat and spent the day doing her hair and make-up so Wade would be impressed. If he was feeling neglected and that was causing his indifference, she wanted to make it up to him.

Wade was late coming home from work again, and Natalie was concerned they would miss their reservations. He didn't comment on her appearance when he walked through the door and threw his keys unceremoniously on the table. He simply asked, "When's dinner?"

Natalie forced a smile. "I made reservations for us for our anniversary. Cedars of Lebanon," she added expectantly, hoping he'd remember.

Wade slumped into a kitchen chair and thumbed through the mail. "I'm a little tired. I wasn't expecting to go out tonight." Natalie watched the realization dawn on him and saw a muscle twitch near his left eye. "I didn't forget," he said. He was scrambling for cover. "It's been so busy at work— you know that—and I assumed you wouldn't be able to get a babysitter on a school night. You caught me off guard." He rose to stand next to her and shot her his mildly irritated look. "You could have reminded me. You know how much I have on my mind right now."

She had tried to remind him—at least she'd tried to encourage him to come home early. But she'd also learned that his work hadn't been too busy for him to take a two-hour lunch with a client, as she'd found out when she'd called his office at different times that afternoon. At the time, Natalie had wondered just who the client was, especially since Wade's secretary had sounded nervous over the phone.

"Give me a minute to unwind, and we can hit the road. A little lamb and couscous sounds good, I guess."

No comment about her hair, her face, her dress. No words of love or even affection. They hardly talked during the drive to the Cedars. Natalie stared at the menu, mentally resolving to leave the conversation up to him; she had been the one to do everything else, after all. He drank his spiced herb tea, dug into his lamb tagine, and tipped the belly dancer five bucks, slipping it into the waistband of her harem pants. Natalie noticed the harem pants of sheer black silk and the gold bangles attached. She also noticed Wade noticing as well. He hadn't looked at her that way—or in any way—for months now. Trying not to sound hurt or petty, Natalie suggested taking belly dancing lessons. "Maybe you'd like it if I could dance like that," she offered shyly.

Wade had looked at her over his cup as he'd sipped his tea. "That's not a bad idea. Maybe it would help you lose all that disgusting weight you can't seem to get rid of."

Natalie stepped from the tub and wrapped herself in her towel. That anniversary, that event meant to celebrate the joining of two people forever as one, had been a major turning point. Life was full of turning points, moments of epiphany, when the clouds parted and illumination shone forth. And there had been events to follow, events that had eventually culminated in the end of her marriage to Wade, leaving two bereft daughters and a son who had guessed at the inevitable and still had felt betrayed.

Tucked into her favorite fleece pajamas and wrapped in her robe, she grabbed her latest read and curled up on her bed to relax. Cleaning houses for others had freed her from her unwanted pounds and had also given her at least partial freedom from Wade. But what she really craved was the ability to care for her and her children without having to rely on anyone but herself. She'd been the little daughter at home, then the reluctant, remorseful, pregnant bride of her so-called high school sweetheart, then the dutiful wife of a distant, critical husband. She'd learned the hard way that she could trust no one else. If Wade was going to pull his child support, then let him. She would not ask again. She would not depend on anyone, any man, ever again. She would get her education somehow. She would go to school and find a career that would support her family.

Wade threatening to stop financial support for the girls wasn't a complete surprise, considering what a deadbeat he'd already been, but it complicated things; she would have to use her carefully saved tuition funds to pay for things she had presumed would be taken care of by the girls' father. So be it. She would not see her daughters or Ryan go without, nor would she be stopped from her course now that she knew what she had to do. That meant finding another house to clean, and soon. She opened her book, feeling resolved on the matter, read one paragraph, and fell into a deep sleep.

Chapter 4

THE INDIAN SUMMER OF SEPTEMBER continued into October, and with it came a summons from the firm to return to New York. Ross's flight back East was an uneventful one. He rode in the business-class section beside a silver-haired gentleman reading the *Wall Street Journal*, and they had nodded a polite greeting to each other before settling themselves into the comfortable disregard of seasoned commuters.

The minute they were at cruising altitude, Ross dragged out his tablet and scrolled through his notes. The prestigious old law firm of Rogers, Goldman, Clarke, and Janofsky had done their best to dissuade him from returning to Utah. Frankly, he himself had been reluctant to leave after fourteen years in the Big Apple and over a decade at the firm. His entire professional life had been there. The agreement they had struck was that he would continue to do work for them, long distance, while he attached himself to a Salt Lake City firm with whom they dealt regularly. It had been easy for Ross to gain entrance there; it had been an inconvenience trying to juggle both locations. At least he was earning plenty of frequent-flyer miles.

Amazing, the things one does for one's family, Ross thought. He shook his head slightly as he skimmed through his notes. He had disrupted his career and uprooted himself all because of a couple of promises he had made to his parents the day he graduated from law school and announced his intentions to take a permanent position at Rogers, Goldman, et al.

"Hmm," his mother, Dorothy, had murmured as he'd walked her across the manicured lawns of Columbia University, her hand neatly tucked into the crook of his arm. "They made you an offer, then?"

"They're giving me a week so I can escort you and Dad around town while you're here; then I'll be putting in regular hours until my bar exam results are in." He'd had no doubt he would pass the New York bar exam.

He'd been on law review and was in the top ten of his class, even with the distraction Liz had been that year. He'd worked for his accomplishments, but he'd worked with the confidence that brains and talent provided. He had always succeeded at whatever challenge he'd faced.

"I will guard every minute that you are with us greedily, then," Ross's mom said. Ross watched her glance over at his dad, who'd been sitting on a bench on the vast campus lawn, a cluster of sparrows hopping around his outstretched feet. Delbert McConnell had always attracted birds, animals, and small children like the Pied Piper.

"I've had twenty-eight wonderful—not perfect but wonderful—years with that quiet, tall timber of a man," she said to Ross. "Your dad and I are so proud of you, son. Will you be able to come home for visits very often?"

Ross knew she'd hoped he would move back home to Utah after his schooling in New York came to a close.

She sighed heavily and hugged his arm.

"I'll be sure to come home a couple of times a year, Mom. You know I can't live without your meatloaf. Or your bad jokes," he added dryly.

She chuckled. "You know full well my jokes are bad and my meatloaf is even worse." She waited a beat, and Ross sensed what was coming. "So, are you seeing anyone special?" The sun broke through the billowing white clouds that gathered at midday. She avoided looking at him by digging her sunglasses from her purse.

Ross could still see everything like it was yesterday.

Oh no, he'd thought. *Here comes the inquisition, concerned-mother version.* The inquisition—concerned-father version—included discussions of finances, Church responsibilities, and family duties. First-son duties, or in his case, *only*-son duties. But inquisition—concerned-mother version—dealt with hearth and home. Daily-life issues. Dating, marriage, and morals. Was he eating well? Getting enough sleep? Did he have a doctor, a dentist? Was he seeing anyone?

He'd been living on his own or with college roommates and mission companions for roughly seven years at that point. But she was his mother, and invariably, every conversation he had with her arrived at this juncture. There were occasional variations on a theme, maybe, but the theme was solid and straightforward: she worried about him and always would. She couldn't be there to take care of him; that meant she wanted him to marry so someone *would* be there to take care of him.

"I'm not seeing anyone currently, Mom, but I'm not worried. There's still lots of time for that." He had never been inclined to burden her with his problems. That year had been a tough one, but he'd buried thoughts of Liz as carefully as he'd buried the engagement ring in the back of his dresser drawer. He gave his mom a reassuring smile, placed his hand over hers as it rested in the crook of his arm, and waited for his gentle inquisitor to go into full swing.

"Ross, that makes you twenty-six with no viable prospects. Brigham Young said single young men were a menace to society at age twenty-five, you know. By now, you're a menace and a half."

He rolled his eyes heavenward. Only in Utah would a twenty-six-year-old single man be considered a societal menace. "I know I'm a menace, Mom. It's a natural gift. That's part of the reason I went to law school. Being a menace is a résumé item most firms look for in prospective attorneys."

She laughed at his meager attempt at humor, and he hoped the worst of the inquisition was past so they could move on to new subjects.

He'd dated plenty in high school. Then there'd been his mission—two years with the opposite sex at arm's length. When he'd returned home, he'd decided the girls he met fell into two categories: they were either completely mercenary about marriage or they weren't interested in marriage at all. The mercenary types spiked interest in him when he mentioned his academic plans—lawyers equaled dollar signs, after all. Others just wanted to be married now, period. Both mercenary variations were annoying.

Ironically, the other category of girls was the one he actually found most interesting. Those girls tended to be smart, attractive, and compelling. They were focused on their education. As a result, they were as interested in their schooling and career plans as he'd been in his own. Marriage wasn't necessarily on their immediate horizon, and that seemed like only a minor hurdle to him. He was focused enough on his own academic goals and getting into law school that he didn't pay serious attention to his social life. He went on occasional dates with a variety of girls, generally avoiding the mercenary husband hunters as much as possible and rarely seeing a girl more than a few times.

So far, it had been enough to keep his mother off his back, for the most part.

"Whatever happened to Josie?" His mother bent over to brush some lint from the skirt of her dress.

Josie Davenport, a girl from his senior year at the University of Utah. One of the few real relationships he'd allowed himself time for as an undergrad. A tall, dazzling brunette whose looks had barely overshadowed her formidable brains. For a while that year, he'd been intrigued. Eventually, though, Ross had discovered she'd been more interested in making a name for herself in broadcast journalism than in a family or church, and he'd ultimately decided he was more interested in letting her pursue that independent of him. "Couldn't tell you, Mom."

"Nice girl. You might have had a baby or two by now if you'd—"

"Uh-uh. Wouldn't have happened." He watched his father stand up in the distance, the sparrows scattering in a flurry of feathers, and amble toward them.

His mother tried another tack. "What's the ward like, son?"

He had to give her points for tenacity. He knew she wasn't going to like the fact that since he graduated, he'd decided to attend the regular ward, not the singles ward. He'd given the singles ward three years of his life during law school, and he'd decided it was time to move on. "I'm actually changing wards right now, what with moving to my new digs. I'll have to get back to you on that."

"How will you ever find a nice girl to settle down with here in Manhattan? You'll only meet career girls or one of those wacky New Yorker types like you find in a Woody Allen movie."

He doubted she'd ever seen a Woody Allen movie in her life—she preferred to spend her evenings reading—but she spoke with convincing authority. She would have made a good trial lawyer.

In New York, it was true, most of the girls he'd met were either students or employees of the university. A lot of them believed school and a career didn't preclude them from having an intimate relationship with a man and even suggested it on a first date. Since that type of activity was a moral and religious problem from his point of view and he'd met few girls with the same moral and religious beliefs he had, he'd put the study of law firmly in the foreground and, for the most part, had put dating on hold. Then he had ceased worrying about it.

"They'll probably approach you, handsome as you are, and offer themselves up to you on a platter," she said.

Girls on a platter, he thought wryly. The girls he'd met at Columbia had frequently offered themselves up like some delicious entrée. It hadn't happened to him quite that way in the singles ward though. He hadn't received any girls on a platter, per se, but he had frequently received cookies on a platter from several girls. Good cookies, several passable casseroles, generally nice girls, no sparks, and part of the reason he'd switched to the family ward. He'd also learned that when someone left food at his house on a platter or in a dish, he invariably had to return the platter or dish. He was sure it was calculated thinking on the part of the girls.

And then Liz had approached him, and his life had spun out of orbit, at least for a while. She'd approached him one morning during his third year of law school. She'd smiled her Liz smile at him and had asked if she could join their study group, saying she was fed up with hers and knew Ross's group, which had also included Bud, was among the class's academic elite. Ross hadn't known her but had definitely noticed her around campus. With her golden hair and graceful figure, she was hard to miss. She had joined the study group, and the more Ross had gotten to know her, the more he'd been lost.

That year had been like a dream to him. He'd found perfection. He'd found his soul mate. It had seemed like perfect timing. They would graduate, set up practice together, weave their lives together. There were a few little details to work out, though, even though he'd been confident in the outcome. Aware of how his mother and sisters would react and the pressure that would ensue if they knew he was serious about someone, he had kept their relationship a closely guarded secret. Only Bud knew. And it had been Bud and his bishop who had helped him pick up the pieces when perfection had shattered.

Ross returned his wandering thoughts to his mother. He'd had his fill of these kinds of conversations with her and his two loving and well-intentioned little sisters in phone calls and e-mails, and now that he was finally free of the rigorous demands of law school, had put Liz firmly out of his mind, and time was his ally, it was time to terminate the subject with his mother once and for all.

And then he had a stroke of genius.

"I tell you what, Mom. I'll make you a promise." He was on a roll. He was certain his idea would stop this particular type of inquisition for a good while, at least, and assure his mom that he was serious in his pursuit of eternal marital bliss. He'd never had trouble attracting the opposite sex. "I guarantee you I will have no trouble bringing a girl home someday soon to meet her future mother-in-law. *But*," he added, "on the off chance I don't, let's say by the time I reach forty—"

"Forty!"

"Yes, forty. Just listen for a minute. You have to give me time to look. If I'm still single at age forty, haven't found that one and only you're so desperate for me to have, I promise you I'll move back to Utah." It was such a no-risk deal—not to mention humorous—that he felt a little heady. "*And I will go on every blind date you, Susan, and Jackie choose to throw at me. Willingly! How's that?*" Yeah. He was throwing caution to the wind with that one. Knowing his sisters, they would line him up with three-legged circus performers, just for spite. Not that it would ever reach that point, he was certain. It was nearly fifteen years away.

"But, Ross, forty will be so *old* if you haven't married by then. And I'll be too old to enjoy your little babies." That comment brought an image of a pregnant and glowing Liz to mind, and Ross winced. "Make it thirty."

"Forty."

"Thirty."

"Forty! I'm not going to budge on that, Mom."

"How about thirty-five?"

His dad had reached them by then, his eyes sparkling amid the crinkled fans of laugh lines. "This little bit of a girl putting you through the paces, son?" He shoved one hand deep into his pants pocket and casually threw the other arm around his mother's shoulder. She didn't make it up to his chin, even standing on tiptoes, but she still seemed to be just the right size for his dad. "It doesn't look like she took any chunks out of you that won't heal."

That comment earned him an elbow in the ribs, hard enough to make a point.

Ross grinned. "The law school held a special forum on dealing with difficult clients. I simply applied the suggested techniques and instantly had this quarrelsome female in the palm of my hand."

His mom snorted.

His dad grinned and hugged her close. "You're going to have to share those techniques with me, son. Your mother's been getting away with murder for way too many years."

"Oh, no you don't, either of you. It took me years to get you properly trained, Del McConnell. I refuse to have all my good efforts undone by some disreputable ambulance chaser!"

Ross barked out a huge laugh. "I knew I should have taken that job with Dewey, Cheatem, and Howe."

Then his mother grew serious. "Ross, I can't bear the thought of you being out here alone. And forty is too much." She sighed.

"Mom—"

"I have a counteroffer," his dad interjected.

He glanced at Ross's mom, then straight into Ross's eyes. "I caught the end of your conversation. I think you can live with forty, Dorothy; it's his life." His steady eyes still held Ross's. "But with one little proviso attached. On the off chance that something were to happen to me, I want your assurance that you will return home so you can take care of your mother. At least during that first year."

Ross watched his mother's eyes grow wide in alarm, and his dad reassured her he was fine; he was only taking husbandly precautions in her best interest. So Ross, with misgivings he couldn't quite define, agreed to the terms of the deal. His father was in the best of health. There had been nothing to worry about. It had seemed as much a nonrisk as Ross still being single at age forty.

The flight attendant announced that the pilot was beginning their descent into JFK, so Ross brought his thoughts back to the present and put his tablet away. So much time had passed since that conversation with his parents. So much life had happened, and so much of it hadn't happened as Ross had expected it would. He now lived in Salt Lake City, commuted frequently to the brownstone he maintained in New York, saw to his mother's needs, and visited his father's grave as often as possible.

And he was thirty-seven and single.

Ross grabbed his bag from the overhead bin, slung it over his shoulder, and made his way down the aisle of the plane. The firm was sending a limo for him like it always did. He glanced at his watch. With airport traffic, he'd be cutting it close. The German dignitaries with whom he was meeting would only be in town this afternoon. A lot of money hinged on the outcome of this particular meeting. Ross had gone through the briefs thoroughly because confidence in presentation was a must; Robert Goldman—*the* Goldman of Rogers, Goldman, Clarke, and Janofsky—had assured him that someone would feed him any last-minute information he needed before he met with the Germans—Engel Tech, to be precise. He felt the beginning surge of adrenaline. In his opinion, matching wits, slicing through details, selling the argument, bringing the client or opposition to his way of thinking was as much a thrill ride as a bungee jump off the George Washington Bridge.

He saw the waiting limo at the curb. George the driver was standing next to it and tipped his hat to Ross in welcome. They'd made many airport commutes together over the last few months, and Ross sensed that today George seemed a little agitated, his eyes glancing quickly from Ross to the window of the passenger seat. "Good to have you back, Mr. McConnell. How was the flight?'

"Routine." Ross walked to the back of the car and set his bags down on the curb. "What's the news in the office?"

"Nothing much to speak of, Mr. McConnell."

Ross had tried for months to get George to call him by his first name and had eventually given up. Now Ross was more interested in the suppressed edginess he sensed from George. "How's Rita?" She was the cute little receptionist George had been secretly eyeing since summer. "Making any progress there?"

George glanced from Ross to the tinted windows of the limousine and back. "Huh? Oh, not much, Mr. McConnell. I been seeing her a lot lately with one of those guys from Schwab. Accountant or some such." He glanced again at the back window of the limo. "How was the flight?"

George had asked him that already. He was a consummate driver. He could outmaneuver seasoned cabbies and NASCAR racers, Ross was sure. The guy had nerves of tempered steel. Ross didn't think he would really feel outclassed by a skinny accountant from Schwab, and he couldn't fathom what could have him so edgy right now. Unless—

George opened the door for him. Long legs in sheer pearl-gray hosiery stretched from here to China. Ross shut his eyes and grimaced inwardly. He was well acquainted with those legs—not intimately acquainted but well enough. They were attached, probably at the armpits, to Gina Rogers, the only child of LaMonte Rogers, founding partner. Beautiful, brilliant, and ruthless, she was a powerful, effective ally and devastating foe.

Ross slid into the seat, and George settled into the driver's seat, glancing in the rearview mirror surreptitiously. If they were lucky, Ross mused, they might make it back to the office without any spilt blood. One never knew with Gina.

"Darling Ross! That fresh country air must be doing you some good. You look marvelous." Gina leaned forward and extended her cheek to Ross for a kiss.

Not responding to her actions, Ross nodded courteously instead. "Gina, as always."

Chapter 5

NATALIE WAS JUST FINISHING HER regular Tuesday-morning cleaning job at the Montgomery home when her cell phone rang. It was a number she didn't recognize. "Hello," she managed as she crammed the phone under her chin and opened the trunk of her Focus.

"Are you Natalie Forrester?" The woman's voice sounded mature but strained somehow.

Natalie managed to lug her tank vacuum up onto the rim of the trunk with one arm. "Uh-huh." She used her hip to balance the vacuum while she shifted her caddy of cleaning supplies to the corner of the trunk. The hose of the vacuum was coiling dangerously around her legs. "Can you hold just a moment?" She set the phone down on the bumper of the car, settled the vacuum and hose into the trunk, and slammed the lid. Now she could actually think and talk at the same time. "Thanks for waiting. My vacuum hose was attacking me like a hungry elephant."

No laugh from the other end. Natalie grimaced.

"Mrs. Forrester, my name is Esther Johnson. I got your name from Valerie Lisle. She says you've been cleaning for her regularly for the last few years."

Well, what do you know? Natalie's eyebrows shot up in amusement. *Mrs. Lisle is aware of the serfs and lackeys in her life after all.*

"I know she is very particular about the people she allows to work for her, and I'm looking for someone reliable like that. I'm afraid I am in need of help."

Natalie leaned against the side of her car. The October air was brisk, but the sun made the body of her car warm, and the rays felt good on her face. She'd been sweating after mopping the floor, and the crisp combination was refreshing.

The woman continued. "I have been cleaning a home for the last few months—just the one house. A little bit of extra money on the side, you know, for the fun things. What? Just a minute, Mrs. Forrester." Natalie could hear murmurs in the background, bells dinging, voices over an intercom. It sounded like a hospital. What was going on? "Thanks for holding—so sorry about that." Her voice sounded even more strained, even weak. Natalie waited patiently, but she could feel a knot in her stomach begin to form. "As I said, I've been cleaning a home for some time now, but an emergency has come up." Her voice broke.

Natalie, alarmed, waited quietly. She didn't know this woman and didn't know what to say, but she didn't want to abandon her either.

"Sorry. I'm okay now. I have to go in a minute. They're . . . Anyway. I'll have to go in just a minute. My husband is ill, and I need someone who can take over this house for me for a while. Do you think you can help me? I'm not sure how long Burt will be . . . I just want to be sure I'm there for him."

"Tell me about the house, Mrs. Johnson, and I'll tell you if I think it will work into my schedule." Natalie hoped it would work into her schedule; it could be the answer to her prayers. Best to act professional and not too eager. Still, how could she not try to help this woman? Natalie could almost hear her crumbling over the phone.

Mrs. Johnson told her quickly about the house. Executive-style home, not too large but tastefully decorated. Quality, high-end furnishings on the modern side, with the occasional antique thrown in for balance and a touch of the eclectic. Single, professional man—an attorney—who traveled quite a lot; the job involved a bit more housekeeping than just the quick dust and sweep up. He paid extraordinarily well—Natalie gasped when she heard how much—but that included carting his clothes to and from the cleaners and an occasional personal errand or two. Mrs. Johnson confessed that the pay had staggered her as well, and as a result—and because she liked the nice young man—she brought in or made meals for him on occasion. After she did that, she noticed her paycheck amount increased even more.

"Wow," Natalie said under her breath. She found herself hoping Mr. Johnson stayed sick for a long time. That led to a stab of guilt. But the money involved—on a long-term basis—would allow her to meet her tuition and possibly allow her to dump the Lisles', despite Valerie's generous recommendation. She imagined never having to pick up Megadeth Lisle's dirty laundry ever again. She shook her head. It was wrong to hope that this poor woman's husband would become chronically ill just for Natalie's sake. But even in the short term . . . Natalie mentally rubbed her hands together in glee.

"I'd be happy to help you, Mrs. Johnson. Tell me what days he normally expects you. Even if I have to do a little juggling"—Natalie was in the second month of a couple of college classes—"I'll make it work and get there this week."

"Oh, thank you! I usually go in on Tuesdays and drop off his laundry on Fridays. I didn't get there today, because—"

"I understand."

"He just left town again for a while. He travels a lot. I don't think he'd mind if you were to work other days, although I always went in on Tuesdays as we originally arranged it, so I'm really not sure."

How could a person who was out of town care what day of the week she cleaned his house? And that would give Natalie the flexibility her schedule dictated right now. "I'm sure it won't be a problem. Do you know when he'll be home?"

"No. He never shares that kind of information with me. I just show up on Tuesdays, clean, and take his shirts to the laundry. I pick them up and drop them off at his home on Friday. If he has errands for me, he leaves a note on the kitchen counter. That doesn't happen very often though. I leave any meals or goodies I feel inclined to make for him in the fridge."

Mrs. Johnson gave her the name and address, told her where the spare key and security controls were, and gave Natalie her cell number just before the doctor arrived and she had to abruptly end the call.

Natalie slipped her cell phone into her purse and did a little happy dance. Then she made an embarrassingly loud whooping sound, looked around sheepishly, and slipped into the driver's seat of her car. She was due at the Raymonds' house in thirty minutes, but this Mr. McConnell professional man's house was only a small detour on the way there. She'd swing by and take a quick peek.

High on the east bench, hugging the hillside, she found a contemporary house—work of art, more like, to Natalie's eyes—made of mountain stone and cedar. The architecture was natural, with clean lines and rough edges combined. It looked settled in its environs as though it was comfortable in its own skin. Scrub oak wrapped around the exterior in a fiery autumn blanket; yews stood as solid sentries of the deepest green. Natalie could breathe in the very masculinity of the place. She was entranced. Her fingers itched to get the key from its secure location and take a quick look around, see if the heart of the house matched the exterior as well.

After a quick call to Mrs. Raymond to let her know she'd be a few minutes late, Natalie located the spare key and deactivated the security alarm. She slipped through what appeared to be a utility room. A professional-grade washer and dryer that looked like they'd never been used stood against a pewter-colored wall, and maple cabinetry and a slate floor accented the room. Natalie's "utility room," if you could call it that, was in a corner of the unfinished basement of her rental house. Her ancient washer and dryer were chipped but reliable. Her floors and walls were pewter colored also, but that was because they were made of concrete. Above her washer was a single hanging lightbulb.

Natalie felt an almost reverent urge to remove her shoes, so she slipped them off and left them next to the utility room door. She had butterflies as though she were a thief. Ridiculous. She'd never had this kind of reaction before when she'd done her job. She'd been in plenty of homes alone working. Shrugging off the feeling as best she could, she made her way to the kitchen. And sucked in her breath.

The kitchen, again, was pewter and maple, its slate flooring rich with mottled colors of charcoal, rust, and jade. The east wall wasn't a wall; it was a bank of windows that looked out onto a sloping hillside of scrub oak and aspen and let in a glorious amount of morning sunlight. French doors opened onto a cedar deck that wrapped around the house. The ceiling was high and angled dramatically. A large mission-style dining table and chairs with a deep cherry finish stood next to the windows so diners could enjoy breakfast with a breathtaking view. She would have called the overhead light fixture a chandelier; it was constructed from a weathered bronze, with twists and angles that made the artist in Natalie want to climb on a chair and stroke it.

The living room wasn't large, but the high ceilings and use of windows gave the room the illusion of spaciousness. Its floor was hardwood, and oversized leather sofas faced each other on a muted Oriental rug. Splashes of color came from a couple of well-chosen throw pillows and a spray of Oriental poppies in a chunky earthenware vase. A huge fireplace of mountain stone held a large oil painting that looked original and old. Probably an antique and by itself worth more money than Natalie would earn in her entire lifetime. Feeling more and more impressed, she walked up the stairs.

The master bedroom took up half of the second floor. It held a huge four-poster bed and some large chests she was sure were also antiques. The carpet was a deep, warm green, the duvet covering the bed a thick brocade of golds and greens that looked rich and European in style. The master bath was Natalie's idea of heaven. It was large and airy, the exterior wall lined with bright windows high enough to let in floods of sunlight without losing privacy. The bathtub was huge and sunken into a slate surround wide enough to sit on comfortably or hold hundreds of wonderfully scented candles. Natalie could see herself sinking up to her ears in bubbles, with the flickering lights of the candles and soft music playing quietly in the background. There was also a large shower with multiple heads at various levels in a glass enclosure.

Natalie had yet to see any evidence of the man who supposedly lived in this amazing house. She had almost decided Mrs. Johnson must work for a phantom or a Realtor who was really having her keep a model home tidy. She glanced at her watch, gasped, and headed back to the utility room door. Her snooping time was more than over. She was going to have to work quickly at the Raymond's to be in time to pick up Em from school. Taking one final look around, she decided this house should be easy to take care of if its appearance today was anything typical. It didn't even look lived in.

She briefly wondered where this Mr. McConnell did his actual living as she pulled out into traffic and headed for the Raymonds', now nearly an hour behind schedule. As beautiful and rich as the house had been, it didn't appear to be much of a home.

Chapter 6

DURING THE LIMO RIDE FROM the airport back to the office, Gina briefed Ross on the latest developments with the German firm Engel Tech, and then they went straight into a meeting with Friedrich Dierdorff, its CEO. It became immediately apparent to Ross that she'd withheld pertinent information from him. Luckily, years in a courtroom had prepared him to think quickly on his feet, but he was infuriated that a team member had deliberately set him up like that in front of a prestigious client. Tattling to Daddy about her was not an option. But after all this time, he had no qualms about letting her have it with both barrels privately after the meeting.

Her eyes grew large in feigned innocence. "How can you accuse me of such things? I am first and foremost a professional. You simply weren't listening during the briefing in the limo."

"You never said anything about their expansion plans."

"I must have. It's here in my notes." She made a fuss of straightening her short skirt and looked up at Ross through slitted eyes. "Come on, Ross. Admit to being human. You were simply off your game."

There was no point in arguing further. He understood her attack methods only too well; he'd dealt with them before, so while she let her arrows fly, he ignored them and stared her down. "Gina, stand warned. Remember the law of the harvest, and remember who your allies in this venture are. Or should be."

She shook her head and turned to look out the office window. He'd been dismissed.

Things between them professionally were colder and more distant than usual over the next couple of weeks, even with their hands as full as they were. Engel Technologien—or Angel Technologies—was anything but. The principals were insufferable, demanding long hours, sometimes fifteen-hour days, working page after page, bullet by bullet on every aspect of their complex international contractual deal. The meetings and the posturing were endless and unmerciful. The law firm brought in translators, then hired different translators when the first ones quit. Some moments were untranslatable and best left that way.

Ross and Gina went the rounds with Engel Tech and then went the rounds with each other on approach and method and everything and anything.

When Ross finally watched Friedrich Dierdorff climb into his limo for JFK, he breathed for the first time in two weeks. Then he caught the first available flight out of New York, a red-eye, which included a short layover in Chicago. Exhausted and suddenly starving, he headed to the Chinese fast-food place in the concessions triangle at O'Hare, wolfed down his purchase, and reboarded the plane.

But now, back on board, instead of the hunger one joked about feeling shortly after eating Chinese food, Ross felt the acute onset of nausea.

Oh joy.

Shortly after takeoff, Ross was crouched over the toilet in the lavatory, retching violently. *And didn't this just cap off two of the worst weeks of his life?* he thought miserably.

Ross had done everything possible to avoid working with Gina on the Engel Tech case but to no avail. He remembered only too well working with Gina shortly after she'd joined the firm five years ago. The darling daughter and heir apparent of LaMonte Rogers, founding partner, and a fresh graduate from Yale, her daddy's alma mater, she had the brash confidence that money, looks, and an Ivy League education could provide. Men swooned over her, and women immediately felt inferior to her. And her daddy indulged her. Initially, Ross had been intrigued by her too, right along with the rest of the bourgeois masses.

They had been assigned to work together on the Watkins case, with Ross as lead counsel, and he'd found Gina to be a bright, passionate young lawyer, fearless to the point of recklessness, but a little too willing to ride on daddy's coattails. Ross had chalked up her lack of restraint to youth and thought grooming within the firm would polish her into an asset for the firm.

He had soon discovered that she was passionate in other ways as well. Gina was a woman who had never encountered the word *no*.

They had been working late on the case one evening after weeks of working closely together. Gina frequently displayed her feminine attractions to her advantage, but this particular evening as they'd worked, Gina had also made opportunities to brush against him, which he'd ignored. She'd frequently flirted with the other men of the firm, including her father, so initially Ross had been unconcerned. As the evening had worn on, however, Gina's advances had become less subtle, until she was looking at him with eyes that bespoke a frank challenge.

Ross had realized he faced a huge dilemma. First of all, he was a man and would have been lying if he'd said her overtures hadn't flattered and affected him. She was an extraordinarily attractive woman and, at that moment, an obvious one. He'd considered himself a seasoned professional, a mature man, and he was a Mormon. He was respected within the firm for his professional skills and his integrity, and he would not undermine that respect by behaving unprofessionally toward a colleague, especially if that colleague was also the daughter of a founding partner.

He also knew he was an aberration of the typical New York singleton. He'd been and still was celibate, as dictated by his religious beliefs. He had stopped trying to explain this moral tenet to his friends long ago in law school when they'd invited him to join them on their weekend binges of booze and willing coeds. His explanations had been so foreign to them, their faces so bewildered as they'd tried to wrap their minds around the concepts, that he had frankly given up. Only Bud had cut him any slack. After that, when others had asked Ross to join their partying, he'd simply said he was busy. Busy reading . . . scriptures. Busy not thinking about the other guys' descriptions of nubile young women. Busy at the gym, working out hard. Busy running cold showers. Just staying busy.

Eventually, he had compartmentalized his personal life, separating it completely from his professional one. Better to be considered a mystery than a throwback to the Middle Ages if he wanted to survive as an attorney. He had to project a tough, confident, alpha-male image, and most of his colleagues automatically presumed that image included as many notches on his belt as possible.

So there he'd been, face-to-face with a huge moral challenge: Gina looking seductive, arrogant, defiant, and formidable all at once. He had tactfully and successfully discouraged unwanted attention from women in the past. He was not inexperienced in the pitfalls of romance. But right then, Ross, with his maturity, his years of professional experience, and his devout religious moral convictions, had faced a young woman who boldly wore the sexual confidence of a pop diva, and he'd known he was outgunned.

He'd looked Gina in the eye as squarely as she'd been eyeing him and had told her they were through working for the evening.

"I hope so," she'd said.

"That isn't what I meant," he'd replied. He'd stood and closed his case file. She'd stood and grabbed the lapels of his suit, pulling herself to him. Placing his hands over hers, he'd gently pried her fingers free and shaken his head. Then, like Joseph of old when faced with Potiphar's wife, he'd left.

Gina had been stunned. And then she'd become enraged. Ross had known that as an attorney, she accepted the challenges of opposition with aggressiveness, but what he hadn't known was that in her personal life, she had eons more experience than he did and had honed her combat tactics down to a vicious and cunning art.

Work on the Watkins case had turned into a cold war. Ross had maintained his composure while Gina had missed deadlines, subtly suggesting in subsequent meetings that Ross had dropped the ball—always with her hallmark feminine allure that made otherwise rational men willing to accept her words.

Eventually, Ross had even been called into Monty Rogers's office, where he had sat silently and listened to Monty's overblown lecturing. Monty had expressed disappointment in Ross's lack of chivalry, slapped him on the back, and said he expected Ross to help show Gina the ropes. Ross had clenched his teeth through it all and had then returned to his office. As he'd passed Gina's desk, she'd shot him a combined victory and warning look.

They said hell had no fury like a woman scorned, but when that woman was also an attorney, even hell needed to watch out.

An office source had informed him that Gina was out to get Saint Ross McConnell, that she was out to teach Mr. High and Mighty a lesson. Ross had prayed mightily that his problems with Gina would eventually blow over. He'd learned otherwise on the Engel Tech case.

Turbulence over the Colorado Rockies sent his already raw stomach back into an uproar. The plane lurched and heaved, and Ross did as well. He was deathly certain the seemingly endless hours he'd spent in the claustrophobic cubicle the airlines referred to as a lavatory were the longest of his life so far, and that was saying something, especially after the last couple of weeks.

He finally arrived in Salt Lake in the wee hours of the morning, gray faced and miserable. It took an interminably long time for his luggage to find its way onto the baggage-claim carousel, but when it finally showed up, he heaved his carry-on bag over his shoulder, grabbed his suitcase and garment bag, and, by sheer force of will, made it to the airport shuttle.

The drive from the terminal to long-term parking was miraculously brief, probably because the moment Ross sat down, he closed his eyes and fell asleep. Fortunately, the shuttle driver, with few passengers at four in the morning, had asked him what section his car was parked in when they'd headed out. When the driver's voice came over the speaker, announcing their arrival, Ross opened an eye, then the other eye, then hauled himself out of the shuttle and toward his car.

Determined to get home alive and in record time, he lowered the convertible top of his charcoal-gray Mercedes. The crisp October air was a sharp slap to his senses; he needed it to stay awake and keep his dulled, depleted wits focused on his driving.

He eventually pulled into the garage, threw the car into park, dropped his head against the steering wheel, and closed his eyes. His body felt like lead. Driving from the airport to his home had taken a Herculean effort. Now that he was here, he wasn't sure he would ever move again. He knew if he fell asleep right now, he would be sitting in his car, in the garage, for several days. Maybe years.

He sat up, hit the button for the automatic garage door to close, and rubbed both hands vigorously over his face. He was sorely tempted to recline the seat. He was sure he would sleep like the dead wherever he was, but his big four-poster and its deep, soft mattress called like a siren to him and lured him from his sleep-deprived haze long enough to at least grab the carry-on with his tablet in it and head into the house. Everything else could just stay where it was for now. He dragged himself heavily up the stairs, set the carry-on on a bedroom dresser, stopped long enough to slide out of his shoes, and fell backward onto the thick duvet.

And instantly fell asleep.

Chapter 7

NATALIE'S HAND SLAMMED RHYTHMICALLY ON the steering wheel of her car to the beat of her classic Beatles CD. She cranked the volume up, rolled her window down, and flew along in ecstasy. Her anthropology teacher had left a note on the door of their classroom saying class had been canceled for the day. Hooray for personal emergencies and the teachers who had them! That gave Natalie an extra couple of hours of unexpected freedom, not to mention a few more days to study for the midterm exam she had expected to sweat blood on that morning. She liked the subject well enough, but the teacher had warned the class that he was tough, and he hadn't been exaggerating. Natalie wouldn't have been as worried if she'd gotten to go over her notes last night, but she'd ended up helping Emma write a paper on Greek mythology.

Now she could get to the lawyer's house, have it spanking clean—that meant dusted and quickly vacuumed, since he was never there and she'd never even seen evidence that he existed—and use his marvelous kitchen space to practice for her tap class midterm. Who knew that tap dancing would count as a physical education requirement? Considering the fact that Natalie had never considered herself very athletic, it had seemed like a fun and less intimidating choice—especially after she'd found a pair of tap shoes at the DI.

She would also be able get her afternoon cleaning job finished by early afternoon and have free time to—what? She had free time so seldom on weekdays she wasn't sure what she wanted to do with it. She could work on her stained-glass creation, study for her anthropology exam, or scour a couple of thrift stores for some hidden treasures.

Pulling to an abrupt halt in the driveway, she grabbed her cleaning tool kit and lightweight vacuum cleaner and headed to the front door.

She had gone through the utility door on her first visit to the house, but the front door was so much closer to her car that she'd quickly made it a habit. On a whim, she went back to her car and grabbed the Beatles CD. Mr. Big Shot Attorney had a first-class audio system wired through the entire house. And she felt like rockin'.

Halfway to the door, Natalie paused and ran back out to her car again. She wasn't in the mood to clean yet. She wanted to celebrate! For so long, her life had felt like the lyrics of a bad country song, and now she had the small miracle of time. She returned the cleaning tools to the car, grabbed her tap shoes, exchanged the Beatles for her tap class CD, unfortunately titled "Best of Vaudeville," which contained a modern remix of some good old tap standards, and ran back to the house. She slipped into the tap shoes, slid the class CD into the audio player, cranked up the volume, and ran to the kitchen to get set.

Feet apart, hands on hips, she mentally thought through the movements she would be practicing. Step, shuffle, lift, cross—darn! What was it? She clicked across the kitchen floor tiles to the spiral notebook she had set on the table just as the music began with a crash. A long, showy drum solo got the first track cranking, louder and quicker, faster and faster, cymbals and snare drums repeating like machine-gun fire, bass drum thumping loudly. She reviewed her notes and ran back to her original position. Deep breath. Step, shuffle, cross, step. Step, shuffle, cross, step. She readied herself for her first steps. The drum solo continued, tenor drums pounding syncopations into her brain. Initially, she thought the class CD was kind of corny—it *was* called "Best of Vaudeville," for heaven's sake. But the more she had listened to it as she practiced her tap-dancing steps, the more it had gotten under her skin. Sheepishly, she acknowledged that she liked it. It was fun. Besides, it reminded her, sort of, of her nana and how she used to talk about the good old days.

The drum solo crescendoed into a big drum roll, and then the trombones kicked in with the melody. *Hands on hips*, she thought, *here we go. This time we are going to stay with the beat.* She'd had a hard time getting her feet to move fast enough to keep up with the music's tempo, but she'd practiced a lot and was almost up to speed. She focused, took another deep breath, and lifted her right foot. Step, shuffle, cross, step, step, shuffle, cross, step. She almost had it. A couple more times through and she was sure she'd be able to stay with the music.

* * *

Ross was as close to unconscious as a person could be. A complete lack of awareness blanketed his senses, his body in a deeply relaxed void. He gradually became aware of gunfire somewhere in the near distance. Enemy artillery, gang warfare. His shoulders bunched and tensed. He was on the streets of New York—not Manhattan or Brooklyn. Somewhere more dangerous. It called for caution. He thrashed in his bed, seeking cover from the gunfire. Sunlight began filtering through the buildings. No, they were the curtains of his bedroom. He was foggy, but he remembered now, he was home. So why didn't the gunfire stop?

Adrenaline pumped fire through his veins as a result of the disturbing images in his dream. The percussive shots hammered at his skull. What was going on? As full consciousness hit, he bolted upright with alarm. Someone was in his house. He leaped from the bed, his head swinging from side to side, searching for a makeshift weapon. Opening the closet, his eyes landed on his practice putter leaning against the corner inside the door.

He grabbed it, then ran his hand through his hair and took a deep breath to calm his jangled nerves. After his ordeal of a trip to New York, it would be just his luck to have a break-in on his first day home. A stroke of inspiration made him pause to grab his cell phone out of his jacket pocket and punch in 911, with his thumb over the send button, before heading out of his bedroom to the landing and quietly inching his way down the stairs.

Halfway down, the gunfire, which he now recognized as drums, turned into some sort of band thing. Jazz, sort of, though he wasn't sure. He heard some strange rapping bursts, like castanets, coming from the kitchen; the "music," he could tell, was being pumped through his audio system. Quietly, he edged his way down the hall to the kitchen door. There, in his kitchen, to his utter surprise, was a petite woman in a lime-green T-shirt and blue jeans, her blonde hair pulled back in a ponytail, tap dancing, of all things. Make that tap dancing, *sort of.* Her arms were flailing wildly at her sides like frantic windmills as her feet hopped up and down and shuffled back and forth. If it weren't for the fact that his head throbbed and his stomach pitched from his sudden movements, he might have found the scene humorous. As it was, she was a stranger, an intruder invading the privacy of his home. There had been a woman in his ward in New York a couple of years back who had gotten into his apartment once. He wasn't sure how, but he'd had his suspicions at the time. He had flatly told her not to bother him again or she could expect him to file charges.

Suddenly, the woman in the green T-shirt let out a blood-curdling scream, slipped on the tiles, and fell in a tangle of elbows and legs to the kitchen floor.

Ross felt every nerve ending in his body explode, especially the ones in close proximity to his head. He clenched his hands, narrowly missing calling emergency, and raised the arm holding the golf putter. The woman's shoulders collapsed, and she was gulping in breaths. So was he, actually.

"Who are you, and what are you doing here?" he asked in a threatening tone loud enough to be heard over the blaring trumpets from the CD.

She looked at him like she didn't speak English, like she was trying to process his simple questions in terms she could understand. Then she replied in a shaky voice. "Natalie. I'm Natalie."

"Okay, Natalie, and just what are you doing in my house?"

Her hand was clutching her T-shirt over her heart, and she paused like she was collecting her thoughts along with her wits. "I was . . . what? I . . . hmmm. Shuffling off to Buffalo?" She slid her knees under her and pushed herself to all fours.

Ross wasn't a dance expert by any stretch, but he'd at least heard the term before, and while still cautious, he started to relax. With the putter still slightly raised in warning, he walked over to the CD player and stopped the music. Gesturing with his head toward his CD player, he said, "And what was that?"

Still breathing hard, staring down at the floor tiles, the woman Natalie said, "'Mississippi Mud.'"

Was she intentionally trying to be funny? Ross crossed his arms over his chest and gave her his best death-sentence stare. Except that she wasn't looking at him. She moved to get her feet under her, averting her face. He put out his hand to help her up, but she ignored the gesture and scrambled to her feet, the taps on her shoes clinking like bad money.

* * *

Natalie tried to catch her breath as she surreptitiously studied the man in front of her who was wielding a golf club. He was tall and dark, his mouth set in a firm line. He had a day's growth of beard showing, and his eyes were dark and intense but shadowed, and he looked—wrinkled. He wore rumpled slacks and a dress shirt, the cuffs rolled up to his elbows, the collar open, the shirttail hanging partially out on the side. Unfortunately, right at that moment, the rumpled slept-in-his-clothes look didn't make him look cute and cuddly. He looked formidable. Why was it that when she encountered a strong male her brain turned to sludge, her tongue became ten pounds heavier, and the words that plopped off of it could have been scripted into a bad sitcom?

Seeing him had scared her to death anyway, but when she'd gotten a good look at him, all broad shoulders and designer clothes, with the rugged-warrior thing going, she'd gone into default wallflower mode. Now, if she could just leave the house with a modicum of poise . . . she'd pack up and get the heck out of Dodge.

He was staring at her, not saying anything, looking at her thoroughly, sizing her up. She realized suddenly that she had been staring at him as well and felt herself go pink. She dropped her gaze and nonchalantly hiked up her jeans. Clearing her throat, she extended her hand and said again, "I'm Natalie. You must be Ross McConnell."

She hoped that the fact that she knew his name would add a sense of reassurance to the situation and was horrified when her vain attempt at an introduction failed. His probing looks suddenly iced over, turning glacial and rigid. He ignored her outstretched hand and leaned the golf club against a wall, then refolded his arms against his chest. "Natalie whoever you are, I am not in a patient mood. I suggest you leave my home right now."

The corners of her mouth turned up in a quivering attempt to smile. "I didn't mean to disturb you. Esther said, I mean—"

"Before I push the send button on this 911 call."

Natalie's mouth dropped into an *O*, then snapped shut. She swiftly moved to the kitchen table, grabbed her things, and slipped out the front door. She ground the key in the ignition, threw the car in reverse, and tore down the road. Her only coherent thought was how glad she was that she hadn't taken all of her cleaning tools into his house yet, how that would have dragged out her entire escape. She didn't notice how badly she was shaking until she was halfway home. And it wasn't until she pulled into her own driveway that she realized she'd left her CD at Mr. McConnell's house.

* * *

Ross locked the front door and headed slowly up the stairs. His head felt like it would fall off any second, and part of him wished it would. Even though his stomach still felt like he'd been on a roller coaster all night, he decided to risk it and take some ibuprofen. He headed back to the kitchen and grabbed the pills, then filled a glass with tap water. His mouth tasted like battery acid, and he felt like he'd just stepped on a bunny. The slogan on the woman's T-shirt had read "What if the hokey pokey is really what it's all about?"

Carrying the glass upstairs with him, he set it on the night table and lay back on the bed. He tried to fluff the pillow and settle it around his throbbing brain. He needed more sleep. He tried to push the image of a female whirligig aside but failed. He could still see the blonde ponytail whipping as wildly as her arms had been, then her falling in a sprawling heap on the floor, her green eyes wide. "Mississippi Mud," he muttered. He probably shouldn't have been so short with her, he knew, but he'd used every ounce of patience he had during his two weeks with Gina and the Germans. Whatever he'd had left, he was sure he'd vomited into the great void at thirty thousand feet. And seeing some strange woman in his house had conjured visions of cookies and casseroles, blind dates gone bad, nice women who turned into desperate stalkers when they scented single male prey. He thought of Liz, who had initially approached him. He'd acted on instinct today, that's all. The tap-dancing woman seemed familiar, for some reason. He couldn't think anymore right then. His eyes felt heavy, the pulsing throb in his temples beginning to ebb. The ibuprofen was starting to work, thank goodness.

She'd mentioned an Esther, he thought, just before he drifted back to sleep.

Chapter 8

THE SKY WAS THE DEEP orange and red it turned just before the night turned to indigo. Ross stood at the window in his bedroom and looked out over the Salt Lake Valley and the first winking of city lights. He had awakened only a few minutes ago. While still not in top form, he felt rested, and his head no longer ached. He was trying to decide what to do about a meal. It was a relief to actually feel hungry again, not that he would be eating mu-shu pork anytime soon. He showered and pulled on his favorite pair of old Levis and a blue polo shirt.

The light on his answering machine was flashing. He used his cell phone for nearly everything but had steered local business to his landline. He'd even trained his family to use the home phone unless it was urgent. The LCD display told him he had sixteen messages in the two weeks he'd been in New York.

He decided to take a minute to go through them. Sitting on the edge of his desk, he grabbed a notepad and pen and pushed the play button.

The first few were hang-ups with no messages left. Fine. The first real message was from his investment broker. That could wait.

"Ross, dear, it's your mother. Be sure to put October 27 on your calendar. It isn't every day a woman turns sixty-five, and you had better plan on being here. Jackie and Suzie have a big family thing planned. You can bring someone along if you like. Or they can bring someone along for you if you're too busy to arrange something yourself." He sighed. His mom and sisters were not going to let up on him until they could see the ring on his finger. "Be safe in New York, honey, and give me a call when you get back to town."

"Hey, Uncle Mac, I know you're not home right now, but I e-mailed you my football schedule. If you can make it to any of the games, that'd be awesome. Braden got injured, so they moved me to first string. So, cool, well, see ya." Brett, his sister Jackie's son, was a junior at East High.

"Mr. McConnell, sorry to bother you—I hope this isn't a problem. Oh, this is Esther Johnson. Listen, my husband's in the hospital, and I had to arrange for someone to take over your housecleaning. I wish you weren't out of town; I would feel so much better getting your approval up front. Anyway, her name is Natalie Forrester. I got references, and they looked good, so I hope it won't be a problem. I'm not sure how long this will take, but Natalie seemed willing to fill in for as long as you need her. I'm sorry for the inconvenience."

Esther. That meant Mississippi Mud was his new—albeit temporary—housekeeper. The case of the tap-dancing stranger was solved. A few guilt pangs knifed through his gut, along with his hunger pangs. Still, she hadn't exactly been doing housekeeping when he'd encountered her, so how was he to know?

"Ross, this is your sister." Susan. Suzie automatically assumed he only had one sister when she called him. Jackie always said, "Mac, it's Jack." His sister with the boy name was the most feminine female he knew. "Megan Howard called me—you remember Megan, don't you? She's the tall Stevenson girl with horse teeth that she had fixed in college? Well, it's Megan Howard now, and I saw her at the mall, and we got talking, and then we got talking about you, and she mentioned she has a sister-in-law who'd be perfect for you. I told her how picky you are, and she said she understands, but she e-mailed me a picture of her sister-in-law at the wedding—Megan's been married ten years, so it's not that old of a picture, and she's really pretty, Ross. So I called her back and said I'd talk to you and see what you think—I mean with Mom's birthday bash coming up, you have to make room in your busy social calendar for *that*, and I don't think you've met anybody, *really*, since you moved back to Utah, so what do you think? Should I give her a call and set something up, or what?" Did Suzie never breathe? "I need to get back to her pretty soon because Mom's birthday is a week from Saturday, and that's not a lot of time. So call me." Her voice dropped to a stage whisper. "What if she's the *one*, Ross? I have a feeling something is going to happen, and it would be so good for Mom to see you happy and settled with kids. She's been waiting for so long." Ross rolled his eyes and sighed. "Call me, Ross. Bye."

Thankfully, there were more hang-ups on the machine after Suzie's call. There was a call from Jackie, quietly telling him that Brett had caught a long pass for the winning touchdown at the game last Friday and she hoped he was having a nice trip. Nice trip, like he was taking in Radio City Music Hall or Madison Square Garden and not going head-to-head with Engel Tech and Gina. Jackie didn't force the females down his throat quite like Suzie did, but she more than anyone seemed to unconsciously remind him that something was missing in his life that he'd forgotten he needed.

He shuffled down the stairs and poked his head into the fridge. He didn't really expect there to be anything edible after more than two weeks back East, although one never knew until one looked. But there, sitting on the top shelf, was a jar of homemade chicken noodle soup. Attached was a Post-it sticker with today's date on it. The soup was fresh.

Chicken soup with homemade noodles. Nothing could sound better to his stomach. He reached into a cabinet for a bowl and noticed a small bag containing three large rolls on the counter. Next to them was a small plate with a stick of butter. Did one of his sisters know he'd gotten home last night? It wouldn't surprise him. Could it have been Esther? He had no idea. He poured a third of the soup from the jar into the bowl, threw a paper towel over the top to contain splatters, and popped it into the microwave. Two minutes later, he was seated at the kitchen table, scooping up a man-sized chunk of chicken as he took a large bite of a soft, buttery roll. Slouching into his chair, he extended his legs and crossed his ankles on the seat of the chair across the table from him. Savoring the bite, he pulled out his cell phone and punched the buttons. A tiny female voice answered, "Hello?"

"Hey, how's my best girl?" Ross took another quick bite of soup and grinned at the squeal that began on the other end of the connection.

"Uncle Mackee! Mama, it's Uncle Mackee!"

"Hush, Lex. Mac? Hello?"

"Hi, Jack. How's the world hanging together?" Ross took another bite of soup.

"Are you back in town? For some reason, I wasn't expecting you to be home so soon this trip."

That left Jackie out as his good soup fairy. "Just got in last night. Red eye. You're my first call."

"You haven't talked to Mom yet?"

How could he explain that he fared better with other family members if he got an emotional barometric reading from his sane baby sister first?

"I wouldn't advertise that fact around Mom and Susan," Jackie said. "Mom is so worked up about this birthday of hers, and Susan is turning it into an event worthy of Ringling Brothers." She chuckled.

Jackie was so much like their dad in temperament. Soothing and affable, easygoing. Her low, husky voice continued. "Mom is ready to remodel her entire main floor. Suzie is talking about a live band and dancing. That could be interesting, don't you think? It's close enough to Halloween that she's even talking about costumes. If you have any feelings on the matter, you'd better get your two cents in now, or you may be showing up at Mom's a week from Saturday dressed as a Smurf."

Over his dead body. "I'm sure Suz can be made to see reason. Tell Brett I plan to make it to at least a couple of his games; I have to go over my schedule first." He ignored the sigh his sister attempted to muffle. "And give Lexie a big smooch from her favorite uncle. I assume everybody in between is doing well?" Jackie and her husband, Rick, had five kids in total.

"We're all great. I'm actually off to watch Jason's soccer game right now. I spend half my life sitting in the stands at sports events these days and the other half driving to and from sports events. Glad you're back in one piece, Mac. I'll catch up with you later, hmm?"

"Yeah. Talk to you soon. Love you."

He was ready for seconds on the soup and another roll. The food tasted great and really felt good in his nearly healed stomach. Did Suzie cook well enough to be responsible for his dinner? She probably could if she was motivated enough, although Caesar salad and grilled prawns would be more her forte.

Suzie didn't answer her phone; Ross left a message. Just as well. He would have been tied up in conversation with her too long for his still-recuperating psyche. He then tried his mother.

"Hey, beautiful," he said when she picked up.

"Oh, Ross, you sweet dear. You're home?"

"Yup. Got in this early this morning."

"Do you get to be home for a while now, honey? No. No, Susan, not that one. The big pewter one on the top shelf. Put that other one back. Sorry, Ross. Susan's been with me all day. We've been trying to get the details worked out for the party she thinks I need to have. I keep telling her I just want a nice, simple dinner with my family, but—" Ross could hear his sister's voice in the background. There was enough bite in the tone to suggest the party planning hadn't been smooth sailing in all ports. "Don't talk to me like that, young lady. I'm still your mother. Ross, tell her."

Ross looked heavenward. It was times like this when he especially missed his father.

"Ross! So glad you're back. Talk some sense into her, will you?" Ross figured their mom had handed Suzie the phone so he could reprimand her. "A person doesn't reach a milestone like this every day. We don't get to do a golden anniversary with Dad gone"—he could hear the choked sound in the words—"so I think we should really do it up big for this. She's just being unreasonable and stubborn."

The corners of Ross's mouth inched upward. He didn't doubt the stubbornness had been two-sided all day long, if he knew his family.

Law school should have offered more classes in family mediation.

"Suz, listen. We'll do what we can to make it nice and memorable, but it sounds like Mom's getting a little overwhelmed. I just got in today—we'll talk in the next day or two, you, me, and Jack, and I'm sure we'll come up with something nice, and we'll still have time to get out the invites. Let me talk to Mom again."

"Okay, but before you do, I talked to Megan Howard. Did you listen to your phone messages?"

"Yup." He ladled out more soup, heavy on the homemade noodles.

"Well, Megan talked to Ashley—she's Megan's sister-in-law—and Ashley says she wants to meet you, but, of course, who wouldn't." Suzie paused, expecting a reaction of some kind from Ross. He just took another bite of soup. "So I told Megan I would send her an invitation to Mom's birthday party, and she's going to bring Ashley so you two can meet."

Ross coughed on a piece of chicken. "Whoa, Suz, back up. I thought we just agreed to talk about the party plans tomorrow, and I'm pretty sure Mom would rather this be a nice, intimate, family gathering. Maybe meeting this Ashley at another time would be better." He would do whatever it took to get out of this forced lineup with an audience, a large audience to boot, everyone watching him with high, hopeful expectations.

He heard her quick exhale of breath. "You made a promise to Mom and Dad, and we are making darn sure you keep it."

He wished his promise wouldn't keep rearing its ugly head at him. A few of those heads actually had been ugly too, as his tenacious matchmakers seemed to be dragging over every available female within a hundred miles to parade in front of him. A very skinny radiology tech with questionable hygiene came to mind. She'd talked incessantly about her cats. He'd let Suzie have it after that one. Did she not know her own brother at all?

There was enough soup left for a quick snack tomorrow. And it was time to end this particular conversation.

"I haven't forgotten my promise to Mom and Dad, Suz. I'm just not sure it's a good idea to set something up during Mom's party when I would rather concentrate on her. Let me talk to Mom again."

He knew his sister well enough to know he really hadn't won this battle; he had only bought himself a little time. He could hear her murmuring on the other end of the line.

"Here's Mom. Just remember, Ross, nothing would be a better birthday present for her than for you to get married."

All right. She wasn't going to let it drop. It was time to enforce a few of his own rules. "I haven't forgotten what I told Mom, Susan. But as an attorney, I am forced to remind you that the particular clause of my promise dealing with lineups does not go into effect until I am forty. That being said, I will endure the well-meaning introduction on occasion. But I am not going to bind myself permanently to or endure a social engagement with just any warm body that happens to be available. I have definite standards, and I expect that if I am to endure these imposed introductions, you all try to adhere to those standards."

"Those being?"

"Well, more than merely being female and breathing, for a start. Attractive. Beautiful, preferably. Intelligent, college educated. That means college degrees. Advanced degrees wouldn't hurt. Successful in her chosen career. LDS, of course. Family oriented. Likes children. Young enough for us to have children of our own but not so young that I have to babysit her as well." He paused. "Single, never married." It didn't sit comfortably with him to think that he might be compared to a past husband.

"Let me see if I have this straight, Ross." He could hear the sarcasm in Susan's voice. It hissed loud and clear through her clenched teeth. "We'll be looking for a beauty pageant winner who was a college valedictorian and is now a self-made millionaire but she's willing to give up everything to become barefoot and pregnant for you."

Ross stuffed the last of his roll in his mouth.

"Just a little clarification—does pageant runner-up count?" she continued. "What if she wasn't valedictorian but is a member of MENSA? What if she has two undergraduate degrees but no postgraduate work? What if her portfolio took a dive, and she is only fabulously wealthy instead of filthy rich? What age is old enough to be mature and young enough to be sufficiently fertile?"

Ross swallowed the roll and waited for Susan to catch her breath. "Not up to the task, sis?"

"Oh, I'm up to the task, but now I know exactly how I need to describe you to these women when I ask them if they'd like to meet you."

"You'll say I'm your smart, successful, good-looking older brother?" He knew it was a smart-aleck answer, and he could tell Susan wasn't in a great frame of mind, but he didn't really expect that a day spent haggling with their mother would push his sister to the edge of her patience. It didn't compare to two weeks with the German Angels or his hellish night flying the friendly skies.

"More like, you're my older brother, getting older by the day. You are so smart you won't allow yourself to look the fool. You are so successful you set standards too high for others to reach, and that absolves you of ever making a mistake. You used to be fun and have a sense of humor, but now you are so rigid they could use you as a template for yardsticks." She paused, and Ross heard her sigh. "You aren't really serious about all that stuff, are you?"

Her assessment of him was a little too close to the mark for Ross's ego and comfort. And not feeling altogether patient on the subject himself, Ross remembered every lineup his sisters and friends had made him suffer through. He remembered every cookie, every casserole, every homemade card, and every apple pie from what seemed like every LDS girl he'd ever met. Then he remembered all the other girls and everything they had offered. They hadn't been offering cookies. He'd *had* to set standards, build those walls his coworker Allen had accused him of.

"I'm serious, Suz. I really won't be settling for anything less. But I'll keep my end of the bargain. If you'll use discretion, I'll be the epitome of politeness. Now let me speak to Mom."

"All right. I'll be more selective if you'll loosen up a bit. Here's Mom."

"What is it, Ross, dear?" His mother's voice had a low, gravelly quality that was somehow soothing, like the rough tongue of a mother cat.

"Nothing, beautiful." Ross rinsed his bowl and stuck it in the dishwasher. Susan had been with their mother all day. That ruled out both of them as the soup donors. "Just wanted to say I love you before hanging up. I'll see you soon."

"I hope we can get on top of all of these party plans. I keep telling Susan I want simple, simple! But she brushes me off and comes up with more names for the invitation list. The idea of so many people coming over to my house, Ross! The walls should be washed, the carpets! Those big windows on the west side will get all the sun, and every single water spot will show."

"Don't worry, Mom; let us deal with all of that. You are the guest of honor, not the hostess, even if it is in your own home. Relax; make a list when you see something that needs doing. Suz and Jack and I will take care of things or find someone who can. Talk to you soon."

One last phone call before he called it quits and got his schedule organized. Scrolling through the contact list on his cell phone, he located the number for Esther Johnson, his housekeeper, and called her from his landline. She picked up right away.

"Mrs. Johnson, this is Ross McConnell."

He heard her quick intake of breath. "Mr. McConnell, you're back in town. I hope you got my message." He could hear the worry in her voice.

"I did. I guess my first question is, how is Mr. Johnson?"

After a quick rundown on Esther's husband, Ross said, "You mentioned the name of the person who has been cleaning my home. I wonder if you can give me her phone number. And an address if you have one."

Esther produced both for him. "I hope there isn't a problem, Mr. McConnell. I was in a bit of a tight spot when I first called her, what with Burt going into surgery. I didn't feel right about sending a total stranger though, and I did manage to meet her later that week. I figured if I met her, I would be able to tell if she was on the up and up, you know? Her references sounded good, but you never can tell about those things." She paused. He was sure she was waiting for some form of reprimand. When it didn't come, she continued. "Mrs. Forrester seemed very honest. I'm sorry, Mr. McConnell, if you feel I betrayed your trust. Mrs. Forrester called me today and said you weren't happy with the arrangements. If you need me to find someone else—"

"Bad timing, Mrs. Johnson, that's all. Let me worry about that; you worry about taking care of Mr. Johnson, okay? I'm sure I can work things out at this end. When exactly did this Mrs. Forrester start working?" He was sure he owed both women money. After ironing out the details with Esther, he looked out the kitchen window, then glanced at his watch. It was early evening, even though it was getting darker faster these days. He decided it was still early enough to run one small errand.

Chapter 9

THE BEST WAY TO OVERCOME setbacks, Natalie thought, was with chocolate. She could really use some right about now. Chocolate chip cookies, fresh from the oven, the chips warm and melting through each soft, chewy bite, would work. Opening the can of fudge frosting she had hidden from the girls in the back of the pantry would be good too. Rocky road ice cream could do it. However, her kitchen was teeming with giggling teenagers up to their elbows in sugar-cookie dough. Not chocolate chip. The girls'-choice dance at the high school was in November, and Emma and a few of her friends were decorating freshly frosted cookies with candy shots, spelling out their names so they could ask the boys to the dance. The last few batches of cookies were on the cookie sheets awaiting their turn in the oven, or cooling, so the girls had temporarily abandoned decorating the cookies so they could decorate each other with flour.

Natalie's wonderful day of freedom had turned into a nightmare. First, the new boss she'd never met until today had caught her—not working diligently scouring toilets and detailing the grout in his kitchen tile with a toothbrush but tap dancing. Tap dancing! Her face flushed instantly at the memory. This great extra job she'd hoped would pay amazingly well was toast now, she was sure. A high-powered attorney like Mr. McConnell would want an actual housekeeper, not a whirling dervish or a really bad *I Love Lucy* episode.

Then she had come home to find a voice mail message from her ex-husband. He'd said he *knew* he'd promised to help financially with Ryan's mission, but he and Sandy decided to remodel their kitchen, and it didn't look like he'd be able to help now. Sorry. Wade wasn't Ryan's real father, but Ryan had only been a toddler when Natalie had married Wade, and Wade and Ryan had formed a bond as the two males in the family . . . If Ryan were to find out, Natalie was sure it would break his heart. At the very least, it meant she would be lucky if she could save even a little each month, maybe only taking one class each semester. She would just have to get through school more slowly, after Ryan got home from his mission. It would have to do for now.

She had still been mulling over Wade's phone call and the pathetic role men seemed to play in her life when it dawned on her that the angry bear of a man who had threatened her that morning hadn't looked well. He'd been sleeping in his clothes, obviously, and his coloring had been a little green, not that she'd had a lot of time to really study his appearance. She'd been too mortified; her adrenaline from the shock had been off the charts. To make amends, Natalie had decided she'd make some chicken noodle soup for her and the girls and sneak some into his refrigerator. Not that she would tell him it was from her—that would be groveling. But it would ease her conscience a little at being caught derelict in her duties.

Natalie's thoughts came back to the present when a handful of flour exploded next to her nose and Emma and her friends Kate, Heather, and Tess squealed. In addition to the girls, Natalie's kitchen was also decorated with flour and pink frosting. As was Natalie. She couldn't help grinning at the girls as she brushed a hand across her cheek, sending up a cloud of flour. If she couldn't overcome setbacks with chocolate, who was to say a good food fight wouldn't work just as well?

Emma lobbed another huge salvo of flour at Natalie. Natalie blinked the worst of it from her eyes. She was covered from head to foot in flour, her hair and face coated with the stuff.

Emma bent over like an old woman and hobbled after Natalie. "You look like a granny!" she said in a squeaky voice. The other girls shrieked with laughter.

"Says you," Natalie replied, then chucked a handful of flour back at Emma.

Callie had been working on a big homework project at a friend's house and was missing all the action—at least until she walked through the kitchen door and got a fistful of flour in her face from Tess, Emma's best friend. Snorting flour like a baby dragon, she immediately grabbed a wad of dough from the nearest cookie sheet and mashed it on Tess's head.

Chuckling, Natalie scooped a bowlful of soup from the still-simmering pot on the stove and set it on the counter—away from the shenanigans. "Here's dinner, Cal-pal. Eat up."

Callie noticed Natalie for the first time and sent up a shrieking laugh, pointing at her.

Not to be outdone, Tess pulled the wad of dough from her hair and fashioned a goatee out of it around her mouth. It stuck amazingly well. In a wobbly tenor, she crooned, "Then I'm an old gramps." She linked arms with Natalie and waggled her eyebrows. "You're looking mighty tasty there, missy!"

Natalie grinned and dished out soup for the other girls. Tess grabbed a spoon and, still in old-geezer mode, intentionally let soup dribble down her chin.

"Tess, you are so gross!" Heather exclaimed as she sat at a kitchen stool and tried to form a false nose on her face out of cookie dough.

"You should talk," Emma replied to Heather, laughing. "You should see yourself. Come on, Kate, let's go get the hand mirror." She grabbed Kate by the elbow and dragged her down the hall to the bathroom.

"I knows what I'm doing," Heather yelled after them. "Get it? *Nose* what I'm doing?"

Natalie could hear the answering groans from down the hall.

The doorbell rang just as the oven timer buzzed, so Natalie, still grinning, bent over to pull the cookies out of the oven. "Get the door, will you, Cal?" Giggling, Callie ran to answer it. Natalie set the sheet on top of the stove and grabbed the spatula to start moving the sugar cookies to the cooling rack. Sensing a change in atmosphere—as in from total silliness to utter silence—she paused, spatula midair, and turned. And gasped.

Standing in the kitchen doorway, hands shoved deep into his pockets, was a man—a not-totally-unfamiliar-looking man—but then again, Natalie was momentarily disoriented. Men didn't show up unannounced on her doorstep. She could count the number of men who had ever shown up at her house on one hand, and this man wasn't Wade, Gorilla Doug, or the disgusting Mr. Childs. This man was tall, with dark brown hair and eyes. His shoulders were broad, and his muscles were well defined under the baby-blue polo shirt he wore. He had a bemused expression on his face, but there were a few crinkles at the sides of his eyes.

"It appears that, once again, I have caught you in an odd moment." He pulled a hand from his pocket and extended it to Natalie.

In that split second, she knew. It was the grizzly-bear attorney from her near-death experience that morning. She stiffened, speechless, and cautiously extended her hand.

He shook it briefly, let go, then glanced down and began to brush the flour off of his hands. He looked back at her and smiled politely. Natalie watched his eyes take in every inch of her. She glanced down and groaned inwardly. She was wearing her old faded apron that read "Kiss the Cook" over her hokey pokey T-shirt. Both were generously dusted with flour. When she looked up, she realized he was trying to keep his expression bland, but his mouth was quivering like he would burst out laughing at her at any second.

He cleared his throat. "Apparently, I am your employer, of sorts— Ross McConnell. And you must be the Mrs. Forrester Esther Johnson told me about—on the voice mail I just listened to this afternoon." His smile broadened a little, and he looked entirely confident and in control.

Natalie smiled faintly back. "Not Mrs. Forrester. Just—"

"Bob!" Kate yelled as she and Emma ran back into the kitchen; then both girls skidded and froze in their tracks.

Mr. McConnell got a funny look on his face, then asked, "Just—Bob?"

All eyes were on Natalie—five pairs of female eyes staring out of what seemed to be statues and one pair of rich brown male eyes under eyebrows raised in question. "No, that would be Natalie. Not Mrs. Forrester, please. And Bob is what my girls and their friends call me. Little family joke." She noticed he didn't offer to let her call him Ross in return. Still feeling like a glaring spotlight had focused in on her, she nervously reached for a plate of frosted cookies. They were perfectly edible, but the letters had turned out funny. "Would you care for a cookie?"

Ross reached for one, then paused, his hand hovering over the plate. "Were any of these cookies facial appendages at any time this evening?"

Heather's false nose chose that minute to sag.

"I can honestly say the answer to that is no. They are quite safe," Natalie answered gravely.

He nodded and took a bite of a cookie that was supposed to say *A* but looked like a wobbly arrowhead instead. "Mmm, very good."

Natalie pulled a glass from the cabinet and opened the refrigerator door. "Let me get you some milk to go with that. The girls are making cookies to ask some boys to the girls'-choice dance. Your cookie happens to be an artistic casualty." She was babbling a little, and she knew it; she was having difficulty getting her nerves totally in check.

Ross took the glass of milk. Cookies and milk were generally irresistible to human beings of any age, and that undoubtedly included him, Natalie thought a little grumpily. She didn't know what to say to him. How was she supposed to play hostess to the man who had very abruptly thrown her out of his house that morning? Well, he had his cookie and milk; that was a lot more than she had received. She turned back to the counter and poured a glass of milk for Callie.

Since her mouth had gone dry, Natalie took a swig of milk from Callie's glass before handing it to her and then looked around. The girls were still standing quite still, all staring at this tall, good-looking man as he chewed his cookie and swallowed as though women watched the way he ate every day. She wondered what to say next. Did he expect her to apologize to him? He obviously knew who she was now. She knew she shouldn't have been tap dancing in his house, really, but he hadn't even given her an opportunity to explain. He'd ordered her out as though she were some kind of criminal. Although, to be honest, her tap-dancing ability did border on criminal. Well, she'd been wrong, but he'd overreacted. It wasn't as though she'd been loading the trunk of her car with his valuables. But she didn't want to say the wrong thing and jeopardize the job cleaning his home.

Buying herself some time, she returned to removing cookies from the cookie sheet and placing them on the cooling rack. She heard him clear his throat, and she turned back around. The girls were still transfixed. Natalie mentally rolled her eyes. He *was* handsome, and Natalie would be lying to herself if part of the reason he made her nervous—aside from this morning's debacle—was that men in general still intimidated her, but attractive men paralyzed her.

"I thought I would come by and introduce myself. Mrs. Johnson explained her husband's situation to me, and I appreciated that she located a substitute to take her place. I would like to go over your references, however, before we set up anything of a permanent nature—assuming, of course, that either of us might be interested in a permanent arrangement."

Natalie's mind took an unexpected jump from the words *permanent arrangement* to the two failed permanent arrangements, otherwise known as marriage, that she'd already had in her life. They had been extremely painful and life changing. Her hands were suddenly clammy, and she wiped them on her apron, shaking loose a fresh cloud of flour.

Ordering herself to get a grip, Natalie said, "I have a list of references I can give you." Turning deliberately to Emma to give herself a moment to regroup her thoughts, she said, "Em, will you go get one of my reference sheets? They're in the top drawer of my—"

Natalie's words shook Emma out of her stupor, and before she could finish her sentence, Emma dashed from the kitchen and returned momentarily with the paper in her hands. Emma handed it to Ross, smiling meltingly at him like he was a rock star. Natalie inwardly groaned. She was going to have to sit down with her girls and explain *carefully* about men and trust and using their brains practically, not romantically.

Suddenly, she felt unreasonably angry. Why did women, even young teenage women, lose all of their brain cells when a man walked into the room? Natalie had certainly lost her brain cells as a teen, when Aaron, aka "Buck," Jacobsen had been anywhere nearby, at least for a while. Until he'd gotten what he'd wanted and left her life in shambles.

"Mr. McConnell," she said politely but formally, "even if my references check out to your satisfaction, perhaps we should just agree to a trial period, see if we each think the arrangement will ultimately work."

Ross pulled his checkbook and pen out of his back pocket and began to write. "This should cover any work you have done so far, according to the information I got from Mrs. Johnson. Let me go over your references, and I'll be in touch with you in a couple of days. I presume you will continue what you've been doing until then?"

When she nodded, he reached for her hand again. Gripping it firmly, he gave her a long, solid handshake and looked squarely into her eyes. She held his look as long as she could and felt all of her righteous indignation begin to dissolve. Was there something familiar about him? The question nagged at her and made her nervous. Dropping her gaze, she retreated by pulling her hand away in an instinctive act of self-preservation.

He shoved his hands back into his pocket and headed to the door. As he turned the knob and opened the door slightly, he looked over his shoulder at Natalie. "Just one question—where did you get the nickname Bob?" He smiled slightly, a bit of humor showing in his eyes.

"Maybe I'll tell you sometime," she replied and bit into her cookie.

He nodded briefly, gave the dreamy-eyed teens a brief salute, and let himself out the door.

* * *

Ross pulled away from the curb and headed away from Mrs. Forrester's small house. No, not Mrs. Forrester—Natalie, he corrected himself. Then he chuckled. No, make that Bob. He briefly wondered again what that was all about. She and her posse of young females had provided a few entertaining moments this evening. Walking in on some sort of flour explosion had surprised him. He'd never encountered anything like that before. Finding out the cookies were intended as treats for boys had knotted his stomach for a moment. It had given him, as a frequent recipient of such "treats," a sense of déjà vu—like once again the female species was using domestic skills to lure in the unsuspecting male—and it had dawned on him that there, before his very eyes, he'd been watching a future generation of desperate females learn the art of male bribery through baking. It was after this realization that he'd noticed the bowls of chicken noodle soup—*homemade* chicken noodle soup with *homemade* noodles.

His mystery was solved, and his conclusions about females were once again reinforced, as was his cynicism. So he'd casually watched Mrs. Forrester—Natalie—Bob—to see if she was checking out his reaction to her cookie offering, but she'd been pouring milk for the youngest girl, not looking at him at all. He admitted to himself now that it wasn't the way he'd expected her to behave.

When they had begun to discuss regular employment, Ross had watched the emotions change in her face with curiosity and interest. Over the years, he had sat across the bargaining table from the most expert lawyers and CEOs. He had dealt with their poker faces handily, and as a result, Natalie Forrester was like reading an open book. She'd been marginally friendly and hospitable, although nervous and edgy. After suggesting they set up realistic working terms, she had suddenly become tense, even slightly hostile. Afterward, she had seemed distant. And it had been more than obvious that she had been ready to bolt.

He cocked a half grin. That bunny image came to mind again—not the bunny he'd stomped flat earlier that morning but a jittery bunny fleeing a predator. When he'd shaken her hand he was sure he'd felt every cell in her body jumping like she was holding hands with the big bad wolf. He was sure she was relieved when he finally took his leave.

He wondered why. He acknowledged he'd been fairly rude that morning, but he'd been intentionally friendly tonight as a result. Did it offend her for him to say he wanted to review her references? He didn't think reviewing references was an unreasonable request, and obviously she didn't either; she'd had them readily available. Maybe his own suspicions and cynicism about her having romantic ulterior motives had come across to her. He wasn't sure. Surprisingly, her mood change had disappointed him. He'd found the whole cookie thing, not to mention the earlier tap-dancing episode, especially now that he'd recovered his health, somewhat amusing.

While shaking her hand, he'd intentionally maintained eye contact with her, a tactic he had learned staring over the table at all of those poker faces during settlement negotiations. She'd held his gaze longer than he'd thought a bunny would, and he had watched, intrigued, as her countenance had begun to soften in a most compelling way. Then she'd lost her nerve and looked down. Her eyes were green—not the light gold-green of hazel eyes but a deep emerald green.

He was suddenly hungry. He wished he'd asked Natalie if he could have a few of those reject cookies to take home.

Chapter 10

ALLEN POKED HIS HEAD IN the doorway of Ross's office. He held up his left arm and dramatically tapped the face of his watch with his right forefinger. He and Ross were due in court any minute.

Ross had been nearly out the door when his office phone had rung. He'd looked at the ID and taken the call. He'd known he shouldn't have answered it, hadn't had time to answer it. But it was Jackie. He'd promised his sisters he'd help them with this birthday thing, but he'd been working twelve-hour days since returning from New York and hadn't found a minute to get to them.

Jackie, in her soft, peaceable way, began the conversation by letting him know he had fallen short of the mark. Susan, impatient, had simply gone ahead and invited half the county, and their mother had stopped sleeping at nights, thinking about all of the people coming to her house. Jackie had spent the mornings helping but was tied up afternoons chauffeuring her kids to and from their afterschool activities. And Ross had done nothing. Susan and she could not do it all; they needed help. And fast.

Ross looked up at Allen and shrugged his shoulders helplessly. "I'll be right there," he mouthed.

Allen gave him a brief wave and walked away.

"Why did you call me on my office line, you little pest of a sister?"

"You know why, you big pain of a brother. You're not answering your home phone or your cell or returning our calls. I figured if you didn't answer your office phone, I could at least get your secretary to pin you down. Knowing you, I imagine you have a similar history of avoidance with her, and she'd be on our side."

Despite himself and the hurry he was in, Ross chuckled. "Listen, Jack, things piled up while I was out of town. Sorry." He was glad it was Jackie who had called. Susan would have given him an endless stream of hysterical exaggerations, and his mother would have made him feel even guiltier than Jackie was. "Things will settle down next week, and I'll be sure to do my part." A sudden idea came to him. "Jackie, I'm due in court, so I have to go. But I have this housekeeper who might be looking to pick up more work." He wasn't sure why he thought that, other than she looked like she could use more money.

He gave her Mrs. Forrester's number. "You can give her a call and see if she can help get the house ready. I don't know—she may even be talked into helping decorate or something." He hadn't called any of Mrs. Forrester's references yet, but if Jackie talked to her and liked her enough to hire her, that would be one less thing for him to have to deal with. He trusted Jackie's judgment.

When Jackie hung up, Ross was only partially convinced he'd pacified her by suggesting Mrs. Forrester as a possible solution. At least she'd said she was willing to call the woman. Hopefully she'd be able to help, and Ross would redeem himself as the hero of the hour. Besides, there wasn't time to be wasted. The party was a week from Saturday, and today was Thursday.

* * *

Natalie showed up on Mrs. McConnell's doorstep at nine on Saturday morning with cleaning tools in hand.

"It's so nice to meet you," Mr. McConnell's mother said. She was a trim, lovely older woman with beautiful dark hair shot through with silver.

"Please, call me Natalie. I'm not really Mrs. Forrester anymore anyway," she said.

"Oh. All right, then, dear. And you must call me Dorothy. You can't imagine what a relief it was for Ross to suggest you may be able to help," his mother said. "What was supposed to be a simple birthday party has gotten out of hand."

"I'm glad Mr. McConnell thought to suggest me," Natalie said. It was especially true considering their only encounters up to this point wouldn't have left him with much confidence in her abilities—or her sanity, in Natalie's opinion.

Dorothy gave her a list, and Natalie spent the next few hours washing walls, floorboards, and windowsills, then set about on the last chore on the list, going over the drapes in the spacious family room with her small tank vacuum.

Out of the corner of her eye, she saw Dorothy enter the room, followed by a woman close to Natalie's age. The woman was tall and slender, with dark, cropped hair.

"Natalie, I'd like you to meet one of Ross's sisters, Jacqueline. Jackie, this is Natalie Forrester, Ross's housekeeper."

"Nice to meet you, Natalie," Jackie said. "I have to admit, the way Ross has talked about his housekeeper these last few months since he's been back, I expected to meet a much older person. He commented that she was always mothering him, bringing him meals."

"That's true," Dorothy replied. "You know, Natalie, as his *real* mother, I was feeling a little jealous."

"Oh," Natalie said, "that was Esther Johnson, not me. She had a family emergency, so I've been filling in for her the past couple of weeks. Although I did take him some soup when I first started. I wouldn't exactly call that mothering—at least not any mothering you'd need to feel jealous of."

"Oh, honey," Dorothy said. "If a cute, young thing like you were the one mothering him, I wouldn't be jealous at all. I'd be thrilled."

Natalie was not expecting a remark like that from Ross McConnell's mother, of all people, and it made her face, already flushed from working hard, heat up even more.

"Well, Natalie," Jackie spoke up quickly and smiled at her with what Natalie interpreted as sympathy. "We'll leave you now and let you get back to work. Mom, let's go plan the menu, okay?" She grabbed her mother's arm and guided her out of the room.

Natalie turned the vacuum back on and resumed cleaning the drapes. How ironic was it, she thought, that Mrs. McConnell had said she'd be thrilled if someone like Natalie were to take care of her son. She knew what Mrs. McConnell had been implying, and the idea was almost painfully ludicrous. Natalie and Ross McConnell couldn't be more different, in education, in experience, in all the ways that mattered, really. They were from completely different worlds.

Someone like Ross would never look twice at someone like her, she thought as she finished cleaning the drapes. And she wasn't sure she'd know what to do if he did.

She walked into the kitchen and found Dorothy and Jackie sitting at the table, working on what she assumed was the refreshment list. She smiled at them as she ran her forearm across her brow to wipe beads of perspiration away. "The jobs on the list you gave me are done, Dorothy. What would you like me to do next?"

Dorothy smiled appreciatively at her. "You can join Jackie and me at the table, have a nice glass of lemonade, and tell us what you think of our menu for the party."

Jackie immediately rose and removed a tall pitcher of lemonade from the refrigerator and three glass tumblers from the cabinet. Then she poured and passed a glass to her mother and to Natalie. Sipping slowly, Dorothy murmured her approval and said, "Take a quick look at this, would you? And give us your honest impression." She pushed a sheet of paper across the table toward Natalie. Natalie set her glass down and picked up the sheet.

Jackie slid back into her chair after returning the pitcher of lemonade to the fridge. She leaned in on her propped-up elbows.

"We want the refreshments to feel homemade and taste yummy, but we have too many people invited to do too much of it ourselves, really," Dorothy explained. "So we're including some catered items out of necessity."

The list included miniature ham sandwiches, chicken puffs, iced shrimp, stuffed mushrooms, cheesecake, petit fours, tartlets with a variety of fillings . . . Natalie's brain automatically heard the cha-ching of a cash register. She thought of the sugar cookies she and the girls had made—on a budget—just last week.

"What about a nice soup, dear?" Dorothy continued. "The evenings are getting that crisp autumn bite. Soup might be nice. Chili, maybe?" She looked expectantly at Jackie, who shook her head.

"Mom, remember how many invitations Susan sent? If we include soup, that means bowls and spoons in addition to plates and forks."

"Not to mention the potential for spills," Natalie murmured. She looked up from the menu. "Is this a party for adults, or are you expecting children too? Because brownies—"

"Oh, Jackie!" Dorothy's eyes widened in horror. "Children!" Turning back to Natalie, she added, "Of course there will be children. My grandchildren will all be there, and I wouldn't be surprised if one or two people showed up with their kids in tow."

"And who knows how Suzie addressed the invitations." Jackie plopped her head onto her arms. "Mom, we need to come up with some sort of plan to keep the kids happy—and us sane!"

"What about having games, maybe some crafts set up somewhere?" Natalie suggested. "Apples on a string, face painting, that sort of thing—"

"Great idea!" Jackie exclaimed. "There might be a fairly big age range—maybe we can hire a couple of teenage girls to keep things generally in control, with one of us checking in occasionally to make sure things are okay."

"I have a couple of teenage daughters who are pretty dependable," Natalie offered. "Unless there are girls you already know who you'd prefer."

"Perfect!" Dorothy beamed. "And since we are expecting you to be here anyway, you can just bring them along. Do they have any friends who can help?"

"I'm sure they do. And my younger daughter especially loves kids. She'll be thrilled at the idea of helping." She paused. "You said you're expecting me here?"

"It would be so lovely if you could help us with the party, make sure the buffet stays filled, that sort of thing. Only if you're free that evening, of course, and willing."

Natalie could feel Jackie suddenly studying her. "You *really* have two teenage daughters, Natalie?" she asked.

"Guilty as charged—and a son on a mission as well. I'd be happy to help next Saturday night in any way I can." Natalie stood and took her glass over to rinse and load into the dishwasher. She dried her hands on a dish towel and turned determinedly to Dorothy. "What would you like me to do for you now?"

Dorothy shot Jackie a pleased look and then sent Natalie outside to wash windows. The temperature was a bit chilly outside, but Natalie didn't mind. The brisk air felt good, and her exertions kept her warm.

The view of the Salt Lake Valley from Dorothy's home was lovely. Natalie had worked hard all day, but the work had been enjoyable as she'd watched Mrs. McConnell—Dorothy—interact with her daughter. Ross had a nice family, she thought, her heart aching. She hoped he realized how blessed he was.

She missed her mom like crazy just thinking about it.

After she finished the windows, she planned to hurry home and hug her daughters and then e-mail Ryan. And tomorrow she'd call her dad and have a nice, long conversation with him. He'd like that.

And so would she.

Chapter 11

Ross PULLED OUT OF HIS driveway and headed to his mother's house, the place where he'd grown up. The party was scheduled to begin in a little more than an hour, and he'd promised to arrive early to make sure all of the final details were in order. Suzie had hired a live combo, his sisters had purchased enough food to feed an army, and they'd arranged for his new housekeeper to help out. Despite his best attempts at rationalization and his generous pocket book, however, he felt guilty that he hadn't played a more active role in the planning of the festivities. He *had* talked to his mother briefly earlier in the week, and she'd seemed relaxed and even excited about her birthday party, so he'd figured things were well in hand. When he walked through the kitchen door, he would know for sure.

Living in New York, he'd been able to compartmentalize his memories of family and home—and his father. When he'd returned to New York after the funeral, he'd dug into his work to separate himself from his feelings and his grief.

He stopped at a red light, checked the time on the dashboard clock, and drummed his fingers on the steering wheel. Moving back to Salt Lake City had been hectic, between juggling time at both law firms and trying to be there as much as he could for his mother. All of it had been rough, but walking into his parents' house every time he visited her was the hardest thing he had to do.

His father should be there. But he wasn't.

Ross had other misgivings about tonight as well. The party needed to be about his mother. He sincerely hoped it would be about Mom. Maybe even about Mom and Dad, and that was okay too. People would come and go; there would be dancing; there would be conversation.

There would be a lot of catching up with family and friends he hadn't seen in years. And that led to the source of those remaining misgivings.

He was afraid too much of the evening would be focused on him, and he dreaded it. Ross didn't consider himself to be vain or egocentric. He knew those invited would be, by and large, interested in wishing his mother well on her birthday. But he also knew human nature, and he was afraid that as the perceived "prodigal son" who had left his roots behind and did not fall into the local stereotypes (i.e., married), he would draw undue attention. He thought it pathetic and irritating that his whole life and character could seem to be reduced to a single word. And that word was, in fact, *single*.

He was sure Susan had invited every person the family had ever known from the beginning of time. That meant he was going to be hit with a barrage of questions—the same questions he'd answered ad nauseam for years. Curious family and friends would be expecting the inside scoop on the life and times of Ross McConnell. "How's work? You're a lawyer, right?" That was always followed by the questioner's favorite lawyer joke. Then they would progress through the usual, "What's New York like? How are the Nicks (Jets, Giants, Yankees, pick a team and fill in the blank) looking this year? Seen any games?" Next would come, "Lots of single women, I bet—" which inevitably led to the rhetorical, "Not married yet? Confirmed bachelor, huh?" followed by the ever popular, "Any prospects? Holding out for Miss Right, are you?" These were invariably accompanied by grinning, punches in the arm, offers of lineups, and/or raised eyebrows. Not to mention his personal favorite—the quote that he remembered hearing, not for the first time but for the first time directed at him—at his graduation from law school: "You know what Brigham Young said about single men being a menace to society . . ." Yeah, he knew. He was a college-educated, successful, wealthy, religious, law-abiding, hard-working menace to society.

He was also nearly certain, knowing Susan and her undying quest to see him hitched, that she had invited every available female within a radius of fifty miles to their little soiree. Probably with ages ranging from sixteen to sixty. So in addition to the arm pokes and the lawyer jokes, he could look forward to twitters, flirtations, and enough heavy perfume to develop allergies.

He pulled into his mother's driveway and parked his Mercedes. Gripping the steering wheel, he took a deep breath, bracing himself for the pre-party chaos he expected to precede what was bound to otherwise be an evening of social torture, and forced himself out of his car. Too soon, he was up the steps leading to the back porch, and there was nothing left to do but open the kitchen door.

Immediately, he was flooded with warm light, delicious smells, and the happy murmur of voices. Taken aback, he paused and closed his eyes briefly. He inhaled the spicy aromas, drank in the warmth, and tried to fill the nagging void inside him before shutting the kitchen door. He could see Jackie giving last-minute instructions to a couple of teenage girls who were tying a long string to the cupboard doorknobs, clothesline style, so it hung across his mother's kitchen. When she was done, Jackie rushed over and threw her arms around him in a tight squeeze.

"Mac! Good. You're finally here." Ross gave her a bear hug in return, lifting her off her feet in the process. She chuckled. "We were just going over the activities for the kids. I'm sure you know Natalie's girls." She grabbed his arm and pulled him in the direction of the teens, who were gaping at him with familiar glazed stares.

"Natalie? Oh, Mrs. Forrester. No, I haven't actually met the girls formally yet."

Jackie let go of Ross and put her hand gently on the shoulder of a slender blonde girl who looked to be about sixteen. "This lovely young lady is Emma Forrester, and this"—she put her other arm around the waist of a petite adolescent with delicate features and large green eyes he'd already come to recognize—"is her younger sister, Callie." Callie flushed bright pink and looked at her feet. She reminded Ross of a forest pixie. "And this young lady," Jackie continued, taking her hand off Emma's shoulder and placing it on the shoulder of a tall girl with long dark hair, "is Emma's friend Tess."

Ross smiled and nodded politely. "Ladies."

Jackie slipped her arm around Ross's and walked him into the hallway. "Those girls' job is to keep the pygmy-sized natives from becoming restless."

"Ah."

"And you are going to pay them handsomely after they do. I may even suggest bribes to the natives themselves so things stay sane."

"My wallet is yours to command, as always."

"Come see Mother's cake. You paid for it too."

"And for the band and for the refreshments, not to mention my little housekeeper."

Jackie looked at him funny.

"What?"

She narrowed her eyes and studied his face.

"What?" he demanded again.

She looked like she was puzzling something out in her mind, but then she smiled at Ross. "Nothing. I was just thinking about something Mom said last week. It's nothing." They heard the front doorbell ring, and Jackie said, "I'll go see who that is. The cake is in the dining room. Go check it out."

The large table in the dining room had been converted into a buffet, the chairs normally around it having been removed to the family room, where they and folding chairs from the church had been placed conversationally for guests to use. His mother's best lace tablecloth covered the dining room table, and in the center was a lovely three-tiered cake with creamy frosting and sugar flowers that looked so real Ross was tempted to inhale their fragrance. Roses in deep autumn colors, golden calla lilies, deep violet pansies, and lily of the valley gracefully wound their way down the cake. Matching sheet cakes on either side assured every guest a piece. There were no candles anywhere. It looked more like a wedding cake than a birthday cake, and Ross was grimly reminded once again of the dual nature of the evening's party.

In addition to the cakes, the buffet table held large, deep platters of iced shrimp, silver trays of miniature puff pastries with a chicken filling, cubes of imported cheeses, small spears of fruit, and open-faced finger sandwiches of various types.

Jackie walked back in and unconsciously straightened a stack of napkins. "Suzie and Scott and the gang should be here by now. I'm going to call her and see what's holding them up. She and I are going to take turns mingling with guests and helping Natalie keep the buffet stocked. Scott and Rick are assigned to take pictures all evening. Your job is to not eat all the food at the buffet, mingle, dance with every female who walks in the door, and look important. In other words, you get to play host."

Well, that pretty much ensured a fate worse than death, although he supposed he'd half expected it and deserved it for being AWOL all week. He would rather stick closer to the food than the females who would invariably cross his path tonight though.

"Fair enough," he said as Jackie scooted out the door again. He was turning to go find his mother to wish her a happy birthday when Natalie walked into the room carrying a large silver tray in each hand. She glanced his way and, startled, nearly upended a tray of berry tarts. Reacting quickly, Ross grabbed the edge of the tray and helped her stabilize it, then took it entirely from her. He set it in an open spot on the table as she placed the other tray next to it.

"Tragedy narrowly averted," he said, smiling at her.

She smiled back, and he noticed she had a small dimple in one cheek. "Thank you. Your timing was perfect. I hate to imagine the mess if you hadn't been there to rescue these tarts."

He picked up a tart and popped it into his mouth. Chewing thoughtfully, he swallowed and nodded. "Mmm. Yes, it was definitely a good thing I was here to rescue these tarts. But I think my perfect timing has more to do with catching you off guard than saving dessert. I seem to do that each time we meet. Maybe that makes it less than perfect timing."

She flushed slightly, but there was a twinkle in her eye that bespoke a sense of humor. "I suppose it depends on your goal. If your goal has been to help me win the big prize on *America's Funniest Videos*, your timing has been pretty good so far."

"Darn! Forgot to turn on my video recorder."

"There goes my ten grand."

"Did you make any of these delicacies?" He asked, gesturing toward the spread on the table. "Those cookies of yours tasted pretty good, and apparently, they make good prostheses too." He smiled as she stifled a chuckle.

"Thanks—I think. I did bring a batch of brownies for the kids, just in case they weren't too keen on stuffed mushrooms."

"Brownies, huh? Fudge brownies with lots and lots of frosting?"

"Of course," she answered seriously.

"With walnuts?"

"One batch has walnuts; the other doesn't, in case some kids don't like them."

"I think it's only fair that you save one big brownie with walnuts for your boss, don't you?" He smiled, his eyebrows lifting inquisitively.

She smiled back, but he saw her eyes cool slightly. "One big brownie with walnuts for the boss." Gesturing her head slightly toward the kitchen, she said, "If you'll excuse me, I'd better get back to the kitchen."

Ross watched her leave, puzzled slightly by her change of mood, and then headed to the living room to give the guest of honor a kiss. It was time to greet his mother and brace himself for the deluge of guests.

In the living room, the curtains had been drawn wide open to show the expanse of windows that faced south and west, overlooking the valley. It was a glorious autumn night, the sky deepening to violet, the first stars peeping out one by one in contrast to the bank of twinkling city lights.

Ross found his mom watching the band set up. Seated comfortably on the sofa, she looked radiant, her hair shiny and curled softly around her face. Ross remembered what she was like when he was a child looking up into her bright brown eyes and dark hair. It hadn't taken many years before he'd been looking *down* into those eyes and that hair had been threaded with silver. He wondered if she had shrunk a couple of inches over the past year; she was thinner, he could tell, but her eyes still sparkled like they always had when she saw him walking toward her.

She gave him her cheek when he leaned over to kiss her. Nodding in the direction of the band, she said, "I was afraid those boys were only going to play rock-and-roll music, and how can a person carry a conversation with that kind of noise blasting around them? But I think we came to an understanding." She looked over at the drummer, who adjusted his stool and winked at her. Ross grinned at him. His mother continued. "I asked that boy there if they take requests. I want to hear 'September Song.'"

Ross tensed, but he asked lightly, "'September Song' in October?"

It was the song his parents had danced to at their wedding. It was their song.

She absently reached for Ross's hand and squeezed it. "Del would have liked it." Abruptly, she shifted topics. "That little girl of yours is quite the find! She had this place spic and span in the blink of an eye."

Pulled back from thoughts of his father, Ross said, "Little girl of mine? Oh, you mean Mrs. Forrester. I'm glad she worked out. The place looks great."

Dorothy patted the seat next to her, and he sat and threw his arm casually across the back of the sofa behind her slender shoulders. "Sixty-five years. Can you imagine, Ross? It seems like only yesterday I was hauling you home by the ear when you got into that fight in fifth grade with—what was his name? Johnny? Tommy?

"Tommy Johnson."

"Oh, that's right. Bud and Elaine's boy. You and he were never very good friends in grade school, I remember. Your dad was fit to be tied when he came home that night and learned you'd blackened that boy's eye. You were grounded for a month."

"Tommy couldn't get it into his head that I didn't want to share my lunch money with him. Some people require more explanation than others."

"And then there was the time Del went looking for you when you were late for curfew on prom night."

Ross's lips curved up slightly. He and Kendra Bennett had been doing quite a bit of very memorable kissing, which was the real reason he'd been late for curfew. Then, after seeing her safely inside, he'd discovered his car battery was dead. He'd quickly returned to Kendra's front door and quietly knocked, and luckily he and Kendra had been wielding the jumper cables when his dad had driven up, his normally mild countenance stern and patriarchal. When he'd seen the cables, he'd visibly relaxed. Ross had been out way past curfew but had dodged a huge bullet, thanks to that battery. He was drawn out of his reverie when he heard his mother chuckle.

"You always thought you pulled one over on your dad that night. But the first thing he noticed was the fogged windows of your car."

"He never said anything to me."

"He figured you'd learned your lesson. You knew he'd hunt you down if you ever missed curfew again, and the looks on your faces told him you were both guilty of something but, fortunately, not too guilty."

Dorothy began to stand up, and Ross rose to lend her his arm. "Ah! Here they are, finally!" she exclaimed as her grandchildren hurried over to give her hugs.

Ross slapped Brett, Jackie's eldest son, on the back and then grabbed the curly-topped cherub who was squeezing both of his legs and tossed her high in the air.

"Uncle Mac! Higher!" she squealed, and he tossed her again, exactly the way she had requested.

"I can't watch when you do that," Dorothy muttered.

With his niece now firmly planted on his left hip, Ross reached out and shook his brother-in-law Rick's hand.

Rick kissed Ross's mom on her cheek and said, "Suzie and Scott are parking their car, so they should be inside any minute." He glanced at his watch when the doorbell rang. "And let the games begin!"

Soon conversation was humming in the living room, where Ross's mother spent most of the evening greeting people. Guests then wandered through to the family room for more conversation, if that suited, and dancing, with music provided by the band. Old standards and classic rock wafted pleasantly through the house. The volume level was low and discreet, and people were enjoying themselves, whether dancing or conversing. Guests also helped themselves to refreshments in the dining room. Conversation areas in nearly all of the rooms throughout the main floor were full of guests. Jackie and Suzie and their husbands took turns visiting with friends and neighbors and refilling shrimp bowls and sandwich trays. Smiling and relaxed, Jackie was the quintessential cool hostess, while Suzie, fueled on adrenaline, flitted from person to person and traded jokes, compliments, and gossip.

Ross, relegated to the job of host, attempted to keep a smile on his face and his real thoughts to himself.

A half century of his parents' friends and neighbors banged him on the shoulder, pumped his arm vigorously, made him guess their names—knowing full well who *he* was while he had no clue who they were—and told him every embarrassing anecdote from his childhood. Distant elderly relatives he may have met only once in his life hugged him and pasted lipstick kisses on his cheeks. This would have been more than enough to tolerate with equanimity, but Suzie had really outdone herself on the invitation list. She had somehow conjured up the name of every childhood friend, every high-school sweetheart and pal, and it seemed, every female to whom he'd ever been introduced. The muscles in his cheeks ached from continuous smiling. He wondered to himself if all of his grade-school teachers would be walking through the door at some point during the evening.

Amazingly, the teachers didn't show up. Most of his local law firm did though, and at that point, he politely excused himself from them, grabbed Suzie by the arm, and dragged her to the back of the house.

"What were you thinking, inviting all of my law colleagues to this? I've only been at that firm for a few months. This evening is supposed to be about Mom. There is no reason for any of them to be here."

"First of all, you were supposed to call and help make plans. When you didn't call, I had to decide by myself whom to invite. And you're wrong, Ross. There is every reason for me to invite them. We've never met any of your coworkers, here or in New York, so I called your secretaries and got them to send me names. This was an opportunity for all of us to see who the people are who you prefer to spend your time with."

"Did you say secretaries—plural? And what do you mean; prefer to spend my time? It's work! Did you invite Scott's and Rick's coworkers too?"

Suzie had the decency to flush. "No. But they haven't been missing from the family for nearly twenty years either."

The arrow hit home. That, in a nutshell, was it. The sisters had families; the families had each other. They were a unit. He, on the other hand, was only an appendage to it, one that had been missing for a long time. Even his mother had his father. Dad was gone, but he still enveloped Mom's heart and the life she led. Suzie had Scott; Jackie had Rick. Ross really had only himself. But now his sister was behaving like a jealous girlfriend, insisting that all his acquaintances be paraded in front of her so she could determine what he saw in them that she was lacking. That, on top of his having to pretend he was some sort of family patriarch while he played host in his mother's home, was the final irony: that they, having each other for all these years, were somehow betrayed by Ross, who had no one. No one! He, forced to play magnanimous host in his mother's home, didn't have a real home of his own anymore.

Ross shook his head, turned, and walked down the hall, back to the guests he needed to entertain.

But he didn't manage to leave quickly enough to miss Suzie's parting shot. "You better be on your best behavior when Ashley arrives to meet you in a few minutes."

By the time Ross reached the living room, more guests had arrived. He had just shaken hands with his mother's new bishop and his old scout leader when he heard a squeal. He turned and found himself crushed in the arms of a woman who seemed vaguely familiar. He pulled back and studied her face.

"Kendra Bennett!" He smiled at her upturned face, still pretty after all these years. "What a coincidence! My mother and I were just talking about a certain prom night that occurred several lifetimes ago." Suzie really had done a thorough job with the invitation list.

"Ross! Look at you! You always were devastatingly handsome, and you still are." She released him from the embrace. "It's Kendra Dickson now. This is my husband, Dave. Dave, Ross McConnell. Ah, prom. It was the only time my date ever told me his car wouldn't work—after I had already gone in the house."

"I used the old dead-battery excuse instead of saying I was out of gas, right?"

The men laughed and shook hands. Ross politely listened while Kendra, his high-school kissing partner, told him about her husband, his company, Dickson Realty, and their three children. She had been a very appealing girl; she was now a lovely woman.

Kendra's husband, Dave, was asking him how the Jets would fare against the Patriots that week when Suzie grabbed his arm. "Sorry to interrupt," she said, "but there is someone I would like Ross to meet."

Kendra's eyebrows arched in surprise at the interruption.

Ross smiled apologetically. "Help yourself to the refreshments, and I'll catch up with you later. Pleasure to meet you, Dave. You're a lucky man." He let Suzie lead him away as Kendra and her husband walked toward the dining room.

"Ross, I'd like you to meet Ashley Howard. Ashley, this is my brother, Ross. Megan, you remember Ross, don't you?"

Ross looked at Megan, who did look much nicer now that her horse teeth were fixed, and then at Ashley. He extended his hand. "A pleasure." Suzie could have done worse, he conceded. Ashley was tall and slender, with a nice, animated face and short, dark hair.

"It's very nice to meet you, Ross," Ashley said. "I understand you're an attorney."

He nodded. He waited for the lawyer joke to come next, but it didn't materialize. That scored her a couple of additional points, he thought. "Boring work, really. What is it that you do, Ashley?"

Ten minutes later, with Suzie and Megan hovering the entire time, Ashley walked out the door having given Ross her phone number. He had promised to call her sometime soon. Ashley was articulate and nice to look at and was the branch manager of a bank. Suzie had done a lot worse in the past. Ross hadn't exactly heard bells and trumpets, but he could abide by his agreement with his sister on this particular introduction.

He decided he'd earned a refreshment break. He loaded a plate with some of everything and headed toward Kendra and Dave, who were sitting by themselves near the designer birthday cake. He overheard Kendra say to her husband, "I *know*, Dave, but it's still such a shock! Imagine, he makes as much money as he does, and she is forced to do this."

Ross stiffened. Were they judging him and his money? Were they talking about his mother?

He was on the verge of interrupting when Dave said, "I sign his commission checks. I know how much he makes, Kendra. He's always trying to guilt me into a pay increase, always complaining about her constant demands and how much he's forced to give her. Are you sure she really said she was *working* here tonight?"

"Yes. I asked her if she was a friend of the family. She looked so embarrassed when she recognized us, I felt just awful. She said, no, that she was working in the kitchen, and then she vanished—Oh! Hello, Ross! Care to join us?"

Ross settled into a chair next to Dave. There was only one person who would classify as kitchen help tonight, and that was Mrs. Forrester. Interesting. "How's the food?"

By the time the conversation ended, Ross had a fairly accurate read on Dave Dickson and his very lucrative real estate agency, as well as some probing questions about his housekeeper's ex-husband. He glanced at his watch. It was only seven forty-five. If this crowd was any indication, this party was not going to end on time, despite the fact that the invitations read seven to nine. They might be lucky to be out of here by midnight. He'd seen Mrs. Forrester a few times, quietly and efficiently restocking the buffet, straightening things up as guests left, generally making herself useful. The words came back to him, *He makes as much money as he does, and she is forced to do this.*

"Ross, darling!"

Ross knew that voice and found himself mentally forming a word that would make his sisters blush. And right about then, he wanted to do more to one of his sisters than simply make her blush. Like something painful. "Gina, Monty. What brings you to our humble city?"

Gina Rogers gave him a quick air kiss on the cheek. "Why you, darling, of course. We met your mother—lovely woman. Just lovely." She looked around with the jaded eye of a connoisseur. "And such a charming home."

LaMonte Rogers offered his hand. "We had business in San Francisco, if you'll recall. When your little invitation came to the firm, Gina suggested joining me and stopping by on the way. Killing two birds with one stone, as it were." He wasted no time loading a plate.

"Yes," Gina purred. "You've meant so much to us over the years." She ran her hand down his arm. "How could we ever say no to you?"

Mrs. Forrester came into the dining room at that moment with a fresh supply of stuffed mushrooms. She stopped dead in her tracks. Ross suddenly felt awkward, like he owed her an explanation. What would make him react that way? He caught Gina's eyes, which had narrowed slightly. The old pro had sensed something—what, Ross wasn't completely sure, but instinctively he knew it meant trouble.

"The goodies certainly look irresistible," Gina said, walking around the table toward Mrs. Forrester.

When Ross realized Gina was looking at his housekeeper and not the food, he clenched his teeth, afraid he'd say something he'd regret.

"Tell me, do you happen to have a bar at this cute little soiree?" Gina asked, then answered her own question before Ross could reply. "Of course you don't, not at the home of Saint Ross. Oh well." She helped herself to some shrimp. "Is there anything to drink around here besides that awful punch? Bottled water perhaps? Milk maybe?" She smirked. "Find me something suitable, will you, miss?"

Ross felt strangely protective of his little blonde housekeeper. Mrs. Forrester didn't deserve to become Gina's newest target simply because she had walked into the room. He needed to do something. "Monty, why don't I take you and Gina across the hall? We've got a fairly decent band in there. I understand they're taking requests."

"Only if you'll promise to dance with me, darling," Gina cooed. "That's *my* request."

Ross gestured to the door and glanced at Mrs. Forrester as she headed back to the kitchen. She was pale, but there was an oddly purposeful look on her face.

The band was playing a slow ballad. Gina led Ross to the floor and curled into him with all the skill of a predatory feline. He subtly eased back from her and looked her in the eye. She was strikingly beautiful, he admitted, but at the moment, he felt he was tangling with Medusa. "Cut the act, Gina. Why are you and Monty here? And don't try to sell the whole sentimental line."

"Darling! How could we resist? That invitation was like receiving an audience with the Pope. I was too curious. I merely told Daddy that as long as he was crossing the country anyway, we owed it to our esteemed colleague to pay a visit. We're staying at a quaint little place somewhere in the mountains for the night if you want to join us later." Gina smiled mirthlessly and ran a finger slowly down his lapel. "This has been so enlightening, let me tell you. Oh—it's about time! I'm parched." She took the offered glass of ice water from Mrs. Forrester, who had a professional and disinterested look on her face. "It has gotten so very *warm* around here all of a sudden." She sipped, and Ross watched Mrs. Forrester slip quietly back to the kitchen.

Why was Gina so insistent on baiting his housekeeper? There was no reason for it, and it bothered him.

Monty was happily absorbed in his food and a conversation with a partner in Ross's Salt Lake firm, he could see. Since Ross didn't care to play into Gina's games, he decided it was time to make a polite getaway. "Excuse me, Gina. I must see to the other guests."

She sent him a slit-eyed look, then sauntered over and seated herself by her father with a fluid motion that had every man in the room staring.

I must see to the other guests—as soon as I've had a few minutes to myself, Ross thought.

He walked determinedly to the back of the house and made his way out the door. The October night air was bracing. He breathed in deeply. The air was pungent with the scent of damp leaves and raw earth. He shoved his hands into his pockets and strolled through the backyard. His mother's prized roses were nearly bare now, with only a few stubborn leaves refusing to succumb to the inevitable. He plucked one and rolled it between his fingers. The brittle edges of the leaf broke away. He felt like the leaf, barely pliable, dead around the edges. The thought disgusted him.

Tossing the abused leaf to the ground, he wandered to the side of the house, where his car was parked. The din of conversation and music seemed far away, like an unconscious thought. He knew he should return to the party; it was barely eight o'clock, and Suzie would send out search and rescue if she lost sight of him for more than five minutes, but he leaned against the hood of his Mercedes and crossed his arms against the cold. Five minutes was all he asked.

He wasn't exactly sure how long he'd been standing there, lost in his thoughts, when he heard the kitchen door open and the sound of footsteps crunching in the gravel nearby. He looked up. The light from the shaded kitchen window briefly caught the highlights of a blonde head walking toward him. It was Mrs. Forrester carrying a bag to the garbage can, he guessed. His eyes were adjusted to the dark; hers apparently were not because he didn't think she had noticed him yet. He moved away from the car and straightened.

She jolted and looked up warily at the sound. Ross knew the minute she recognized who was out there in the dark with her because her eyes flared. The thought nagged at him again—where had he seen her before? He was certain he had.

"Oh! I'm sorry. I didn't mean to disturb you." She slipped past him in the dark. He heard the bag land in the garbage can and the crunch of the gravel beneath her steps as she returned. She headed toward the kitchen door.

"Wait, Mrs. Forrester." Why did he say that? He'd come out here to be alone for a few minutes.

She paused on the first step and silently turned to look at him.

"I wanted to thank you for your help tonight. I'm sure my sisters and mother appreciate all you've done."

"No thanks are necessary."

"Oh, I think they are. You've done more than merely keep the food going. You've given my mother and sisters peace of mind. And that, Mrs. Forrester, deserves my undying gratitude."

He could sense more than see her smile in the darkness. "Well then, you're very welcome." She turned back to the stairs.

"Mrs. Forrester—"

She stopped with her hand on the kitchen doorknob and turned back again.

"Have we—I keep getting the impression that we've met before. It seems unlikely, I know, but I've been wrestling with it for a—" And then he knew. His simple reference to wrestling brought Mr. WWF into full focus. And her green eyes. "Little America."

She audibly gasped. "The dark knight," she whispered.

Ross cocked his head. "No, it wasn't dark that night. It was early September, as I recall. And early evening. You were with pretty interesting company, I remember." He waited a beat. "Boyfriend?"

"Doug. What? *No.*"

"Maybe I'm putting my foot in it here, but he didn't exactly seem the type to go for tap-dancing wannabes."

Mrs. Forrester smiled slightly. "Not many men do, I suspect. No, it was a blind date."

"Ah." Why did he feel relieved? Probably because he was finding out she was a nice, helpful person, and he'd been genuinely concerned for her that evening. That had to be it. "I've been on a few unusual blind dates of my own over the years; although I confess none of them sported Maori body art. At least not that I could see."

"I imagine not."

"Well, I'll confess to having been concerned at the situation that evening. It was apparently misplaced." He raised an eyebrow in question, though he doubted she could see it in the dark.

"I've learned that sometimes first impressions are deceiving, Mr. McConnell."

"That's true." He wasn't sure if she was complimenting her tattooed friend or pronouncing a judgment of some kind on him.

She opened the door, and the resulting slice of blinding light and noise jarred his senses.

"I'd better be getting back to the kitchen now," she said. "Please excuse me."

* * *

The dining room, at present, was fairly quiet, so Natalie decided it would be a great opportunity to replenish the chicken puff tray. She stepped into the dining room and slipped to the back of the table, where she was better able to access the tray and stay out of the way of any hungry guests who decided to wander in. Two women were loading their plates and talking in hushed tones. Natalie tried hard not to listen, but when she heard Ross's name, she immediately tuned in, despite her best intentions.

"So, did you see him? Ross?" The woman, who looked to be about Natalie's age but with the leathery complexion of years in the tanning salon, glanced around quickly, then turned back to her friend.

"Uh-huh. Very dishy." The second woman, who was a little bit on the plump side, pushed a stuffed mushroom into her mouth and placed two more on her plate.

"He was so hot in high school. I remember doing whatever I could to hang out with Suzie so I could come over to the house and stare at him."

The second woman swallowed. "Did he ever ask you out?"

The first woman sighed. "No. He was dating Kendra Bennett at the time and never even looked at me. She's Kendra Dickson now. Do you know her?"

"I don't think so. I was a year behind you in school, remember?" The second woman was munching on a tiny ham sandwich now.

"Oh, that's right. And Suzie and I were just sophomores when he was the big senior everything. Suzie told me he's never married. I couldn't believe it."

"Really? That's weird, don't you think?" She shoved the remainder of the ham into her mouth and licked mustard off her finger.

"Kind of. He's been in New York. I imagine he could have all the women he wants. Although his mother would probably kill him if he did— have them, if you know what I mean." She chuckled at the implied double meaning in her words. The leathery woman picked up a berry custard tartlet and slid it onto her plate. "I think I'll go talk to him, see if he remembers me."

"Your divorce from Mike is final, then?"

Natalie pulled herself away from the table when the conversation took this tangent. She went to the kitchen, filled the tray with chicken puffs, and returned to the dining room. The women hadn't budged from their spot.

The first woman was loading her plate with cocktail sauce and cold shrimp. "And Suzie was furious at him. They had it out again earlier tonight, and I couldn't get her to stop ranting about it. Then she told me that he'd given her a list of requirements that a woman has to have for him to be interested in her. She said he wasn't kidding either. She was so angry at him. She said he'll never get married, and it'll serve him right."

Natalie busied herself straightening napkins.

"So what was on the list?"

"Well, the first item on the list is single, as in never married, although at his age, that will be next to impossible, and it won't stop me from saying hello to him." The woman glanced back out the door and didn't see Natalie glance up. Determining the coast was clear, the woman continued in her overloud whisper. "College grad, beauty queen, professional, a financial success. The whole package."

A previously smooth napkin wrinkled in Natalie's hand.

The second woman paused with a chocolate cream tartlet halfway to her mouth. "Well, that explains it."

"Explains what?"

"Why he's not married. He's looking for the perfect woman. But the perfect woman doesn't exist. You'd have to put Mother Teresa, Eleanor Roosevelt, and Oprah in a blender, along with a Victoria's Secret model, to get the woman you're talking about. And that leaves him free to entertain himself with all those women you said he's got available to him back East." She paused in thought and took a moment to set the tartlet down on her plate. "And if no one meets the requirements, it's not his fault. It gives the impression he's still looking for a relationship. He doesn't have to actually find one."

Natalie and the first woman both stared in amazement. The second woman shrugged. "I saw a show on cable about men who won't commit."

The first woman sighed. "I'd take Ross McConnell for one evening, no commitment necessary, if I could. I imagine there are a lot of women out there who would as well."

"Well, that would be all you would get, if you were lucky, since you didn't graduate from college and you aren't a rich beauty queen." She laughed and grabbed a slice of birthday cake.

Natalie refused then and there to be one of obviously dozens—no, *hundreds*—of women drooling after Ross McConnell. He was her boss. She was an ordinary, undereducated, divorced housekeeper with three kids and crow's feet. She may have the same employment as Cinderella, but that was as far as the parallel went. Natalie had given up on fairy tales and happily ever after. Buck Jacobsen had put a huge dent in her dreamy-eyed view of love when she was a young girl, and Wade Forrester had finished the job off completely and then stomped on it. She had to get away from these women and their talk, so she headed back to the kitchen and safety.

I am a fool, an utter fool, Natalie thought. She grabbed an apple and fastened it to one of the many strings tied to the clothesline crossing Mrs. McConnell's kitchen. The apple-eating contest for the grandkids was about to begin. Natalie decided she was going to hang out in the kitchen and keep a low profile for a little while. It would allow Wade's boss, Mr. Dickson, and his wife plenty of time to leave, the gossipy women would disappear, and, hopefully, the nasty goddess of beauty would slither back to her fiery cave. Natalie also vowed to put the idea of Ross McConnell as her dark knight safely on the shelf, out of sight.

She couldn't get over the fact that he was the man she'd encountered during her blind date with Doug. She had been so flustered at the time. Her usually reliable visual memory had put together only his essence, tall and dark, strong. Handsome. That essence had become her fictitious hero. There had been a couple of days recently when she had felt overwhelmed with life, when Wade had been at his nastiest and she had envisioned this dark knight coming to her rescue, saving the day, like he had tried to do in the restaurant lobby. It was silly nonsense, Natalie knew, but it felt therapeutic, just like her art projects did. It had given her a creative release, a happy ending, and had put a smile on her face. She knew she could rely only on herself, so she had kept her knight to herself and trudged on. Now that this storybook hero had an actual name and face, *his* name and face, she wanted to laugh and then weep from embarrassment.

She was glad it had been dark outside, or she was sure Mr. McConnell would have seen straight through her. It was bad enough that every time he walked into a room Natalie stopped breathing. After what she'd gone through with Wade and Buck, she'd sworn off men, and then bam! The first attractive man who came along reduced her to the behavior of a silly, dumbstruck fool. Of course, it had become apparent that she wasn't the only one to behave like that. There had been many females in close proximity to him all evening. Very attentive, clingy females vying for his attention. Virtually every female here, in fact, from the curly-headed niece she had witnessed him tossing in the air to the devastating siren who had ordered Natalie around like her personal slave.

It was enough, she thought as she picked up an apple and shined it on her apron before tying it onto a string. She had to take herself firmly in hand. A faceless fantasy knight may have been pathetic but had been virtually harmless. A knight who was Ross McConnell, on the other hand, was dangerous. He was too attractive, too successful, too everything for her to think about. He had too much power. She knew all about what giving her power to someone else could do. Natalie didn't have much power to begin with and what she did have had been hard won. Besides, she thought as she tied the last apple to its string, someone like Ross McConnell would never look twice at someone like her, except to point out a streak she might have missed cleaning the bathroom mirror.

"Okay! Who's ready to play?" She looked around the kitchen. Thankfully, no guest children had been brought to what amounted to a grown-up's birthday party, which had left only Dorothy's grandchildren to be entertained. Suzie's two children, Riley and Regan, knew their cousins well, and Jackie's older kids were used to running herd on the younger ones, so the atmosphere was stress free and fun. Callie had quickly developed a fast friendship with Jackie's fourteen-year-old daughter, Mindy, and a deep crush on Mindy's twin brother, Matt. Emma and Tess had already exchanged cell phone numbers with a ruggedly handsome young man named Brett while they'd been up to their elbows in pumpkin guts. Natalie thought Brett was Jackie's son too. The teens had already cleaned out four pumpkins to make into jack-o-lanterns and were nearly done scooping the seeds out of a fifth, while Callie and Mindy entertained the younger children by making ghosts out of Tootsie Pops and Kleenex. Earlier in the evening, Natalie had observed Matt prowling from the buffet table to the older teens, all the while keeping a nonchalant eye on Callie. It unnerved her that some *boy* was checking out her baby until she noticed her baby was surreptitiously checking out said boy. "Let's get this contest underway," she said.

Emma, Tess, and Brett rinsed pumpkin from their hands and arms and quickly selected apples conveniently located next to each other. Mindy chose hers, and Matt grabbed his spot.

"There are two more apples," Natalie said. "You in, Cal-pal?" Callie had been happily carrying three-year-old Lexie around and watching Matt from beneath lowered lashes.

Callie now looked at Matt and blushed. He grinned back at her, and she said, "Sure. Lexie wants to, don't you, Lex?" When the toddler nodded vigorously, Natalie smiled and moved a chair into place next to one of the remaining vacant apples for Lexie to stand on.

"How about you, Bob?" Tess called out. Natalie hesitated, but then Emma and Callie joined in, chanting "Bob! Bob!" followed by the others.

Natalie peeked quickly out the door at the buffet table. Things were still slow for the moment, and there was plenty of food. "Oh, okay. But I'll be tough to beat!"

The boys shouted their objections at that.

"Callie, if you're going to be helping Lexie, why don't you also be the judge to see who wins?" Natalie suggested.

"Great!" Taking her newfound authority very seriously, Callie looked around and called, "Everyone ready? Get set. Go!"

Apples on strings started swinging like pendulums as laughing mouths and teeth tried to grab hold of the slippery apple skins.

"Hey! No hands, Matt. That's cheating," Brett yelled, which was followed by a maniacal laugh from Matt.

There were a few muffled sounds of pain as swinging apples bumped into faces. Natalie had almost taken a bite, but her apple was too smooth and didn't have any of those nice nubby spots where she could easily sink her teeth in and gain an advantage. At one point, she noticed that Callie was holding Lexie's apple for her so Lexie could take tiny nibbles.

Natalie had finally taken a good first bite and had half of her apple eaten when she heard Brett yell, "Done!"

"Stop, everyone!" Callie said as she checked his apple.

It was clean to the core.

Brett started to dance, his arms swinging up in victory.

"Brett won, Uncle Mackie!" Lexie called out. "He won!"

Grinning, Natalie turned toward this Uncle Mackie and froze when she saw who he was. Darn it! Why did he always catch her doing stuff like this? This time she was attacking a hanging apple like a demented giraffe.

Well, at least she wasn't wearing her tap shoes.

"I was watching, Lex." He shot an amused glance at Natalie that made her feel like she was seven. "Well done, Brett," he said and clapped his nephew on the shoulder. "You're keeping the proud McConnell legacy alive, I see."

Brett laughed.

"Uncle Mackie, are you gonna carve pumpkins with us? We're gonna carve pumpkins next! Please, Uncle Mackie?"

He picked Lexie up off the chair and plopped her comfortably on his hip. "Probably not, kiddo. It's my job to talk to the *grown-ups*."

Natalie assumed that comment had been directed at her and her participation in the apple contest. Setting her teeth, she fixedly ignored Ross and turned to Brett. "Brett, does your grandmother have a paper and pencil handy around here? And a magic marker?" As Brett hustled around the kitchen to investigate, Natalie sat down at the kitchen table and continued. "Lexie, what would you like your pumpkin to look like? We'll draw pictures, and you can choose."

Lexie wriggled out of Ross's arms as Brett returned with paper and pencil. Natalie picked Lexie up and placed her on her lap. Emma and Tess got busy watching Brett draw on his pumpkin—although, really, it looked like they were more intent on looking at handsome Brett.

"A scary witch? A Halloween cat? A Frankenstein monster? What would you like, Lex?" Natalie quickly sketched out a few ideas and then laid the pencil down to let Lexie study what she'd drawn.

Natalie noticed Ross take a quick glance at the sketches as well, and she breathed a sigh of relief when he quietly left the kitchen after that.

"Ooh, I want that one," Mindy said, grabbing Natalie's drawing of Frankenstein to use.

Lexie still hadn't said anything, so Natalie gave her a quick squeeze and whispered again, "What would you like your pumpkin to look like, honey?"

Lexie's fingers had slid into her mouth. She whispered back, "Not scary."

"Okay, honey. Not scary."

"A princess."

A princess. It seemed like only yesterday that Emma and Callie had been Lexie's age and asking for princesses. "Cal, it looks like we are going to be paid a royal Halloween visit again," she said.

Callie giggled, and Emma looked up from what Brett was doing. "Princess Pumpkinseed!"

"The very lady."

"Is she a real princess?" Lexie asked.

"Oh yes. She is the princess of All Hallows Glen." It had been an interesting challenge to come up with a nonthreatening Halloween figure Natalie could carve on pumpkins when her girls were little. Princess

Pumpkinseed had been the result. Ryan had insisted his own pumpkin be as terrifying as possible, and he and Wade had made it a challenge each year to make the result more and more menacing. The girls would scream and avoid the front porch as long as the "men's" creation was lurking there. Princess Pumpkinseed had reigned merrily in the kitchen. Back during some of the better times.

Natalie slid Lexie off her lap onto the chair next to her. "Sit here and I'll tell you all about her."

Lexie propped her head in her hands and listened spellbound as Natalie drew and cut and carved and spun stories of Princess Pumpkinseed, stories Natalie had woven over the years for her own girls' enjoyment. Eventually, Princess Pumpkinseed sat regally in the center of the kitchen table, surrounded by her royal court: Frankenstein, a traditional Jack, a rather lopsided vampire, and Prince Bart Simpson, his hair forming a perfect jack-o-lanternish crown. But by then, Lexie's head had settled itself on her crossed arms, and she was sound asleep.

"I'll put her on Grandma's bed," Brett whispered to Natalie as some of the other grandchildren made their way out of the kitchen, and he gently lifted Lexie into his arms. Natalie nodded and, figuring the coast was probably clear by now, decided to check on things once again. It was past nine, but there were still a surprising number of guests milling about.

Making rounds through the rooms to clear away refreshment clutter, Natalie refocused on her resolve. She'd enjoyed her time with the kids, but she was here to work tonight. She wasn't a guest. She headed toward the family room and deliberately set about straightening chairs and generally tidying. The band was still playing, and Natalie saw that Mrs. McConnell—Dorothy—was dancing with her grandson Matt. Ross was dancing with five-year-old Regan, her small feet settled atop his while Ross moved to the beat. Jackie and Rick were snuggled closely together, swaying intimately to the music. Looking away, Natalie quickly picked up abandoned clutter left by guests. Eventually, her hands were full of napkins and used plates, so she turned to leave.

As she started walking out, she heard Dorothy say, "No, no, don't cut in, Ross. I'm having such a nice time with Matthew here. Find yourself another partner."

Natalie was almost to the door when a deep voice behind her quietly said, "Well, you heard the general. Do you know any steps that don't require tap shoes?"

When Natalie looked over her shoulder, she saw Ross there, a smile in his eyes and his eyebrows lifted in inquiry. She held up her hands, full of refreshment clutter and shrugged apologetically.

More than his eyes smiled then, and he took the piles from her and stacked them on the floor. "I'm pretty sure those will still be there after the song ends."

He offered her his hand, and she, utterly dumbstruck, took it. She was unprepared for the jolt that ran up her arm.

The band was playing a slow ballad. The electric shock she'd felt when he'd taken her hand had been nothing compared to the lightning bolt that struck when his other hand slid around her waist. She laid her free hand on his shoulder and willed herself to stop shaking. She wasn't sure if he had felt it too. She didn't want to admit to feeling it herself—but she was sure he would sense her tremors if she didn't get them under control.

They danced quietly for a minute, and then he said, "The tap lessons must be paying off, Mrs. Forrester. You're very light on your feet."

She was preoccupied with breathing evenly, and it took her a moment before she realized he was making light conversation. "Thank you," she murmured, then added, "Please, call me Natalie."

"Okay. Natalie." He said it with finality, but he paused a moment. "Not Bob?" he asked.

He was teasing her, trying to get her to relax, she assumed, but his manner and close proximity were making her heart race. "The kids call me Bob. You're not a kid, are you, Mr. McConnell?"

"It's Ross. And do I look like a kid to you?" At that moment, he pulled her in against his body and spun her around in a couple of tight turns. Then he kept her there and slowed his pace. "Why *do* they call you Bob? You promised you'd tell me sometime."

"I think I said 'maybe.'"

"Oh, I'm pretty sure it was a promise." He gave her a wicked half smile.

Being so close to him felt warm and exciting and—surprisingly nice. And it was precisely those feelings that reminded her to stay on her guard. Her Bob story would provide a distraction, and she hoped it would give her time to get herself back on an even keel. "All right. It started when my son, Ryan, was a little boy."

Ross stopped dancing. "You have a son as well?"

She'd forgotten he didn't know about Ryan. "Yes. He's on a mission right now." She could see his mind at work, mentally assessing her and doing the age-related math.

"You barely look old enough to have a daughter Emma's age," he said.

"Thank you."

"Where is he serving?" Ross asked.

"Scotland. He's been gone five months now." She gave Ross a minute to absorb the revelation; it seemed to affect a lot of people this way when they learned about Ryan, so she should be used to it. She watched his face and could tell he made a conscious decision not to pry. It surprised and relieved her. She continued. "Anyway, when Ryan was a little boy, about seven, he caught a horrible cold. He was miserable. I can still see his sad little face: red, puffy eyes, goopy nose, and a cough that could blow the trade winds off course. Nothing seemed to help. I gave him medicine, but it didn't ever work for very long. I would just get him to sleep and be helping the girls with something, and this hoarse little voice would croak, 'Bob! Bob! I deed you.'" She smiled warmly at the memory. "After a few days, he started feeling better, but he still had that horrible stuffiness in his head. And he was so bored he was turning into a little tyrant. So I decided to talk to some of his friends' moms and got a couple of them to allow their boys to come play for a while in the afternoon, despite the germs. We did a lot of hand washing that particular afternoon."

"I can imagine."

She continued. "Ryan would walk into the kitchen and say, 'Bob, cad we have a dodut?' 'Bob, cad we play video gabes?'"

Ross chuckled, and he spun her around again.

Natalie smiled back at him. "The funny thing is, his friends started teasing him about it. They would come find me and say, 'Bob, cad I have a dodut?' too. Then my girls, who were quite little at the time—Callie was only a year—started to mimic him as well. Callie was just forming words, and she toddled around the house saying, 'bob, bob, bob,' at everything and everyone she saw. The boys thought it was hilarious, and it egged them on even more. By the end of the day, it had stuck. Now all my kids and their friends call me Bob."

Ross smiled at her. It was a gentle, amused smile, and it awakened a part of Natalie's heart she hadn't been sure even still existed. The side of Ross she'd seen tonight was such a contrast to the hard man who had regarded her humorlessly during the tap-dance fiasco. She told herself it didn't mean anything. Ross was only being polite, nothing more. The silly dark knight business she'd created on a whim was a childish fantasy as fictional as Princess Pumpkinseed was.

Ross interrupted her thoughts, murmuring, "What are you thinking?"

She made herself look up at him. She couldn't tell him what she'd really been thinking, that he was handsome and compelling, that she was attracted to him against her wishes and her better judgment, and that she knew she was so far from his ideal woman that it was pointless. So she said, "It seems only yesterday that my children were that little. It goes by so quickly, and then one day you wake up and realize those sweet years are past. You wish for them back. At the very least, you hope you have spent them well, with no regrets."

"Have you spent yours well?"

"In some ways, I hope. I have three wonderful kids who are fairly well adjusted, all things considered. But I definitely have regrets." She didn't regret, would never regret, having her wonderful son Ryan in her life. But she definitely regretted the choices she'd made that had resulted in her becoming a teenage mother and tying her, at least temporarily, to a resentful teenage husband. She also regretted allowing her desire to give Ryan a daddy to blind her to the red flags in Wade's character.

"Everyone has regrets."

"I don't think so. Not everyone. Not the really big regrets." She paused, thoughtful. "I suppose every choice leads down a certain path, and that path leads to lessons learned. I believe I'm a stronger person because of what I've learned. Would I have learned them if I'd made different choices? Possibly. Who can say? I *have* definitely learned I need to be philosophical about it though. When my regrets weigh on me, I try to balance those feelings by remembering what I have learned. It helps, sometimes." She paused again, embarrassed that she had rambled. She hadn't realized they had stopped dancing. Neither of them moved for several moments. She wondered if Ross had regrets; it was obvious he wasn't going to volunteer any. He probably didn't. A man like Ross McConnell, smart and confident, knew and plotted every step along his illustrious and successful course in life. "The music stopped." She began to pull away. "I should get back to work. Thank you for the dance."

Ross let her go. She could feel his eyes on her as she stooped to pick up the refreshment clutter. She was irritated at herself, and she felt depressed. She'd meant to move away from dangerous conversational territory when she'd talked about how fast time had gone by. Instead, she'd not only plunked herself smack-dab in the middle of a touchy subject, but she had also allowed things to get almost maudlin. And while she'd used brave words, touting lessons learned, she did have many regrets in her life, real, deep-seated regrets, and they plagued her daily. The first had been naively allowing Buck Jacobsen to charm her and take her innocence when she was barely seventeen. She understood now why she'd allowed it to happen and had taken full responsibility for her actions; that was part of the "lessons learned" mantra she told herself in difficult times. It had included a lot of soul searching and repenting. But that specific choice had also changed the course of her life and had led to other regrettable life choices. If someone had told her a decision made when she was so young and vulnerable would impact her for her entire lifetime, she wasn't sure she would have believed them. She could preach the sermon eloquently now.

Natalie returned to the kitchen and found Emma and Tess busily boxing up leftovers. Callie was nearly asleep at the table, just as Lexie had been just a few minutes ago. Natalie shook off her melancholy and pitched in. She needed to get them all home and into bed. Wade had allowed his girls to miss a Saturday with him for the sake of earning a little spending money. But he was picking them up early Sunday morning for the day, and Natalie had also forfeited her Thanksgiving with the girls as part of his hard-driven bargain.

Yes, she thought, she definitely had regrets.

Chapter 12

ROSS HAD FULLY INTENDED TO write checks for Natalie and her girls before they left the party, but Susan had cornered him before he got to it. By the time he'd been able to break away from her, she had grilled him about Ashley Howard, lectured him about his lack of contribution in preparing for the party (did his money count for nothing?), tried to firm up family plans for the upcoming holidays, and made him miss Natalie leaving.

That conversation alone had been enough to give anyone a migraine. As it was, the conversation had followed what had been, for Ross, a trying event, however successfully it had turned out. He loved Suzie and appreciated her willingness to take up the reins when it came to family matters but wished she would adapt her style and timing.

Finally, her husband, Scott, found them and, throwing Ross a sympathetic look, tossed his arm affectionately around his wife and dragged her home.

Since Ross was scheduled for a quick trip to Washington, D.C., the following week, he took a moment the next morning to write checks and left them on his kitchen table, knowing Natalie would find them Tuesday when she showed up to clean. He'd given each girl a generous amount and figured Natalie would kiss his feet when she saw the size of her check. She had two teenage daughters and a boy on a mission. Was this ex-husband of hers helping her at all? He had to be, Ross thought. But he thought again about what Kendra and her husband had said: *He makes as much money as he does, and she is forced to do this.*

Well, at least this month she would have extra to put toward that mission fund, he hoped. He'd felt oddly disturbed by Natalie at the party. She'd worked hard all evening. She'd stayed busy, going from one helpful thing to the next. He'd been impressed by her impromptu sketches; he'd found himself amused at her blushes when he'd teased her about the apple-eating contest. In fact, their conversations had helped divert him from the pressure he'd felt playing host. But it had also seemed like every time he could tell she'd begun to relax, something would happen and she would vanish. Or worse, she'd distance herself emotionally from him.

It was ironic, he thought. For nearly twenty years, women had used every ploy imaginable to pursue him. He wasn't a fool—he knew he was a pretty good catch, all things considered. But the dating game had become tiresome and old. So here was a woman going to apparent great lengths to avoid him, and he was feeling put out. *I must be perverse. I should be relieved and thanking her*, he thought. Instead, he'd purposefully baited her, flirted in a way he hadn't since high school. He had thought for sure her coy act would crumble when they'd danced. Instead, she'd grown serious, talking to him about regrets. It had been that conversation that had affected him the most. And then she'd vanished again.

He could guess what those regrets of hers could be. She was divorced, her ex was obviously a clod of some kind, and that alone would lead to regret. But he'd looked closely at her when she had spoken of it, and she'd had a look of utter sadness. Sadness, resignation, but also resolve. Her eyes had darkened to nearly black when she'd been talking about having regrets and learning lessons. He wondered, really wondered, what depths she had experienced to warrant such a profound expression. And it had moved him. He'd experienced depths of his own.

Ross decided that as long as he was on the East Coast, he would make a quick stop in New York. Gina and Monty were undoubtedly still enjoying the fine sights of San Francisco, and it was a great opportunity to get current on Engel Tech without Gina manipulating things to her advantage and his chagrin. It also gave him a chance to visit an old friend, his former bishop. That bishop, in addition to Bud Atwood, had helped him through the aftermath of Liz. Bishop Daynes, now just Neil to Ross, had been a compassionate spiritual leader at the time and was a close friend now. Ross seldom went to New York without seeing Neil, and he was a frequent guest for Sunday dinner at their home on those occasions.

Ross pulled out his cell phone and quickly made the necessary changes to his airline schedule.

* * *

"Ross! Over here." Neil Daynes waved Ross over to the corner booth, where he was seated at Levin's, a popular deli located near Ross's office. Ross was only going to be in New York for the day, and between both of their busy schedules, this brief lunch was all they could manage. Over the years, they had been regulars at this particular deli, so Neil had taken the liberty of ordering ahead for both of them. One never knew what the traffic from LaGuardia to downtown would be like, and with this visit, time was at a premium.

Ross asked LaTaundra for a bottled water, shrugged out of his overcoat, and slid into the booth. LaTaundra didn't exactly fit the profile one would normally expect of a deli employee, since she was African-American and Southern Baptist, to boot—definitely not a New Yorker or Jewish. But Wally Levin, proprietor of Levin's, had admitted to Neil and Ross on more than one occasion that he'd grown fond of the way she hummed gospel hymns while she built sandwiches. He had recognized a great cook and dependable employee when she'd walked through his door from Tupelo, Mississippi, and the customers loved her. He'd been right on, Ross thought.

"How's your mother?" Neil asked.

"She's doing pretty well," Ross said. "We just celebrated her sixty-fifth, actually. Big bash under the minimalist direction of my sister Susan. Don't take it personally, but I think you were the only person in the Western Hemisphere who wasn't invited. Blame me if you feel slighted."

"Sorry, old boy. I am horribly offended to have been snubbed. I would have hopped on the nearest plane if I'd known," Neil said.

"I'm afraid I bugged out on the planning end of the festivities, and Sister Suzie took it upon herself to invite everyone who'd ever been within ten feet of me since birth—everyone but those acquaintances who fall into the black hole known as New York City, which left you off the hook, by the way, except for the entire firm of Rogers, Goldman, et al. She actually managed to get old Monty Rogers and Gina to travel cross-continent to put in an appearance."

Neil chuckled. "Ah, the gorgeous Ms. Rogers. She certainly knows how to wage battles with tenacity and flair."

"Yeah, well, don't laugh yet. That wasn't the worst of it. I had to dance with her. I was expecting her to ram a stiletto between my ribs at the very same time she was whispering sweet nothings in my ear."

"I am always sadly struck that such beauty is truly only skin deep."

"Skin and silicone deep. Ah, here are the sandwiches. LaTaundra, your culinary talents are exceeded only by your singing abilities."

She settled the plates in front of them. "Humph. Always was more talk than action from the likes of you. Eat up now, hear?"

Both men grinned at her retreating figure, a symphony of jiggle and jive.

Ross regaled Neil with stories of the birthday party while they devoured their Reuben sandwiches and chips.

"So your sisters are still intent on securing your eternal happiness, it seems," Neil said around a bite of corned beef.

"Oh yes." Ross shrugged. "They mean well, I suppose, but Suzie goes after it like a fury and won't let up. Although one of her introductions at least holds some potential."

"Oh?"

"Branch manager of a bank, nearly has her master's in finance, quite pretty, conversation was surprisingly good. I'll be giving her a call when I get home. Nice girl." Nice enough, Ross thought, and she had enough of the qualities on the list he'd given Suzie that he needed to take her out at least once so his sister wouldn't out-and-out kill him.

"Uh-huh."

LaTaundra returned at that moment. "You gentlemen fixin' to put away some of my fine spicy apple pie à la mode this afternoon?"

Both of the men groaned in unison and then both said yes.

"I'll go get that for y'all, then," she said with a victorious look before heading to the dessert case.

"How does she do that?" Neil mused. "Destroy all of my self-control with only two words: *apple* and *pie*?"

"Janis is going to kill you," Ross said. "You know she watches your diet like a hawk."

"Tell me about it. But what that woman right there"—he gestured at a humming LaTaundra, who was now settling mammoth portions of pie in front of each man—"can do with apples is downright magical and undoubtedly sinful."

She gave Neil a smug smile and sauntered off, humming.

"Speaking of apples," Ross said, "we had a little apple-eating contest at Mom's birthday bash. And . . ." He gave a dramatic pause. "I'm sure you will be interested to learn there is actually a woman in the world who appears to be resistant to my manly charms."

"Obviously a woman of rare intelligence." Neil took a huge forkful of spicy apple pie à la mode and nearly swooned. "Mmm, I think I died and went to heaven."

Ross chuckled and took a bite of pie himself and then closed his eyes in ecstasy. LaTaundra had definitely outdone herself. "I seem to have a talent for catching this woman at the worst possible moments. In fact, we started off on the wrong foot entirely. Literally. Since then, I've tried the standard approaches to see how she'll react—but just when I think there may be a breakthrough and all the typical female reactions I'm expecting are about to emerge, she beats a hasty retreat."

"Typical female reactions," Neil murmured as he took another bite of pie. "Not a very flattering description of the fairer sex."

"You know what I mean." Ross forked up a big bite of pie. "At any rate, my enormous male ego has been taking a beating."

Neil paused with his fork halfway to his mouth, and Ross suddenly felt uneasy. Maybe he had said too much, confessed to something he hadn't intended.

"Sounds like you've got a story to tell me here. What did it have to do with apples again?" Neil ate the bite of pie and followed it up with another forkful of ice cream.

"Natalie, that's her name, was helping with Mom's birthday party. The kids were in the kitchen having the apple-eating contest. Not bobbing for apples, the apple-hanging-on-a-string kind." Neil nodded in acknowledgment, so Ross continued. "She was the only adult participating. I happened to walk into the kitchen when the contest was in full swing." Ross could still see her bright eyes twinkling with humor as she went after her apple. "Brett won, by the way," he added.

"Great young man."

"That he is. Then the kids carved pumpkins, and Natalie drew sketches of ideas for carving. They were good too. I left after that, but when I checked back a little while later, she was telling my niece a Halloween story. Brett told me later she'd made it up herself. Clever." He'd been surprised and impressed. Housekeepers weren't generally known for having artistic abilities or storymaking skills.

Neil looked up from his plate. "But this Natalie is immune to your magnetic charisma, and we know this how?"

"I asked her to dance. Well, technically, I asked Mom to dance, and she blew me off and told me to find another partner. Natalie was in the room, so I asked her. We danced; I swung her around, plied her with my best moves, and used all my charm. To no avail." He smiled with mock chagrin.

"How'd y'all like my pie?"

Ross forked up a huge bite and winked at LaTaundra.

"Honey, if I weren't already married, I'd be down on my knees begging," Neil said.

LaTaundra grinned and threw a hand on her hip, striking an alluring pose. "I could fatten you up plenty too, sugar. You all just bones. But you'd have to fight my man DaRonne for me, and DaRonne would knock you into next week. He don't like sharing me with no other men. Even if they do appreciate my fine cooking skills."

Neil threw his hands over his heart as LaTaundra turned and left them again. "Wounded!"

"DaRonne is one lucky guy. And Janis will be relieved, I'm sure," Ross said.

"Mmm. So what's the next step with this Natalie?" Neil asked.

"There is no next step. I only thought you'd find the story entertaining, considering my history with women," Ross said.

"She seemed to be spending a lot of time in the kitchen with the kids. Doesn't that seem unusual for a guest?"

"She was working for us that night. Part of that included supervising the grandkids, I guess. My sisters made the arrangements." Come to think of it, if Natalie had been involved with the grandkids too, she'd done even more than he'd realized. He was glad the check he'd written for her had been a generous sum.

"So, tell me. Is she someone you could see yourself dating or in a relationship with?" Neil asked.

Ross realized he'd let his guard down too far with his old bishop and had said too much. He could tell where this line of questioning was leading. And the answer, not that he was going to share it with Neil, was that the kind of relationship he intended to have with Natalie Forrester was the employer/employee kind. She was attractive, yes, with her blonde hair and curvy figure and her big green eyes, and, yes, her talents had surprised him. But being a single mom with three kids, one of them old enough to be serving a mission, was enough of a warning sign to make anyone stop and consider what a date with her might mean.

"It's not what you think, Neil. Natalie is my housekeeper. I get the impression she was lucky to even graduate from high school. That is definitely not the type of woman for me, no matter how green her eyes are." Ross paused and waited to see if his old friend planned to argue the point with him. He didn't, and Ross relaxed. "Now tell me how Janis and the boys are doing."

After finishing catching up, they dropped cash on the table to cover the tip. It had been a quick lunch, both men with fully booked afternoons, and Ross was taking an early flight out the next day.

They shook hands and said their farewells, but Neil seemed reluctant to leave.

"Ross," he began. "I know it's a sore subject, but I need to ask. Do you ever hear news about Liz?"

"Elizabeth Turner Bancroft, attorney at law," Ross said, trying to keep the acid out of his voice. "Last I heard, she'd accepted a position with a Boston firm. But that was a few years back. Why bring her up now?"

Neil grimaced. "The gossip around town is that her firm is opening an office in Manhattan and she's on the short list to relocate here. Whether she does or not remains to be seen. But I thought you should know."

Despite himself, Ross's stomach knotted. He'd moved on from Liz years ago. And yet, hearing Neil talk about her brought some of the pain back. He fought it. "Well, then, it's a good thing I'm spending most of my time in Utah these days, isn't it?" He pulled Neil in for a quick hug. "I appreciate your concern for me, Neil, more than you know. But I'm fine. It's been a long time. I'll see you the next time I'm in town."

Neil looked relieved. "I'm glad to hear it, old friend. And next time you're in town, you're coming over to the house for a home-cooked meal. Janis will insist on it."

"It's a deal," Ross said.

As he pushed his way through the revolving door of his building, Ross tried to reassure himself that he'd been telling Neil the truth when he'd talked about Liz.

Chapter 13

THE FIRST THING ROSS NOTICED when he walked into his home from the airport was a stack of money sitting on the kitchen table with a note from Natalie simply stating, "Too much." He thumbed through the bills, quickly calculating that she had deducted what would have amounted to her hourly rate for both her time at the party and the Saturday she had spent helping his mother. The balance was now in his hands.

He shook his head and chuckled. He couldn't help it. He was mildly irritated and begrudgingly impressed. She hadn't waited for him to return to ask him to write a different check. That would have required a confrontation with him, something he already knew she would avoid if at all possible. It had also allowed her immediate access to funds he was sure she needed without waiting for him to return from his trip. Since his trips were frequent and frequently long, this was a prudent step on her part if she needed the money quickly. She may not have a college education but she was no dummy, this one.

What would happen, he wondered, if he were to force a showdown about it with her? The thought was intriguing. He, seasoned attorney that he was, wasn't one to back away from a confrontation. But Natalie Forrester would wriggle and look for an escape. That could be interesting. His previous encounters with her had all been fairly amusing. He hadn't been this entertained in years. He'd forgotten how it felt, actually. And it felt pretty good.

By the time he'd showered and checked his watch, he'd decided he was going to do it. He'd promised Brett he'd catch part of his football game because the season was winding down, but he figured he still had a small window of time before heading to the high school. He was going to face her down about the money. She was being foolish. He didn't need the money, and she did.

But more than that, he felt devious and slightly wicked. He never knew what to expect from her, and the thought of pinning her strategically and watching her try to maneuver out of it made the legal shark in him smile.

He pulled up in front of her tiny home fifteen minutes later. Her little Ford Focus sat in the driveway, so he was fairly certain she was there. He briefly wondered why she didn't park in her garage, but the thought passed as he rang the doorbell. He waited a few minutes and was about to ring again when he heard, "Come on in!"

Ross quietly shut the door behind him. He could hear Natalie talking, apparently on the telephone, then she yelled, "I'll be right there! Get comfy." So he did.

He hadn't really paid attention to Natalie's home when he'd been here before, so he took a moment to look around. The living room was exactly that—a "living" room. It breathed. The furniture was clean but worn, arranged for comfortable conversation over a faded carpet, the striped slipcover on the sofa mostly neat, with a slightly sat-in look. Pillows in bold florals added energy but also looked soft enough to stick behind his head while reading a book. And on the subject of books, there was a large stack on an end table next to a unique, eye-catching lamp. He browsed through the stack: Jane Austen—no real surprise there—a compilation of Greek myths, a paperback copy of *Othello*, and *The Great Gatsby*. Pretty eclectic, he thought. There was a comprehensive volume on ancient civilizations, and, of all things, a how-to book on papier mâchè. He picked it up, thumbed through the pages briefly, and noticed it was a library book. They all were.

There were framed photographs on the wall, as well as on the simple wood mantel above her fireplace. Some black-and-whites of Natalie's girls and a tall, dark-haired young man he assumed was her missionary son. Funny, Ross thought. He had pictured her son looking different—more like her. Ross noticed a closely cropped photo of a grizzled old man, his light eyes piercing and direct. It was the type of photo he thought could win an award of some kind, somewhere.

Who was this Natalie Forrester who cleaned his house, tap danced horribly, and carved pumpkins into works of art? He glanced toward the kitchen; he could hear her still speaking on the phone. He didn't want to eavesdrop, but she wasn't really trying to keep her voice down either.

"It isn't worth it . . . I *have* talked to him. I talk to him more than I'd like . . . no . . . Dad, no. I have to keep the girls' feelings in mind. I can't just

. . . I appreciate it, really, but I'm fine. We're fine. No, don't you dare. You need that money for . . ." There was a long pause. Ross felt uncomfortable listening, but the room was small, and the sound carried without much effort on Natalie's part. "I'll only send it back if you do. I mean it. I need to go now; I have company. No—heavens, no! Not that kind. Tori. Yes, I'll tell her. Love you. Talk to you soon."

Ross grabbed the closest magazine, which thankfully was the *Ensign* and not some woman's fashion rag, and proceeded to look busy reading. He figured it would create a more believable picture than perusing a book on papier mâchè.

He glanced up at her gasp, innocent expression firmly in place. He started to smile until he saw the look on her pale face. It held more than just a look of surprise, which was what he'd expected to see. Layered on top of it was a world-weariness he'd not expected. He'd never seen it on her before. It twisted something inside of him.

"You're not—" she started.

The phone rang.

She took a moment to check the caller ID before answering the call. "Tori," she said quietly, and then she was silent, just listening for a few minutes. Ross laid the *Ensign* down on the table and straightened. "No, it's okay. Tell her I hope she feels better soon. We'll do it another time. I'll call you tomorrow." She closed her cell, obviously distracted.

"Big plans cancelled?"

"Just a girls' night with my friend."

"Sorry."

"It's not a big deal." She seemed to realize suddenly that he'd shown up unexpectedly at her house and asked warily, "Why are you here?"

Ross knew her earlier phone conversation with her dad had included a confrontation about money. From the looks of her, she didn't need another one, not even in jest. His wicked plans of torture dissolved on the spot. He would play straight with her. "I got home from D.C. today and saw that you'd left money on my kitchen table." He held his hands up, palms forward, when she started to object. "I was going to hassle you about it. I'm not going to now."

"It was too much!" she said indignantly. "I couldn't take that kind of—"

"You worked for it."

"I don't charge that much for what I do."

"Maybe you should in this case." He gave her a teasing smile. "At the firm, we constantly factor in damages for pain and suffering."

"Helping with your mother's party wasn't painful."

"Maybe not for you, but it saved me a boatload of pain and suffering to have you help her, and you should be compensated for that."

"Do you know what the hourly rate would have been if I'd taken that money?" She looked like she wanted to start pacing, but she stood there stiffly instead.

He shrugged. "Roughly." He hadn't figured it out to the penny, but he was aware of how much he paid her on an hourly basis. His check for the party had been for significantly more, but he'd felt relief that it had gone well—and was over.

"It's what professionals, doctors, you know, that type of—make. I don't—" She was struggling to find the words. "I'm not—" Her mouth was a firm line, but he thought it quivered a little. She raised her chin just a little. "You don't pay someone like that just to clean toilets."

"I don't think you realize—"

"Housekeepers aren't worth that kind of money."

"Okay." *What's the big deal if she gets a little windfall?* he thought, feeling irritated now.

"And I won't take charity, not from you. Not from anyone."

"Okay," he said again. He took in her face, her determination and pride, and his irritation evaporated. "Good for you," he said.

"Don't patronize me!" Her face flushed pink, then paled. She expelled a huge breath and walked to the window. "I don't know why I said that. I shouldn't have spoken to you that way. I'm sorry."

Ross studied her tense shoulders, watched her massage her temples. He had a fleeting urge to rest his hands on those shoulders and ease the burden that seemed too large for them. It would just be a friendly, comforting gesture from an employer to an employee. Nothing more. And yet, some very primal instinct warned him that if he did, he would be stepping on dangerous ground, ground he had long avoided. He compromised and offered conciliatory words instead. "I'm sure it was the disappointment from having to cancel your plans and the shock of seeing the big bad wolf at your door."

She tried to smile. He gave her credit for that. He almost saw that single dimple start to emerge.

"Whatever the reason, there is no excuse," she said. "I'm sorry."

"All is forgotten."

"And you're not exactly the big bad wolf."

Yeah, he figured her big bad wolf was some jerk of a guy with the last name of Forrester.

Suddenly, she brightened. "You *can* do me a favor, since you're here. I have a gift for your little niece. Will you take it with you? Will you be seeing her anytime soon?"

"Probably." Why would she have anything for his niece? Was this some kind of back door way of ingratiating herself with him? His well-developed suspicions went on alert.

"Great! I'll be right back." She headed through the door into the kitchen.

Curious, Ross followed. It was an old Formica and linoleum kitchen, but she'd managed to make it cheery. He saw her go through another door, which had to lead to that unused garage.

"What's in here?" He peeked in after her and saw worktables and boxes all over the place and no room for a car. That explained the Focus in the driveway. All over the worktables, resting on open newspapers, were white blobs of something in various shapes, roughly the size of his fist.

She opened a cupboard, removed something small, and was placing it in a brown bag when he came behind her and looked over her shoulder.

"Let me see."

He heard her take a deep breath as she reluctantly drew the item out of the bag. She quietly held it up for his inspection.

There, in her hand, sat a fairy, or an elf; he wasn't sure exactly which. She had a round little face with apple cheeks and a mass of auburn hair. She wore a vivid orange dress that plumped out around her and was trimmed with curling grape vines, the purple polka dots of grapes just peeking out along the hem of the skirt and at the neckline. A little crown of vines sat on her head, and tiny pale wings showed from the back. She held a cornucopia filled with red apples and gourds. This enchanting little person had a slightly rustic, nubby texture, and Ross's hands itched to hold her and look at her more closely. He reached out. "May I?"

She handed him the little fairy, her hand shaking slightly. Ross wondered why.

He studied the little fairy and could have sworn it was watching him back. "This is for Lexie? Where did you get it?"

"Her name is Princess Pumpkinseed, and . . . I made her. Sculpted her. Out of papier mâchè."

Ah, the library book. "You made it." It was a fairly elaborate offering for a kid she'd met only once. He was definitely suspicious now. He kept his voice carefully neutral. "You made a painted sculpture from papier mâchè specifically for my niece?"

"She's the one who got my mind working, and the resulting idea it gave me actually solved my Christmas gift problem. So I made a Princess Pumpkinseed for her as a way of saying thank you." She took the fairy from Ross and placed it back in the bag. "At your mother's party, Lexie asked me to carve her pumpkin into something not scary. When my girls were little, they would ask me to do the same thing. I came up with Princess Pumpkinseed a long time ago for them." She smiled, her eyes looking someplace faraway. "My own little spinoff from Celtic mythology. I'd totally forgotten about her. Anyway, I carved Princess Pumpkinseed for Lexie that night and couldn't get her out of my mind. The princess, that is. So I crafted her out of papier mâchè. It's inexpensive, and it got Princess Pumpkinseed out of my head through my fingers."

She went back to the cupboard, and Ross found himself staring after her. Celtic mythology? "And then I pushed some more papier mâchè around in my fingers, and he showed up." *He* was a pear-shaped Santa, plump and purple and looking like he'd delivered toys for hundreds of years. "Now I am making Santas to give as gifts this year, and I owe the idea, indirectly, to Lexie, so I wanted to thank her. It's silly, but that's the way it is."

He gestured toward the little white blobs on the work table. "These, I presume, are Santas in embryo?" What a convoluted path she had followed to arrive at something like this. Gifts on the cheap that looked like a million bucks. When did she have time to do this sort of thing? The little sculptures were clever, truly. Whimsical and original and artfully done, at least to his eye. "May I have one?"

She looked shocked. "You want one?"

"Yes. May I have this one?"

"All right. I guess so." She handed over the Santa and watched as he inspected the old elf's violet-hued robes and frothy beard. "Does this mean I don't owe you a Christmas present later? This will count as the traditional employee-sucking-up-to-boss holiday gift?"

So occasionally there was a little bit of spunk and humor in her. "Of course not."

"Well, your employer-appreciation-for-not-tap-dancing-in-your-kitchen-ever-again gift had better be pretty darn good, then." The dimple was there in full force that time.

He laughed. "Deal."

He checked his watch. The football game was in full swing. He needed to go so he could keep his promise to Brett. When he looked up, he saw that she was picking up each blob, checking to see if it was dry, and replacing it on the newspaper. Her head was lowered. So quickly she'd retreated away from him. Every other woman he knew would be hanging on his every word, urging him to stay, offering him food. Not Mrs. Forrester, oh, no. What was it with her, anyway? He'd felt a spark from her when they'd danced, not that it had meant anything, really. She was his housekeeper after all. Nothing would come from this. But the puzzle, the challenge—it was almost too tempting to ignore. He decided to kill two birds with one stone.

"Listen—I'm on my way to watch Brett try to catch a couple of footballs for East High. Jackie and the family will be there. I think you should give the gift to Lexie yourself. Come along with me." When she started to shake her head, he added casually, "I'm not planning to stay for the entire game; I have other plans later this evening. We'll just go, watch a few plays, you can give Lexie her fairy, and then I'll bring you home." When she still seemed to hesitate, he said, "Come on. It will get your mind off the bitter disappointment of missing an evening of chick flicks and chocolate."

"Chick flicks and pizza. I never get over the need for chocolate. And thanks, but—"

"Does that mean you're not up for a wild night of high-school football? I know it's not quite the same as a good old tear jerker. There isn't as much kissing and crying at football games. Well, maybe the same amount of crying, at least for the losing team." He waited a beat; as an attorney, he knew timing was everything. "Brett will appreciate it. And Lexie will be thrilled."

She looked wary. He should probably hope she told him no again. His family would blow this simple invitation way out of proportion, he knew, but he and Mrs. Forrester were only delivering a gift. It was an errand, nothing more. And if his family did blow it out of proportion, he'd simply set them straight.

And the idea of getting Natalie Forrester to crack—just a little bit— was a challenge he couldn't resist now. Maybe it was the hokey pokey T-shirt; maybe it was her proud refusal of money. Maybe the little orange fairy had cast some sort of crazy spell on him.

He gave her his most charming summation-to-the-jury smile. "What do you say, Bob?"

Her dimple faded briefly, then her smile seemed to overbrighten. "All right, I guess. I haven't enjoyed a high-school football game in twenty years."

He thought her reply seemed cryptic, but he decided to keep his question to himself for the time being.

* * *

Natalie was shivering. In her thin leather jacket, her hands stuffed in the pockets, she could feel herself shake from the cold. To say she'd been shocked when Ross had invited her to the football game was an understatement. It always surprised her when a man invited her to do something—maybe that was why she was constantly caught off guard and then typically caved in. But this time, ironically, her inability to gracefully decline had put her in the worst possible place to be for her emotional well-being. It was daunting enough to be here with this impossibly attractive, intimidating man, but to be at a high-school football game? It was at a high-school football game that her road of regrets had begun. She wasn't sure being here with Ross McConnell was the best way to face old ghosts.

Teens screamed and yelled at football plays they didn't understand and huddled and flirted in the deep shadows cast by the stadium lights. There was a rich smokiness in the crisp autumn air, laced with the scent of hotdogs and burning leaves. The pep band wailed off tune; the drums pounded out an upbeat tempo. Amid the shrill whistles and cheers, the music wove through the wind like the ghosts of her memories. She shook her head to clear it. This evening she had an opportunity to rise above memories and enjoy the moment, start fresh. Bury regrets.

"Where do you think the rest of your family is sitting?" she asked. The bleachers were filled to capacity, and Natalie didn't know how they would ever find them.

Ross craned his neck to search the crowd. "Jackie usually likes to show up in time to get seats close to the fifty-yard line," he said. "I can't see her though. We'll find a couple of seats for now and look for them at halftime."

Ross located a place near the end zone for them to sit, and Natalie followed. He'd lugged a couple of stadium blankets from the trunk of his car and folded one of them to cushion their seats; the other he handed to Natalie, which she wrapped around her legs.

She glanced over at Ross. He was sitting casually, his forearms resting on his thighs, his jacket unzipped. *Why don't guys seem to feel the cold?* she wondered. The occasional breeze that seemed to only ruffle his hair sent frigid spasms through Natalie. She flipped her jacket collar up to shield her neck. It was early November, and the temperature was in the forties, but Natalie, who generally liked cold weather, was a popsicle and hoped she survived. And if she was honest with herself, part of the shivering came from nerves and chilled memories, not just the nighttime breeze.

She tried to concentrate on the game. It was the second quarter, and Brett had already caught a couple of short passes and taken one long bomb in for a touchdown just since they'd arrived. She watched Ross watching the game, quiet but intense, only yelling at the refs a couple of times. She still couldn't believe she was here. She'd walked out of her house toward his amazing car, smelled that luxurious expensive leather upholstery smell, and had nearly bolted back into the house. She'd been struck speechless, but he'd managed to keep the conversation light and continuous and mainly one-sided, so she hadn't felt too awkward. And now the aloof, aristocratic attorney Ross McConnell was sitting by her at a high-school football game. It was like she'd stepped into an alternate universe.

In her safe little universe, she would be home watching a movie with Tori. Emma was at her school's football game with Tess and Kate, and Callie was sleeping over at Gwen's house. Natalie and Tori were supposed to be having a simple girls' night. A nice, peaceful evening with a happily-ever-after movie. She wasn't supposed to be at a high-school football game. She had learned twenty years ago that high-school football was bad for her health and happiness. And she definitely wasn't supposed to be in the company of her boss, the most unnerving man she'd ever met.

It was nearly halftime, and Natalie could swear the temperature had dropped another ten degrees just from the number of people leaving the stands to buy concessions. She hoped Ross had been caught up enough in the action and satisfied enough with her attempts at enthusiastic responses not to notice that she was turning blue.

The whistle sounded, ending the first half. The drill team began marching out onto the field as the players jogged to the locker room.

Ross turned to Natalie, grinning. "Brett's playing great. When their safety flattened him at the fifteen, I thought they were going to have to scoop up what was left of him with a spoon." He chuckled, then his brows came together. "You're cold. I wish you'd told me. Do you want to move around a bit to get your blood pumping again, or would you like to shiver here bravely while I go get you a large hot chocolate?"

"I think I'll take a little stroll toward the ladies' room, actually."

"Okay. When you get back, I'll get you that chocolate you say you can't live without. Then we'll go find Lex and the rest of the family."

Walking felt good, even though Natalie's joints were stiff from cold. She hoped the bathrooms were equipped with hot-air hand dryers. If she was really lucky, they would have the nozzles that rotated up so she could defrost her face.

Maybe coming to the football game with Ross had been a good thing. He was being nice, the game had been action filled, and Natalie wasn't looking at every player on the field and seeing Buck Jacobsen instead. At least, not so far.

Then, as she headed toward the school building, she saw a couple pressed closely against the wall. The boy was murmuring to the girl, who clung to him like a second skin, giggling. Natalie could guess what the boy was saying. She'd heard words like his at their age. The girl gazed at the boy worshipfully. Natalie knew that look too. She'd given that look to Aaron "Buck" Jacobsen at the Bear River High School football games twenty years ago. Before and after the games, at least. He'd been the star running back, nicknamed "Buck" for his style against the defense and his prowess on the rodeo circuit. And Natalie had worshipped him from afar.

She had lost her mother during her junior year and, as a result, had lost her father to his grief. Lonely and hurting, Natalie had focused her dreams on the most amazing boy she'd ever seen. So when Buck asked her to dance at an after-game stomp early in the autumn of her senior year, her heart flew.

The dance led to dates and lots of time spent in the cab of his rusty Dodge pickup. He made her feel wanted. He made her feel alive. She didn't feel empty anymore.

He whispered crazy love words to her against the school walls. He promised her everything would be okay. He told her he needed her. It was love, he said, and if she really loved him she would understand this. She would show him she loved him. Really show him. Something deep inside her quietly told her it was a huge risk, but when his urgent mouth was on hers, when he whispered words in her ear, the quiet voice inside got quieter and quieter until it disappeared.

She relented. She gave him what he asked her for, pushed her for. In the end she wanted it too and gave it freely. She trusted him, loved him, or so she thought.

The quiet voice returned though, dogging her mind with cautions, telling her to stop. She blocked it out and relished the joy of feeling like a part of something whole again. She gloried in the weight of his arm on her shoulder in the school hallways, the wink he would send her as she scurried off to class. And then the pregnancy showed her the true Buck and changed her life forever.

As a result, Natalie had learned to doubt the reality of dreams at the age of seventeen. When a girl lost her mother at sixteen and her innocence and freedom at seventeen, there wasn't a lot of room left for dreams. Even in an empty vessel.

Natalie pulled herself back to the present as she dried her hands using the hot-air dryer. She punched the button again and crouched to let it warm her face. It was time to return to Ross, smile, and replace old memories with new ones. She vowed they would be happy ones this time.

"You a little warmer now?" Ross asked as she slipped back into her seat next to him.

Natalie thought she was until he smiled at her and shivers ran straight up her spine. It was just a reaction to all of those teenage pheromones permeating the air, she thought frantically. Let him think she was freezing; it was safer. He pulled off his jacket and threw it around her shoulders. It was big and warm and smelled of leather and aftershave and something that was distinctly Ross.

"Now you're going to get cold," she managed to say with slightly chattering teeth.

"Nah, I'll be fine for a while. If the hot chocolate doesn't do the trick, we'll leave. I've seen enough of the game to give Brett a good report." He turned and strode down the bleachers.

Natalie gazed around her. The students looked young, fresh, and full of promise. The loudspeaker crackled with the booming voice of the announcer, who was highlighting upcoming school events over the din of noisy teenage activity. She glanced over to see Ross returning to the bleachers, a large steaming Styrofoam cup in each hand.

"Here, drink up. It's really hot though—don't burn your tongue."

She held the cup close to her face and let the steam unthaw her nose. It smelled heavenly. "Mmm. Thank you."

"Mac! Hello!"

Natalie looked up from her chocolaty cloud and saw Jackie striding up the bleachers toward them, Lexie in tow.

"You made it. I'm glad," Jackie said. She pointed toward the fifty-yard line. "Everyone is sitting over there. Brett will be thrilled you're here. You did see that touchdown, right?" She smiled warmly at Natalie, obviously noting Ross's jacket around her shoulders. "Nice to see you again, Natalie." She glanced back at Ross.

Ross gave his sister a quick hug. "We saw the touchdown. Watching Brett snag that ball out of midair was like watching the Bolshoi Ballet. It was art in motion. What's the word on scholarships?"

"He's not sure he wants to play college ball, but he has so much ability. Rick and I keep telling him to go for it, just give it a try, but he's resistant. He's so intent on law school, and he thinks football will distract him. He remembers what you said about your football—"

"Football? You played football?" Natalie looked up suddenly from settling Lexie on her lap.

Ross shrugged. "I was quarterback. It was a great way to go through high school, but I'd already decided I was heading to law school, and I didn't want to be sidetracked."

"And Brett is determined to be just like you, you know. I wish you'd explain to him that he has options, that he doesn't have to mimic you."

"I'll talk to him if you want me too, Jack. But ultimately, you have to let him follow his own path."

"I know." She sighed. "Do you like football, Natalie?"

"She must." Ross grinned. "She knows the game quite well."

Natalie was surprised that he'd paid attention to her occasional comments. "I'm not what you would call a huge fan, but I understand the basic rules."

"And she agreed to come with me tonight regardless of her disinterest in the game. Can you believe it?"

Natalie couldn't let that one stand. Patting Lexie on the shoulder, she said, "It had more to do with Lexie than football or you. Lexie, I have a gift for you." She reached into her purse and gave the little brown bag to her.

"What is it?" Lexie asked, wide-eyed.

"Open it and see." Before she could even finish, Lexie had torn the bag open and was holding the orange fairy reverently in her tiny hands. "Mama, look!"

Jackie held the fairy up out of the shadows cast by the stadium lights. "Oh my. It's darling! Where did you find it?"

Lexie tugged Natalie's sleeve. "Is it her?"

"Yes. It's Princess Pumpkinseed." Natalie tucked an errant blonde curl behind Lexie's ear. "She's fragile though. You have to be extremely careful with fairies. They get their feelings hurt very easily."

"Natalie made it," Ross told Jackie. "I have a Santa in the car."

Jackie's eyes widened. "She gave you a Santa?"

He grinned. "Only after I twisted her arm."

After freezing all evening long, Natalie could now feel heat flooding her cheeks.

Jackie looked like she wanted to question Ross further, but the cheering crowd announced the return of the teams onto the field. "Come on, Lex. Let's go back to Daddy and the kids."

Natalie saw Ross glance at his watch. They'd accomplished their task, and she remembered he'd said he had plans later.

Just then, Lexie threw her arms around Natalie's neck. "I want to stay with Bob. Please, Mama, can I stay with Bob for just a little while?"

"Bob?" Jackie said.

"Long story. Don't ask," Ross replied.

Natalie tried to ignore him, squeezed Lexie, and said, "We're leaving now, so maybe another time, okay?"

Lexie's vise-like grip around her neck only tightened, and Natalie glanced at the others for help. She couldn't read the expression on Ross's face. He glanced at his watch again.

Big killer eyes used to getting their way turned their lethal charm on Ross. "Just for *one minute*, Uncle Mackie?"

The corner of one side of his mouth curved slightly. "One minute. And that's all."

Jackie gave him a quick kiss on the cheek. "We're sitting right over there. Bring her back when you're ready to go. I'll take the fairy princess with me, Lex."

One minute turned into a bag of popcorn, several sips from Natalie's now-lukewarm chocolate, and a mildly successful attempt from the crowd to do the wave. Natalie rose in her seat, hoisting Lexie in the air while Lexie stretched her arms up and squealed. Ross sat, and only when Lexie scolded him did he make a halfhearted attempt to raise an arm when the wave went by again.

By the end of the third quarter, Natalie could tell Ross had removed himself to someplace unreachable. She nudged his arm gently. "We can go."

He shrugged. "Fine."

They returned Lexie to her parents and headed toward the parking lot and his car.

* * *

Natalie reread the paragraph she'd just finished, then closed her book when she realized she still didn't know what it said. She'd been sitting in her living room, waiting for Emma to return home for quite a while now. It was past her curfew, and she hadn't answered any of Natalie's calls or texts.

Ross had dropped Natalie off a few hours ago from the football game. She'd spent the rest of the evening painting Santas, until Emma's curfew had come and gone. Then she had cleaned up her paints and taken a sentry position in the living room, where she could see the front door when Emma finally walked in.

Her daughter wasn't late very often, and she usually sent Natalie a text to let her know what was up and when to expect her. It hadn't happened this time, and after all the teenage regrets Natalie had been reminded of earlier tonight, she'd automatically gone into worry mode.

The door opened. Thank goodness.

"You're late," Natalie said.

"I know. I'm sorry," Emma said, shutting and locking the door.

"And . . . ?"

No response.

"Why didn't you answer my texts or phone calls?" Natalie asked her, trying to control the edge in her voice.

Emma gave her a confused look and tugged her cell out of her pocket. Her face cleared. "Oh. It looks like I forgot to take it off of silent mode when I got out of class. Sorry."

Seriously, *why* was she paying for her daughters to have cell phones if it wasn't going to make her parenting job any easier? "Emma, come on. If you knew you were late, then you also knew I'd want to know what was going on."

"Honestly, Mom, I didn't realize I'd left my phone on silent. We were at the game, and then Kate wanted us to go with her to a party at this guy's house—"

Natalie felt her heart start to pound. "What guy?"

"Just some guy Kate met at the mall. They've been texting each other a lot, and Kate has a thing for him. But when we got to his place, the party looked kind of, I don't know. Wild or something. We weren't there very long, I promise. We finally talked Kate into leaving, and then we went to Tess's house to watch a movie and accidentally fell asleep."

Natalie studied her daughter's face. Emma hadn't lied to her before, but lately, between the strain of dealing with Wade, her friends, and high school in general, Emma had seemed distant. "It's *so* not a good idea to go to a party at some strange boy's house," Natalie chided. "You know better than that. And you should have called me the minute you woke up."

"I know. I really am sorry, Mom."

"All right, then." Natalie sighed. "Go to bed. There will be consequences for tonight, but we'll discuss what they are in the morning."

"Okay. Good night, Mom. I love you," Emma said. She gave Natalie a quick hug.

"Good night. I love you too."

Natalie watched her daughter head back to her bedroom and shut the door before she flipped off the table light next to her and went to her own bedroom. She sighed with relief. It had been a long night. She hadn't said anything to Em, but Natalie had been mere minutes away from calling Tess's and Marie's parents or even calling the police. Thankfully, Emma was home and safe and apparently no worse for wear. Natalie was sure she would have been able to tell if anything really bad had happened. She knew her daughter.

Which was also why Natalie was also sure Emma hadn't told her the entire truth about what she'd done that night.

Chapter 14

ROSS STEPPED OUT OF THE shower and grabbed his towel. Five miles on the treadmill and an intense session on the Nautilus hadn't dulled his edginess. So he'd run some more. And that was just this morning. After dropping Natalie off last night, he'd gone straight to the gym and worked out. And first thing this morning, after a sleepless night, he'd been right back at it. He rubbed a clear spot in the foggy mirror with his hand and stared at the haggard face staring back. He should shave. It would make him feel more in control.

They'd hardly spoken a word to each other on the drive home. She'd been looking out the window, seemingly lost in her own thoughts. He'd had plenty of thoughts himself and hadn't been disposed to share them with her. He'd been curious about what she was thinking but wasn't sure he really wanted to know. So he hadn't encouraged conversation, and she'd sat there like a stone. It hadn't been a smart idea to invite her to the football game. He wished he could figure out her tactics. He was sure she had them, and he didn't like not knowing what they were. He felt outstrategized.

He grabbed his razor out of the drawer and started shaving. There were reams of documents sitting on his desk, waiting for his review this afternoon; he didn't have time to waste being distracted by some little housekeeper. He sucked in his breath when he nicked his jaw and grabbed some tissue to stanch the blood. He could see her in his car, sitting with her hands folded in her lap, quiet. Then his mind flashed to seeing her do the wave with Lexie, radiant with happiness, their arms outstretched. He saw her dabbing chocolate from Lexie's chin, stroking Lexie's curls when she'd given her the fairy. He impatiently rubbed the remaining blobs of shaving cream from his face. She was an undereducated divorcee with practically grown kids. He didn't want to see her at all. Especially not in his mind.

He stalked through the bathroom door into his bedroom to get dressed. "Oh!"

Startled out of his thoughts, he looked up to see a pink-faced Natalie frozen briefly in her tracks. Then she turned and retreated.

"Stop."

Natalie paused, her hand on the door leading to the hall. She turned slowly and kept her gaze focused intently on some invisible spot on his rug. "I'm sorry. I didn't know you were here."

"Uh-huh. Where would I normally be on a Saturday?" He could tell his voice sounded terse.

"I don't know. Where you are every other day. Not here. Not home."

"You didn't hear water running?"

He watched her look up, look at his bare chest, his face. She turned back to the door. "I'll leave your dry cleaning hanging on the doorknob outside."

That's when he noticed the hangers full of clothes clutched in her hand. It ought to have absolved her, but right now all he saw were years of chicken casseroles and cookies. Calculated entrapment. "Not good enough."

She turned and faced him. "I just got here. I didn't know you were home. You usually aren't during the day. Your laundry is supposed to be ready on Fridays, but it wasn't this week."

"You didn't mention it last night."

"I didn't think to mention it. I'm sorry. I really didn't mean to intrude."

"Yes," he muttered to himself, "but you *do* intrude." He saw her flinch as though she'd been slapped. She slipped through the door and quietly shut it.

"Wait a minute." Inwardly cursing himself, he started after her and felt his towel slip. He wouldn't go chasing Natalie through his house wearing only a towel. It was demeaning; it felt too close to begging. He wouldn't do it.

He ought to apologize, except he shouldn't need to apologize—she was the one who'd walked in on him. And when he'd seen her looking at his chest, he'd wanted to grab her by the arms and—this kind of thinking would not do.

Ross stalked back into the bathroom, splashed cold water on his face, and then grabbed his cell phone. He had a call to make, and now was the time to do it.

A female voice answered after a couple of rings. "Ashley? Ross McConnell. We met at my mother's—you do remember? Great. Listen, I know it's late notice, but I wondered if you were free for dinner this evening. Super. How's eight? Good. Eight o'clock it is. See you then."

* * *

Natalie'd had better days, including ones with Wade that were so bad she'd previously vowed to block them from her mind.

It was Tuesday, the day she was supposed to clean *Mr. McConnell's* house. She'd had to leave Callie home in bed alone suffering from the stomach flu, she'd had an argument with Em about the too-revealing outfit she'd chosen to wear to school, and Natalie's anthropology teacher had assigned the class a ten-page paper this morning as part of their upcoming final. She needed to register for next semester, and she still wasn't sure what she was doing.

Wade had made good on his promise to cut financial support for Ryan's mission, so that meant she had a huge payment due a week from Sunday, larger now than she'd originally budgeted. Not to mention tuition for her as yet undetermined classes. Make that class—singular. Where all the money would come from, she didn't know because she would be cleaning one house fewer after this week.

And all she could think about was how badly she did not want to step foot on Mr. McConnell's property today, not when she could tell she was falling for him and he'd flat out told her she was nothing but an intrusion.

She'd done everything she could think of to avoid the inevitable. She'd checked in on Callie after anthropology class, balanced her checking account—of course, subtracting nothing from nothing didn't take much time—and even done a little grocery shopping. A very little, due to the state of her finances. And despite the moths that had fluttered out of her wallet when she'd paid the cashier, she'd also called Esther Johnson to see if she was ready to take back her old cleaning job. The woman could have her "nice young man" back. But Mrs. Johnson hadn't picked up, and Natalie had been forced to leave a message, which hadn't been returned yet.

And next week was Thanksgiving. It would be a Thanksgiving alone— the deal she'd made with Wade so Emma and Callie could help with the party. Along with all of the other frustration she was feeling for Ross, the McConnells' party had cost her the holiday with her girls.

Then, to top it all off, Mrs. McConnell had called and left a message on her machine, asking if Natalie would come over and get a few boxes of Christmas decorations, of all things. She'd said she was sure Ross didn't have any decorations of his own and she wanted to be sure his house looked festive this year, since it was his first Christmas back home in so long. It had also been implied that Natalie would do the decorating.

Natalie chalked the request up to being part of her final duties as Ross's drudge. Besides, his mother didn't know she would be slapping a formal letter of resignation on his kitchen table today, and Natalie hadn't found the heart to inform her of that fact. But then, of course, considering her luck, it turned out that a "few boxes" ended up filling the trunk of her car and the passenger seats as well. Great.

She pulled into his driveway. First things first. She marched to the door, punched in the security code, and tentatively opened the door. She listened carefully. No footsteps. No running water.

Fine. Good. She could get those boxes out of her car and store them in his basement. She would bet money he never went down there, so in storing the boxes there for the time being, she wouldn't *intrude* on him. It took her awhile to lug all of them out of her car and down the stairs; when she was done, she was filthy and sweating, and she hadn't even started cleaning his house yet. She looked at her watch. Wiping sweat from her forehead with her sleeve, she decided if she hurried and watched out for speed traps, she could go home to get her cleaning supplies—she hadn't had room for them in the car before—and get his house done before he got there. He was only getting minimal service today, anyway, she thought begrudgingly.

When she ran in the door at home, a grim Emma greeted her.

A grim Emma still wearing that awful outfit.

"Dad called," she said.

Oh, wonderful. Natalie waited for Emma to continue.

"He wasn't very happy when he found out Callie was sick and you weren't here with her."

"Callie's thirteen, not three. Although, maybe I should have called him so he could come sit with her while I worked to keep a roof over our heads." She regretted the words the minute she said them, but watching tears form instantly in Emma's eyes made it that much worse. "I'm sorry, honey, I shouldn't have said that."

But the tears she'd mistaken as a reaction to her comment were really tears of frustration and anger. "Why does he get so mad at you working,"

Emma cried, "when he doesn't even send you money anymore? I know he doesn't because I heard what he said to you. He's always on our case. I hate it! I hate him!" On a huge sob, Emma bounded out of the room.

Natalie heard the bedroom door slam shut.

She started down the hallway toward Emma's room, sighed heavily, and knocked on the door. "Emma?" She could hear crying. "Em, honey? Do you want to talk?"

She heard a muffled no through the door and more sobs. Natalie's thoughtless comment had opened the floodgates. She felt horrible. "Em, I need to go to Mr. McConnell's house. You rest and check in on Callie, and we'll talk when I get back, okay?"

Discouraged, she turned down the hall and retrieved her cleaning tools. She needed to talk to Emma and make sure she was okay, but they were both too upset; having a little time to calm down would be good for both of them. Besides, if she didn't get Mr. McConnell's house clean today, she wasn't sure when she'd be able to do it. And there was no way she was going to set herself up for a lecture on her failures and incompetence from him. She'd had more than enough of that from Wade, even after all these years.

When Natalie got back to Ross's house, she worked like a wild woman, vacuuming, dusting, and doing cursory work in the bathroom. Ross would have to wait a week for the deluxe—and final—cleaning treatment there. She glanced at her watch. Six thirty. Thankfully the man was a workaholic. It would be a close one, but she just might make it out of there before he showed up.

She was stowing the broom and dustpan when she thought she heard a car approach. Growling to herself, she quickly gathered her tools and headed toward the front door. If she was lucky—although *lucky* definitely wasn't the word of the day—he would take a few minutes in the garage and she could make a clear getaway.

But instead of it being Ross, the doorbell rang. When Natalie opened the door, there stood a beautiful, tall woman in a designer suit, with short, stylish brown hair and a startled look in her eyes.

"Oh! Hello. I'm here to see Ross." She glanced curiously at Natalie first, then over Natalie's shoulder. "Is he here?"

Despite her best efforts at denial, Natalie felt a sick twisting in her stomach. She discovered with horrible clarity that she was not only jealous of this woman, but she had also been quickly dismissed as a rival. Not that she *was* a rival; she was an *intrusion*, she reminded herself. Ross had certainly made that point clear enough.

"No, he's not at the moment. Is he expecting you?" Natalie asked, relieved that her voice was steady.

The woman smiled. "Yes. We agreed to meet here." She looked over Natalie's shoulder again. "His home is lovely."

Natalie realized she was stuck. She couldn't ask the woman to remain outside if Ross was expecting her, and she couldn't leave the woman alone in Ross's home either. "I'm sure he'll be here shortly, then. Why don't you make yourself comfortable. I'll be right back."

She lugged her equipment and his laundry to her car and popped the trunk. The woman shut the front door. *Come on, hurry*, she thought as she dumped his laundry bag in the trunk and hoisted the tank vacuum to do the same with it. He was certain to be here any minute, and the last thing she wanted was for him to see her wrestling a vacuum hose and then going inside to greet Ms. Perfect Professional.

She slammed the trunk and fumbled with the lock on her car door. She needed a few seconds to sit and collect herself before returning to play hostess to Ross's attractive guest. It wasn't as if the woman was going to snatch the family heirlooms and make a run for it. She yanked the car door open, and as she prepared to climb in, a large hand grabbed the top of the door, holding it open. She froze.

"Hello."

It was Ross.

Of course it was. That was the way her luck was running today, wasn't it?

She stared at his hand.

Had she detected a trace of humor in his voice? Funny, she herself didn't feel very humorous right at the moment. Guilt, embarrassment, anger—those she felt. And the beginning burn of tears. She would not look at him. Wade had told her countless times that her tears were merely a show of weakness and a pointless waste of time. She couldn't let Ross see them.

"Listen, about last Saturday—"

"You have a guest waiting in your house for you, Mr. McConnell. And I have a sick daughter at home. So, if you'll excuse me." She didn't know where she'd found the voice to speak, shaky as it was.

"Natalie—"

Now she did look at him. She lifted her chin and willed the tears welling up not to fall. His brows instantly furrowed.

"Callie is waiting for me. And your guest is waiting for you," she repeated.

She looked deliberately at his hand on the door and then back at him. He didn't move it; he put his other hand on the top of her car, boxing her in. He studied her face for a long time, and to her utter surprise and relief, she was able to hold his look with only a few rapid blinks to fend off the threatening tears. Finally, he glanced at the house and back at her. He nodded, turned, and strode away.

Natalie choked on a sob as she cranked the ignition and threw the car into gear. She had made it only a few blocks away before the tears streaming down her face made it impossible to drive. She pulled to the curb, buried her head in her hands, and wept.

* * *

Natalie looked up when the doorbell rang. Tori opened the door and poked her head in. "Nat? It's me."

Natalie waved her in as she set a cup of soda and a few crackers on the end table next to a white-faced Callie, who was tucked snugly in a blanket on the living room sofa. Natalie crouched down and stroked her hair back from her forehead. *The Price Is Right* announcer told the next contestant to "come on down."

"Can I get you anything else, Cal?" she asked.

"Not right now. Thanks, Mom. Hi, Tori."

Natalie rose to her feet.

"Hey, kiddo," Tori said. "I hope you didn't catch this nasty thing from Sarah when you two hung out last week. She was sick all weekend."

Callie just sighed and blinked at the TV. A contestant was jumping up and down, having been told she had a chance to win a new car.

Natalie motioned to Tori to follow her into the kitchen so they could leave Callie in peace.

"I'm surprised you actually took a day off," Tori said. "Isn't Callie usually pretty good about staying home when she's sick?" She glanced back into the living room. "Is she that sick?"

"Wade found out I was gone working yesterday with Cal home by herself. He's always looking for leverage, you know. Ways to make me look like a terrible parent. He really laid into Emma about it yesterday. I decided I had better play it safe and stay home today. Not that I can afford it." She dropped bread into the toaster and grabbed jam and butter from the fridge. She was wound tighter than a top. "Have you eaten, Tor?"

"Yes. I'll join you in a slice of toast though."

Natalie broke a couple of eggs into a frying pan, resisting the urge to throw them against the wall instead. "Today, you are going to help me decide what I want to be when I grow up."

"I am?"

"Yes. You are." Natalie scrambled the living daylights out of the eggs in the pan.

"There are a lot of good-paying jobs out there, you know, that don't require a college education at all. You wouldn't have to put yourself through all of this."

"It's more than a job. It's more than a career, even. It's a dream." She looked up from the frying pan and gazed out the window, then glanced back at Tori before returning her attention to the eggs. "You know I gave up on my dreams a long time ago, Tor. But I want to get just one of them back, as well as take care of my kids."

"Okay." Tori sighed, picked up the university class schedule Natalie had left on the kitchen table, and flipped to the section with the heading "Majors."

Natalie set the plate of buttered toast on the table with a clank, dropped a few more slices into the toaster, and went back to the stove. "Are you sure you don't want any eggs?"

"I'm sure, but thanks."

Natalie dumped the eggs onto a plate and sat down across from Tori. "What are some good-paying majors? I was hoping to take a few more classes to get a better feel for what I might be good at, but I don't have that luxury now."

"What about accounting? Or business?" Tori traced her finger down the page.

Natalie blew on her forkful of eggs. "I don't think I'm very good with numbers. Wade used to say the only way I could balance a checkbook was if I put it on the bathroom scales."

Tori picked up a piece of toast and slathered jam on it. "I don't know, Nat. You were always better at math than I was. You could do it, despite what your lousy ex-husband says. Although, honestly, I'm not really sure accounting or business are exactly this dream you say you gave up on. What about art? That's more like you than accounting is."

"Art." Natalie said around her mouthful of eggs. "The history, the self-expression. I would love to study art." She moved to the fridge and got a carton of milk. "But the reality is, there are enough starving artists, and I need to keep food on the table, at the very least. I already spend too much time and money on my crazy projects." The next two slices of toast popped, and Natalie buttered them and brought them to the table. "Do you want some milk?"

"No, thanks." Tori picked up her toast and took a bite. "But studying what you enjoy would seem more like this dream you're talking about, if you ask me. And for you, that would be art."

"Wade always said my art was a big waste of my time and his money. What do you think about nursing? There's always a demand for nurses, and the pay is good." She ran her fingers through her hair and slumped back into her chair.

"Nursing. That's an honorable profession."

"I heard a 'but.'"

"You're right. *But*," Tori continued, "I can't see you as a nurse. You're caring and nurturing enough, but I think the facts and tables and memorization that you'd have to do would drive you crazy. You have a creative mind. You should find something that will allow you to use it. By the way, where did you go Friday night? Jim got home early from work, and since Sarah had gone to sleep, he said I should still come over and watch movies like we'd planned. I figured you'd be here, so I just drove over, but when I got here, no one answered."

Natalie's entire body instantly tensed. "I was at a football game."

"You hate football. Ever since Buck—"

"I was with Ross McConnell."

"Ross McConnell? As in scary, handsome, boss Ross McConnell?"

"As in *Mr.* McConnell, my former boss. At the end of the month."

Tori leaned toward Natalie across the table. "Okay, I'm listening."

"He just showed up at the door. I was talking to Dad on the phone; I thought it was you, so I yelled to come in—so he did. He was going to give me back the money I left; you know how I told you he paid me too much. Instead, for some reason, he invited me to go to his nephew's football game."

"Keep talking."

Natalie rinsed her plate and dropped it into the dishwasher. "It started out fine. He was being nice. At the half, his sister came over to say hello, and we kept his little niece with us. I thought we were having a good time." Natalie dried off her hands on a dish towel and dropped back into the chair. "Lexie is a darling; she reminds me of Em at that age. Then, all of a sudden, he got silent, wouldn't speak to me. He'd mentioned he had plans for later, and I thought maybe he was angry that I'd let Lexie stay with us. Although it wasn't really me who said Lexie could stay with us. I told him we could leave if he wanted. He hardly spoke the rest of the evening. Then on Saturday, I went to his house to return his dry cleaning. I went into his bedroom and"—Natalie flushed—"and caught him in only a towel."

Tori coughed, obviously trying to cover her laughter. Natalie gritted her teeth. "What did you do?" Tori asked in between the coughs.

"I excused myself and tried to leave."

"You *tried* to leave? *Tried*? You didn't leave right away? Tell me, Nat, how does scary, handsome Ross McConnell look in a towel?"

Natalie's flush deepened.

Tori grinned. "That good, huh?"

"Stop it! I told him I was sorry I'd intruded. He told me I always intrude." She slapped both hands palm down on the table and rose. "Well, I didn't mean to intrude. And I don't plan to intrude again. I called his old housekeeper to tell her she could have her job back, but she didn't pick up the phone. If Wade hadn't—" She broke off, avoiding Tori's eyes.

Tori froze. "If Wade hadn't what? Natalie—"

She looked bleakly at Tori. All the years of pain, resignation, and failure flooded back. Natalie had earned a full university scholarship when she'd been a senior, despite everything she'd gone through with losing her mom the year before. She'd given it up to take care of her new baby. After Buck had walked out of her life, it had all fallen to her. She'd been a girl with the promise of a bright future in high school; now she was a woman with little hope. Even Tori, with her lackluster grades, had gone off to college and actually graduated.

"Nothing. Never mind." What good would it do anybody to talk about Wade or what-ifs?

But Tori was persistent. "If Wade hadn't what? You may as well tell me because I'm not going to let it drop."

Natalie took a deep breath and spoke the words aloud for the first time. Somehow saying it made it too real. "He's stopped supporting Ryan's mission."

"What? No way. He agreed to go halves with you on that. He promised."

"Now he has other priorities."

"It would kill Ryan if he knew. He loves Wade. Wade always acted like he cared for Ryan too."

Natalie pressed the heels of her hands against her eyes. "I think Ryan saw enough toward the end that he wouldn't be surprised. Still, it's the kind of thing he doesn't need to hear, not when he has more important things to occupy his time. So he won't find out. Not from me."

"You can't afford to make up the difference."

Natalie shrugged her shoulders. "I'll only take one college class this semester. That will buy me a couple of months. By then, I'm sure I'll have found a replacement for Mr. McConnell. It'll all work out. The Lord will provide, right?"

"Absolutely. But seriously—couldn't you just tell this McConnell guy you changed your mind?"

"No. He's right. I do intrude, I guess. I do all the wrong things, make people upset." Wade had said so on more occasions than Natalie could count.

"That's not true."

"Well, it doesn't matter." She dragged the catalog across the table and stared at the open page. "How far into a new career can I really get at one class a semester? Nursing it is for now. And it looks like I'm taking biology." She slapped the catalog shut.

She wouldn't let her dreams haunt her.

Chapter 15

"WHAT DO YOU THINK ABOUT Ashley?" Susan asked Ross on the phone.

Ross needed peace, and he needed it now. His caseload was demanding, and New York was on his back to make another visit. His mother was pressuring him to commit to more time with the family during the holidays.

Then there was the little business of a resignation letter from Natalie that made him want to throttle her.

"Ashley's very nice," he replied.

"She hits all the major points on your little checklist, doesn't she?" Suzie's voice sounded a bit too smug.

"I'm still getting to know her." His secretary was supposed to have returned the Langley file to him. He thumbed through the files on his desk.

"You wanted someone college educated. Professional. Religious. Attractive. Bing, bing, bing, bing. And I know for a fact that she's interested in you."

"Ashley is very pretty and very successful." At dinner, after listening to her valiantly pursue every conceivable topic of conversation, he'd realized he wasn't interested. Nice, pretty girl, just not interested. He had made a meager attempt to contribute to the evening, doomed though he'd decided it was, by mentioning his collection of jazz and offering to loan her a couple. Big mistake. As a result, she'd shown up unexpectedly at his house to borrow a couple of CDs—at the worst moment possible, when he wasn't there but Natalie was. After Natalie had driven away, he'd politely loaned Ashley the CDs, explained he had a meeting (with his elliptical machine, but she didn't have to know that), and sent her on her way.

It bothered him that Natalie had been the one to greet her, especially when Ross had already decided he wasn't interested in Ashley. It complicated things, not the least of which was that he was losing his housekeeper. Not that Natalie would ever admit to it, but Ross suspected the run-in with Ashley had been part of it.

"And . . . ?" Suzie asked.

"And?"

"Don't you want to know what Ashley thinks of you?"

Nope. "Sure, Suz, why don't you tell me?" He couldn't see the Langley file in his inbox either.

"I should make you beg. I shouldn't try so hard to find nice girls for you, but Mom worries about you so much, I have to do it."

"Uh-huh." *Where is the Langley file?* He searched through the stacks on his desk while his sister spouted at him.

"You're such a brat, Ross. Anyway, Ashley said it's been a long time since she went out with anybody who compares to you."

Not on his desk. He opened his file drawer and thumbed through the folders there.

"She's really interested, Ross, but she isn't sure how you feel about her."

He wandered over to his office door and mouthed "Langley" to Tina.

"She really appreciated you loaning her the CDs," Suzie droned on. "She's never liked jazz before and thought it meant something for you to trust her with them."

He gave Tina a thumbs-up sign when she handed him the file. He went back to his desk.

"Well, did it?"

There was a lengthy pause as Ross tried to recollect what Suzie had been saying. Coming up blank, he opted for generic. "She's very nice, Suz."

He could hear her hiss of frustration. "That isn't what I asked. Were you even listening? I *asked* if loaning Ashley the CDs meant that you, you know, are *interested*. In *her*."

He knew he hadn't been very attentive, but he'd still inferred enough to know that Suzie and Ashley had been discussing him like a couple of boy-crazy teens. And he didn't much like the invasion of privacy he felt as a result.

"I said she's nice, Suz. And that's enough for now. *If* things work out, they'll work out on their own at this point, without you running interference. She can even keep the CDs," he added, "but that doesn't mean I've decided to buy her a ring yet. Is that enough of an answer?"

"I told you how she feels about you, Ross. She thinks you're amazing, the total package. She can't help how she feels. You're you, after all. You're everything on your own checklist and more. But I know, as your sister, that your checklist also includes other things, and they aren't all sterling. Sure, you're handsome, smart, and successful. But you're not very charitable these days. I would tell you that I think you're only concerned with your own feelings, except lately, I find myself wondering if you even *have* feelings at all. You're not the brother I remember." There was a sadness in her voice that surprised him.

"I apologize for my less-than-attentive behavior. I'm swamped right at the moment, and I have a lot on my mind. I also recognize that those are excuses, not necessarily reasons. Forgive me?"

A pause. "Okay." Suzie tended to react emotionally, but thankfully, she usually settled back down quickly afterward.

"I can't make any guarantees with Ashley," Ross warned her. "I *won't* make any guarantees with Ashley." He flipped to the last couple of pages in the Langley document and made sure the corrections he needed were there. "I appreciate your taking an interest in my eternal happiness"—he'd hoped to get a chuckle out of her but thought he heard her sigh instead—"so let's let things play out naturally now, huh?" For him, that meant a natural death.

"I do want you to be happy, Ross. I'm not sure that you are. I'm not sure you have been for a long time."

He wasn't, not really, and particularly not at that moment. But she didn't need to know that; it would only worry her and fortify her matchmaking resolve. "I am. Don't worry."

"I love you, you big lunkhead."

"I know; me too. I have to go."

"Okay. See you at Mom's on Thanksgiving. Two o'clock, remember."

"I'll be there." He ended the call and grabbed his coat. His conversation with Suzie was the final straw.

"I'll be out of the office the rest of the day," he said to Tina, his secretary. "If anybody needs me, tough."

Peace. A moment of peace would help him find perspective. It would enable him to think clearly, define priorities. He'd always prided himself on his cool, objective nature. Maybe he'd been cool and objective only because he'd been in New York and a thousand miles from familial females. Being in close proximity to them seemed to have driven the word *objectivity* right out of his vocabulary. He knew he could deal with the demands of his work—from both locations. He could handle his mother just fine. He even understood her need to have all of her children together for the holidays—the first one without his father. But his personal life, time limited as it was, had become the focus of too much sisterly attention. And that personal life that had been so nicely contained for so long was suddenly becoming complicated. He needed to find his objectivity again, so this afternoon he was giving himself the time to find it. Time and peace. The place for peace was the temple, so that was where he was going.

It was the Tuesday before Thanksgiving, and the afternoon traffic downtown was fairly light. He reasoned that it might mean fewer people in the temple than usual because they were busy with Thanksgiving and other holiday errands.

The fewer people the better. He was peopled out.

But when he got there, the Salt Lake Temple was humming with people. Ross still found plenty of time to sit quietly, undisturbed, and he was relieved. It took awhile to decompress from work. Now he could feel the serenity of the place seep into his bones. He breathed deeply and felt his tense muscles relax.

He needed more than peace from his time in the temple this afternoon. He needed to sort through his head and heart. The situation with Ashley wasn't the issue, nor was his conversation on the phone with Suzie. Suzie had been right though. He had become uncharitable and unfeeling. His well-meaning family didn't realize how monotonous it was to meet woman after woman, year after year, and question if any of them got past their own super-guy checklist to the real Ross. The human Ross.

Out of the corner of his eye a petite woman with blonde hair caught his eye. Was it Natalie? A second glance said no.

Natalie. What to do about Natalie Forrester? It bothered him that she hadn't returned his call this week. It bothered him that he'd unthinkingly blurted out that she intruded. It bothered him that she *did* intrude. She intruded into his thoughts more and more frequently. It bothered him that she was divorced, that she had nearly grown children, that she'd never been to college. It bothered him even more that those things should matter. It also bothered him that she was a superb artist. That she had a collection of library books his college educated sisters wouldn't glance at in a lifetime. It bothered him that she was poor but determined to be independent. That he wanted to punch her ex-husband in the face. That he itched to discover if her cheek was as soft as it looked, if her lips tasted as full and sweet as he imagined. That he wanted to know if he'd feel electricity again if he touched her. And that bothered him the most.

Was it asking too much to want the ideal? Was it too much to want a wife who belonged to him only, someone he wouldn't have to share with some former spouse? Compete with memories of another man? To want a fresh innocent who would bear his children, his eternal family, all his own? Was it asking too much to search for a woman who matched him experience for experience? He was well known and respected, here, in New York, and in D.C. A man wanted a woman on his arm who would make a statement about him, someone his colleagues would recognize as an asset to the attorney, as well as to the man.

He settled deeper into his seat and attempted to shift his thoughts back to the proceedings. A professor had told him once that when you reached an obstacle in the creative process, it was best to shelve things for a while, whether it was for a few days or simply a few hours, and focus on something else. This advice had been a great resource to Ross as an attorney, allowing him to use his time and his mind in the most effective and efficient way possible. It relieved his conscious mind and allowed his unconscious mind opportunities to work on solutions of its own. Now Natalie was an obstacle, an obstruction to his clear, objective thinking. He would tune her out for a couple of hours.

He tried. He prided himself on his disciplined mind. But ironically, he found the temple wasn't providing him the kind of peace he had expected. The words spoken, lessons learned within its holy walls, were about eternity and family and promises, poignant subjects that called to his heart. Eternity, as things stood right now, would be a long, empty void without someone who truly completed him, without children of his own. He'd felt a glimmer, the hope of completeness once, with Liz. He hadn't felt anything close to it since. Maybe he hadn't allowed himself to feel close to it. Since then, there had been no one, not a single woman who had sparked the desire of eternity in him. There'd been no motivation to take the risk again. Feeling his mood drop, he redoubled his concentration on the words he was hearing.

But quiet whispers began to penetrate his thoughts once again. Why was Natalie talking to her father about money? Why wouldn't she take Ross's cash from the party? Why was such a bright and artistic woman cleaning houses? She seemed unsure of herself, but he knew that despite her lack of confidence, she was reluctant to accept help from others. When she was relaxed or unaware that he was observing her, she was bright, her wit quick. She was generous with her time. Her interests were varied and unusual. He didn't know a single woman, no—a single *person*—who carved pumpkins into works of art, created original stories based on Celtic legends, read books on ancient civilizations, and tap danced. Or bobbed for apples on a string.

The bigger question was why, when all of the women he encountered seemed more than happy to receive his attention, was Natalie Forrester so resistant? He'd felt her respond to him when they'd danced. He knew he had. He'd seen what was in her eyes at that moment. But he couldn't manage to keep her in the same room with him. A lot of it was his fault, he knew. It was difficult to be irresistible to someone when you ordered them from your house, threatening to call 911, he thought wryly—or told them they were intrusive, which was even worse. Or turned into a sullen stone of a man at a football game. Apparently, his personal super-guy list didn't have a check mark next to "charming."

He smiled, feeling better now than he had all day. It had been a productive afternoon, a peaceful time in the temple after all. He didn't know what eternity held for him at this particular juncture, but he at least knew the next step. He would make amends with his pretty puzzle of a housekeeper. He made no promises to himself about what that meant or what his intentions were. He only knew that he had behaved badly toward someone he thought was truly beautiful, inside and out, and he needed to fix what he'd done. And there was an undeniable spark he was curious enough to pursue—for the time being.

As he walked along the corridor of the temple on his way toward the exit, the quiet whispers prompted him again. Two weeks ago, his encounter with Natalie had driven him to make a phone call—to Ashley. It had been the wrong one.

He had a different phone call to make now, he thought as he nodded in farewell to the man by the temple exit. Two phone calls, to be precise. He'd allow himself a quiet ride home and enjoy the peace he'd worked so hard to find this afternoon, and then he would make the first call—to Jackie. And after that, he intended to search the Church's website so he could learn the name of Natalie's bishop and have a conversation with him as well.

Chapter 16

As Thanksgivings went, Natalie thought, this one was just a Thursday. Wade had picked the girls up the night before, informing her not to expect them back until late Sunday. She'd attempted to put a positive spin on things, calling this her personal holiday—freedom from everything. She'd slept in as long as she could, which wasn't as late as she'd hoped. She'd spent the morning putting finishing touches on her papier mâchè Santas. And she planned to spend the afternoon at Ross's house putting up his holiday decorations.

When his mother had given them to her, she'd ask Natalie what she was doing for Thanksgiving. Natalie hadn't been about to tell this nice woman she'd bargained away the holiday with her girls because of her party. Besides, it had given them some much-needed spending money. So Natalie had remained politely vague, saying her plans were small. Dorothy hadn't needed to know it was a gathering of one.

Dorothy had talked at length about her own plans for the holiday. She seemed to feel comfortable with Natalie. Natalie liked her tremendously, despite her son. And so it happened that Natalie knew Ross was expected at his mother's home on Thanksgiving at two o'clock. Natalie figured that gave her at least a solid four hours to get the decorating job done, if she factored in everything Dorothy had mentioned: appetizers, dinner, dessert, football. Lots and lots of football.

That should be long enough. It might even put her into enough of a holiday spirit to pull out her own decorations. With the loss of Ross's income, she'd be lucky to put many presents under the Christmas tree for her kids. So if they weren't going to be treated to an extravagant Christmas, they could at least enjoy a feast of the senses. She would let decorating Ross's home stir her creative juices, and then she would put her whole heart into making her own family's holiday as memorable as she could. With that noble thought in mind, she pulled on a pair of worn jeans, her favorites despite the tear at the knee, grabbed a few tools from her garage, and jumped in the car.

* * *

Ross was surprised. Thanksgiving with the family was turning out to be more pleasant than he'd anticipated, not that he'd expected it to be unpleasant. While he'd typically made it home for a few days each Christmas, at least most years, they'd been hectic days. He'd used the time to do his shopping, and his sisters were always rushing to meet their spouses' family obligations. To have everyone relaxed, with no other plans this Thanksgiving, was rare and felt wonderful.

The afternoon started with some touch football for the guys. Ross, Rick, and Scott, aka the geezers, against Jackie's boys, Brett and Matt, the punk kids. Seven-year-old Jason tried valiantly for about twenty minutes to keep up with his big brothers, and six-year-old Riley mostly managed to get tangled up in everybody's legs, which made for a more level playing field.

After a quick shower, Ross became the honored guest at an imaginary tea party hosted by Lexie and her "big-girl cousin," five-year-old Regan. If he'd actually eaten all of the invisible cookies and drunk all of the pretend tea with cream and sugar the girls had put in his pink plastic teacup, he'd be ten pounds heavier. And that was before the real food, the Thanksgiving spread, passed through his lips.

At dinner, Rick handed Ross the carving knife and fork, officially making him patriarch for the day. After the quick stab of pain and longing for his dad subsided, he carved the turkey and slid into the role of family elder with only a bit of discomfort.

Now he was sated from the meal, watching the New York Jets play the Dallas Cowboys and beginning to feel restless. He could hear Jackie and his mother chatting quietly as they finished washing the dishes. The kids were in the basement playing video games. Suzie had snuck into the family room to snuggle with Scott, and Ross watched from the corner of his eye as she curled into Scott's lap, slipped her arms around his neck, and tucked her head under his ear like a contented kitten. An image of Natalie flashed into Ross's mind, her eyes a dark jade, her fingers entwined in his hair. He leaped from his seat on the sofa and wandered into the kitchen.

His mother was drying the last of the casserole dishes, and Jackie was getting out the plates for pie. "Good, Ross, you're just in time. Will you put this dish up there? How's the game?"

He slid the crockery onto the top shelf of the cupboard. "Dallas is up by ten."

His mom hung up the dish towel and started dishing pumpkin pie. "Jackie, will you get the whipping cream out of the refrigerator?" She glanced at Ross. "Do you need something, dear?"

He smiled at her and walked over to gently massage her shoulders. There was something he needed, someone he wanted, but his mother couldn't help him with it. "No, gorgeous. It's been a great day, thank you. You're going to be tired tomorrow."

He could feel her chuckle softly under his gently kneading hands. "Today has been so wonderful; I wouldn't care if it laid me up for a week." She paused. "I only wish your father—"

"I know." He didn't think he could bear to hear her talk about his dad at the moment.

"Mom," Jackie said, taking her by the hand, "I'm banishing you from the kitchen, effective immediately. Where did Suz disappear to? Oh well. Ross and I will finish dishing up the pie, won't we, Ross?"

"Absolutely." He patted his mother's shoulders and gave her a gentle push in the direction of the door. "You heard the boss. Out you go."

She offered a weak protest that made Ross and Jackie both laugh, and then she was gone.

Jackie gave Ross a conspiratorial look and whispered, "You won't believe what I have to tell you."

His eyebrow arched. "I'm listening."

Jackie moved closer to him and lowered her voice. "I called my friend who owns the boutique, like you asked. It's an upscale place in Park City, lots of rich tourists. We had lunch yesterday. I showed her both of them, the little autumn witch and the Santa I picked up from your house. Needless to say, she was *very* impressed." She folded her arms across her chest and grinned at him.

Ross felt his pulse jump. *Cool and objective*, he said to himself. "Yes, go on."

"I asked her to tell me what she thought people would be willing to pay for sculptures like those." She told Ross the figures, and he whistled. Jackie was practically vibrating with excitement. "Ross, she said she's always looking for items to sell on consignment, especially around the holidays. And she said she'd take as many as she could get her hands on. So what's the next step?"

He would have to approach Natalie, of course, but first he had a little employer relations mess to resolve. In addition, he knew she believed her art was just a whim, nothing serious. He wondered if he told Natalie she could sell her Santas in an upscale boutique if it would excite or intimidate her. She might not even agree to the proposition. He would have to approach her with some care.

Now he was anxious to leave, to plot his next move. Finding his mother settled comfortably on the sofa, feet propped obediently on an ottoman, he kissed her cheek and made his farewell. "I have some work I need to get to this evening," he said. When she started to protest, he pressed his fingers to her lips and said, "Save some pie, and I'll stop by to share it with you tomorrow. Happy Thanksgiving."

* * *

Low clouds had gathered during the afternoon, and a light snow was just beginning to fall. Ross drove home, barely aware of the weather or the roads. He wanted to speak to Natalie as soon as possible. If they couldn't move quickly, she'd miss some prime sales opportunities.

If he was honest with himself, he simply wanted to see her, be with her. Touch her again. But first he had to mend fences with her. That could take some delicate maneuvering. He'd seen firsthand her reaction to what she considered charity. If she knew what other machinations he had in place, he thought wryly, she might never forgive him.

As the snowflakes flew at him from the other side of the windshield, he mentally calculated how many little white blobs he'd seen in her garage workshop.

He was so preoccupied with his plans he almost didn't notice her car parked in front of his house. *Why is she here?* he wondered. He knew darn well she wasn't delivering any goodwill casseroles, not to him. Intrigued, he wondered briefly if it was better to park in the driveway and quietly enter through the front door before she had a chance to bolt or make a noisy entrance through the garage. As often as he'd caught her haplessly off guard in the past, he opted for noise and hoped for the best.

When he entered the house, he stopped cold. It wouldn't have mattered which approach into the house he'd taken. Cheerful Christmas music filled the air, and he could hear Natalie's voice weaving in a low harmony. Orange and chocolate and cinnamon and evergreen scents filled the air. The place had been magically transformed, and the effect was warm and inviting. He realized with a start that it was the first time his home here had actually felt like exactly that—a home. He liked it. Very much.

Bing Crosby was counting blessings instead of sheep as Ross walked into his living room. He couldn't believe his eyes. A large Christmas tree was fully decorated, covered with heirloom ornaments he recalled vividly from his childhood. It stood in front of his large picture window, the drapes drawn open. Behind the tree's twinkling splendor, the city lights were just beginning to blink on. Snowflakes whirled and danced outside in the multicolored glow. Natalie was perched on a stepladder in front of his fireplace mantel, looking like she belonged there, humming to the music and arranging evergreen boughs. His childhood stocking, admittedly dog-eared, hung dead center. The corner of Ross's mouth curved up. That mother of his. How had she managed to arm twist Natalie into this little project?

Now that his shock was wearing off, he saw the immediate potential of the situation. Before Natalie could sense that he was there, he slipped out of the room. He wanted a few more minutes to gather his thoughts after this surprising turn of events.

She'd already tackled the kitchen. A large evergreen centerpiece adorned the table, its deep red candle flickering. Large fragrant bowls of potpourri sat on the buffet. The shelves of his kitchen hutch were loaded with Christmas curios and draped with more evergreens. Garlands arched over each doorway.

He made his way to the bedroom and saw she'd been busy there as well. Holiday pillows nestled comfortably with the others on his bed, and there was a simple arrangement of candles of differing shapes and sizes on his dresser. On the bathroom counter, a fat ceramic Santa in polka-dot underwear was grinning at him. He couldn't help it; he grinned back. He didn't remember ever seeing it before. It must have been a white elephant gift from his mother's jaded past. But it provided just the right touch here.

It was time to put his plan into action, he decided. He was surprised that the thought of proceeding made him nervous. He hadn't had any real nerves before presenting a case in years. But he was feeling them now. Forcing them down, he returned to the living room.

Natalie had just picked up a large, empty ornament box. He watched her eyes widen with surprise at seeing him, then narrow and look away.

"I'll be out of your way as soon as I put this box in the basement, Mr. McConnell. Excuse me." Her voice was cool in contrast to the cozy atmosphere he'd been enjoying.

He would try humor first. He had successfully dealt with irate clients and adversaries that way for years. And with her. "You've been busy today, and on Thanksgiving of all days. You looking for time and a half?" It came out sounding miserly, not clever like he'd hoped. He grimaced inwardly.

"This one's on the house. Literally." She headed past him to the door.

"That was meant to be a joke."

Her eyes glimmered with an anger he'd never seen in her before. She dusted her hands off like she was brushing him away. "Mr. McConnell, I don't want time and a half or double pay or anything from you. I don't want your money. I don't even expect polite conversation from you anymore. So if you'll excuse me, I just want to get this favor for your mother finished so I can be officially done here. There are a couple more boxes of decorations downstairs, if you're interested. I'm sorry I wasn't able to get to them before you got home. Good-bye."

There was a sharp finality to her tone that speared through his stomach, its intensity catching him by surprise. He grabbed her arm to stop her. Something strong and potent seared through him this time. "Let me take that for you." He gestured to the box.

She looked at him warily before handing over the box. "All right. Thank you." She picked up her bag and started toward the front door.

"Wait! Please." He set the box down abruptly and strode over to her. "Please stay a moment."

He noted abstractedly that there was mistletoe hanging above them in the entrance by his front door. He had the sudden urge to take the opportunity but thought she'd probably slap him, considering the look in her eyes. He took her free hand instead and led her back to the living room. "I want to speak with you. Won't you have a seat?" When she continued to stand, he added roughly, "I'd like to apologize, if you'll let me."

She sat stiffly on the edge of the sofa, a closed expression on her face. He had a lot of damage control to do, obviously. Even more than he'd realized.

He turned down the music and returned to stand in front of her. "The house looks terrific. Thank you. I don't know how my mother talked you into doing this, but I appreciate it very much." She was carefully studying her clasped hands on her lap. He waited for her to look up. When she didn't, he let out his breath and sat down next to her. "You know, I was in New York for all those years, and I never took the time to decorate my flat. Not even once. I had a wreath I dragged out and stuck on the door—when I remembered to—but that was it. I was at the firm more than I was anywhere else and didn't stop to think about Christmas until I was on the plane heading back to Utah each year. I knew Mom would have the tree up; Dad would be serving up his own version of eggnog . . ." He paused, struck silent for the second time today by the flood of longing for his father. He turned away to give himself a moment. He needed to be in control of his emotions if he was going to persuade her to do what he hoped.

"I guess my mother decided I needed an extra dose of hearth and home this holiday. She was right. Thank you again. But even she wouldn't have expected you to give up your Thanksgiving to do this. Where are your girls? With their father?"

She nodded stiffly, silently. He wasn't out in the clear yet. He'd leave that particular subject for the time being and try a different tack.

"I'd also like to apologize for my poorly chosen words a few Saturdays ago." He chuckled softly, hoping it would ease the tension he could feel radiating from her. He was feeling strangely tense as well. "We seem to catch each other at the most unexpected moments. What are the odds of that, do you think? I can honestly claim never to have found a woman tap dancing in my kitchen before you."

She blushed, just a tiny bit.

He was charmed. She was irresistible. He wanted to reach for her, touch her.

"Or caught one in the middle of a cookie-dough fight," he added in a low voice.

She groaned and dropped her face into her hands. He truly couldn't resist now. He picked up a strand of her hair, playing with the ends. Soft. "Just when life seems back in balance, there she is—upsetting the equilibrium. My equilibrium. Saturday was no exception." He tucked the strand behind her ear. "Can you forgive me?"

She sat very still but wouldn't look up. He could feel his pulse pounding in his throat. Time slowed to an impossible crawl. When she finally did speak, it was to herself, not to him. "He was right."

"Who was—what?"

She looked at him now. Her eyes had deepened to that jade color, and the angry spark was nearly gone. "I forgive you."

"Does that mean I can tear up your letter of resignation?"

She looked back at her lap. "I don't think that's a good idea."

"You must not have forgiven me, then. Either that, or you're willing to be frightened away by a little show of temper." Her eyes sparked at him again. Good. That little spark showed some of the backbone he knew she had. The backbone it took to raise three kids on her own. He was also sure she didn't realize she had that backbone. He crossed his arms over his chest and stared back. He fought down the urge to smile. He fought down the urge to run his finger along her jaw.

Her chin went up fractionally. "I do forgive you. And I'm not frightened by you." He suspected she may be stretching the truth a little there. "But I'm not certain that continuing to work for you is the best idea."

"Why?"

She hesitated. "Maybe I found a better offer."

Nice try, honey. "Did you?" he murmured, shifting a little closer.

She took a deep breath. "Maybe."

"Maybe I'll make you a counter offer."

She stood quickly and moved to the window. He could tell she was muttering to herself. "What did you say?" he asked.

She shook her head. "I'm a fool. I never learn. Wade always said—" She stopped.

"What did Wade always say?"

She looked at him now. "That it didn't matter what he did, I'd always forgive him. Because I was weak. And he was right. I always did forgive him. Just like I forgive you."

Ross found he hated, *hated* being lumped with this ex-husband of hers. The guy must have done a real number on her over the years, and Ross hated that too. He clenched his jaw. A fire was beginning to build inside him, making him feel violent toward this faceless ex of hers and, at the same time, making him want to melt and consume her, make her part of him. He felt something he had no words for, something he'd successfully buried for years. He struggled to choose his words carefully now. He prayed silently for help. "Is it a weakness to forgive others? Or a strength? Don't the scriptures say to forgive our trespassers seven times seventy?"

"Oh, but that's the trap. You forgive, but that forgiveness turns into permission for some people. They take advantage. They hurt you. And you forgive them again and again until the hurt is too big. Eventually, you learn that forgiveness is not enough anymore. You forgive, but you also have to draw the line, if you still have the strength to do it by then."

He crossed to her. He realized that he had hurt her, badly, with his careless words. Worse, because it was in the same way she'd been hurt before by her ex-husband. That knowledge was bitter. Humbling. He wanted to comfort her but didn't think she would accept it, not from him. Not yet. He leaned slightly toward her, almost imperceptibly. She responded by turning her head to look out the window and running a shaky hand through her hair. His hands itched to tangle themselves in that hair.

"Is that what you're doing with me? Drawing the line?" he asked.

"Yes. Partly." She turned, and he found he was mere inches from her beautiful, sad face. "I have to think of my children. Take care of them and protect myself."

Now he allowed himself to trace her jaw with his finger, just the lightest whisper of a touch. He wanted to take this step toward her. He wanted to do more. "Protect yourself? From what?" He watched her eyes flutter. "From whom?" He leaned closer, let his lips glide softly over hers. "From me?"

He barely heard her whispered answer. "From myself." Her hands moved tentatively to clutch his arms. He heard her shuddered breath. "Oh no," she whispered.

His fingers threaded through her hair—finally, finally—and he brought her to him, brought her mouth back to his. Her lips were full and soft and warm. Heaven. His hands gently stroked her shoulders, and then he lowered them to enfold her in his arms.

Ross absorbed the scent, the feel, the rightness of her, and found himself enveloped in emotions, sensations he hadn't anticipated. He felt her hands creep up to his shoulders, her fingers pressing into him. Staggered by her sweetness, he only gradually became aware that she wasn't pressing to be closer but was pushing back. Away. Easing his hold on her, he brought himself back to earth and tilted his head to read her expression. Her eyes were heavy, her lips slightly downturned and trembling. He simply couldn't resist and kissed her briefly once more, on the cheek this time, then rested his forehead against hers. He was sinking fast, so hoping to lighten the mood, he asked, "Still 'oh no'?"

Her breathing was uneven. "Oh, um . . . yes."

He chuckled. "Okay." Intentionally misunderstanding her, he dropped his head to kiss her lips again, sink into them and savor them. Eventually, remembering her earlier reluctance, he pulled himself away. "Sit with me." He led her back to the sofa and drew her down next to him. Loath to break the intimacy created by their kiss, he linked his fingers with hers and put his other arm around her shoulders. He sat quietly for a moment with her that way. Now he felt a peace like he'd found in the temple earlier in the week. He wondered if she could feel it too. He hoped so.

"This is nice," he said, "with the tree and lights. The snow. With you."

She was quiet, too quiet, and he felt her tension starting to return.

"Ross, I can't afford to . . . I know how I do things. This can't happen. I'm not safe for myself or my kids with something like this."

"Natalie," he said as he stroked her shoulder, "are you so dangerous that you need protection from yourself?"

"I don't have a sterling track record when it comes to . . . I've made poor choices. My kids pay daily for that. I owe it to them to consider their needs first. I won't put them through any more upheaval than they've already experienced. My girls or my son."

"Your son. Ryan, right?" He wanted to, had to, distract her from her train of thought.

"Yes, Ryan. He's in Scotland on his mission. I'm so proud of him. I was very young when I met Ryan's father. Too young."

"Tell me about his father."

She hesitated, and he wasn't sure she would tell him.

"Oh, he was a teen girl's crush," she finally said. "Football hero, rodeo star. Charm and danger rolled into one. I'd worshipped Buck from afar for a long time—the quiet, studious girl with no hope of being noticed." She looked wistful. "Then I was noticed."

It wasn't difficult for Ross to imagine why. He'd have noticed her if he'd been at her high school, he was sure.

"I couldn't believe it. It was a dream. He was calling *me*, asking *me* out. Girls—pretty, popular girls—were giving me looks like I was a force to be reckoned with. Boys I'd never dared speak to were smiling and saying hi." She looked at Ross. "I liked it, the attention, the new friends. Especially the attention from Buck.

"Anyway, it didn't remain a dream. I realized Buck didn't want to be a father a little too late, and before I knew it, I was a single mom."

Ross gave her a minute and thought about what she'd said, what she hadn't said. He suddenly remembered her comment to Jackie at Brett's football game, how she wasn't a big football fan. Now he understood why.

He stroked his hand gently down her arm, drew her in a little closer. "And then you met Wade Forrester."

"Wade." She said his name sadly, and Ross's heart broke a little for her. "I think I fell in love with Wade because he fell in love with Ryan. And I really needed somebody to love that little boy."

"Ryan's father doesn't—"

"No. When I met Wade, he swept me off my feet. He would take the three of us on dates. Ry was barely two at the time. We'd bundle him into Wade's car, and off we'd go. The zoo, the park. They'd dig in the dirt together, play with toy trucks. It melted my heart.

"I felt like I'd let Ryan down, not choosing a father who would be there for him, who would stick. When Wade came into our lives, it seemed like such a blessing. Things were good for a while. Then it seemed like I couldn't do anything right; no matter how I tried, I couldn't make Wade happy. Maybe I missed clues; maybe if I hadn't been so thrilled at the prospect of a daddy for my little boy, I would have seen things with clearer eyes." She looked at him then. "Ultimately, it isn't a very good foundation for marriage when the man you love loves your son more than he loves you. Now Wade doesn't even bother with Ryan."

Ross hated what he saw in her eyes—the pain, the harsh disappointment.

She continued. "Obviously, he still sees the girls, as you can tell by my grand Thanksgiving plans. I always pray he's tucked a little quality time into their visits. The girls need it."

"You have your doubts?"

"Sometimes." She sighed. "Frequently." She carefully pulled her hand out of his and stood. "Listen, I'd feel much better if I finished the decorating, then I can leave you to enjoy what's left of your holiday."

Despite the tone of the conversation and the fact that his thoughts were in a state of flux, he realized he *was* enjoying what was left of his holiday, just being with her, learning about her. He needed to proceed cautiously, not push too hard. He stood. "All right. But only on the condition that you let me help." He led the way down to the basement to retrieve more boxes.

They spent the next hour hanging swags above doors and loading every conceivable corner of his house with the Christmas knickknacks from his childhood.

"Last box," he exclaimed as he lugged it to the top of the stairs. "Then I insist on a hot-chocolate break." He smiled. "I remember you have this thing for chocolate."

"Every female does." Natalie opened the box and drew out a bubble-wrapped item. "Oh, look! It's beautiful." She held up a porcelain angel, delicately hand painted, for Ross to see.

"My crèche. I'd forgotten all about it. Mom has an entire collection of crèches from all over the world. Some elegant, some more whimsical. She gave me this one when I got home from my mission. I think she was hoping I would be starting a family shortly, continuing a tradition. That has to go on the mantelpiece. Let's make room."

Natalie carefully shifted some evergreen boughs. "Did you ever want to? Start a family, I mean?"

"I guess that was always the plan."

"But . . ."

"Didn't happen." He smiled tightly. "Obviously." He'd wanted to distract her from her plans to leave, but he wasn't particularly excited about the direction the conversation was headed now.

"Uh-huh." She nodded and gave him a look that spoke volumes and began rearranging the figurines on the mantel.

"Uh-huh what? Would you care to elaborate?"

"If someone like you isn't married, it's by choice, not chance."

"What makes you say that?" He intentionally dropped his voice to a quiet, cool tone. His practiced, objective lawyer tone.

Natalie just laughed humorlessly, shaking her head.

"You think I've chosen to be single," he said. "You think I've dealt with speculative looks, cold showers, and the daily abuse of my mother and sisters—for decades, mind you—by *choice*? You don't think location or opportunity is a component in this? The world at large looks at basic attractions, basic interests, and compatibilities, and voila! You have another eHarmony success story. And that success can stay as uncommitted and transitory as the parties involved prefer. No strings. Now, factor in a religion like ours that bases life in the eternities on your choice of mate, permanent choice of mate, and what do you think it does to the odds?"

"You forget that I've seen how women behave around you," she countered. "How every woman behaves around you. You are trying to tell me there hasn't been—"

"The interest has to be mutual."

"Have you ever even been in love?"

That stopped him. Cold. "Yes. Yes, I have."

"Not enough to marry her."

"Not true. I wanted to marry her."

She turned from the mantel then to look at his face. He didn't want to be analyzed. He moved to the window to watch the snow blanketing the world with a soft coldness.

"But you didn't—"

"I asked her."

She walked over to him and stood there quietly, waiting, not pushing him to speak.

"Her name was Liz," he said finally. "We were in law school together. It was a long time ago."

"I'm sorry. I understand," she said. "Buck was just a young girl's crush, but the pain when he left was horribly real at the time."

"I'm sure it was," he said.

He stood there next to her, viewing the snowy scene outside his window, thinking. Then he spoke. "Natalie, there is something happening here between the two of us. I have to believe you feel it as much as I do. What if we take things one step at a time? Find out what it is, what it might be. For both of us."

She reached out and rested both hands on the windowsill. Ross waited.

Finally, she turned to face him. He was surprised to realize he was holding his breath.

"All right. One step at a time. But—"

He'd already started to exhale, but now his breath was cut short again. "But, what?"

"I've made the poor choices in the past, Ross, and have had to take responsibility for my children growing up in the aftermath of those choices. I have to feel like I'm not dependent on you, that I'm not your subordinate and reliant on you for my welfare and my children's well-being. I have to be free so my feelings are my feelings alone, not determined by a sense of obligation."

"I can live with that," he said. He knew how badly she needed money, but now was obviously not the time to tell her about some of the steps he'd taken to help her financially, about the plans for her sculptures. He was absolutely *not* telling her about the large check he'd written out to her bishop. He didn't intend to ever tell her about that. It was a gift to a missionary, and he intended for it to stay anonymous.

"So the resignation stands." She bent once again to pick up her purse.

"All right," he agreed, relieved. It didn't mean he wasn't above trying a little old-fashioned guilt on her though. "I accept your resignation, with no hard feelings, understanding where you're coming from. I won't think about how difficult it will be to find a replacement during the busy month of December. Esther isn't quite ready to return to the job." He smiled when she looked at him, her eyebrows drawn together. He'd hit the mark. She was such a marshmallow.

"Well—"

"I do have a favor to ask. Nothing to do with cleaning," he added and tried to maintain a poker face. He spoke in a low, conspiratorial tone. "Jackie just loves that little fairy you made for Lexie and the Santa you gave me. She commented on how she would like one herself." He watched Natalie carefully. She was curious. Good. "So I want to purchase some Santas from you for Christmas. What do you think?"

He watched her jaw drop open and couldn't help grinning.

"Some? How many?" she asked incredulously.

"Oh, I was thinking somewhere in the neighborhood of twenty, to start." When she began to splutter, he added, "I have no time to shop for gifts. I might even need to buy some more when it gets closer to Christmas. And since you *have* refused to work for me any longer . . ."

"I could probably fill in until the first of the year if you really need me to."

"That's great; maybe I'll take you up on that occasionally. And you can use the extra time you would have been mopping my floor to make masterful creations." He understood now how Buck and Wade had taken such easy advantage of her generous nature. One nicely crafted phrase, and she was willing to set aside her personal needs to accommodate him. That was a quality to cherish, not abuse.

Sensing by the look on her face that she was still speechless, he moved ahead. "How much would you charge me per Santa, do you think?"

She looked at him in utter confusion. "You want twenty Santas?

"To start."

"I haven't got a clue. They're just paper and glue and paint."

They were much more than paper and glue and paint. "They're collectibles, cleverly and artistically rendered." Ross recommended a number that was a nicely padded version of the price Jackie's friend had suggested. He watched Natalie do the mental math. Her look of utter amazement amused him, to say the least. He felt part of the wall he'd carefully crafted around himself over the years fall away.

"You can't be serious," she said.

"I won't agree to less." He pressed his advantage with a little bit of logical persuasion. "I usually spend double that on gifts, so I'm still coming out ahead, especially since I'm asking for a rush job." He glanced at her out of the corner of his eye. "Do we have a deal?"

"Okay, I guess." She smiled and shrugged. "Why not?"

"How many can I pick up tomorrow?"

"Tomorrow? But Christmas isn't for a month. Do you really need—"

"The sooner I have them, the sooner I'll know how things stand. Giftwise," he added. He knew he was steamrolling her, but he wouldn't lie to her. He intended to give one as a gift to Jackie, one to his mother, and, worse-case scenario, proudly give any that didn't sell at the boutique as gifts to colleagues and friends. Between what he was paying for them and what the boutique would charge, she'd make a nice chunk of change. But before he told her about the arrangement with the boutique, he wanted to see how things went. He was confident they would sell, and sell quickly, but he didn't want to build any premature expectations in her yet, for either success or failure. Considering her self-deprecating view, he wasn't sure which way she would respond.

"Well, let me see," she said. "I have six completed, a few that only need a couple of finishing touches—"

"Great. I'll come by first thing tomorrow to get the finished ones, and I'll pick up whatever you can give me next week."

They were under the mistletoe now. This time he didn't hesitate. He slid his hand around the back of her neck and lowered his mouth to hers. Her remaining hesitance evaporated, and she became open and welcoming. Her generous response, in light of her history and fears, touched Ross and brought down even more of his emotional wall. His lips made a path along her jaw to her ear, and he kissed her there and then whispered, "I will definitely be seeing you tomorrow."

Chapter 17

LIFE WAS A DREAM, AND Natalie was terrified that she would wake up. She picked up her pile of research notes and sank onto her living room sofa. She had that ten-page research paper to write for her anthropology class, and the deadline was next week. She needed to concentrate, but right now, all she wanted to do was pinch herself. Or not pinch herself—in case doing so woke her up. She wanted to savor this dream. The dream that had continued the day after Thanksgiving when Ross had taken eight Santas, written her an outrageous check for them, and then cheerfully hung her outdoor holiday lights for her before flying out for a week of business in New York.

The following Sunday she'd pulled out her checkbook to pay her monthly missionary obligation when the ward clerk had told her to put it away. "No need this month, Sister Forrester," he'd said. "Donations have covered the amount in full. Merry Christmas early!" When she'd asked who had donated, he'd given her a vague shrug. "Couldn't say. Bishop said they wanted to remain anonymous."

Natalie had spent the entire time she'd been at church looking at ward members, analyzing their behavior toward her, mentally evaluating their financial status, trying to figure it out. By the time she'd arrived home, she'd realized she hadn't heard a word of the meeting, nor was she any closer to solving the mystery. But it had felt terrific.

The girls had arrived home from their weekend with Wade in relatively decent spirits. He'd let Emma use his old Honda Accord (he hadn't traded it in when he'd upgraded to the SUV) and had dropped hints that he might give it to her at some point in the future. Natalie wouldn't tell Emma that whatever future point Wade had mentioned was probably when pigs flew. Emma was too full of happy anticipation for Natalie to burst her bubble.

And frankly, Natalie was relieved. Emma had seemed to be under a lot of strain lately, and this week it actually felt like she had her daughter back.

Being a Friday night, Em was at Kate's house, along with Tess. Callie was babysitting for the neighbors, so Natalie decided to use the evening to polish the rough draft of her paper. A reread of her notes reminded her of some information she wanted to include, so she quickly circled the paragraphs and marked their location in her pages.

Grabbing a red pen, she pored over the pages and furiously rewrote sentences. She needed it clean and concise so she could spend as little time as possible on campus typing it on one of the computers there. She really wished she'd been a little more assertive with Wade and his demand for all of the electronic equipment. The computer and printer would have come in handy about now. She could have typed the rough draft, for starters. Think of all the time she would have saved.

She was curled over her papers, halfway through the rewrite, when her cell phone buzzed. She gave the caller ID a quick preoccupied glance, then bolted upright at full attention.

"Ross! Hi." She unconsciously straightened her hair.

"Hello, gorgeous. My flight just landed, and I was hoping I could drop by to see you later."

Natalie looked down at the remaining pages she had left. "No problem."

"That's great. I need to stop by the office for a minute, and then I'll swing by."

That plan was more than all right with her, paper notwithstanding.

"I was also wondering how your week went making the little Santas," Ross continued. "Do you have anything for me?"

She had several Santas and a whole heart load of feelings she was having difficulty controlling, not that she dared tell him. She'd learned from Buck and Wade that men can kiss you, even want you, but not necessarily love you. "Yes, I do, as a matter of fact."

"That's great, sweetheart. I'll be there in about an hour, then." His voice lowered, gentled. "It'll be good to see you."

It would be good to see him too, Natalie mused as she resumed her editing, since she thought about him most of the time anyway. But this was the part of the dream that was terrifying to her. She was falling in love with him and falling fast. And no matter how she tried, she just couldn't see a happy ending between a high-powered attorney and a humble housekeeper. Ross needed someone as educated, elegant, and professional as he was. He'd argued cases in front of the Supreme Court. He socialized with senators and corporate moguls, intellectuals and movie stars.

What had she ever done?

But he made her feel wonderful, important. He'd finally confessed to her over the phone that he'd placed her Santas in a boutique. The fact that all of them had sold within a few days had amazed her. When he'd told her what they'd sold for, she'd had to sit down.

She got through another page of editing before she gave up. The words continually blurred into an image of Ross, his deep brown eyes, the sculpted lines of his face, the intelligent warmth of his smile. She could hear his laughing comments as she'd untangled cords of outdoor lights, could see the banded muscles in his legs as he'd climbed up and down the ladder. Strength. Strength and polish and humor. And more kindness than she'd originally thought when he'd ordered her from his house under threat of police that first time.

Not really the first time, she reminded herself, as she freshened her make-up and hair. The first time had been at the restaurant when he'd checked on her to see if she was okay. He'd reminded her then of a dark knight. Gallant, aware, and ready to assist. She hadn't needed any assistance at the time but had still been grateful. It had supported her, enabled her to face Doug squarely and ultimately rise to the occasion.

She heard the doorbell and forced herself not to run to the door, not to read too much into things too soon. She took a calming breath and opened the door. Snow had begun falling, and his shoulders and hair were dusted.

"There's a sight for sore eyes." Before she could open her mouth to reply, he pulled her into his arms for a bone-melting kiss. She clutched the lapels of his coat and held on. "Utah never looked so lovely and warm."

His words felt wonderful and dangerous at the same time. When she knew her legs wouldn't collapse beneath her, she led him to the couch. "You've had a long day, so relax. I'll go get what I have finished from the garage. I did something different this time, and I'd like your opinion."

He eased into the cushions, stretched out his long legs, and sighed contentedly. "I'll be waiting right here. Just wake me up when you get back. I'm beat."

She practically danced into the garage to retrieve the papier mâchè creations. Her heart sang, even as her head tried to issue a stern warning.

Slow down, Natalie. Buck had filled in the void when she'd lost her mother. Wade had stepped in as the father her child lacked. She'd felt empty for a long time. It was a huge risk to allow this feeling of wholeness she felt to be anything more than a temporary salve to help her heal. But it could at least be that—a friendship and temporary respite, a chance to heal and believe. Believe in others. Believe in herself.

She returned to the living room with a half dozen sculptures and sat next to him, carefully placing the Santas on the coffee table.

"Impressive," he said.

"You haven't even looked at them yet." She picked up a rustic Santa with a long curling beard, his suit bronze and ochre, rather than red. "What do you think? Not quite traditional, but still. And I came up with this new character thinking ahead to Valentine's—"

"Not the Santas, though I'm sure they're as remarkable as ever. I mean this." He rattled the sheaf of papers he was holding.

He'd been leafing through her rough draft.

"Impressive? Oh, I don't think so, but thanks anyway. Any input you'd care to offer?" She reached for her pen and avoided eye contact with him in case he noticed how skeptical she was of his compliment.

"Really, you're off to a great start," he said. "Just a couple of suggestions so far . . ."

She watched, silently, while he read, pondered, shook his head occasionally, adjusted a word or two, crossed out sentences. He asked her questions and made her clarify her answers.

When he laid the last page down a little while later, he studied her with fresh eyes. Serious eyes.

"It's very good."

Well, Natalie thought, "very good" was better than anything Wade had ever said to her and was a lot more believable than "impressive." "I appreciate your help, Ross. It's my final exam, and I want to do well. You really think it's good?"

"Not good." He still had that sober look. "Very good. Excellent, in fact. And enlightening on many levels."

She smiled, almost willing to trust his compliment. "It was a lot more work than my tap-dancing final was. By the way," she added with an impish grin, "I aced that one. Of course, it was a class for beginners."

He smiled back. "I expect a performance from you, then."

"Not on your life. Oh, wow." She turned as Emma blew through the door with Tess in a flurry of snow. "Look how hard it's been snowing."

"Hey, Bob! There's almost a foot, and it's still going strong. You know what that means."

Natalie hesitated, then shrugged with a smile. "I guess a tradition's a tradition. Go make the calls." Emma and Tess squealed and ran off to the kitchen. "And don't forget to call Tori and Jim!" When Ross looked at Natalie questioningly, she only said, "I'll bet you're hungry. And you're going to need your strength if you want to go midnight sledding with us. Let's see what I can throw together."

* * *

During the time it took for Natalie to whip up a tasty and satisfying meal of what she called "whatever spaghetti" and for them to devour it, a horde of people arrived at her house. Natalie's friends Tori and James Matthews and their young family had joined them, along with a dozen teenage girls, ages thirteen to seventeen, and a few teenage boys, Brett included, which surprised Ross, but it worked to his advantage, since Brett brought along enough ski gear from home to keep both him and Ross warm and dry in the snow.

"Mom won't believe it when I tell her you went sledding at midnight." Brett laughed. "I'm not sure I'll believe it until I see it, Uncle Mac. It's not exactly touch football."

"Yeah, she'd probably insist you take a polygraph test or ask if you'd suffered a recent concussion." Ross was personally glad he'd dressed down for the flight home and was only tucking a mildly expensive pair of chinos into the old ski pants he was pulling on instead of one of his Italian suits. The tie had been abandoned long ago. And the verdict on this brand of adventure was still out—but at least he was game.

Callie's girlfriends passed around extra gloves, scarves, and mittens, sampling and discarding as they went for the more stylish ones.

"I just love the first midnight snow party of the season!" Callie exclaimed to no one in particular, her face flushed pink, a purple knit cap pulled snugly down to her sparkling eyes. She was standing next to Ross, and her bubbling excitement and joyous anticipation of an obviously long-standing tradition was infectious.

Who but Natalie Forrester would have a family tradition like this? Not anyone he knew, Ross was sure.

The falling snow had slowed by the time they reached their sledding destination, and the clouds had parted in places. The occasional star flashed like a diamond, and the moon wove its pearly light among the contrasting velvets of cloud and sky. Midnight and moonlight. Was any combination more spellbinding? he wondered.

He listened to the kids' muted laughs and shouts as they dragged the sleds and tubes up, then zoomed and crashed down the hill. Natalie reminded everyone to keep the noise level down so the neighbors wouldn't complain, and Brett and the other boys challenged each other to hotdog dares and races. And Ross had to admit after the first few passes he'd taken himself that it was exhilarating.

He decided to take a hot-chocolate break and watch Natalie head down the hill backward on her tube with Callie in her lap. Emma gave them a spin right as they took off, and Ross took a sip of the steaming chocolate and chuckled. Both Natalie and Callie's arms waved about wildly. And after all her cautions about noise, Natalie was shrieking hysterically.

"Having a good time?"

Ross looked over his steaming cup at Jim Matthews. "Yeah. A great time, matter of fact. Bitter cold out here though."

"This is nothing. Last year there was no cloud cover, and it was colder than Hades. Best thing to do," he gestured to the right, "is to keep hiking up that hill and sledding. Keeps your blood pumping and your mind off the temperature."

"I think I'm good for a few more runs."

"Glad to hear it." They both glanced up at a sudden burst of squeals. A tube chain made up of Brett and Emma and several of the others rumbled down the hill like a clumsy caterpillar. Jim cleared his throat. "Um, I hope you don't mind, but I've been assigned to play concerned guardian tonight. Tori's orders."

"It's been a long time since I had to answer to a protective dad. You're not going to pull out your shotgun and start polishing it, are you?"

"Nah, nothing that extreme. It's just that we think pretty highly of Bob—Natalie."

"You call her Bob too."

"Yeah, when the nickname started, it just stuck. Anyway. She's family, you might say. We're only looking out for her best interest. We don't want to see her hurt anymore."

"I don't plan to hurt her."

"I don't expect you do. Not intentionally, anyway. What do you know about her?"

I know she's amazingly artistic, intelligent, gentle, and thoughtful of others. I know she's not afraid of hard work, has an adventurous streak, and takes care of her own. I know she's beautiful and fun and braver than she thinks she is. I know her eyes sparkle like emeralds when she's happy and turn deep as the sea when I kiss her. I know she fills me in ways I haven't thought mattered in years. "I know she's special, Jim."

"What do you know about her past?"

"She's been married a couple of times. She doesn't talk about it much, but she seems to blame herself."

Jim cursed, emitting a cloud of steam. "Sorry about that. Tori'd shoot me if she'd heard. But when I hear stuff like that, I want to—never mind. Let me tell you what I know about Natalie, let you decide for yourself where the blame lies."

Jim proceeded to tell Ross about Natalie's secret crush on football star Buck Jacobsen, her mother's diagnosis of cancer, the strain of her mother's treatments and her eventual death just mere months later, how withdrawn her father had become, grieving for his wife, and how lonely that had left Natalie, grieving herself.

"Tori did all she could to be there for her, but what does a kid know about that sort of thing? Needless to say, Natalie had it rough and still managed to pull straight As. Tori said Nat didn't smile much back then. Didn't want to hang with her friends.

"It didn't help that her dad wasn't coping. He'd work long hours, then go home and drink just enough to numb the pain. While her mom went through treatment, Natalie cooked, cleaned, and did all the necessary stuff. He's a good guy, don't get me wrong. I think he got used to it, her doing everything for him. So when her mom finally died, he forgot she was a kid. She'd taken care of so many of the grown-up things."

"Where is he now?"

"He eventually remarried and lives in Oregon. They stay in touch; things are good. Natalie seems to like the new wife, though I doubt she'd say differently. Anyway, that summer, Tori decided it was time to get Natalie back among the living. She talked her into going to the dance that kicked off the school year. That's where Buck got a look at her, and that was all it took. You know Natalie. You can tell exactly what she's thinking the minute you look at her eyes. Well, Buck saw adoration in the form of a pretty girl and knew just what he wanted to do about it.

"To hear Tori tell it, Buck swept her off her feet at a time when she just plain needed to be loved, and badly. He made his move, got what he wanted, then left her high and dry when the going got rough." He waved at Tori, who was giving him eye signals. Natalie was approaching. "It looks like we'll have to continue this later."

Natalie was breathless and, Ross thought, more beautiful than ever, blonde tendrils escaping her knit cap, the moon making her skin luminous. "Come race me, slacker," she called to him. "A final showdown before it's time to unthaw the kids. Five bucks says I'm taking you down."

Ross grinned at her and fought down the hard ball that had formed in his stomach listening to Jim. He had nieces who were nearly the age Natalie had been when this had happened. He'd flay the skin off any boy who tried it with one of them.

"That's big talk, coming from a sassy little girl," he called back. "You're on. Double or nothing." He crunched his Styrofoam cup menacingly at her and glanced at Jim. "We'll finish this later."

"Yeah. And my money's on Bob, buddy. Sorry."

* * *

When Jim actually called Ross to set up lunch for later the following week, Ross was surprised but definitely interested in continuing the conversation they'd started at the midnight sledding adventure. He'd thought of little else and had plenty of questions.

He was even more surprised when Tori showed up for lunch as well. Jim shrugged. "Tori knows more about it anyway, so I thought I'd let her tell you firsthand."

As Ross listened to Tori tell the story, he could hear the guilt she felt for encouraging Natalie to go to the dance, her inadequacy at protecting Natalie, and her own successes and happiness in contrast to Natalie's life of hardship.

Buck had always been successful with the girls, always had at least one on a string. Tori had known of his reputation and was afraid he would tire of Natalie and move on, like she'd seen him do with other girlfriends in the past. Natalie only knew she was in love and Buck seemed perfect.

Tori's worst fears were realized that Thanksgiving when Natalie informed her that she'd missed her period, and Tori was sworn to secrecy. When Natalie's father became suspicious of her ongoing flu symptoms, he confronted her, and she tearfully confessed. Natalie's very solemn and sober father invited Buck to have a chat, and when he left that evening, it was with the clear understanding that he would be marrying Natalie in the immediate future.

Two weeks later, she secretly became Natalie Jacobsen, with only their parents in attendance at the county courthouse. She stayed at home to hide her pregnancy and worked to get her diploma while Buck continued to live with his parents and finish up his senior year.

Tori would never forget the day she broke an awful reality to Natalie, that Buck had been seeing different girls at school. Natalie had gone pale and denied it was true. Buck wouldn't do that to her. But Tori suspected from the forcefulness of Natalie's words that she was mostly trying to convince herself.

When Natalie questioned Buck about it later, he angrily told her they had a marriage on paper only and that if she thought she could trap him by getting pregnant, she was mistaken. She countered that he was as responsible for their situation as she was, that she was a prisoner in her home while he strutted around school as though he were free. And he wasn't—not any more than she was. He slammed the door on his way out.

She sat at home on graduation, swollen with pregnancy, feeling like she was being kicked on the inside by a bucking bronco. Aaron "Buck" Jacobsen walked across the stage wearing his cap and gown and then took a cheerleader he'd been seeing to an all-night graduation party up Logan Canyon—Tori saw him there, and when she confronted him, he just blew her off.

On the Fourth of July, as Tori and Natalie and her father watched the fireworks in the distance from the front porch, Natalie went into labor. Just before dawn on the fifth of July, she welcomed a nine-pound boy into the world and named him Ryan. On the sixth of July, Buck's father visited the hospital with a small gift for the baby and divorce papers in his hand. Buck also stipulated that he was relinquishing parental rights. Mr. Jacobsen flatly stated that Buck had given the baby his name, if it even was his baby, and that was more than enough for any eighteen-year-old boy with a bright future to do. Mr. Jacobsen didn't touch his grandchild.

"She'd been awarded a four-year scholarship to Utah State. Instead, she stayed home, divorced, with a baby, a job as a waitress, and a broken heart—at eighteen." Tori laughed bitterly. "It sounds like an awful country song."

Tori's comment reminded Ross of the first time he'd seen Natalie. Beautiful, tense Natalie staving off the advances of the Hulk while his coworkers joked about out-countrying each other with heartache stories. Natalie won the contest hands down, owned it, and didn't complain about it.

Tori continued. "I was still away at college when she wrote and asked if I'd be her maid of honor when she married Wade. It should have been nice. Wade was nice looking, Natalie was thrilled, and Ryan was adorable in his little tuxedo. I had this feeling though.

"I thought I was being silly, cautious for Natalie's sake. When she'd written, she'd told me it was a civil wedding, that there were a few things keeping Wade from the temple at the time, but they didn't want to wait. That made me wonder. After everything she'd been through with Buck, she'd really relied on her faith to get through. Church had become really important to her. She'd write and tell me how she was going to do things right the next time around. So when all of a sudden I got this new line of thinking from her, I was concerned. She kept saying, 'Look at the two of them together.' Wade and Ryan, you know? 'Doesn't it melt your heart?' Well, it was pretty cute, so I started to relax a little."

"How did this—Wade—how was he with Natalie?" Ross asked.

"Well, like I said, he was cute with Ryan, piggyback rides, things like that. He seemed crazy about Natalie, really. I did notice that he liked things his way, and she was always eager to please. I know now that he's selfish; he didn't love her enough to begin with and didn't care enough to make it last."

"That's pretty harsh. Doesn't it take two people to make or break a marriage?"

Ross was just playing devil's advocate, but Tori bristled more than he'd anticipated. "Do you know why Natalie cleans houses? Because this bright woman who earned a four-year academic scholarship was convinced by her 'loving' husband that she wasn't competent enough to do anything else.

"She was competent enough for him to marry. After that, she did everything he demanded of her, but she never did anything good enough to make him happy. Eventually, she heard rumors about other women. It decimated her. Her only escape for years was her kids' lives and her art. She was committed to keeping her family together, tried hard to make her marriage to Wade work. But the rumors persisted. When she finally got brave enough to confront him about it, he didn't deny it, and he convinced her it was her fault. When all you've heard about yourself for years is how pathetic you are, you believe it. It was the final straw. But not the way you think." Ross watched Tori twist her napkin. His stomach twisted too. "She wasn't the outraged wife, cutting the loser loose. She was giving him his freedom because she couldn't make him happy, because she didn't have the qualities he needed in a wife. She heroically fell on the sword for that selfish bully."

Ross had heard about all he could stand. He took a long drink of water and breathed deeply. "He took her to the cleaners in the divorce."

Tori snorted. "Yeah, he knew just how to play it. And Natalie was under some misguided idea that if she could keep things amicable, it would be better for the girls. Wade still knows how to play that with her."

"It sounds like Natalie could use a new attorney."

Tori and Jim eyed each other, smiled, and nodded. "Know anybody?"

Chapter 18

NATALIE SPENT CHRISTMAS EVE DAY with the Emma and Callie, baking cookies and delivering them to the neighbors. After an early dinner, they opened gifts, read the traditional Nativity account from the New Testament, and curled up on the sofa together to watch the *Grinch*. Then Wade showed up to take the girls to his house for the rest of the evening. It was his turn to have them for Christmas.

But at least this year she wouldn't be spending Christmas home alone reading or watching old movies on TV. Ross picked her up first thing Christmas morning and took her to his mother's house. Dorothy welcomed her with a warm hug. "I'm so glad you're here, dear. The old place needs some brightening up, and you're just the ticket."

After what Ross called their traditional Christmas breakfast of eggs and sausage a la Ross and waffles loaded with berries and whipped cream, compliments of Dorothy, he dragged Natalie into the family room for some serious board-game competition. He beat her soundly at chess, but she managed to actually outdo him in a heated game of Scrabble. Before she knew it, it was nearly eleven o'clock. Then the doorbell rang.

"Let's see who that could be." Ross took her by the hand, and they went to the door together. There were Emma and Callie, with Wade standing uncomfortably behind. As she hugged the girls, Wade said, "The girls wanted to be with you when Ryan called. They said you'd be here. I told them they could stay for a half hour." He shot a scowl at Ross and headed back down the sidewalk to his car.

He'd told her only yesterday when he'd picked up the girls that he wasn't going to interrupt his Christmas morning lugging them back and forth to speak to Ryan. Now here he was, and here they were.

"Wade!" Natalie called. He turned. "Do you want to come in?" she asked.

Wade glanced back at Ross, then at Natalie. "Nah, it's okay. I'll stay in the car. Tell Ryan hello for me."

"I will. And, Wade," she said as he started back down the walk, "thank you. And Merry Christmas."

"Yeah. Thirty minutes, Em."

"Okay, Dad."

The call from Elder Ryan Jacobsen was wonderful and frustrating. He sounded happy, teased his sisters like normal, and tried to make the telephone conversation last as long as he possibly could. By the time he had described every member of his small branch in Falkirk, all of the elders in his zone, and each tie he'd collected while in Scotland, Natalie knew she'd have to be the tough one who ended the phone call. It was well past the allotted half hour.

Natalie was pretty sure Wade wouldn't ring the doorbell and throw his weight around in front of the McConnells, but she didn't want his ire to upset Emma and Callie's holiday or their conversation with their brother. Maybe he'd leave it be since it was Christmas, but she couldn't count on that being the case.

Emma and Callie each gave Natalie a final hug and danced out the door. "See you tonight, Mom," they sang. "Dad says he has one more present to give us. We'll tell you all about it tonight."

Ross came up behind Natalie as she waved good-bye to them from the doorway. He and Dorothy had left her alone with her girls and son. He placed his hand on her shoulder and gave it a squeeze. "How's the missionary?"

Natalie smiled and brushed away a lone tear that had managed to escape. "He's great. Really great. I could even hear a bit of a brogue when he spoke. He told the girls to expect a present in the mail. I got the impression they're getting clan tartans. Forrester is a clan name." She thought for a minute. "Is McConnell?"

In his best Scottish impersonation, he told her, "Nay, lass, we're but a wee family that owes our allegiance to the MacDonalds." He dragged her toward the family room. "And right now, I want a rematch at Scrabble."

Natalie laughed. Her heart was full. Her girls were happy; her son was doing well. "All right, laddie, but stand warned. Ye havna seen the best of Nat Forrester yet."

And she was right. She beat him two games straight. Granted, their scores were close, but she beat him fair and square. She also saw him get a look in his eye that she was sure had intimidated many an opposing counsel. During the third game, he placed his tiles on the board.

"Ross, *voxism* is not a word."

"Sure it is."

"No, it's not. You made it up."

"Voxism. From the Latin, *vox*, meaning 'voice', *-ism*, meaning 'the state or quality of.' Voxism, therefore, is the state or quality of the voice."

"Totally made it up."

He grinned. "You wanna bet?"

Well, she didn't. Not with Mr. *Columbia Law Review*.

"That's a triple letter score for the *X*. Thirty-four points for me. Write it down."

"Wait a minute."

"Thirty-four points, gorgeous."

He should take up high-stakes poker, Natalie thought. And he was closing in fast on her lead. That meant only one thing: it was time to match fire with fire. She looked at all the letter *A* tiles she kept picking out of the pile and said, "Okay, buster, you asked for it." She laid down her tiles. "Using your *V* and the double letter and the double word score, that's forty points." She picked up the pencil.

He laid a heavy hand on her wrist. "Hold on there, sweetheart. You think you can get away with *aviaqua*? *Aviaqua*?"

She smiled at him smugly. "From the Latin, *avi* meaning 'bird.' *Aqua* for 'water.' Aviaqua. Waterfowl."

Ross choked. Then he threw his head back and laughed. Natalie wrote forty down on the score sheet, picked six replacement tiles, and groaned. Three more *A*s. Ross was still laughing. She took the time he needed to compose himself to rearrange her new tiles into potential words.

"What is going on in here?" Suzie asked as she pulled off her jacket. Ross continued to laugh, wiped his hands over his face, and pointed at Natalie.

"I'm beating him at Scrabble," Natalie said simply.

"Nobody beats Ross at Scrabble," Suzie said. "He knows too many fancy words."

"He cheats."

Ross started laughing all over again.

Suzie glanced suspiciously at Ross. "I don't get the joke."

"I'm being toppled as king of the hill." He leaned over the table and kissed Natalie loudly on the mouth, shocking both Suzie and her.

"You're one in a million. Come on, I bet I can cream you at Halo. If we can beat the boys to the Xbox, that is."

* * *

Natalie set a steaming cup of cocoa on the table and settled in next to Ross on the sofa in her living room. He watched her take a cautious sip from her own cup. "Ooh! Still hot." She fanned herself. "You may want to give it a couple of minutes."

"Uh oh, you got burned. We need to kiss it better." He leaned over and brushed his lips over hers, letting the kiss linger. He could feel her lips curve up in a smile. "There. All better now. At least I am." He smiled back and scanned her face.

"Merry Christmas, Ross."

"It has been, for me at least." Today had been a perfect day. He had enjoyed being with her and hadn't enjoyed a Christmas as much as he had this one in more years than he could remember. He studied her again, this time more seriously. "Has it been a good day for you?"

"Yes, it's been wonderful."

He was happy that she'd enjoyed the day. It couldn't have been a perfect day for her, with her girls spending most of Christmas with their father, but Ross had done what he could to at least make the day nice for her. "My mother loved the little papier mâchè nativity you made for her. I think her exact words were, 'I never knew funky could be so religious.' I didn't know my mother knew words like *funky*."

"It was my small way of thanking her for letting me spend the holiday with her and her family."

"By the way, what did you end up making as Christmas gifts for your friends, since I commandeered all of your Santas for the boutique?" he asked.

"Oh, I managed to squeak out a few you weren't able to get your hands on." She smiled. "I made a couple of gifts out of other odds and ends. I also broke down and bought a few gifts at the very last minute. Nothing too expensive, of course, but it was still nice to feel like I could actually afford to do it." She shook her head. "Who could have imagined that my silly little creations would sell as well as they have? It's unbelievable."

"Not silly. And not unbelievable at all." He'd already heard from Jackie how well Natalie's sculptures were continuing to sell, but it pleased him no end that she had told him herself.

"Well, it still seems that way to me," she said. "I needed to pinch myself when I got the second check from the boutique yesterday. It was enough money that I'll be able to pay for Ryan's mission for the next few months without Wade's help and still have enough to add a chemistry class to the biology class I'm taking next semester. Plus, the boutique owner wants to arrange a meeting so she can see what other things I've done. I already have a few more ideas for Valentine's and Easter."

She didn't know yet that he'd already paid Natalie's bishop enough to cover Ryan's entire mission. The only mystery that remained for him was why she was taking chemistry and biology, as artistically gifted as she was.

"Speaking of chemistry and biology . . ." Ross said, but Natalie stopped him with a gesture.

"Stay here," she said. "I'll be right back."

She sprang up and was out of the room before he could react. He wondered if she misinterpreted his intentions with his reference to chemistry and biology. He grinned. There was plenty of chemistry between them, that was certain. But she'd seemed nervous just now for the first time all day, for the first time in weeks, actually.

She returned to the living room carrying a large wrapped box and sat back down next to Ross.

"What's this?" he asked. He slid their mugs to the side as she set the package down on the coffee table.

"Merry Christmas, Ross." She choked a little on the words, and when he looked up, he was surprised at the emotion he could see in her misty eyes. "I guess my voxism is a little unsteady tonight."

He chuckled at the Scrabble allusion. "Yes, the quality of your voice seems a little impaired at the moment. Do you want me to open it now?"

She nodded, words gone. He shot glances at her as she waited, seemingly breathless, while he tugged off the bow and slipped a finger under the taped edges and pulled off the lid. And then he sat silently and looked at what was inside while his heart beat wildly in his chest.

"It's not much—"

He turned abruptly and looked at her.

Looking embarrassed, she explained, "I was going to make a fanlight for my front door," she gestured with her hand, "but when I saw that magnificent window in your kitchen and the sunshine that pours through it in the morning, I changed my mind . . ."

Ross gently lifted the object from the box. It was a large stained-glass diamond shape with a rich wood frame that had been polished until it gleamed. But it was the image the bright colored shards of glass created that made him catch his breath. It was the rising sun, a blaze of abstract flames in all the colors of the rainbow. It burned and bloomed. He could already envision the explosion of colors it would create. It was glorious.

She was glorious.

He eased it carefully back into the box, then pulled her into an embrace. Overcome by emotions he wasn't quite ready to name, he held on, his face buried in her hair.

She held on to him too. He could feel it.

"It's a sun catcher," she whispered.

"What?" It took him a moment to pull himself back from his thoughts.

"A sun catcher. Not a traditional one, obviously. This one is a lot bigger, but your window is so large, so amazing, that I wanted it to be in proportion. Then the pieces just started coming together." Her hand crept to his shoulder. "I could see the colors flooding the room." She pulled back from him and smiled into his eyes. "You'll have a sunrise all morning long."

He framed her face with his hands, stroked his thumbs along her cheeks, and gave her the sweetest, most tender kiss he possibly could. This was no casserole or plate of cookies. He was keenly aware that she had given him a part of herself, a very intimate part of her soul, in that gift. He wished he could explain what he'd felt when he opened the box and looked at it; the art itself evoked feelings powerful and thrilling. That she had made it herself humbled him. That she'd made it for him shook him to the core. He had no words to express any of it. He allowed the kiss to speak for him.

Ross wasn't sure how much time elapsed when the door blew open and an excited Callie yelled, "Bob! Where are you? You won't believe it! Bob!"

He and Natalie drew apart slowly as Callie and Emma flew in, pink from the cold. Ross lingered over Natalie a couple of moments longer, basking in the warm glow of her face before turning his attention to the girls. Wade Forrester hovered in the background, not looking at anyone but still managing to look like he wanted to pick a fight. Ross's lawyer instinct immediately put him on alert and warned him to prepare for a confrontation of some sort.

"What won't I believe, Cal-pal?" Natalie pulled her into a tight squeeze, and Ross saw her eyeing Emma before giving her a hug too.

"Tell her, Em!"

"Bob, I know it's your turn to have us for the rest of Christmas break," Emma began, "but Dad—"

"We're going to Deer Valley!" Callie interrupted. "Dad got us ski passes for the whole, entire holiday and snowboards and new gear and everything!" She was shaking with excitement.

Ross watched Natalie jerk her head in Wade's direction and tried to analyze the emotions he saw flash over her face. Ross knew her ex had cut off support of her missionary son and had held up making the support payments she was due. But he'd just blown a bundle on the girls in order to take them from their mother when it wasn't his right. And Natalie's face showed it all: shock, anger, betrayal, and then resignation. It was the resignation in her face that set his jaw. Wade stood right inside the closed doorway, his expression smug, his arms crossed over his chest, just asking Natalie to take him on. Ross could see that in his face too.

Emma touched Natalie's arm entreatingly but said nothing. Ross couldn't contain his fury as he watched Natalie's glorious countenance shatter. The air in the room was brittle. She looked at Wade. "What do you expect me to say?"

Wade shot Ross an indifferent glance, then looked at Natalie. "That you care more about your girls' happiness than some stipulation in a divorce decree." Natalie visibly recoiled, and it took all of Ross's will power to keep from stepping into Wade's face.

"Emma, Callie, would you please go to your rooms for a moment while your father and I talk this over?" She spoke in low, even tones, but Ross watched her fingers flex and knot. "Wade, let's go in the kitchen."

It tore Ross to bits to stand in the living room alone, feeling powerless. He could hear the quiet, angry hissing of their voices, the occasional bark of punctuated words. He looked at the stained glass, sitting dimly in the tissue-filled box, a joyful fire wanting to blaze but now lightless. Eventually, Wade stalked out of the kitchen, a look of arrogant triumph on his face, a withdrawn Natalie behind.

"I'll leave it to you to give the girls the good news. Have them packed and ready to go at nine tomorrow. I want to be on the road early."

The door slammed. Ross opened the door and followed, jaw still clenched, as Wade headed down the porch stairs. "Forrester. I'd like a word."

Wade turned and glared at Ross.

"You pull any more legal end runs around Natalie, you'll be dealing with me in more ways than you'd care to imagine."

"Threats from a boyfriend don't worry me too much."

Ross's voice was quiet and cold. "As her 'boyfriend,' as you so impotently termed it, I would only be inclined toward violence." Ross smiled grimly and stepped closer to Wade, nose to nose. "But as her newly appointed legal counsel, I am prepared to keep you in litigation until you have grandchildren if you so much as modify a comma in the terms of your divorce decree without her prior knowledge and consent. Do we understand each other?"

Wade made no reply as he stalked off to his car, but Ross was confident Wade had a clear understanding of the situation now.

* * *

Ross came back in the house and quietly shut the front door. He was silent, but Natalie could sense an intensity about him that hadn't been there before.

"Is everything okay?" she asked.

"Your ex-husband and I just reached a little agreement," he answered blandly.

"I can handle Wade," she said. "And I need to do it my way for the girls' sake."

"I know you can, sweetheart. And I'll let you. But I wanted to let him know that you have some firepower backing you now."

"What does that mean?"

"It means that I told him you have new representation who won't let him take advantage of you."

"I can't . . . Oh, Ross, I can't possibly let you—"

He ran his hand gently over her hair. "You can. And don't worry. I have a feeling my little warning will be enough. I doubt Wade will actually challenge it." He kissed her on the nose. "I'd better go now so you can spend time with the girls before they leave again in the morning."

He carefully picked up his present and shifted its weight so he could hold it with one arm. Then he wrapped his other arm around Natalie and walked with her to the door. "Thank you for the gift," he said. "It means more to me than you know. I have a gift for you too—"

"Oh, Ross, I didn't expect—"

"I have a gift for you too," he repeated, silencing her with a couple of fingers over her lips. "But now is not the time for me to give it to you. I'll see you tomorrow, sweetheart." He stroked her cheek, kissed her soundly, and was gone.

* * *

After Ross left, Emma took Natalie aside. "Dad was really excited about taking us boarding. I know it's your holiday week for us, but thanks for saying we could go and not fighting about it. Dad told us not to get our hopes up, that you would probably give him flak like you always do, but you didn't."

You would probably give him flak like you always do? What was Natalie supposed to say to that? She'd certainly not given him flak over Thanksgiving or this unscheduled custody switch—or his lack of financial support the last six months. Apparently, as long as he provided snowboards and luxury resort time, he was doing his duty as father and provider. Money for food and shelter wasn't nearly as much fun or impressive. "Do you think I'm always giving him flak? You don't, do you?"

"No. He says you do, but I know you don't, even though I haven't told Callie what I heard." She gave Natalie a hug. "But thanks for letting us go. You're the best."

When Wade set her up like he had this time with expensive gifts and preparing the girls for her objections, Natalie knew she had no choice, or she'd be the villain. Not him. No, sir. She'd reached the point where if he was going to make her out to be a villain, maybe she would become just that and start pushing back.

But not this time. This time she had conceded to his manipulations, consciously recognizing his tactics but allowing him to win. Next time would be a different story.

Despite her upbeat words, Em seemed subdued, so Natalie pressed her. "Are you okay? Is something bothering you?"

Emma shrugged. "It's nothing, I just . . . Kate's been weird lately, and I wanted to hang with her a little to see what's up. But it's okay."

"Weird how?"

"She's got this boyfriend and everything—you remember, the party guy?—and she's acting different now. Tess is so mad at her she hasn't talked to her for a week. Jeremy isn't my fave, you know? But it's nothing. Dad says I can live without my friends for a week. I'll hook up with Kate when I get back."

When Emma said Kate's boyfriend's name, Natalie felt a chill. She wished that hearing the name Jeremy didn't make her automatically think of the icky Lisle twins, Jeremy and Justin. Besides, Kate had more sense than to hang with one of them, Natalie was sure.

* * *

"Em, Callie, your father's here to get you," Natalie called out right before the doorbell rang. She could see the black SUV sitting in the driveway. She opened the door. "They'll be right out."

"Tell them to hurry." He turned and went back to the SUV without stepping inside the house. That was a first, Natalie thought. Usually he liked to come inside and criticize something about the place.

She grabbed Callie's suitcase and hustled out the door with Emma trailing behind. Wade was in a particularly foul mood, which meant the best thing for everyone involved was for him to get on his way with the girls. Ross had definitely upset Wade last night.

While Wade stowed the girls' gear in the back of the car, Natalie smiled as brightly as she could and told Callie and Emma to have a great time. "Be good, do what Sandy tells you, and I'll see you—"

"I'll have them back before school starts on the fifth," Wade interjected.

He was really pushing it with her. "Fine." Quietly, to Emma, she said, "Call if you need anything, but only if you do, so your dad stays happy. Got your cell?"

"Yeah. Bye, Mom."

Then they were gone, with Callie waving furiously through the window of the SUV.

An unexpected week without her girls. Since it was the holidays, she wouldn't even have work to keep her mind occupied. How would she fill the hours to keep from missing them?

Natalie wandered aimlessly around the kitchen, straightening chairs that were straight, wiping up nonexistent spills. The house hollowly echoed her loneliness off its walls. She decided to call her father first, remember what a real father was like, and thank him for their Christmas gifts. His new wife, Marie, had knit sweaters for them. Natalie didn't know people still did things like that.

"Yello." Ray's drawl was smoky and mellow like a campfire at twilight. "Natalie, is that you, little girl? Well, what do you know. Marie! Marie, get on the other phone. It's Nat and the girls."

"It's just me, Dad. The girls are with Wade."

"Ah, well, shoot. I wanted to hear their voices—"

"How were the sweaters, dear?" Marie's voice chirped in over the extension. "Were the colors all right? Did they fit?"

"They're gorgeous, Marie. I don't know how you manage the time each year to hand-make every gift." The cable-knit sweaters were oversized but soft and cozy. "They're just the thing for snuggling in on cold days."

Marie murmured a pleased sound. Natalie smiled. Her dad had chosen well for wife number two. He and her mother had loved each other, and watching him fall apart had been as hard on Natalie as her mother's illness and death had been. She was grateful he'd come through it to find joy again with Marie.

"Got a package from that son of yours."

"From Ryan?"

"What other son have you got? From Elder Ryan Jacobsen, to be exact."

"He gave him a tie!" Marie piped in.

Natalie had seen her father in a tie only on two occasions that she could remember: the day she'd married Wade, and her mother's funeral.

"Kid thinks I'm gonna wear it, he's forgotten who he's dealing with."

"Now, Dad—what does it look like?"

"It's a crisscrossy thing. Ryan said in his letter it's a Brown tartan tie, but it's red and blue and black. Not a bit of brown."

"Dad." Natalie chuckled. "It would be the plaid worn by the Brown family in Scotland. Our family."

"Is that so? Didn't know the Browns came from Scotland. Well, I'll be. Kid thinks I'm supposed to wear it to church sometime. Maybe I will, too, when he gets home."

"That would make him feel great."

"Well, he's a good boy. A good boy, Natalie. That's your doing—don't forget it. And he's going to have some stories to tell that I plan on hearing when he gets home, so you plan on Marie and me showing up at your door about then."

"It's a date. Of course, you could show up before then. The door's always open, you know."

If anybody could get her father inside a church building, she thought as she hung up the phone, it would be her son. She'd enjoyed talking to her dad, and it had temporarily distracted her from her restlessness. The house was clean, the dishes were done. The bed was made. She'd finished a couple of her library books. She could go hunt the stacks for something new to read, she supposed. But her hands were starting to itch for something to do. And when that happened, it meant only one thing.

Natalie went to her workroom to see what kind of creation was begging to exist. She grabbed a sketchbook and started to draw. Before she knew it, she'd filled one page and nearly another with sketches.

"It's quiet in here."

Natalie jumped at the sound of Ross's voice. "You didn't answer the doorbell, but I knew you were here. Hope you don't mind that I let myself in."

"No! No, not at all." She suddenly realized what she'd been doing and hastily closed her sketchbook before standing to give him a hug. She could tell by the expression on his face that he'd seen what she'd been drawing, and her face reddened.

"Let me see that," he said and made a move for it.

She grabbed the book and clutched it to her chest. "No! It's nothing."

"Then a little peek won't hurt if it's nothing." He playfully reached for it again, but she countered and scurried around her worktable. "Come on, sweetheart, give it up. You know you want to."

She giggled and backed toward the kitchen door. He'd been calling her sweetheart a lot lately, and every time, it made her insides melt. He might call his secretary sweetheart for all she knew. She had to keep reminding herself of that. Just in case . . .

He followed her into the kitchen, grinning wickedly, and soon had her trapped against the counter. Putting a hand down on either side of her, he went in for a smoldering kiss. If she'd melted before, she was a puddle now. The moment he knew she was totally distracted, he neatly grabbed the sketchbook from her and started flipping through the pages.

"Hey!" She blinked, trying to clear her head, and lunged for the book.

He made a quick, evasive move, flipped through a few pages, and found what he was looking for. Rough sketches of his face, eyes, and hands filled the page. The expressions she'd captured of him varied: thoughtful, fiery, fun. Eyes that twinkled in amusement in one drawing burned with intensity in another. A rendering of his hands. Through her eyes, they appeared strong.

On the next page was a study that caught his attention. It was the drawing of a medieval knight, mounted on his horse, dark tunic and chain mail, shadowed, surveying the distance. He recognized the face and the posture and manner of the knight. They were his.

"That's me, isn't it? I'm not exactly your knight in *shining* armor," he teased, stunned once again by her ability but even more by how astutely she had captured him, his character, on paper; even translated into another period of time, it felt authentic to him as a person.

"The knight in shining armor gallops in, arriving in a blaze of glory, vanquishing all before him, and sweeps the damsel into his arms and rides off into the sunset, much to the awe of the admiring crowds."

"You make it sound cliché."

"It is cliché. For me, at least." She took the sketchbook from his hands and traced her finger over the solemn lines of the knight's face, the strong angles of his arms. "This is the dark knight. He holds the same rank, the same power as the shining knight but without the bravado. He stands in the shadows, ever watchful, and then acts incisively. He rescues the damsel without fanfare, then goes about his business."

"Not nearly as romantic a fellow, I'm thinking."

"Oh, but he is. He has left his mark on her. She will never be the same, for he has quietly stolen her heart. No, that's not quite right." She brushed her fingers over the drawing, then closed the book. "She has given it to him, willingly." *If he only knew.* She smiled up at him. "Why are you here?"

"Took a day off work. Wanted to see how you're holding up with an empty nest."

"I'm all right." Needing to lead the conversation away from her girls and her growing love for Ross, she added, "I'm glad you're here. I need someone to eat this fudge. One of the neighbors brought it over, but I'll eat it all in one sitting if I so much as have a taste."

He obliged and then led her to the sofa. "We have a little unfinished business."

"We do?"

"Yes, we do. You gave me a Christmas gift, but we were interrupted before I was able to give you mine."

"But you didn't . . . I never expected you to—I just wanted to give you—"

"I fully intended on giving you this present last night. Remember that, okay? Then when everything happened all at once, I thought it best to wait. I'm hoping today that it makes your week a little—brighter." He suddenly seemed less confident, anxious even, as he pulled a small packet out of his coat jacket. "It's not nearly as impressive as original artwork, but I hope . . . Never mind. Just open it."

Natalie took the packet, slipped the ribbon off, opened it, and gasped. Inside was a plane ticket to New York, departing in three days with a return date of January fourth. "What is this?"

"I need to go back East tomorrow. You would think the German consortium I've been dealing with would be more traditional when it comes to their holidays. Instead, they're insisting on meetings. In fact, they're making a special trip from Europe to deal with some issues they want addressed, ASAP.

"At any rate, the firm was already planning a party at the Ritz-Carlton for our clients, as well as some of our law associates. This year, for some obtuse reason, someone decided to make it a New Year's bash. Since it involves making nice with the consortium, as well as other high-rollers, I have to be there. I thought, maybe, you'd be willing to come as my guest."

Natalie looked at the ticket in her hand, speechless.

"You'll be staying there, at the hotel. I booked you a suite. I have to work part of the time, but I'd like to show you some of the sights, introduce you to some friends. I wasn't sure how you'd feel about coming to New York, wasn't sure how you'd feel about leaving the girls for a few days, although I still intended to ask you and give you the choice. My mom offered to let them stay with her. So did Jackie, although I didn't know how you'd feel about having Em and Brett under the same roof, however supervised they might be. They've gotten to be pretty close.

"So, when your ex pulled his little Christmas stunt, I was angry for you, knowing he'd manipulated you out of days with Emma and Callie. Afterward, I thought, well, good. It worked into my plans perfectly—although I suspect if Wade knew he'd become the convenient babysitter for this little getaway, he wouldn't like it."

"Oh, Ross. New York. I've never been there—what's it like? Is it cold?—of course it's cold at Christmas. What am I thinking? Oh my gosh. New York." Nervous butterflies were battling the bubbles of excitement in her stomach.

Ross wrapped his arms around her waist. "While we're there, I'll be taking you to a formal party. I wasn't sure what you had in your closet besides a hokey pokey T-shirt, so I already talked to Jackie. Since I have to fly out tomorrow, she said she'd help you throw together enough of a wardrobe to get by. I've given her my credit card and instructions not to let you refuse anything. It's my invitation, and I want to make sure you have what you need without it being a burden. What do you say? Are you up for the adventure?"

"Oh my goodness, Ross. I can't think. It's too much; it's too generous. I can't accept all of this."

"Natalie, sweetheart, money I have in abundance. Who have I been able to share it with? No one. Let me do this. I want to." He whispered in her ear, "Think, Natalie. Imagine. The Statue of Liberty, the Empire State Building. The Met, the Guggenheim, the Museum of Modern Art."

She shut her eyes. "The art museums," she whispered. "Oh. It would be worth it just for the art museums."

"I was hoping it might be worth it to be with me."

She opened an eye and smiled at him. "Well, there is that. The Museum of Modern Art is a pretty close second though."

He grinned. "Then you'll come?"

Natalie opened her eyes and nodded, then threw her arms around his neck. "I'm still in shock, but, yes, I'll come."

Chapter 19

"HOW ARE YOU ENJOYING YOUR stay in New York City?" Ross's former bishop, Neil Daynes, asked Natalie as they sat at a booth in Levin's Deli. Ross had been stuck in a lengthy meeting since early that morning, so Neil and his wife, Janis, had taken on the roles of Natalie's host and tour guide. Ross was hoping he would be able to meet them for lunch, but they'd received no word from him yet.

Natalie picked up a huge, crispy fry and nibbled thoughtfully. "It has been beyond all of my expectations. But then, my biggest adventure up until now was Disneyland, when the kids were small. It may be the happiest place on earth, but New York definitely creates its own kind of magic."

Neil smiled at Natalie, then passed Janis the ketchup though she hadn't asked for it.

Janis murmured, "Thanks, honey," and squirted a huge puddle of it on the edge of her plate. When Natalie raised her eyebrows, Janis just smiled. "I know. Ross teases us all the time about our 'EMP,' as he calls it. Extra marital perception. He says we've been married so long we anticipate what the other is about to say or what they want."

Neil gave Janis an affection pat on the arm. "It does seem to happen pretty often."

Janis leaned conspiratorially toward Natalie over the table. "I just think that after so many years together, Neil doesn't have any more original thoughts left in that brain of his that I don't know."

"And I've heard everything in hers at least twenty times by now, as fast as she talks." He chuckled at her squawk of outrage and threw an arm over her shoulders for a quick, tight hug. She was soon chuckling right along with him.

Natalie smiled at them and felt a twinge of envy. It seemed she'd spent a lifetime trying to read Wade's thoughts, trying to anticipate what would make him happy, but she'd never succeeded. She would love to have that kind of emotional closeness with someone, with Ross, but didn't dare think about it. She still couldn't believe she was here, with him, in the first place.

The last two days had been a dream. Her first day in town he'd arranged for an afternoon off work and taken her to Liberty and Ellis Islands, and they'd gone to a show on Broadway that evening. The next day he'd given her free rein at the Metropolitan Museum of Art. There, she'd wandered joyfully, absorbing the passion of the paintings, the colors, the shapes, the genius of each work. He'd stood by her side, asking probing questions, pointing out observations. Walking through all of that artwork with Ross had been enlightening in regard to both the artwork and her relationship with Ross. Everything had clicked.

They'd filled their evenings with quiet conversations and soft kisses. She was happier than she remembered being in years.

Ross's meeting with the German company that morning would wrap up his obligations to them this week, he'd told her. The New Year's Eve party was that evening, and Natalie was fighting down the butterflies in her stomach. She couldn't decide if she was more excited or frightened by the prospect of being on Ross's arm and meeting his colleagues. Wearing the gorgeous dress Jackie had sent with her and seeing Ross in a tux was like living out a Cinderella fantasy. Facing his coworkers and clients and hoping she didn't trip over her feet or her tongue, however, was giving her a bad case of nerves. She made an attempt to eat another french fry.

"So how did you and Ross meet?" Janis asked before taking a bite of her club sandwich.

"It was nothing, really. I was substituting for his regular housekeeper when her husband became ill."

"That isn't the way I heard it," Neil interjected, shooting her a sly look.

"Oh? Why didn't you tell me about this?" Janis gave Neil a glare that Natalie herself used on Emma and Callie frequently. It usually sent them running for cover.

"Now, Jannie, you know old bishop habits die hard. When Ross told me, I wasn't sure if it was in confidence, and I erred on the side of caution. That's all. But now that we all know each other so well, I think Natalie here will share it with us herself, won't you, Natalie?" He hid a grin behind the rim of his water glass.

He may be a former bishop, Natalie thought, *but he acts more like a sly old dog*. Over the last couple of days, she'd found she liked him and Janis immensely. "Well, if you must know, he caught me studying for a college exam at his house."

Neil snorted. "There's more to the story than that."

Natalie looked sheepishly at Janis. "Okay, okay, I confess. I *was* studying for a college exam," she said, "but it just happened to be for my tap-dancing class."

Neil roared and slapped a hand on the table. "Can you *believe* it? Jannie, I swear I busted a gut when Ross told me. He'd flown home on the red eye, with food poisoning of all things, and was dead to the world. Next thing he knows, a gang war sounds like it's taking place in his kitchen."

"He wasn't very happy that day, that's for sure," Natalie said.

"I'd have given anything to be a fly on the wall." Neil grabbed Janis's napkin off her lap and wiped his eyes.

"Thankfully, we've gotten past the strangeness of our first introduction. We're good friends now, I think."

Neil's countenance immediately sobered. "Natalie, you may not realize this, but you have wrought a miracle on that man. And I suspect—no, I *know*—Ross considers you a lot more than just a friend."

Natalie hoped but didn't *know* if what Neil said was true. She only knew she loved Ross, despite her constant warnings to herself. Buck's rejection had been painful; Wade had made her doubt everything she believed about herself. And Ross, in contrast, had given her confidence, valued her intelligence, and encouraged her art. Because he had given her so much, she knew that if—when—he moved on and found the woman who was his real match, it would truly break her heart, but she would be a better person and grateful to him always. "I think he is the one who has wrought the miracle. Not the other way around."

"I suspect it's just like you to say something like that." Neil smiled fondly at her. "The more I've gotten to know you, the more I see that I like." He glanced at his watch and grimaced. "I've got to head back to the office." He tossed his napkin on the table and leaned over to kiss Janis. "I'll be leaving you two lovely ladies to do those mysterious things women do before their hot New Year's Eve dates."

Janis snorted. "As if a game night with the kids is a hot date."

He smiled affectionately at his wife, and once again, Natalie felt that tug of envy. "It isn't exactly the games with the kids I'm thinking about, honey." He kissed Janis again and winked at Natalie. "It's been a pleasure getting to know you, Natalie. I hope we get to see you again before you head back to Salt Lake."

Natalie watched him stride out of the deli. She turned her attention to Janis. "You two have such a great marriage. I always wanted something like what you have. I worked hard enough at it, but . . ." She took a sip of her drink to wet her suddenly dry throat.

"I have learned over the years that marriage involves the love and dedication of two people," Janis said. "I know I'm blessed having Neil for my husband. We've had rough patches, don't get me wrong." Her eyes twinkled a little. "But somehow, we've been able to use those patches to make our relationship stronger.

"Marriage—love, for that matter—is a two-edged sword. If handled with care and intelligence, it can be a source of strength and power. If neglected, it becomes dull and ineffective. If handled poorly, it becomes dangerous and leaves mortal wounds. Neil and I decided long ago that we would do whatever it took to keep our marriage—our sword—sharp and strong."

Natalie knew that what Janis had said was true; she'd tried valiantly— but on her own, in both marriages. "You also have to choose the right partner to help you forge the best sword you can. A weak sword can be sharpened and polished to look strong to those on the outside, but it will still buckle and break in a real battle. And a sword cared for by only one of the partners creates imbalance and adds to its weakness."

"Is that what happened to you? Do you think you chose unwisely?"

"The first time, definitely. I was too young to see beyond my feelings for the person I was willing to give them to. The second time—"

"You've been married *twice*?"

Natalie always hated this part. Marriage and its permanence was such a vital, all-important subject. Having two failed marriages left her feeling like an eternal waste of time for a man. Who could possibly want to deal with the baggage left over from two previous husbands? Besides that, it tended to make others think she was cavalier about commitment, that she didn't take it seriously, or bailed when the going got tough. Explaining was useless; it sounded apologetic and weak. Only she really knew how dedicated she'd been to making each marriage work. Only she knew how the pain of each failure had devastated her. "Yes, I have." She spoke quietly, expecting to see a shift in Janis's eyes, a passing of judgment.

Instead, her eyes were filled with compassion. "You've dealt with a lot, haven't you? I'm so sorry about that. Perhaps that's why things seem to be working out so well with Ross."

Natalie's heart skipped a beat. "What makes you say that?"

Janis shook her head and smiled sagely. "Natalie, what do you know about Ross? About his past, I mean."

"Not much. I've met his family; I know he lost his father last year. We talk about a lot of things, just not the past. He's fairly private." Suddenly worried about Ross, she leaned forward in her seat. "Why? What about him?"

"We've known Ross for more than a dozen years. Neil had just been called to be the bishop of the singles ward, and we met Ross there, at church. He was in law school at Columbia at the time and was in our home a lot. I'll never forget one weekend when I had the flu—"

She paused and smiled at the waitress as she left the check, then continued. "It wasn't just me; the baby had it too. Neil had stayed up a couple of nights straight taking care of little Matt and doctoring me, and he was exhausted. Ross came over one evening and watched our sick baby so Neil could get some sleep. He was great."

Natalie thought back to Dorothy's birthday party and a gallant Uncle Ross dancing with Regan, the little girl's feet planted on Ross's, matching him step for step. "He has a big heart."

"He does. But for more than a decade, that big heart has been locked away."

Natalie's already nervous stomach tensed even more. She remembered Ross telling her that he'd proposed to someone named Liz and that she'd turned him down. She wondered if that was what Janis was referring to. "Why are you telling me this?" Natalie asked.

"Because you need to know. For the past eleven years, we've watched him throw himself aggressively into his work like he was obsessed. He has rejected every woman he's met, has stood aloof, and has passed cynical judgment over everyone and everything he's encountered. He's gone through the motions and done what was expected."

A light went on in Natalie's mind. "The list," she whispered.

"List?"

"There's a list, a set of requirements for his perfect woman. I heard someone talking about it at Dorothy's birthday party. How he had a checklist, and Susan was furious with him because of it."

"I can just imagine his requirements, especially if their existence has anything to do with his sister Suzie," Janis said. "He's mentioned before that his family, especially Suzie, has been overzealous in the matchmaking department."

"It's an impressive list, from what I was able to hear." Natalie gave Janis the details. "But Ross is pretty impressive himself. He deserves the very best." Natalie took a deep breath and let it out slowly. "This all goes back to the girl he proposed to, doesn't it? Liz somebody."

"Liz Turner. So Ross has told you about her, then?"

"Only that they were in law school together, that he asked her to marry him and she said no."

Janis nodded. "He was smitten. More than that, he really thought she was the one. You have to understand Ross back then. He always succeeded. Whatever he set out to do, he accomplished. He met Liz and just knew, with the confidence of someone who is never wrong, that she was right for him. They were a beautiful couple, the perfect couple."

"The perfect couple," Natalie echoed.

"Yes. Ross asked the missionaries to teach her. And when she seemed genuinely interested in the Church—she'd even set a baptismal date—everything seemed to be falling perfectly into place.

"He didn't call us for a few days after he was supposed to have proposed. But I knew he was busy with school, so I wasn't the least bit worried. I figured he'd call when he could.

"But when he did finally call, he didn't say anything to me on the phone, just asked me to put Neil on the line." Janis was losing her battle to hold back her emotions. Her eyes were brimming.

Natalie just waited; she could barely move a muscle. She knew how it felt to suffer through rejection; imagining Ross in so much pain was breaking her heart.

"Neil wouldn't tell me anything about what happened when he went to Ross's flat, being bishop and all. He would only say that what he'd found was worse than he could have imagined." Janis blotted her eyes with her napkin. "When I saw Ross for myself, it tore me apart. He said Liz had turned him down. I know guys aren't supposed to cry, but I still expected some tears, something, I guess. But there weren't any tears. Just an anguish like I'd never seen. The next time I saw Ross, he'd changed, and not for the better." She looked back at Natalie. "His eyes were blank, like he'd filed Liz away—and everybody else, for that matter.

"I think Neil and a friend of Ross's at the school are the only ones who know the full story, even to this day. I don't think his family knows. It took Ross a long time to get over Liz, and even then, he wasn't the same old Ross. But this week I've begun to see glimmers of the old Ross. And it does my heart good."

"I'm so glad," Natalie said.

"You love him, don't you?" Janis asked quietly.

Natalie looked at her. She knew her feelings showed clearly in her face. She nodded, a small movement, nothing more. Just acknowledging it that much to anyone was terrifying. "I'm afraid I fall way short though. It's too much to hope—"

Natalie's cell phone buzzed to let her know she'd received a text, jarring her entire system. She pulled her phone from her bag with shaking hands.

"It's from Ross. Someone named Dierdorff is apparently still nitpicking over contract details. He says to tell you thanks for taking care of me and he'll pick me up for the party at eight."

Janis patted Natalie's hand. "From what I can see, you don't fall short, and it's not too much to hope." She pulled out her debit card and slid out of the booth. "Well, my dear, if Ross isn't going to make it for lunch, we're out of here. There's a salon appointment waiting for us, and I intend to make sure you look devastatingly irresistible when Ross picks you up tonight."

* * *

It was nearly eight o'clock, and Natalie gave herself one last look in the cheval mirror. Janis and she had indulged in a spa treatment, as well as a manicure, pedicure, facial, and massage. In some respects, she felt like a new woman. She definitely looked like a different woman from the one who usually smiled back at her in the mirror.

The dress she wore was on loan from Jackie. Natalie had held her ground about having Ross pay for formal wear, and Jackie had finally relented. She'd insisted in return, however, that Natalie borrow something from her and had loaned her what, to Natalie's mind, was the perfect dress: a deep forest-green creation that sparkled and gently hugged Natalie's figure, then fell straight to the floor from her hips. Its high neckline and long, snug sleeves were elegant, and a cutout at the back of her neck hinted of smooth skin while maintaining the dress's modest allure. She'd pulled her hair up in a loose twist, and simple diamonds, again on loan from a generous Jackie, winked on her ears. Since the party was in the hotel where she was staying, she didn't have to worry about a coat.

Natalie decided to be more daring than usual with her make-up, going a little dramatic for her first big New Year's Eve. She smudged up her eyes a bit and went a little deeper on the lipstick color than her normal daily lip gloss. She was breathless with excitement and nervousness. She felt generally pleased with the overall effect; she hoped Ross would be too.

Ross. She still couldn't believe she was here, in this amazing hotel, in this magical city, waiting to attend a fairytale event with the man of her dreams. Beyond her dreams. Janis had told her she'd helped Ross heal from his heartbreak. If she could do only that much for him, if their time together only allowed her that as a way to thank him, she would be grateful.

The real miracle had been what Ross had done for *her*. He didn't treat her like she was his housekeeper, beneath his notice. He talked to her, challenged her, questioned her like an equal. Just the other day at the art museum while she had been analyzing a Vermeer oil, he had asked, "You are majoring in art, aren't you?"

"Artists don't make a living, Ross. I'm going to school so I can provide for my family."

He'd given her a look of disappointment that had surprised her. Then he'd said, "You're already providing for your family. And art isn't about making a living. It's about giving the rest of us mere mortals joy and an awareness of life and our humanity. You know that. Someone with your gift should cultivate it and share it."

She'd felt incredibly guilty and intensely pleased. No one had ever shown that kind of confidence in her artistic ability before, not since her mother. Her dad loved and supported her, but he just didn't understand its importance. Ross did. And it deepened her love for him.

He also made her feel desirable. He always reached for her hand, put his arm around her waist, touched her cheek, her hair, played with her fingers. And the kisses. Hello kisses that made her feel like he'd been bereft without her. Good-bye kisses like he needed to fill his soul before he could leave. Playful kisses that made her glow and tender kisses that melted her heart.

How could she not love this man? And tonight would be a special evening with him, one she would cherish always.

A knock on the door pulled her from her reverie, and she hurried to open it, anxious to be with him.

He exhaled sharply, and his eyes softened when he looked at her. Seeing his response made her heart beat faster.

"You take my breath away." He took her hand and just looked at her, his eyes flowing like warm honey all over her. Then he held her fingers to his lips and kissed them. She hummed with the pleasure of it. "I could just stand here and look at you for hours."

"You look wonderful yourself." What was it about a tux that made a man look like the hero of a romance novel? "I will be the envy of every woman in the ballroom tonight, because tonight, you belong to me."

The right corner of his mouth tilted upward. "Only tonight?"

"For as long as you want." It had been too much to admit to out loud, Natalie knew. She could tell by how serious he grew after the comment. But she had to tell him, in even a small way, how much she felt for him, what he meant to her.

He gently ran a finger down her cheek. "Well, gorgeous, I guess it's time to brace ourselves and go face the madding crowd."

She slipped her hand into the crook of his arm. "With you, I can face anything."

* * *

The party was well under way by the time they reached the ballroom. Natalie's senses were flooded with the brilliance of the chandeliers, the smooth sound of jazz floating over the murmur of voices, the fluid blending of exotic perfumes with the crisp masculine scent of aftershave. The perimeter of the room was forested with evergreens ablaze in white, twinkling lights. She could see clouds of silver and white balloons overhead, held at bay by netting; when the word was given at midnight, they would pour down on the throngs of partygoers with elegant whimsy.

Natalie had never seen so many beautiful gowns, so many elegant men and women. She had a sudden flashback of her early days waiting tables in Tremonton, Utah, dressed in her jeans and focused only on earning enough to keep Ryan in diapers. Trying to be pleasant enough to ensure generous tips without encouraging the ever-eager truckers who frequented there. She could never have imagined herself in such upscale surroundings, and she suddenly felt she would be more at home behind the buffet table, refilling trays like she had at Dorothy's party, than she was right at the moment. If Ross hadn't been by her side, she'd be lost.

"Ross! Good, you're here." A tall, barrel-chested man with steel-gray hair and eyes pounded Ross on the back. With Natalie's thoughts still on the birthday party, she realized she'd seen this man there. "And who do we have here?" He turned to Natalie in greeting. "Monty Rogers, my dear." His brows drew together slightly, as if he were bemused.

"This is my—this is Natalie Forrester, my guest this evening." Natalie briefly wondered what he'd been planning to say. *This is my housekeeper?* "Natalie, may I introduce LaMonte Rogers, one of the founding partners of the firm."

"Charmed." He took her hand in an old-fashioned gesture and gently pressed his lips to it.

"Thank you. I'm thrilled to be here."

"I have a pretty good recall of faces, and I have to say, you look familiar. Have we met?"

She glanced at Ross, who gave a slight shake of his head but was smiling reassuringly. Was Ross ashamed to be with her, or was he just eliminating awkward details that weren't necessary to explain? She *had* seen Monty Rogers at the birthday party but hadn't actually met him. "No, sir, we haven't had the pleasure. I'm certain I would remember being introduced to someone as engaging as you."

He grinned, looked her over thoroughly one more time with what Natalie recognized as the eye of a connoisseur, and slapped Ross on the back a second time. "She's quite a find, Ross. I wouldn't let her out of my sight this evening, if I were you. Too many disreputable types lurking about. Me included."

"Don't worry," Ross said as he put a protective arm around Natalie's waist. "I intend to be vigilant."

They made their way to the bar, where Ross ordered each of them a club soda. Afterward, they made the rounds as he introduced her to associates, clients, and the formidable Friedrich Dierdorff, who defied Natalie's mental image of him. He was short and lean, fastidious, and formally polite to her, bowing slightly and crisply when they met.

"He's very nice," Natalie whispered as she and Ross made their way through the crowd to the dance floor.

"To a beautiful woman like you, perhaps, especially on a festive occasion. Trust me; he is tenacious when there is something he wants."

Ross calling her beautiful warmed her; the casual way he'd just thrown it into the conversation, as if her being considered beautiful was a given, stunned her.

The band was playing a waltz, and Ross placed one hand in hers; his other hand closed around her waist. They whirled as Ross held her close, and Natalie was breathless. His eyes looked at her so warmly, so intently, and Natalie found herself trapped by them—wishing, hoping that it was possible he might love her even a little. The next dance was slow, and he drew her in against him, resting his face gently on top of her head. Natalie leaned her cheek against his shoulder and breathed in his warm male essence, a blend of spice and soap and strength. The comfortable feel of it, the rightness, lulled her into a state of bliss. Her fingers crept up to play with the hair above his collar.

"Ross, darling," a sultry female voice purred behind her. "Our little German friend is asking for you."

Natalie pulled herself from her reverie and saw the woman from the birthday party, the one who'd made certain Natalie knew she was hired help and nothing more. Recognition dawned on the woman's face when she saw Natalie too.

"Well, look who must have found a fairy godmother! Away from the ashes and at the ball with the prince, it appears."

Natalie smiled as politely as she could. She could tell Ross wasn't pleased. She hoped it was because of this woman's poor manners and not embarrassment at being discovered he was here with the scullery maid. His face was rigid. "Gina, this is my friend and *guest*, Natalie Forrester. Natalie, Gina Rogers. Monty's daughter—and an associate at the firm."

With formalities out of the way, Gina said, "Friedrich is waiting for you in the hotel lounge, darling. He thought it was too noisy in here to talk business." She smirked. "It's New Year's Eve, and he wants to do business. Thankfully, I convinced him he could handle matters sufficiently with just you." She ran a bloodred fingernail down the sleeve of his tuxedo. "I told him I was otherwise occupied."

Ross sent Natalie a concerned glance. She laid her hand on his arm. "I'll be fine. This is a good opportunity for me to powder my nose anyway."

He looked hesitant and glanced at his watch. "It's eleven thirty. Save midnight for me." He looked longingly at her lips. "Promise?" he added.

"Promise," Natalie whispered as she watched Ross stride off toward the exit.

She heard a soft laugh behind her and turned. Gina was looking down her nose at her. "Look at you. Aren't you *sweet*? Lovesick over our little Ross. Saint Ross the Divine. Do you honestly think you're the first woman to set her sights on him? And trust me on this, these are women who have a lot more to offer him than you do—unless he's such a neat freak that the idea of having a little live-in tub scrubber appeals to him in some twisted way." She chuckled at her own joke.

Patting Natalie on the arm, making her feel like a child, Gina continued, sarcasm dripping from her tongue like acid. "Oh, I think I've hurt your feelings. I didn't mean to. I mean, it's certainly possible that the Ross I've known for the last several years has changed his colors. He very well may have suddenly decided he'd rather saddle himself with a woman who wipes up spills and collects bar tips rather than one with a pedigree and accomplishments that naturally complement him." She swallowed the rest of her champagne and then, to make a point, handed the empty flute to Natalie and whispered, "But I really don't think so."

Natalie stared at the empty glass in her hand. Gina's deep red lipstick was a violent smear along the rim, sneering back at her. Part of her was angry at this pretentious woman who didn't know anything about her and had already passed judgment. Gina didn't know how much Ross had done for her; frankly, it didn't sound like she knew Ross very well at all. But she *had* worked with him for years, so it was possible she had a knowledge of his past relationships. Natalie honestly didn't know if he'd had any women in his life, other than Liz. Janis had said he'd become a different man, jaded and cynical. It didn't preclude him from seeing people, just changed how he responded to them. It had been more than a decade, after all. It was hard to imagine he'd not seen any women socially during such a long period of time.

The Ross she'd initially met had been like that man—aloof and wary. The new Ross, with his sharp edges of wariness smoothed away, had given her confidence in her talents and intelligence. Had made her feel worthy.

But Gina was also right on one level, and Natalie began to feel pangs of despair. Ross was the most amazing man she'd ever met, a man she never could have imagined existed. When she'd idolized brash, arrogant Buck or fallen for Wade's initial charm, she'd never dreamed of someone like Ross. Her youthful experiences hadn't prepared her enough to conceive of someone like him.

He was the epitome of intelligence and success. He was strikingly handsome and carried himself with a confidence that only came from deep within. A man like Ross deserved a woman who was like him in all those ways.

She knew he cared for her. He'd invited her to New York, shown her the sights, and introduced her to his friends. He wouldn't have done that if he hadn't had some feelings for her, she was sure. But he'd never told her he loved her. Of course, she hadn't ever told him those exact words either.

"I will be the envy of every woman in the ballroom tonight, because tonight you belong to me," she'd said to him.

"Only tonight?"

"For as long as you want."

He simply had to know how she felt. He had to know she loved him with all her heart.

A quick glance at the large clock hung especially to count down to the new year showed there were only a few minutes left before midnight, and still, Ross was nowhere to be seen. She discarded Gina's champagne flute and her own warm soda and made her way carefully through the crowds toward the exit doors she'd seen Ross go through earlier. She'd promised midnight to him, and she would do what she could to keep that promise. For Ross and for herself.

She was nearly through the tangle of the increasingly celebratory crowd when she saw the doors open and Ross walk through. Ross looked rigid, his jaw set. Natalie felt an urge to go to him and put her arms around him, smooth the wrinkle from his forehead and tease the sparkle back into his eye. She knew the exact moment when he saw her. The corners of his mouth lifted, and his eyes began to warm. And then his eyes broke contact with hers, focused on someone behind her, and widened in shock.

"Hello, Ross." A quiet female voice spoke behind Natalie, and Natalie turned sharply.

Behind her, to the left, was a dazzling woman, tall and elegant in a shimmering gold dress the exact color of her hair. She looked as if she had descended from Mount Olympus, as regal and perfect as she seemed in every way. The goddess smiled slightly, a look of gentle affection warming her rich coffee-colored eyes. What else did Natalie see in those eyes? Regret?

She felt a sharp stab in her stomach. The women she'd seen at Dorothy's party, the woman she'd met at Ross's house, that sultry witch Gina Rogers, had been intimidating. Natalie realized now that they were nothing. This woman, this goddess, was the real threat. Natalie knew who she was the instant she watched Ross compose himself to take care of the formalities.

"Liz! What a surprise." He smiled woodenly at Natalie. "Natalie, may I introduce Liz—Elizabeth . . . Bancroft. Liz this is Natalie Forrester. She's . . ." Natalie inwardly winced at his pause, realizing full well he struggled to label her in front of the woman who'd broken his heart. "She's a . . . friend . . . of mine."

Natalie forced an overbright smile on her face and took Elizabeth Bancroft's outstretched hand. Natalie briefly felt the urge to curtsey and fought through it and her shallow breathing to shake hands and collect herself. Liz held Natalie's hand gently but firmly and looked her straight in the eye. Natalie got the sense she was being thoroughly probed.

"It's a pleasure to meet any friend of Ross's."

Natalie could hear the education and elegance in the cultured tones of Liz's voice.

Liz released Natalie's hand and turned back to Ross. Her affection was intensely apparent to Natalie, her face soft with it, her eyes gleaming. Something in the back of Natalie's mind warned her not to look at Ross, but how could she not? She turned to him and immediately regretted it. His face was like stone, his color ashen. A muscle twitched in his jaw. But it was his eyes that were her undoing. The shock, the intensity of the emotion she could see there sent her heart from its throbbing place in her throat to the floor. He still loved this woman. He had to.

How could he not still love someone as beautiful, as perfect as this Elizabeth Bancroft seemed to be?

Natalie watched Ross collect himself. He blinked a few times and forced the corners of his mouth into a semblance of a smile. "How long have you been in New York, Liz?"

Natalie swallowed hard and looked away briefly, unsure what to do. She noticed the New Year's clock. It was only a couple of minutes to midnight.

"I've only been here a few weeks," the golden goddess said. "The firm opened an office here in town, and I relocated." She paused for a few moments and straightened her back. "Clay and I are divorced. It seems you were right all those long years ago, Ross." She smiled ruefully, shaking her head. "You were even right about becoming Mormon. I was baptized a few years ago. It's what got me through all of this."

Natalie could sense Ross's growing agitation. She also started to notice the crowd getting noisier. Suddenly, they all shouted, "Ten! Nine! Eight . . ."

What was she to do? Well, she couldn't really *do* anything. She wouldn't embarrass Ross by making a scene; she had no concept of how to stop her own internal bleeding with social grace. She would simply have to follow Ross's cues.

The crowd's jubilant cheering continued. "Four! Three!" Natalie held her breath and considered closing her eyes against what she was sure was about to happen. "Two! One! Happy New Year!" The noisemakers squealed, the massive outlay of balloons in the ceiling started their ethereal descent. Confetti rocketed through the air. The band played a sugary version of "Auld Lang Syne."

And then, just as she'd feared, the worst happened. Ross leaned toward her, his face a mask, and gave her a brief kiss on the cheek. "Happy New Year," he said softly. Then, before Natalie could find the breath to respond, he turned to Liz and kissed her cheek as well. "Happy New Year, Liz."

Twin brotherly kisses on the cheek. All of the ardor she'd seen in him earlier was gone. And why shouldn't it be? Here was his ideal woman, the woman who matched his wish list to the letter. She recalled what the women had gossiped about at Dorothy's party. *"College grad, beauty queen, professional, a financial success. The whole package. He's looking for the perfect woman. You'd have to put Mother Teresa, Oprah, and Eleanor Roosevelt in a blender, along with a Victoria's Secret model, to get the woman you're talking about."*

The perfect woman existed right here in the form of Elizabeth Bancroft. And because Ross hadn't held Natalie's divorces against *her*, he definitely wouldn't hold Liz's against her. Even the final barrier had been dealt with, the last hurdle Neil had mentioned.

Liz had joined the Church.

Natalie could feel herself shutting down. She'd been a single teenage mother and had faced as best she could the disappointments and failures in her marriage to Wade. She was well versed with rejection and pain.

But this was killing her.

It took everything she had to smile serenely at Ross and Liz. She hoped she got enough of the smile into her eyes to make what she was going to say next convincing. She laid her hand gently on Ross's arm and then pulled it off as though she'd been burned. "Ross, I can tell you two have a lot of catching up to do. And I promised the girls I'd check in, tell them all about New Year's in New York. If you'll excuse me, I'm going back to my room now."

She saw Ross's eyes clear and his brows furrow. "Natalie—"

"Please!" She made a point of looking at her watch; in a subtle way, it drove the point home better than looking at the New Year's clock. "You know what worriers the girls are." She was afraid if she looked at him even a moment longer she would break down. She turned quickly to Liz. "It was so good to meet you. Now, if you'll both please excuse me."

"I'll walk you to your room."

But if he did, she would fall apart, right there in front of him. She wouldn't do that to him or to herself. She didn't think she'd survive if she did. "It's just a little elevator ride, Ross. I'll be fine. Please." She glanced again at the golden goddess, Ross's ideal woman, but didn't dare look at Ross. "Good night."

Natalie turned and walked as swiftly as she dared to the exit. She knew if she moved too quickly, Ross would sense her upset, and she didn't want to upset him in return. This was his opportunity to get his perfect woman—the woman he'd wanted for more than a decade. The best thing she could do, for both of them, was accept the inevitable and get out of his way.

New Year's revelers swarmed the lobby, locked in drunken embraces. Shouts and giggles flayed her senses. The elevator ride to her floor was long and depressing. A middle-aged man in a tropical print shirt grinned lewdly at her and squeezed next to her in the corner when more partygoers crowded in at the fourteenth floor. When the elevator finally reached her floor, she gritted her teeth and nudged him enough to slip past. She didn't want to think about the pat on her backside she felt as she made her escape.

She fumbled with her room key, finally getting it inserted the correct way. Taking a moment to steady herself, she pushed away from the door and moved to sit on the edge of the bed. What was she to do? Ross had invited her on this trip and had paid her way. She couldn't just leave, although that was what she wanted to do. She didn't think she could bear to face him when he told her he needed to consider getting back with Liz.

Restless, she stood up and paced, sat, and then paced some more. She'd told Ross she'd promised the girls a call. It wasn't the truth; she felt horrible about lying, but she'd really just sought a plausible, polite way to get away. And yet, what mother didn't need to talk to her children? Especially when it seemed they were the only people in the world who loved her.

She needed to hear their voices. Her children had given her a reason to exist for years. The only reason, many times. She desperately needed to talk to her girls right now.

She picked up her cell phone from the top of the hotel dresser and noticed she had a couple of voice-mail messages. A quick look revealed that the first message was from Callie. The second was from Wade. That in and of itself was odd.

A sense of foreboding settled grim and gray on top of her bleak mood. Bracing herself, she listened to the first message. A hysterical Callie was begging her to pick up the phone. Natalie could barely discern the words through Callie's sobs and tears. What could possibly have happened?

She went on to the next message, the one from Wade. After Callie's hysterics, she braced herself for the worst. Wade's voice growled into her ear. "Nat, where are you? Pick up that phone and call me *now!*"

She did, with shaking fingers. He immediately picked up. "Wade, it's Natalie. Tell me what's going on."

"I'll tell you what's going on. Your daughter has gone and gotten herself hauled off to jail! I'm on my way down the canyon right now, and you better be there with me when I get there."

"She's in jail? What on earth happened?"

"I don't *know* what happened! What kind of friends have you allowed her to associate with? What were you thinking?" He was practically yelling, then he muttered, "This is all I need, to have a kid who's turning into a criminal."

That was it. Natalie gripped the phone until her knuckles were white. "Emma is not a criminal. There has to be an explanation for this, a logical one. How did she get away from you anyway? You're all supposed to be at Deer Valley together."

"I don't know, I don't *know!*" Now Natalie could sense the worry, the fatherly concern beginning to override his selfish initial reactions. "She left when Sandy and I went out, just some free time for ourselves. The girls said they'd watch the little kids. Then we got the call from the cops. I still don't know much. Sandy has the other kids at the condo still; I want to meet you at the station."

"That won't be possible, Wade. I'm not in Salt Lake right now." The last of her world was crumbling apart, but she would do what she could to get to Emma's side.

"Where are you?"

"In New York." She could hear Wade's gasp of surprise, but she couldn't go into it with him, make any explanation at all. "Listen, with the holidays, I'm not sure what the airlines are going to be like, but I'll get on the first plane available. I'll call you as soon as I know my flight. And Wade . . ."

"What?"

"Emma truly wouldn't do something like this without a reason. Something else is going on. Believe me on this, and believe in her until I get there." She quietly added, surprising herself, "You've been a good father, Wade, and Em's a good girl. I'll be there as soon as I can."

Natalie ended the call and rang the front desk from the hotel phone. And then she changed out of the beautiful green gown and began to pack.

Chapter 20

IT WAS NEW YEAR'S DAY in New York. The sky arched in full blue glory over the harbor and Lady Liberty, the air bracing and sharp with icy needles. Gusts of wind tore at Ross's coat and whipped his cheeks into fiery redness. What few people he passed on the sidewalks were bundled in layers of wool, scarves wrapped around their heads and necks, only their reddened eyes visible. He wondered if their bleary state was due to the biting temperature or overindulgence from the night before. Bellhops and valets slapped their crossed arms and rubbed their hands in a feeble attempt to draw warmth. The exhaust of limousines and taxis and people puffed out the only clouds in sight.

It was a glorious day in New York.

His thumb, nearly numb from the cold, ran smoothly over the soft velvet of the small blue box in his pocket. Ross felt a sense of grave determination. The last time he'd carried a ring in his pocket his life had changed forever and not necessarily for the good. It wouldn't happen this time, not again. Life and its lumps had prepared him this time. And his life would change again today, but for the better. He had to believe it. A taxi changed lanes abruptly; the Lexus behind it laid on its horn in retaliation. In the distance, a harbor ferry blew a ghostly echo. Pulled briefly from his thoughts, he realized his destination was only one block away. He was nearly there. And he realized oddly that, despite the cold, he was sweating.

Ross was in love. And he was terrified.

His plan had seemed simple and straightforward this morning. He wanted to surprise her, like she'd surprised him. When he'd seen her last night, she'd looked so breathtakingly beautiful that he'd felt like a teenager again, awkward and speechless. She'd been a sylph, an enchantress, with a smile that had promised happiness and eyes that couldn't hide how she felt for him. He hoped she'd seen what was in his.

His happiness, his life, depended on what Natalie said to him today.

He hoped she liked the ring. He'd been tempted to pick out something huge to let her know with a show of sheer extravagance what she meant to him. Natalie was worth it. She deserved to have someone make a big fuss over her for once. Heaven only knew it had been the other way around for her for too long. On the other hand, she was also a subtle woman with a style all her own. When he'd chosen the ring, after some searching, he'd known it was the right one. He wanted it to clearly show her how special she was, how unique, how perfect.

And she was perfect.

Life was full of ironies, he thought wryly. He had thought he'd found perfection a decade before. The perfect woman, his match in every way. And in many ways, Liz *had* been his match. They'd both been ambitious, career driven, competitive. He'd known exactly what he'd wanted and what was important to him. So had Liz. She was beautiful and intelligent; she had challenged him.

Seeing Liz last night at the party had shocked him. No, shocked didn't begin to describe how he'd felt. Thunderstruck. He hadn't seen her since law school. He'd assumed she was in Boston, and even though Neil had said she might be relocating to New York, Ross hadn't expected to see her, especially last night. He'd consciously chosen not to think about her years ago. Yet, there she'd been, smiling at him, arms open in friendly welcome. She was glorious, just as he'd remembered and had suspected she always would be, even a decade later. Golden and graceful and glorious. And the only thing he'd been able to think about was Natalie and how he hoped he could restore his wits and do some damage control before she suspected anything. He was glad he hadn't ever gone into any kind of great detail about Liz with her. As it was, he was pretty sure he'd made a hash of things last night.

He'd stumbled right out the gates with the introductions. "Natalie, this is the woman I wanted to marry. Liz, I'd like you to meet the woman I plan to marry" would have been laughable and uncomfortable for everyone. As a lawyer, he thought wryly, maybe he should have pled the poor introduction off as temporary insanity. Introducing Natalie as his girlfriend sounded juvenile; calling her an acquaintance was too aloof. On impulse, he'd opted to play it safe. So he'd referred to Natalie as his friend, hoping it was an affectionate middle ground, but he'd watched some of the light fade from her eyes.

There had been something else in her eyes as well—a sense of recognition without being told that Liz was the woman from his past. That had alarmed him. He'd been about to clarify things when she'd made her apologies and left. He had known they were merely excuses. There was no way she had planned to call her girls on New Year's Eve, not when she'd given him such a smiling promise for midnight earlier in the evening. Running into Liz had thrown her just as much as it had thrown him. So he'd allowed Natalie to go, knowing he'd owe her a full explanation later. But at the very least, it had given him time to talk to Liz.

And in doing so, he'd found closure.

He and Liz had found a quiet corner and had talked into the wee hours. It had been a satisfying conversation on many levels. He had realized he'd not been far off the mark when he'd set his sights on Elizabeth Turner Bancroft. He respected her devotion to making her marriage work and her coolheaded acceptance when it had eventually fallen apart.

Liz had recognized that Natalie was more than a friend and had asked Ross about her. While he'd been willing to tell her about Natalie's amazing artistic abilities, her wit, and her gentle nature, he hadn't wanted to share his deeper emotions for Natalie with Liz. He'd suspected she'd sensed it anyway; they'd been close enough when they'd been together for her to read him; even though it was a decade later, she would still have understood how his mind worked. He had been willing to let Liz suspect his feelings for Natalie, but he hadn't been willing to share them with her. Not when he hadn't even shared them with Natalie herself yet.

He felt as if some nagging ghost had finally been laid to rest to haunt him no more. What haunted him now was Natalie's quiet departure, the smile she'd given him that didn't reach her eyes and wavered a little at the edges. When he'd knocked on her hotel room door after saying a final good-bye to Liz, Natalie hadn't answered. He hadn't wanted to disturb her sleep, so he'd gone home to his brownstone apartment.

He felt like a coward. He wanted to walk straight past the hotel and head back to his brownstone. It was a brilliant New Year's Day in New York, a day of goals, resolutions, hopes for the future. Verdicts from juries and rulings from Supreme Court judges didn't hold a candle to what this petite blonde woman with emerald eyes had the power to do to him today. And whereas he'd been full of confidence when he'd approached Liz a decade before, he was afraid this time that it wasn't a done deal yet.

Ross entered the lobby and nodded a greeting to the bell captain. As he made his way to the elevators, he strategized for the hundredth time. He would tell her how wonderful the past months had been with her. He would tell her he wanted to stay by her side and be her partner, her love forever. He hoped her brilliant eyes would fill with tears of joy and that her single dimple would emerge when she smiled at him in response. He would pull her into his arms and kiss that soft, sweet, smiling mouth. He would tell her how proud he was of her, how her art moved him, how her quirky intelligence challenged him, how she'd reminded him how much joy there was in just living, and how he wanted to do that living with her at his side.

The ding of the elevator jarred him from his thoughts and announced his arrival at her hotel floor. The door to her room loomed threateningly. Taking a deep breath, he knocked. His hand trembled. He clenched his teeth and shook his head to clear it. He, Ross McConnell, fast-tracking his way to partner, fearless before peers, judges, and CEOs, was shaking like an untried boy. Simply because he would be asking a petite blonde, whom he'd met cleaning his house, to be his wife.

He swallowed hard and ran a hand over his face.

The door opened a crack, and he could hear a vacuum cleaner droning. Nudging it open a little farther, he saw that housekeeping was making its appointed rounds. It seemed a little early for that, considering it was New Year's Day and the majority of the city, certainly the bulk of the hotel's guests, were still undoubtedly comatose from the night's revelry.

He walked in and tapped the maid on the shoulder.

She shrieked and crossed herself religiously several times before regaining her composure.

Glancing around briefly, he said, "I'm looking for the woman staying here."

Patting her chest and breathing deeply, the maid managed to say, "No, señor, is checked out from room. Sorry."

Ross refused to believe what he could already see for himself. He walked past the maid to the bedroom and then checked the bathroom. It couldn't be true. No luggage, no clothing, no toiletries, no Natalie. She was gone, and without a word.

His hand balled tightly around the small velvet box in his pocket. An ominous sense of déjà vu crept over him while a thick coldness seeped into his bones. He thought about her, this woman who'd found the way to break down the barriers and unlock his heart. This woman who had made him willing to risk, made him willing to live.

Gone, just like that. He couldn't draw in a breath.

Ross turned and walked out of the room. He didn't look back, could barely think as he rode the elevator back to the lobby. Outside, the drone of traffic beat at his frayed senses. Rogue gulls screamed at him accusingly. History was repeating itself, only this time the woman had simply fled.

New York was cursed.

Chapter 21

THE MINUTE THE FLIGHT ATTENDANT announced that the passengers could begin to disembark, Natalie had her cell phone out and on. The flight out of LaGuardia had begun at the crack of dawn; it was now past noon in Salt Lake City. There were only two messages, both from Wade. The first one was a terse question asking when her flight was scheduled to arrive. Since she had already given him that information—she knew she had—it meant he'd been so upset he hadn't paid attention. That wasn't unusual, and since Natalie herself was upset, it was a sure bet that Wade's emotions were off the charts. The second message was from a slightly calmer Wade, telling her that he had Emmaline, that they were at his home, and she was to go directly there when she arrived in Salt Lake City.

There was not a message from Ross. And that summed up her worst expectations.

She'd been so upset about Emma when she'd spoken to Wade, so focused on arranging for a flight home, that she'd had to compartmentalize the fact that Ross was still in the hotel picking up where he'd left off eleven years ago with his perfect woman. She hoped she'd appeared calm and gracious when she'd left the ballroom; the situation had jarred her, leaving her more numb than anything.

She'd dealt with it by concentrating on the task at hand: booking the flight, packing, arranging for transportation to the airport. She'd called Ross's cell phone, but it had gone straight to voice mail, so she'd actually spent a few minutes looking around the ballroom for him. When she hadn't been able to locate him, she'd written a note and given it to the concierge. He'd promised to locate Mr. McConnell when he had an opportunity, and Natalie had been resigned to leave it at that.

During the ride to LaGuardia, she'd decided to try calling Ross again. She wouldn't have phone service until she arrived in Salt Lake, and although she'd been certain he was preoccupied with matters other than her, she owed him for the few days of heaven she'd had with him in New York City. She owed him for showing her there were men of honor in the world and that she deserved not to settle for less than she was.

And he deserved not to settle for less than he was. He deserved someone as accomplished as he, and she hoped he would be happy in his life with Liz. She hoped her own heart stopped bleeding at some point.

Dashing away tears, she'd tried his number again during the cab ride to the airport—and had been relieved when he hadn't picked up so she could leave a voice mail this time. She'd thought out in her mind exactly what she needed to say; she'd written basically the same thing in the note. She'd had to choose the words carefully so he wouldn't be alarmed or offended at her hurried departure. An urgent family matter had arisen, and she'd had to leave abruptly. She'd had a wonderful time in New York—*every minute with you*, she'd wanted to say—and thank you. She would remember these days with fondness.

She'd been afraid she would say too much, pour out too many of her feelings to him, which wouldn't have been fair to either Ross or Liz. Natalie hoped she'd struck a delicate balance between saying too little and too much.

Now she needed to put her heartbreak away and focus on the crisis ahead. She didn't know why Emma had been taken to police headquarters. She wasn't sure what Wade's emotional state was going to be, but she was confident that, somehow, she would be to blame. She had too many years of experience with him to think otherwise.

Wade answered the door, looking both smug and grim, if that were possible. Sandy sat primly in the living room, her two young children from her first marriage on the floor at her feet working on a puzzle. Callie and Emma sat on the sofa, side by side, stricken, Callie's face swollen and tear blotched, Emma's ghost white. The pulsing knot in Natalie's stomach turned to lead. Wordlessly, Wade pointed to a vacant chair, inviting Natalie to sit. She did and waited for him to take the lead. She didn't have to wait long.

"It seems your daughter keeps regular company with drug users. Were you aware of this?" he asked accusingly.

Natalie looked at Emma with shock. "Who—" she started to ask.

"Mom, I can explain! It isn't what you think—"

"Shut up!" Wade snapped, then turned his attention back to Natalie. "She deliberately lied, snuck out of the condo, and joined these so-called 'friends' at a party where illegal drugs and alcohol and who knows what else were in abundance. The neighbors were so tired of the continual nuisance, they called the police."

"Oh, Emma," Natalie moaned in dismay. "Who?"

"It's Kate's boyfriend, Mom. I just went there to talk her into leaving with me. I swear."

"So you say." Wade dragged both hands through his hair and stood so his full authority could be felt. Natalie took a deep breath and straightened as if bracing for a blow. "The bottom line, Natalie, is this: it's obvious that the time spent in her mother's care has not been beneficial to Emma. I intend to remedy that. In addition, the police released Emmaline into her father's custody. *My* custody. I plan to make sure nothing like this ever happens again. Therefore, until you are officially notified by my attorney, I am keeping both girls with me. Our current custody arrangement is void."

Natalie reeled from his words. Both girls were sobbing. She rose to her feet, shaking with anger and dread. "She was in your care when she slipped out, not mine, Wade."

"She's done it before. She admitted it to me when I picked her up at the station."

"What?" Natalie swung around to stare at Emma. Her pinched face grew even paler, if that was possible.

"Mom! It isn't what you think—"

"I will be following you with the girls to your house, Natalie. They are to pack their clothes quickly. We're taking care of the essentials right now. We'll deal with the rest of their belongings later."

"No!" Natalie almost yelled it. Realizing nearly too late that the only way to deal with Wade was to remain rational, she took a deep breath. "Wade. Listen. I haven't even heard a complete explanation. I am not simply going to give up my legal custody without knowing why. I want to speak with Emma. Alone. You owe me that much."

Wade stared at her for a long, agonizing moment. "Sandy, get the kids out of here. Callie, out." He stalked out of the room, the others following in his wake.

Natalie sat down by Emma and took her hand in both of her own. "Em, what's going on? What happened?"

"It was New Year's Eve, and Callie and I were stuck babysitting so Dad and Sandy could go out. It was totally unfair, but whatever. And then Kate called and said she had a New Year's resolution she was going to make, but she was scared. And that made me scared, Bob. I was afraid her creep boyfriend Jeremy was going to make her do something stupid."

Natalie knew only too well that stupid teenage mistakes could follow a person for a lifetime. "Wait. Her boyfriend's name is Jeremy, right?" It couldn't be. It had to be a coincidence. "It isn't Jeremy Lisle, is it?" *Please, please say no.*

"Yeah, Jeremy Lisle, and he has an even creepier twin brother."

Natalie's squeezed her eyes shut.

"I didn't dare let Kate go to the party at his house by herself. He'd told Kate it was a party for adults and she was a baby and a waste of his time. I was afraid of what she'd do to convince him she wasn't. So I asked Callie to cover for me."

"And then what happened?" Natalie asked, even though she was afraid to hear the answer.

"Kate snuck me out of the condo, and we drove to Jeremy's house. And when we went in"—she blushed—"well, it was, you know, bad. People were drinking and smoking pot, and doing . . . other stuff. But Kate didn't want to leave until she'd at least talked to Jeremy. I called Tess, but she didn't answer, so then I called Brett."

Ross's nephew. Well, if things weren't already over with Ross, that little piece of news would certainly be the final nail in the coffin.

Emma's mascara was running all over her cheeks. Natalie searched through her purse for a Kleenex and handed it to her. "And what did Brett do?" she asked.

"He told me to get out of the house as fast as I could. He said his Uncle Ross was a lawyer and he'd warned him that cops would assume everyone was involved in whatever illegal stuff was happening at a party like that. And that he'd come and get me. But Kate wouldn't leave, and before I could get out, the cops showed up."

"Well," Natalie started, "sneaking out of the condo wasn't the right thing to do, obviously. Neither was going to the party with Kate. But I'm glad you were only trying to protect your friend."

"Of course that's what you'd say," Wade interrupted, coming back into the room. Sandy and Callie stood in the doorway and watched.

"You had no right to eavesdrop," Natalie said.

"I had every right to eavesdrop. It's my house. You're so pathetic; you'd find any excuse for Emma, no matter what she's done." In his most patronizing tone, Wade added, "It should be very simple to understand, even for you, Natalie. Emma lied, she snuck out, she was at a party where everyone in attendance knew there were illegal substances, and she was picked up along with everyone else by the cops. Considering who her main example and disciplinarian has been the last few years, I think it's obvious she needs a change of friends, a change of rules, and therefore, a change of address."

"Wade, it happened on your watch. You can't—"

"I can, and for the girls' sake, I intend to. And don't forget, it was you yourself just last night who said I was a good father. Remember?"

"You were upset. I was being supportive. I can't believe you're using my own words against me like this." Natalie paused, trying to take a deep breath. "I would never, *never* consider taking the girls from you like you are doing to me, and I will do everything in my power to get them back."

"Yes, well, we all know how pointless that effort will be."

"This isn't over by half, Wade." She looked wildly about the room. "Sandy, you're a mother. Say something! Make him see—" Sandy's gaze dropped to the floor.

Wade stood. "Enough. Grab your coats, girls. I want to get this over with."

Natalie rose numbly and opened her arms. Both girls rushed to her embrace, crying and holding on tightly. Natalie simply stood and looked over their heads, seeing nothing now. Everything she'd ever done, everything she ever did, was for her children. And now she'd lost them. She had no fight left, at least for today. She was exhausted from her ordeal in New York, from a long, sleepless night of worry, and she had no more defenses against Wade. She was beyond fatigue.

Maybe with a good night's rest she'd see things in a more optimistic light. Maybe she'd see a way of getting Wade to see reason. Maybe her heart wouldn't feel like a dead weight.

But she doubted it.

* * *

Ross had turned his cell phone off before the party, and he'd forgotten to turn it back on until he'd discovered Natalie had gone. He'd noticed there were a number of missed calls and a couple of voice mails. Now, after a long, restless night without sleep, he decided to listen to them. It had taken him some time to even be willing to do that. Ultimately, though, he had to know if she'd bothered to tell him she was leaving.

The first was from Natalie.

"Ross," her voice sounded subdued, "something urgent has come up, and I'm afraid I have to leave on the next available flight. Thank you so much for the wonderful time. I enjoyed every minute—I will think back on everything fondly. I know you'll be happy . . ." He heard her pause. "Good-bye, Ross." There was a sense of finality in that good-bye. Ross clenched his jaw. Well, he'd received a message, after all. And he'd gotten the message, all right.

The next one was from Brett. His nephew simply said, "Uncle Ross, I hope this isn't a bad time, but I need to ask you a question. What do you do if a person gets picked up by the cops, but you know the person is innocent? Do they still need a lawyer? It's not me, I have this friend . . . I just want to help her if I can."

It was an odd phone message, but since Brett had left it on New Year's Eve, Ross figured one of Brett's high school friends had gotten caught in a little bit of underage activity and the crisis had probably passed, especially now that it had been a couple of days since Brett had left the message. Brett was a decent kid to worry about his friends that way. Ross would check on it later, when he could stand the idea of talking to anybody in his family. He remembered that Brett and Natalie's daughter Emma had become friends. Chances were that Brett wouldn't ask him anything about Natalie, but if Jackie knew they'd spoken, she'd be on the phone to Ross and pestering him for information. He knew his sisters. They were relentless when it came to this sort of thing.

The idea of talking to anybody about Natalie right now made him physically ill. He had to get the gnawing cold in his gut controlled first. He looked at his watch, judged it to still be business hours in Salt Lake, and called the firm there. He told them that unforeseen circumstances made it impossible for him to return to Salt Lake for a few days. He'd be in touch.

New York City and some physical distance from Natalie Forrester suited him just fine for the time being.

Chapter 22

JANUARY WAS A MONTH OF contradictions, Natalie thought as she picked up her book. It was still so seasonally dark, but there were days when the brilliance of the daytime sky hurt her eyes. Or maybe it was just she herself who was contradictory. It was the season of new beginnings and optimistic goals, but Natalie felt that, for her, doors had been slammed shut. The New Year's goals she'd set had been hard ones. Not having her girls was a constant wound to her heart. She missed Ryan. She was so alone and so lonely she thought she would perish. Yet, when she'd looked out her window and seen the well-meaning ladies of her ward on her porch, hearts and hands laden with sympathy and homemade bread, she couldn't bring herself to even answer the door.

Apparently, a well-intentioned neighbor, observing Wade loading the girls' belongings into his car, had informed her bishop about Emma and Callie. The fact that he'd already known had been a relief. Natalie hadn't had to say a word to him when she'd gone to church on Sunday. He'd invited her to his office and had sat quietly by and had handed her a box of tissues and let her go at it while the tears had flowed.

After she'd cried off all of her make-up and the tears had finally ebbed, he'd told her she didn't need to worry about paying for Ryan's mission. It was completely funded. He wouldn't tell her who had done this and wouldn't even give her a hint. She was mystified but grateful for the blessing. She'd had few enough of those—blessings, that is—in the last week. So she was especially grateful for this one. It was the silver lining on a very dark cloud of a month so far.

She missed her girls. She ached for Ross.

She tried not to think about him or wonder how things were progressing with Liz. But at times, it seemed like she had only two choices: wonder how her girls were, or wonder how he was. And both hurt terribly.

She opened the book, a text on art in western civilization, and started reading where she'd left off the previous day. She'd dropped the class so she could put the tuition money toward attorney's fees, but she'd been reluctant to return the textbook she'd picked up before the holidays. The pictures reminded her of all the museums she'd seen in New York with Ross. Was it merely a week ago that she'd last seen him? She ran her finger down a photograph of *Winged Victory*. Ross had taught her at least one thing about herself. Her true passion was her art. Nursing, for her, would be a waste of time. When all this business with Wade was settled, she would follow her passion and see where it led her. The boutique sales were holding steady, even though Christmas was over. It wasn't enough to stop cleaning houses, but that was okay. And the additional income would also help her offset the costs she would be facing as she fought Wade for her girls. There was also the anonymous benefactor who had taken care of her son's mission, God bless him or her. Her one shred of hope. Natalie actually felt financially able to call her attorney.

She might be making monthly payments to him into the Millennium, but at least she'd be able to afford a monthly payment. She had an appointment with him for the following week. She suddenly remembered Ross's generous offer to represent her legally, how he'd confronted Wade on Christmas Day. She couldn't hold him to his offer now. It would be too painful to see him, to pretend she didn't love him. It would be unfair to both of them.

She closed the book and stood. It was growing late. She had to clean Valerie Lisle's house tomorrow, so she ought to go to bed. Mrs. Lisle herself had told Natalie that Jeremy and Justin had fallen into a bit of legal trouble on New Year's Eve. The boys were home under a form of parentally induced house arrest, so Natalie expected the messes to get worse as the boys' dispositions unraveled. She wasn't looking forward to tomorrow morning. But it was work.

She wasn't cleaning Ross's house anymore. She'd called Esther Johnson as soon as she'd flown into town and had turned that responsibility back over to her. Esther's husband was doing a lot better, and she had been more than happy to resume the duties.

She couldn't stop thinking about Ross. Was he back in Salt Lake? Had he stayed in New York so he'd be closer to Liz? He was so handsome, and Liz was so breathtaking. They would be a beautiful couple. A perfect couple.

* * *

Ross was staring out the window of his study when it became obvious to him that the incessant buzzing at his door was not going to stop. Shrugging, he walked to the door and pressed the intercom button.

"It's about time, Ross. Let me in right now, or I'll call 911 and say someone's having a heart attack." Neil's growling voice sounded irate even to Ross's indifferent ear. He pressed the button to disengage the outdoor lock and waited for the invariable hammering at the door of his flat. He didn't have to wait long to open the door to a red-faced Neil, and Ross stretched his arm out to usher him inside in an exaggerated manner.

Once inside, Neil wheeled to face him. "What's going on? We expected to hear from you after you took Natalie to the airport, remember? But no word. Nothing. You don't return our calls. Jannie has been beside herself with worry, especially after what happened the last time. She's hardly slept a wink since. Neither have I as a result," he muttered. "She's not going to let me back in the house without some sort of explanation. And frankly, I'm not about to leave without one either."

Ross just shrugged. He leaned against the doorframe with his ankles crossed, arms folded across his chest, and watched dispassionately as Neil paced the room. "Tell Jannie not to worry. I've been busy."

"Busy. He says he's been busy." He glared at Ross. "Do you take me for a fool? We knew what you were planning. I saw the ring. What happened when you talked to Natalie? What's going on?"

Ross had dealt with his old friend too long to think he would get out this conversation easily. Honesty, even in as limited quantities as possible, was the best and most efficient policy. And why not? Ross would laugh at the irony of the situation himself if it weren't for the squeezing pressure in his chest. "I never got the chance, old pal. She left. Changed her flight and flew the coop. Left a nice little phone message, saying thanks but she had to go."

"That's not right."

"No kidding, that's not right!" Ross moved away from the door and stalked over to Neil. "She makes up some cockamamie story New Year's Eve about how she needs to leave the party and call her girls. Leaves me standing there with Liz, of all people, and then—just gone."

"Liz was there?" There was something in Neil's voice that put Ross on guard.

"Yes. Floored me, I can tell you. But that shouldn't have had any bearing on Natalie's actions. She met lots of women that night. And she handled our lovely friend Gina like a pro." Still, there had been something in her eyes, something almost resigned, when she'd met Liz. He'd been so caught up in the anxiety he'd felt coming face-to-face with Liz after all these years that he'd forgotten about it. Until now.

"Um, you may need to rethink that, Ross."

Neil rubbed his face with both hands. The tension in his movements gave Ross that guarded feeling again. "What are you talking about?"

"That meeting Liz had no bearing on her actions."

Ross's uneasiness increased. "What do you mean?"

Neil cleared his throat and looked Ross squarely in the eye. "Janis and Natalie had a little chat at lunch the other day. She wanted Natalie to know how grateful we were that she'd brought you back from the dead. And you were dead, Ross." He paused. "As part of that, she told Natalie what happened with Liz all those years ago."

"Exactly what did she say happened?" Ross asked in a low voice.

"Oh, you know, how Liz seemed so perfect, how things turned out. That sort of thing."

"Great," Ross muttered. He went into the kitchen, filled a glass with water, and downed a couple of aspirins.

Neil followed him. "Ross."

"What?" He gulped down the rest of the water and immediately refilled the glass.

"She told Janis she loved you."

Ross didn't move. "What?" he whispered.

"Well, she didn't exactly *say* it; she nodded when Janis asked her point-blank."

Ross could feel his hands beginning to shake. He gripped the glass tighter.

"I'm telling you, if she went home without a word, there's a reason. I believe that. Especially after seeing the two of you together. She loves you, Ross."

Ross was quiet for a minute as he allowed this new information to settle. Neil wouldn't just say something like that. It gave him pause to think.

"Tell me about the list," Neil said.

"Hmm? What list?"

"Janis said something about a list. The perfect woman or something like that."

"Oh, that. It's nothing. Just a list I gave Susan to get her off my back. She was throwing every female she could find at me until it was getting

ridiculous. I finally had to set some ground rules. So I made tough ones."
He smiled mirthlessly. "Susan was ticked."

"What was on your list, if you don't mind my asking?"

"The usual stuff, I guess. The kind of things any guy would say if he
were describing the ideal woman. Suz was such a pain about it that I got
pretty specific with her. She needed a big deterrent."

"The usual stuff *any* guy would say. Uh-huh." Ross watched Neil
nod his head as if he'd just grasped a huge new concept. "What usual
stuff is that? I'm curious. Give me those specifics."

Ross could feel himself getting irritated. "Fine. Beautiful. That's a
no-brainer. Then intelligent."

"How did you define intelligent?"

"Well, the obvious definition was college educated. I think that
was what I said to Susan—yeah, college educated. Advanced degrees an
additional plus." His irritation made a sharp turn toward foreboding.

"And the next requirement?"

"Um, financially successful in her career . . ." His voice trailed off. In
the back of his mind, he was beginning to hear Susan's sarcastic response.
*You're looking for a beauty pageant winner who was her college valedictorian
and is now a self-made millionaire. Does pageant runner-up count? What if
she wasn't valedictorian but is a member of MENSA? What if she has two
undergraduate degrees but no postgraduate work? What if her portfolio took
a dive and she is only fabulously wealthy instead of filthy rich?* By the end,
the words were screaming through his head. He knew the answer to the
question he was about to ask, but he had to ask it anyway. The only way
Janis could have heard about it was from Natalie.

"Janis knew about the list?"

"Yeah." Neil's eyes said it all.

That stopped Ross cold. If Natalie had gotten wind of that blasted
list he'd shot at Susan, he now understood the look she'd had on her face
the minute she'd met Liz.

Natalie wasn't college educated. She wasn't fabulously wealthy. Her
career-to-date had been cleaning houses. There wasn't a thing on that list,
the way he'd worded it, that applied to her. And yet, he had discovered
that she was more than the sum of her parts. Much more.

He'd also been with her enough the last couple of months to know
how battered her opinion of herself had been. He'd worked hard to help
her find her value, see herself as he'd begun to see her. He'd watched her
carefully at the party on New Year's Eve. She'd been gracious, poised—

but under stress. He'd hoped that placing her in that environment would help her see she had the caliber to fit in with that crowd. She'd managed to be gracious to Gina, which was a challenge for anyone. But after Ross had excused himself to deal with Dierdorff, had Gina done something else to shake Natalie's confidence? He wouldn't put it past her.

He hadn't read anything additional into Natalie's reaction to Liz because he'd been thrown off by Liz's presence himself. Now, knowing that Natalie was fully aware of their past, it showed her actions in a new light. When he added her detailed knowledge of that obnoxious list he'd conjured up to get his sister off his case, he thought he knew at least part of the reason she'd left New York: she'd bowed out of the picture to make room for Ross's perfect woman.

He didn't understand her need to rush away in the middle of the night like a thief, though. He remembered the first time he'd seen her at the restaurant. How certain he'd been that she'd ditch the guy she was with but she hadn't. She'd dealt with the guy face-to-face, despite the anxiety he'd seen in her when he'd followed her to the lobby. She wasn't one to run. So why had she?

Natalie loved him. That's what Janis had told Neil. He wanted to believe it. He could see Natalie's face when she'd promised her New Year's kiss to him and how it had subtly changed when she'd seen Liz. That could mean only one thing.

"I think I need to call the airlines," Ross said.

Neil nodded and clapped him on the shoulder. "I think that's a good plan. You do that." Then, grabbing his coat, he headed out the door.

* * *

It was midafternoon when Ross arrived at his Salt Lake home, and the January sky was a bright blue bowl. Crystals of fresh snow shot the sun's rays skyward in icy brilliance, and he was nearly blinded by it.

He unlocked the garage door that led past the utility room, deactivated the security system, and dropped his suitcase heavily to the floor. The house felt different to him. He didn't have to move from his spot to know that Natalie wasn't taking care of it anymore.

The knowledge left him feeling empty. He'd half hoped he'd walk in to find wild music blaring, hear the semiautomatic staccato of her tap shoes, or smell the scent of pine and cinnamon lingering in the air. He found he was reluctant to move from his spot by the utility room and have his gut feeling confirmed.

Taking a deep breath, his mouth set in a grim line, he grabbed the suitcase and headed down the darkened hallway. As he approached the kitchen, a curious thing happened. The hall got lighter from the big windows located there. He was used to that, but there was something different this time. Colors in the light that hadn't been there before blazed all around him: tongues of orange licked up the walls, reds flashed fire. Cool blues and purples, greens, and yellows leaped to join the fray. What was causing this kaleidoscope of color in his house?

As he entered the kitchen, he found the answer. There, hung at the very top of his spacious kitchen window, was the stained-glass creation Natalie had given him at Christmas. A sun catcher, she'd called it. Even with just the midafternoon light coming through his east-facing windows, his kitchen was awash in color. It pulsed and breathed and radiated life. It radiated Natalie's essence. She must have hung it after she'd returned from New York.

He laughed and slowly turned around. The daylight enveloping him was warm in itself. But Natalie's stained glass captured the sunlight, turning its natural brightness into something more glorious. It focused it, splintered it into a million different suns, each with its own hue and glory. It engulfed him in the center of sunrise itself, with all of the color and hope the sunrise brought to each day. Her simple creation was made, he knew, of odds and ends collected along her daily path, raw materials with humble beginnings, and the end result was more than the sum of its parts.

Just like Natalie.

She had forged herself in much the same way. She'd been down a hard road, picked herself up time and time again, brushed herself off, and carried on. Carried on with a smile on her face and joy in the process. She'd crafted the pieces of her life, the odds and ends and raw materials, and had made a work of art.

Standing in his kitchen, surrounded by so many colors, a new palette emerged in Ross's mind: the zippy green of a hokey-pokey T-shirt, the sugary pink of cookie frosting, the buttery blondeness of her hair, the indigo of a midnight sky while freezing on a sled. She'd filled his life with color.

She'd simply filled his life. He couldn't remember the last time he'd laughed so much or felt so light. He suddenly couldn't figure out how he'd gone for so many years without her. And he didn't intend to continue without her. He loved her. He firmly believed—all right, if he was really honest, he just plain *hoped*—that Neil and Janis were right and that Natalie loved him.

This time he would strategize beforehand. He would chart every angle, have all of his facts in hand. As anxious as he was to see her again, he would give himself the couple of days it would take to prepare. He would plan his approach as carefully as if he were battling his most formidable legal adversary. Natalie wasn't an adversary, obviously. She was the prize. And Ross had every intention of winning.

The first step was to listen to his home phone messages to see if there was anything to learn there. He'd been right; Esther Johnson had left a message saying she was thrilled to be back on the job; her husband was doing much better. There was a message from Jackie, telling him Natalie had returned her green dress to her. She was dying to know how the trip had gone; she hadn't been able to pry anything out of Natalie other than she'd had a wonderful time. Well, Ross thought, so far he'd learned that Natalie was tying up any loose ends that dealt with him. No surprise there, really, but it was still a blow.

The last message was his sister's voice again, and her tone immediately drew his focus. "Ross, it's Jack. Maybe I should break your rule and call you on your cell. I don't know if this is important or not. It's about Brett and some problem with Emma, Natalie's daughter. They've become friends, you know. I overheard him on the phone talking about not seeing Emma since New Year's. Then he said something like, 'He's more like a prison warden than a dad.'

"Has Natalie said anything to you? Brett's been really upset ever since the holidays. When I ask him about it, he doesn't say much, only that Emma's living with her dad right now. What's going on? Any light you can shed on it would be so helpful."

Ross couldn't shed any light on the situation for Jackie, but her message had shed a great deal of light for *him*. Now Brett's cryptic message New Year's Eve made sense. Something *had* happened on New Year's that had sent Natalie rushing back home. Ross was sure of it.

He picked up his cell and called his nephew. Very quickly, Brett filled him in on Emma's frantic call from the house party—info he'd apparently felt unwilling to share with his mother—and the subsequent arrival of the police. The girls were now with their father, and Emma had been banned from all of her friends. Ross knew Natalie must be devastated, but he also knew that, despite Wade's bullying, she wouldn't take the loss of her girls lightly. She would fight, even if it meant fighting alone.

What Natalie didn't know yet was that this time she *wouldn't* be alone.

Chapter 23

NATALIE COULDN'T UNDERSTAND IT. SHE should be more nervous. Usually when she went up against Wade, she was shaking from intimidation, but she wasn't shaking this time. She wouldn't exactly say she felt calm, but she felt at peace. He had virtually barred her from her girls, with no legal grounds that she could see, not that she was an expert, but somehow she knew things were going to be okay. She was meeting with her attorney later that morning, and she was more than ready to begin the process of getting them back. She would do whatever it took, whatever the cost. What good were her personal goals and aspirations if the people she loved weren't there to share them with her and reap any benefits that might come? Without her children, her achievements would be hollow.

Wade monitored the girls like they were parolees and had confiscated their cell phones. Sandy took them to school and picked them up daily. The one time Natalie had attempted to talk to them, Wade had found out and made their lives miserable. He had left her another terse voice message telling her to stop contacting them, and a crestfallen Natalie was anxious for her attorney's input in the matter. She wasn't going to face Wade unprepared. She would plan her approach carefully since she was battling her most formidable adversary. Her girls, her very family, were the prize. And Natalie had every intention of winning.

Heaven help her. She had spent so many hours on her knees the last few weeks; she desperately hoped it would turn out right. She had to hope. The alternative was unbearable.

She'd gone through her entire wardrobe, paltry as it was, and found her most serious outfit, a gray suit she'd found a few months back on clearance at an outlet store. Feeling like she needed a little emotional firepower, she tossed on a bold silver necklace and some wrist bangles and pulled her hair up in a serious twist. Giving herself one last look in the mirror, she decided she was ready and realized she had more than an hour to wait before it was reasonable to leave. So maybe she was a little nervous after all.

She sank to her knees one last time and prayed with all her heart that she would find the strength and fortitude to endure what was sure to be a long and costly battle. She prayed that she would know what boundaries to hold, what concessions to make, what to do to keep Wade in her girls' lives in the most productive way possible. The girls needed their father. She would never ask of him what he was demanding of her right now.

Why couldn't he just be reasonable and really see what was in their best interest? Why did he insist on making her girls the bargaining chips for power over her? She prayed for wisdom and compassion and hoped desperately she wouldn't fall short there. She vowed on her knees that she'd sacrifice whatever the Lord required of her to get her girls back. She prayed that when all was said and done she would still have a home to which she could bring her girls.

It was time to count the plusses before she became too discouraged. She would still have her son and her health. Her father and stepmother loved her. She had friends like Tori and Jim. Her bishop and ward were great. It would have to be enough to start again.

Starting again sounded like so much effort. She would have to have faith that she would survive the worst-case scenario and that it wouldn't come to losing everything in the end.

Please, she prayed, *please help me. Please guide me through this; please give me the peace to cope. Please soften Wade's heart and help him realize his girls need their mother, and help him be generous in understanding that I need them just as much. Please help the large hole in my heart that is Ross to not ache so badly. Please give me the support and strength I need to face what lies ahead, to take this first step.*

Well, she thought as she got to her feet, faith was all about taking that first step. She'd taken tough steps by herself before—when Buck had left her a single mother, when she'd discovered Wade's infidelities. She knew she'd never been more alone than she was right now. Yet, as she stood and straightened her skirt, she realized she didn't feel alone anymore. So, strangely, she wasn't surprised when she heard the doorbell ring, although she had no idea, other than Tori, who would be stopping by at this time of day.

Still preoccupied with her own thoughts, she wedged two fingers between the slats of her window shades and peered out. Her heart stopped, then started racing. The strength ran out of her limbs like water. Ross was standing outside on her front porch.

She threw the deadbolt and opened the door.

Looking tall and serious and more than a little determined, Ross stood there, his hands slung deep in the pockets of his wool overcoat. There was a long, awkward moment while Natalie groped to find her voice. She was unsuccessful.

Finally, a slight curve formed at the corners of his mouth. Bemused, Natalie couldn't stop looking at it.

"Hello, Natalie. It's good to see you. I've missed you." He took in her hairdo and gray suit. "Are you going somewhere? You look wonderful, by the way."

"Appointment with my, um, lawyer." She thought once again of how a short few weeks ago—a lifetime ago it now seemed—he'd told her he'd help her with her legal matters. He had to know that was impossible now.

"Ah." His eyes dropped. "I see. Brett told me what happened with Emma. I'm so sorry. I wish you'd told me."

"I left you a voice message. I also left a note for you with the concierge. Didn't you—"

He shook his head. "No. And your voice message didn't really explain much. I was hurt, Natalie. You left. Without much of an explanation."

"Oh, Ross, I never intended to hurt you. I'm sorry. But you were busy with—and when I got the call about Em—I had to get home as fast as possible. I shouldn't have gone to New York with you in the first place—" Her voice broke despite her best efforts, the awful guilt flooding her again.

"Natalie," he said on a sigh. For a moment, Natalie caught herself wondering how her heart, so fragile at the moment, didn't simply shatter like glass. When she finally glanced up, she saw Ross looking bleakly at her. "Something like this was bound to happen with Wade and the girls. Don't take the blame for this. Don't regret New York. May I come in?" he asked quietly. "Please?"

She backed out of the way and opened the door wider so he could enter. He gestured for her to join him on the sofa in her living room. She obeyed and perched next to him as he sat. Her heart was still thumping wildly.

"We still have some unfinished business," he said.

Unfinished business. Her racing heart skidded to a halt. "Oh. I suppose
we do. Mrs. Johnson was more than happy to resume her housekeeping
arrangement with you, since our agreement was only through December."
As long as she kept talking, she didn't have to hear him actually tell her he
was terminating her employment, that he was happily reunited with the
golden Elizabeth Bancroft, and that he would be moving permanently
back to New York. "I hope that's all right with you. I assumed it was, since
you'd seemed happy with—"

He cut her off by placing his fingertips gently over her lips. "Not
that kind of business, sweetheart. Our New Year's Eve business." He
framed her face with his hands and pressed his mouth to hers. His lips
were cool, and Natalie's hands slid up to his shoulders of their own
volition as his found their way around her and drew her in closer. It
seemed like only a moment, or a heavenly forever, before he broke the
kiss and brushed her cheek with the back of his fingers. "Better late than
never, wouldn't you say?"

Natalie's brain was so fuzzy she could barely string her thoughts
together. "But I thought . . . You and she . . ."

He lifted her chin until she looked him in the eyes. "I'm supposed to be
the dark knight, remember? Ever watchful, acting incisively without fanfare,
then going quietly away. Not you." He kissed her again, lingeringly. "On
New Year's Eve, I faltered and failed you. It won't ever happen again."

"She's beautiful, Ross," Natalie couldn't bring herself to say Liz's name,
but he knew who she meant, she was sure. "She's everything you've always
wanted." She touched his cheek; it might be her final chance. "And you
deserve to be happy and have what you've always wanted. What you've
waited all these years to have." Natalie rose from the sofa and moved
restlessly across the room. "I saw her with my own eyes. She's breathtaking.
She's an attorney, smart and successful like you. You have everything in
common. College and careers—"

"But there's a problem."

"What?" He'd stopped her midsentence and thrown her off balance.
"What problem?"

Ross rose and walked toward her. "I have a list—a list of requirements
for my ideal woman."

"I know about that. I know all about—"

"Shhh, darling." He followed up with another soft kiss. "My ideal
woman is beautiful. She has a smile that warms me and eyes that brighten

my day. My ideal woman is intelligent. She is curious about the world around her and has an enthusiasm for knowledge. And she's been to the school of hard knocks and graduated with honors." He placed his hands on her shoulders and ran them down her arms, taking her hands in his. "My ideal woman is successful. She has learned to take the nuts and bolts of life and turn them into living works of joy. She turns cookie dough into parties and pumpkins into fairy tales."

"Oh, Ross." Natalie could barely breathe.

"My ideal woman," he whispered as he pulled her close, pressing his lips to her ear, "knows how to catch the sun and give it to me as fire. But most important of all, my ideal woman has to love me as much as I love her."

Natalie's eyes were brimming with tears. "Ross, do you really?"

"Really. I love you, Natalie."

"I love you, Ross. I love you so much."

"Well, that's a huge relief." He reached in his pocket and pulled out a small blue velvet box. "Then this is for you, if you'll accept it." He handed the box to her.

Natalie tried to control the shaking of her hands while she opened the box. Inside was a diamond ring, intricately sculpted, unique. It was breathtaking.

Ross took the ring from the box and slid it on her finger. As he did, its diamond caught the daylight and shot it into a rainbow of lights. "Perfect," he said, smiling at her. "Now, let's go meet with this attorney of yours and get our girls back, shall we?"

Epilogue

One year later

Natalie stood near the baggage claim of the Salt Lake City International Airport, anxiously waiting for the passengers on the plane that had just landed to disembark and make their way through the terminal—actually, she was waiting for one passenger in particular: Elder Ryan Jacobsen.

Standing next to her were her dad and stepmother. They'd made the trip down from Oregon to be here when Ryan returned home, as they'd promised they would. Marie held a large bouquet of helium balloons, and Natalie's dad proudly wore a conspicuous Scottish plaid tie, the gift from his missionary grandson, Natalie surmised.

Next to them were Emma and Callie, each brandishing a homemade poster welcoming their brother home. Natalie sighed with contentment. She'd gotten her girls back shortly after Ross's arrival at her front door. Once all of the details of what had happened on New Year's Eve had come out and the cops had cleared Emma of any wrongdoing, it had been much easier to get Wade to back down from his threats, return the girls to her, and leave custody as it had always been. It hadn't hurt having some strong legal firepower at her disposal. Natalie had learned that it was handy to have a good attorney around when you needed one.

And considering the fact that Natalie and Ross had been married for a while now, the best attorney she knew—her favorite one, in fact—was around a lot. After notifying Monty Rogers of his intentions, Ross had relocated to Salt Lake City full time.

He'd also converted one of their spare rooms into a studio for Natalie and had convinced her to transfer to the university and study art full time.

And she had—at least until her doctor had said she needed to take it easy. She would get back into her studies soon; her art was important to her. But right now, she wanted to spend time with her husband and her family. And today she'd finally have all of her family together again.

Natalie looked over in time to see Scott and Suzie and their two kids and Jackie and Rick and their entire crew walk through the terminal doors, carrying more signs and balloons. Brett quickly made his way over to Emma, and Lexie skipped up to Ross with her arms outstretched.

"Let me see, let me see," she cried, dancing with excitement.

Ross crouched down so Lexie could peer at the pink bundle he was holding. "Say hello to baby Marissa, Lex. I'm sure she wants to say hello to her big-girl cousin."

"Ooh," Lexie cooed. "Hello, Marissa. Can I hold her, Uncle Mac?"

"That's probably not a good idea right now, kiddo. It's a busy airport, and she's brand-new and just a tiny girl. But Grandma's sitting on the bench over there. Let's take Marissa to her, and you can sit down and talk to her better. Okay?"

"Okay," she said.

"I'll be right back," Ross said, winking at Natalie before taking Lexie's hand and walking over to where Dorothy was sitting.

Natalie smiled. She had delivered baby Marissa just a couple of weeks ago. She wasn't as young as she used to be, and she had a ways to go before she'd feel like her old self again. She was sleep deprived and weak. But she wouldn't have missed being here today for the world.

She took a moment to look around her and simply enjoy herself. Emma and Callie were joking and laughing with their new cousins. Scott and Rick were already busy shooting random photos of everyone.

Here were the people who mattered most to her in the entire world. It was unbelievable to think that when Ryan had left on his mission, Natalie hadn't even known most of the people who were here supporting him today. They were all family now.

Jackie and Suzie walked over and exchanged hugs with Natalie. "How are you feeling?" Jackie asked.

"Yes," chimed in Suzie. "How are you feeling? Do you need to sit down? And where is that baby?" She began scanning the group. "I need to hold her. Oh! Mom's got her. Mother—" Suzie was off like a shot.

Jackie's eyes twinkled at Suzie's hurried exit. "You look great, Natalie, especially for someone who recently gave birth. Oops, it looks like I need to go supervise a few of the natives. Sorry!" And she dashed off as well.

Natalie watched Ross as he murmured to Lexie and tucked the blanket snugly around the baby. Natalie's heart soared. Ross was smitten with his new daughter. Natalie had always known he'd be a devoted father, and he'd proven her right. She was so blessed. Her life and her choices had taken her down a difficult path, one that had taught her a lot about herself and, ultimately, made her stronger. She was a person who had made mistakes early in life and had experienced the consequences of them. But a loving Father in Heaven had given her blessings along the way to help her deal with those consequences. A wonderful son and two beautiful daughters who had helped her get through the hard times. And now she'd been blessed even further with another healthy, beautiful child and a husband who loved all of her children—and her.

Ross wandered back over to stand by Natalie. "How are you feeling?" he asked her, placing his arm around her shoulder and holding her close.

Natalie wrapped her arm around his waist and drank in his solid, reassuring strength. "I feel wonderful," she said.

Just then, a handful of young men in suits emerged from the concourse. Among them was a tall, dark-haired one who was agonizingly, breathtakingly familiar.

Elder Jacobsen. Ryan. Her son, Ry.

Emma and Callie dashed over to him, hugging him tightly and crying. The others cheered and whistled and then crowded around to introduce themselves and offer their greetings. Natalie watched as Ryan searched the crowd until he found her, grinned, and headed her way.

As she smiled back at her oldest child, tears welled up in her eyes. "I feel wonderful," she repeated softly to herself. "Absolutely wonderful."

About the Author

Karen Tuft was born with a healthy dose of curiosity about pretty much everything, so as a child, she taught herself to read and to play the piano. She studied composition at BYU and graduated from the University of Utah in music theory. She was a member of Phi Kappa Phi and Pi Kappa Lambda honor societies. In addition to being an author, Karen is a wife, mom, pianist, composer, and arranger. She has spent countless hours backstage and in orchestra pits for theater productions along the Wasatch Front. Among her varied interests, she likes to figure out what makes people tick, wander through museums, and travel—whether it's by car, plane, or paperback.